THE HEALING SEASON

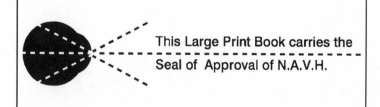

This Large Print Book carries the
Seal of Approval of N.A.V.H.

THE HEALING SEASON

RUTH AXTELL MORREN

THORNDIKE PRESS

An imprint of Thomson Gale, a part of The Thomson Corporation

THOMSON

GALE

Detroit • New York • San Francisco • New Haven, Conn. • Waterville, Maine • London

THOMSON

TM

GALE

LIBRARY OF CONGRESS CATALOGING-IN-PUBLICATION DATA

Morren, Ruth Axtell.
   The healing season / by Ruth Axtell Morren.
     p. cm.
   ISBN-13: 978-1-4104-0380-3 (hardcover : alk. paper)
   ISBN-10: 1-4104-0380-7 (hardcover : alk. paper)
   1. Surgeons — Fiction. 2. Actresses — Fiction. 3. Poor — Fiction. 4.
London (England) — Fiction. 5. Large type books. I. Title.
PS3613.O7553H43 2008
813'.6—dc22
                                                         2007037853

Published in 2008 by arrangement with Harlequin Books S.A.

Printed in the United States of America on permanent paper
10 9 8 7 6 5 4 3 2 1

For Justin, Adája and André.

Thanks, guys, for putting up with a writing mom. When I dotted the final *i* and crossed the final *t* on this one, André said, "Great, that means you won't be on the computer 24/7 anymore."

Only until the next story beckons . . .

But unto you that fear my name shall the sun of righteousness arise with healing in his wings.

— *Malachi* 4:2

The Bible is a book of reversals. Old things become new, the dead come to life, the lost are found. Even those who were the vilest of sinners are now empowered by grace to become the virgin bride of Jesus Christ.

— Francis Frangipane,
Holiness, Truth and the Presence of God

CHAPTER ONE

London, 1817

The sight that greeted Ian Russell as he stood in the doorway of the dark, malodorous room gave him that sense of helplessness he hated. It was in stark contrast to those times when he was setting a bone or stitching up a wound, knowing he was actively assisting a person in his recovery.

This situation was the kind where he knew his pitifully small store of skills would be of little use.

Here, only God's grace could save the pathetically young woman lying on the iron bed in front of him, her life ebbing from her like the tide in the Thames, leaving exposed the muddy rocks and embankments on each side.

Blood soaked the covers all around the lower half of the bed. Ian crossed the small room in a few strides and set down his square, black case at the foot of the bed.

The women were always young: fourteen, fifteen, twenty, sometimes even thirty — if they lived that long. Women in their prime, their lives snuffed out by the life growing within them. This one didn't appear to be more than seventeen or eighteen.

As he began drawing back the bedclothes, he looked at the only other occupant of the dim room — a young woman sitting beside the bed.

"Will . . . will she be all right?" she asked fearfully. He spared her another glance and found himself caught by her breathtaking loveliness. Large, long-lashed eyes appealed to him for reassurance. Strands of light-colored hair framed delicately etched features as if an artist's finest brush had been used to trace the slim nose, the fragile curve of her cheek, the pert bow of her lips.

He blinked, realizing he'd been staring. "I don't know," he answered honestly before clearing his mind of everything but saving the life of the pale girl lying on the sodden bed.

"Can you tell me what happened?" he asked, attempting to determine whether it was a miscarriage by nature, or a young woman's attempt to abort an unwanted life.

As he lifted the girl's skirts and measured the extent of dilation, he listened to the other woman's low, hesitant account.

"She had . . . tried to drink something . . . several things, I think . . . but nothing worked. I think she grew desperate and tried to get rid of it herself." She raised her hand and showed him the knitting needle. "I found this beside her."

It didn't bode well. Blood poisoning could already have set in. If the girl contracted a severe case of fever, she'd be dead in a few days. He prayed she hadn't punctured anything but the membranes.

Sending a plea heavenward, Ian set to work to stop the bleeding.

"Can you remove her stays?" he asked the young woman sitting by the bed. Would she be able to handle what was in store, or was she too squeamish?

The young woman stood and gingerly approached him. As she hesitated, he repressed an impatient sigh. Pretty and useless. Probably a lightskirt, he decided, like the one lying unconscious. His heart raged with the familiar frustration at how easily a young woman's virtue was lost in this part of London.

But he had no one else to assist him. It was two in the morning, and he'd been summoned from his bed, with no idea what

11

he would find when he arrived at his destination.

The edges of the young woman's sleeves were stained with blood as if she'd already tried to help her friend. At his bidding now, she leaned over the bed and began to lift the girl's dress higher. Her hands were shaking so much they fumbled on the lacings of the corset.

"Here, let me," he said, barely concealing his annoyance. He took one of the scalpels from his case and slit the corset up its length.

It was a wonder the girl hadn't already miscarried, the way she was bound so tightly. She was further along than he'd supposed.

He addressed his reluctant assistant. "It's important that we stop the bleeding. In order to do that, I'm going to have to remove the unborn child. Do you think you'll be up to this? You're not going to faint on me?"

The woman stared at him, her pupils wide black pools within silvery irises. She bit her lip. "I'll . . . I'll try not to."

"You've got to do better than that." He tried for the note of encouragement he used with students around the dissecting table for the first time, but his mind was more concerned with the young girl bleeding to death. They had a long night ahead of them.

Dawn was lighting the interior of the room when Ian straightened to massage the kinks out of his lower back.

He glanced at his young assistant. Her pretty frock was ruined, the front and sleeves spattered with blood.

She hadn't fainted, he'd give her that, although many times he thought she'd be sick. She'd clasped her hand over her mouth more than once. Now she wiped the perspiration from her forehead with her sleeve, pushing back the damp golden strands of hair that had fallen from their knot.

"The bleeding has abated and her pulse, though weak, is regular. We've done all we can for now." He turned away from the bed to the basin of water to wash his hands.

After dumping it out the window and pouring some fresh water to wash off his instruments, he asked, "Can you see if there are any fresh linens for the bed?"

She started, then glanced around the dingy surroundings. "I don't know if she would have anything."

"Perhaps the woman who let me in earlier. Can you ask her?"

She pressed her lips together. "I doubt she

would be so obliging."

"I suggest you find out. Bribe her if you have to. Your friend can't lie in that bloody mess." He nodded curtly toward the soiled linens.

The young woman straightened her back and gave him a look that told him the words had stung. It was the first hint of anything other than fear he'd seen in her all night. He'd rarely had such a jittery nurse. He was surprised a woman her age — at least twenty, he'd judge — hadn't been around a delivery room before.

She left the room without a word.

Ian forgot her as he dumped cranioclast, regular forceps, crochet and hooks into the basin. The water immediately clouded red.

He had little hope the girl on the bed would survive. If the loss of blood didn't kill her, childbed fever likely would.

The other woman returned as he was drying the instruments.

"You had some success," he said, noting the folded linens she carried in her arms.

"Not with the landlady." She laid the gray sheets down on the vacated chair and eyed the bed. "The neighbor upstairs whose boy went to fetch you last night gave me what little she could spare."

As she continued standing there, he approached the bed. "Here, I'll show you how." He began to strip the soiled sheets from under the patient, again amazed at the woman's ignorance in changing a bed for an invalid. "If you can procure some fresh ticking for this bed later today, it would help."

She nodded, taking hold of the sheet on the other side of the bed. After they had done the best they could with the limited supplies available, Ian took up the bucket with the remains of the night's work.

"I'm going to see about a burial."

Once again the young woman looked queasy. She averted her eyes from the bucket and nodded.

Ian found the lad who'd brought him the night before and had him fetch a shovel.

Out in the small, refuse-filled yard, he dug a hole deep enough to keep stray animals from uncovering it, dumped the remains into it, and filled it with the dirt.

Dear God, he began, then stopped, not quite knowing what more to say. A poor half-formed child, destined for a miserable existence if it had come to term. And yet, he felt the familiar sense of defeat over every lost life, life that hadn't yet had a chance to live.

Thank You for sparing the mother, he finally

15

continued. *I pray You'll watch over her in the coming days that she might heal. Bless this infant. Welcome him into Your kingdom.*

He gave a final pat with the back of the shovel to the unmarked grave and returned it to the boy. "Thank you."

"Sorry for getting you up in the middle of the night. Mum and I 'eard the screams. 'Twas awful. Sounded like she was dying." He sniffed. "Mum'd 'eard as 'ow you don't charge people wot 'aven't got 'ny blunt."

He nodded. "You did the right thing."

Ian trudged back upstairs. He reentered the room and gathered his things to depart. Ignoring the other woman, he bent over his patient and felt her forehead. If fever didn't develop over the next twenty-four hours, she had a fighting chance.

Lord, grant her Thy healing, if it be Thy will. Show her Thy mercy and grace.

He straightened and turned to the young woman who had been sitting by the bedside. Once again he was struck with her beauty. Ethereal and fragile . . . how deceiving looks could be.

In another few years she'd probably be poxed and coming around to St. Thomas's to be treated, like so many of the women he saw.

"I'll be by later in the morning to check

16

on her," he told the young woman. "There isn't much you can do for her now, except keep her warm and give her some water to sip if she wakes." He handed her a small parcel from his satchel. "This is ergot. If you stir a little in water, it will help stop the bleeding."

She took it gingerly. He tried to give some words of encouragement, but didn't want to get her hopes too high. "Try to get some rest yourself," he said simply.

She made no reply, so he gave a last look toward the girl on the bed. What she needed was divine intervention, and he was too exhausted to pray.

Ian departed the room as silently as he'd come.

Eleanor woke to the sound of low voices. Her maid knew better than to disturb her before noon.

Her eyelids protested as she forced them open. Two men stood by the bed. Frightened, she sat up, finding herself in a chair. She didn't remember falling asleep here. Why wasn't she in her bed?

Betsy! Recollection came back in a heap of nightmarish images. Her friend had been bleeding to death when Eleanor had found her.

Aching muscles in her neck and back shrieked in outrage as she looked toward the bed. The tall, young doctor who'd arrived in the wee hours of the night was standing at Betsy's bedside now, another man beside him.

He'd come back as he'd promised.

Had Betsy made it? Eleanor couldn't see past the two men.

Standing, she winced at the pins and needles shooting through her feet. What time could it be? It was difficult to judge from the overcast day visible through the small, dirty window. Had she really been able to fall asleep after all she'd seen last night? Eleanor shook her head as she walked softly toward the bed.

Hearing her approach, the doctor turned. "I'm sorry to disturb your slumber."

She passed both her hands down the sides of her head, trying to smooth her hair. She must look a fright.

"How is she?" she asked, made even more self-conscious under the doctor's steady gaze, which seemed to miss nothing from her tangled locks to her rumpled, blood-stained dress.

"About the same," he answered, turning his attention back to Betsy. "That's good news, actually," he added, his tone gentler than it had been the previous evening when he'd barked orders like a ship's commander. Last night she'd put up with it only because she was so desperately frightened for Betsy's life. The doctor had seemed so competent, never hesitating in his rapid actions, his hands skillful and steady.

But this morning was a different story. Betsy was out of the woods, it appeared, and the doctor didn't look quite so fierce.

Eleanor wet her lips, considering how to play this scene. The grateful friend . . . the composed nurse . . . the weary toiler . . .

She studied the doctor a few seconds before turning a questioning glance in the other man's direction.

The doctor answered the unspoken question in her eyes. "This is my apprentice, Mr. Beverly." The man was only a youth from what she could see.

"Pleased to meet you, Mr. Beverly," she said graciously, extending her hand. "Excuse my appearance. Dr. . . . ?" She raised an eyebrow to the dark-haired doctor.

"*Mr.* Russell," he supplied for her. "I'm a surgeon," he added, explaining the lack of title.

She nodded and addressed herself to the youth. "Mr. Russell can tell you how we spent our evening. I haven't had a chance to go home and change my garments."

The boy was blushing furiously and stammering protestations.

"I would introduce you," the surgeon said, "but as we didn't have time for the niceties last night, I am afraid I am still ignorant of your identity."

"Eleanor Neville." She never tired of the sound of the stage name she'd given herself. It had the ring of quality. The syllables rolled off her tongue with self-assurance.

"Mrs. Neville," the youth stammered. "It's an honor to meet you."

"Thank you." She gave a demure smile. It was obvious he recognized the name.

The surgeon made no sign that her name meant anything to him. "Has she awakened at all?" he asked her.

"Once," she replied. "She was thirsty and I gave her a few sips of water as you suggested with the powder. That was all she could manage."

He nodded. "Yes, it's to be expected."

"I haven't had time to go home yet. I wanted to ask you — can she be moved? It would be much easier to take care of her in my own house."

"I'm afraid she has lost too much blood to be moved this soon."

Eleanor frowned. "I don't know how often

I will be able to stop in to see her. Perhaps you could recommend a nurse. I could pay her." She turned an apologetic smile toward the younger man. "I must be at work most afternoons and evenings."

As he nodded in understanding, she turned to find the surgeon's eyes on her. They held a censure that made her wonder what she had said that was so wrong.

In the light of day she saw that his dark hair was actually auburn, its coppery shade deepened to chocolate-brown in the eyes focused on her. Before she could speak, his attention shifted to his apprentice.

The two men spent the next couple of minutes discussing Betsy's case. Eleanor heard words like *erysipelas, necrosis,* and *blood poisoning.* Mr. Russell took the woman's temperature, felt her pulse and finally said to Eleanor, "Continue giving her the ergot. Also, comfrey tea. It will help bring down any inflammation and stanch the bleeding. I'll be by tomorrow, but if she takes a turn for the worse, send the boy around again."

She nodded. "I'll do my best, but as I said, I must leave her in the evening to work."

He looked down at her, and again she felt strong disapproval emanating from those dark irises. "Can you not forgo your evening's activities for one night?"

She stared at him for a moment. Forgo her evening's performance at the theater? What did he think she was — a mere chorus girl? She glanced at the young man, and seeing his cheeks turn deep red, she felt vindicated. Obviously *he* understood the impossibility of the suggestion.

She drew herself up. "I couldn't possibly 'forgo' my duties tonight."

"Are you so popular with your clientele that you cannot give up an evening's earnings for the sake of your friend here? May I remind you she is still in grave danger?"

Her eyes grew wider.

"Ian," the apprentice began hesitatingly, "Mrs. Neville isn't . . . er . . . uh . . . "

As Eleanor glanced from one man to the other in puzzlement, it suddenly dawned on her. The good surgeon thought she was a prostitute! Her nostrils flared as she drew herself up.

Abruptly, she clamped her mouth shut on the set down she was about to give him. Putting both hands on her hips, she thrust one forward, shaking back her hair away from her face.

"Well, I don't know now," she drawled in her broadest cockney. "I got me clients, and they 'spect to see me regular. Kinda like yer

22

patients, I should imagine. Wot 'appens if you don't come callin', eh? Go to the next quack down the block, I shouldn't wonder."

She blew on her fingernails and polished them against her bodice, as she gave the young man a firm nod. His mouth hung open and his eyes stared at her.

"There're so many gents callin' theirselves doctors nowadays, a cove's gotta watch out for 'is business, ain't it so, Mr. Beverly?"

"Oh . . . uh, yes, ma'am." His jaws worked furiously, as if they needed to catch up to his words.

She began strutting around the room, hands still on her hips, swaying them just as she saw the women outside the theater do. "So, you see 'ow it is, Doc. I got me rounds tonight, just like you."

She turned back to them and gave the doctor a long, slow look up the length of his tall, slim physique.

When she reached his eyes, she detected the same stern look he'd worn throughout the night as he'd battled for Betsy's life. She flicked a glance at the young apprentice. He'd lost his dumb stupor and was actually grinning. He must have figured out she was playacting.

"Oh, we understand, perfectly, Mrs. Neville," Mr. Beverly told her with a vigorous nod.

"All I understand," said the surgeon, "is that your young friend's life is hanging by a thread. Her only hope lies in skilled nursing help."

As Ian strode from the building, he experienced the impotent fury he did every time he saw a young woman unmindful of the consequences of her street life. Hadn't Mrs. Neville learned something from seeing her friend nearly bleed to death?

He clenched his jaw. The woman was more beautiful than she had a right to be. She might be able to ply her trade for a few short years, but then what? If she'd seen the ugly results he dealt with every day from women dying of the pox or clap, she'd rethink her occupation.

He chanced a glance at Jem, his young apprentice, already regretting having brought him. The woman had enthralled him in a few minutes of conversation.

In reality Jem was his uncle's latest apprentice at the apothecary, but Ian knew how important it was for an apothecary to get practical experience with patients, so he took him on his rounds whenever he had a chance.

The boy was whistling a cheerful tune that Ian didn't recognize. "You can't let every pretty face discompose you, my boy," Ian chided, remembering the boy's blushes around the beautiful Mrs. Neville.

Jem's pale complexion turned ruddy again. "But that wasn't just any pretty lady, that was Eleanor Neville!"

"Is she related to royalty?"

The boy stopped in his tracks. "Don't you know who Mrs. Neville is?"

"Not a clue. Should I?"

"She's the greatest actress on the stage."

An actress? He stared at Jem in disbelief. Then he remembered her strange turn-around, one moment a frightened young woman, her speech too refined for her mean surroundings, the next talking like any common streetwalker. She had been pulling his leg! He shook his head. He had misjudged her, and she had turned the tables on him. He couldn't help a grudging smile.

"An actress, is she?" he asked thoughtfully. "I've heard of the great Mrs. Siddons and Dorothy Jordan, but of Mrs. Eleanor Neville, not a whisper."

"That's because those others are at the Drury Lane. Mrs. Neville plays in the burlettas at the Surrey."

Burlettas! The word conjured up images

of women prancing about a stage, singing bawdy songs.

"Don't look like that! You should see her sing and dance. And she's funny. She has more talent in her tiny finger than all the actresses at the Drury Lane and Covent Garden put together."

"I guess I'll just have to take your word for that." Ian resumed his walk, unwilling to spend more time thinking about a vulgar actress. The description belied the delicately featured young woman who had fought beside him throughout the night.

"You can joke, but someday you'll see I'm right," Jem insisted.

"I doubt I shall have such an opportunity since I rarely indulge in theatergoing, much less musical burlesque." He glanced at the street they were on. "Let's get a hack at the corner and go to Piccadilly. We'll visit Mrs. Winthrop and then stop in and see how Mr. Steven's hernia is doing."

As they continued in silence, Ian noticed Jem shaking his head once or twice. Finally the boy could keep still no longer. "I can't believe you didn't recognize Mrs. Neville. Why, her playbills are posted everywhere. She's been taking London by storm in her latest role. I've heard even the Prince is enchanted."

"Well, then I must be the only one in London who has not yet succumbed to Mrs. Eleanor Neville's charms. She was almost useless as an assistant." Again, a different picture rose to his mind, of a young woman overcoming her terror to save a friend's life. He shook aside the image. An actress was little better than a prostitute.

"I was afraid I'd have to divide my time between reviving her and keeping my primary patient from bleeding to death," he added cuttingly.

"Poor thing! She must have had a rough time of it. I wish I'd been there with you!"

Ian looked at the young man with pity. "To help my patient or to hold Mrs. Neville's hand?"

Ian couldn't help picturing those slim hands with their almond shaped nails, how they'd smoothed back the patient's hair from her brow, and remembering her soft voice as she encouraged her friend throughout the night's ordeal.

An actress? The image wouldn't fit the one formed last night. How long would the innocent-looking, ladylike woman be impressed upon Ian's memory?

CHAPTER TWO

As she sat before her mirror, her maid dressing her hair, Eleanor was gratified to note that a full nine hours' rest followed by the special wash for her face made of cream and the pulverized seeds of melons, cucumber and gourds had left her complexion as fresh and soft as a babe's.

She touched the skin of her cheek, satisfied she would need no cosmetics today.

With her toilette completed, Eleanor went to her wardrobe and surveyed her gowns. The mulberry sarcenet with the frogged collar? She tapped her forefinger lightly against her lips in consideration. No, too militaristic.

The pale apricot silk with the emerald-green sash? She had a pretty bonnet that matched it perfectly. Too frivolous?

She ran her hand over the various gowns that hung side by side, organized by shades of color. Blues, from palest icy snow to deepest midnight, greens from bottle to apple, reds from burgundy to cerise, and so on to the white muslins and satins. She enjoyed seeing the palette of colors. Gone forever were the days when she was lucky enough to have one dirty garment to clothe her back.

She pulled out one gown and then another until she finally decided on a walking dress of white jaconet muslin with its richly embroidered cuffs and flounced hemline. With it she wore a dark blue spencer and her newest French bonnet of white satin, trimmed with blue ribbons and an ostrich plume down one side of the crown.

When she had judged herself ready, she stood before her cheval glass for a final inspection. Her blond tresses peeked beneath the bonnet, with a small cluster of white roses set amidst the curls. She fluffed up her lace collar. White gloves and half boots in white and blue kid finished the outfit. The picture of maidenly innocence and purity.

"How do I look, Clara?" she asked the young maid.

"Very pretty, ma'am. The colors become you."

Eleanor smiled in recognition of the fact. Good. If her appearance didn't put Mr.

Russell to shame, her name wasn't Eleanor Neville.

She took up the shawl and beaded reticule her maid held out to her.

"Is the coach ready?" she asked Clara.

"I'll see, madam," Clara answered with a bob of her head and curtsy.

"I shall be in the drawing room below," Eleanor said.

She had found out from the young boy in Betsy's rooming house that Mr. Russell had a dispensary in Southwark, in the vicinity of Guy's and St. Thomas's Hospitals. They were not so very far from the theater, she thought, as she sat in her coach and rode from her own neighborhood in Bloomsbury and headed toward the southern bank of the Thames.

She needed to accomplish two things on this visit to the surgeon: firstly, to find out about proper nursing care for Betsy, and secondly, to clear up a few things to the good doctor.

She would present such a composed, elegant contrast to the woman he'd seen the night before last that he would fall all over himself with apologies.

She was *not* a streetwalker and had never been. It mortified her more than she cared to admit that after so many years, someone could so easily fail to notice her refinement and see only the dirty street urchin.

It hadn't helped that she'd behaved like such a poor-spirited creature during Betsy's ordeal. But it had been awful finding Betsy like that. Eleanor still felt a twinge of nausea just thinking about it.

She gazed out the window of her chaise, no longer seeing the streets, but recalling the terrified young girl, younger than Betsy, when she'd gone into premature labor. She rarely ever called up those memories, but last night had summoned up all the horrors of those hours of painful labor in vivid detail.

Her own delivery had ended successfully in the birth of a child who had survived, but the ordeal for a scared, undernourished, ignorant girl had almost killed her.

She folded her gloved hands on her lap. Those days were far behind her. She was a different person, one older and wiser in the ways of the world, and few people knew anything of her past.

The coach arrived at the surgeon's address, and the coachman helped her descend onto the busy street.

The building looked respectable enough. Mr. Russell must have achieved some success in his profession to be able to open his own dispensary.

Several people stood in line at the front. As she neared the brick building, she noticed the brass plaque by the door.

Mr. Ian Russell, licensed Surgeon, Royal College of Surgeons

Mr. Albert Denton, Apothecary-Surgeon

Below it appeared: *Midwifery Services.*

She pushed past those waiting, ignoring their angry looks and murmurs, and entered the brick building.

Immediately, she took a step back. The place reeked of sickness and poverty. The waiting room was packed with unwashed bodies — young, old, and every age in between. By their dress, they did not look like paying patients. The rumors must be true that Mr. Russell served one and all.

Every available wooden bench was occupied. Some huddled on the floor. The rest stood leaning against the walls.

Eleanor braced herself and ventured farther into the waiting room. She was surrounded by the lowest refuse of life, those that inhabited Southwark and other similar London neighborhoods. She saw them lurking at the fringes of the theater every night when she departed in her coach. Hard work and determination had enabled her to escape these surroundings, and she had no desire to ever live in such conditions again.

She took a few steps more and found a bit of wall space to lean against. Daring another peek around her, she saw that some of the sick had even brought a form of payment: a pigeon in a small wooden cage, a handkerchief wrapped around some bulky item — a half-dozen potatoes or turnips to give to the good surgeon in exchange for his services.

She heard moans of pain beside her and, looking down, she saw a man holding his wrist gingerly in his other hand. Beside him sat another with an exposed ulcerated leg propped up in front of him.

Eleanor brought her scented handkerchief to her nostrils, fearing the foul miasma that permeated the air. She couldn't take the risk of exposing herself to some perilous humor and sicken.

All eyes were upon her — at least of those patients not too caught up in their pain. She read admiration and some envy in their glances. She was accustomed to that look and bestowed smiles on one and all alike before retreating behind an impersonal gaze above the crowd.

The closed door opposite her across the room suddenly opened and she recognized Mr. Beverly, the young apprentice. She waved her handkerchief at him. He saw her immediately and nodded in greeting, a wide grin splitting his face. She smiled graciously, relieved to see that he immediately made his way toward her.

"Mrs. Neville, what are you doing here? Has the young woman taken a turn for the worse?"

"No, though she is still very weak. But it *is* about Miss Simms that I am here. If I could speak with Mr. Russell for a few moments?" She gave him a look of gentle entreaty.

"Yes, of course, madam. Let me inform him that you are here." He took an apologetic glance about the room. "As you can see, he's quite busy today, but I know he'll see you as soon as I let him know you are here."

"I shan't require much of his time."

He was gone only a few moments before returning to beckon her through the door.

Mr. Russell was finishing bandaging up a patient's arm.

"That should do it, Tom," he told the burly young man. "Let's hope you fall off no more ladders for a while, eh?"

"You're right, there, Mr. Russell. I've got to watch me step from now on."

"All right. Come by in a week and we'll see how you're mending."

As soon as the man had left, Mr. Russell came toward her. The smile he had given the male patient disappeared and he was back to the frowning surgeon. Eleanor suppressed her vexation. All the trouble she'd taken with her appearance and she didn't detect even a trace of admiration in those brown eyes.

He probably knew nothing of fashion. Look at him, in his vest, the sleeves of his shirt rolled up to his elbows. Her physician would never so much as remove his frock coat when he came for a visit.

"Mrs. Neville, Jem tells me you've come about your friend."

She cleared her features of anything but concern. "Yes, about Betsy Simms. I'm quite distraught. I haven't been able to stop by to see her since early yesterday afternoon. She felt warm to my touch. I brought fresh linens and some broth, but I greatly fear her being alone there. I tried to talk to the landlady, but she didn't care to involve herself in any way."

"What about the boy's mother? The one who lives upstairs."

"I tried her, too, but she works all day. She promised to look in this evening."

"She has no family?"

Eleanor shook her head sadly. "None that

I know of. She is a singer at the theater where I work." She wondered if the words meant anything to him, but saw no reaction in his eyes.

"When she missed a performance, I stopped by her room on my way home. I didn't want her to be dismissed from the troupe. I found her doubled over, bleeding . . . well, you saw her condition."

Again his eyes gave her no clue to his thoughts, though he listened intently. She scanned the rest of his face, noticing again the reddish tints of his hair. She wondered if he had the fiery temper to match.

"I see," he replied, his tone softening. "You said she had taken some potions?"

"Yes, she told me she'd been to a local herbalist who'd given her a remedy to take, but to no avail. Then she'd bought something from a quack. It made her awfully sick, but still . . ." Her voice trailed off at the indelicate subject.

"No menses," he finished for her.

"Just so," she murmured, looking down at her hands, which still held her handkerchief.

"I'll stop by to see her again today."

"That would be most kind," she said with a grateful smile. "Are you sure she cannot be moved?"

"It would be highly risky at this point. You

36

cannot nurse her yourself?"

"No. I can look in on her every day and bring her fresh linens and refreshment, but I usually have rehearsals in the afternoon and performances in the evening. My evenings are late, so in consequence, my day begins later than most."

He was weighing her words. Finally, he said, "It may be possible to find her a nurse through a Methodist mission I work with. There are many worthy women who give of their time there to help the poor and infirm."

"If they could send someone, I'd gladly pay her. I meant to tell you as well to send your medical bills to me."

He dismissed her offer with an impatient wave of his hand. "Don't worry about it. Why don't you go to the mission and inquire about a nurse? They are usually shorthanded themselves, so I don't promise anything."

"Very well. Where is this mission?"

"In Whitechapel."

"Whitechapel?" Her voice rose in dismay. That was worse than Southwark.

"Yes."

"You want me to go there alone?"

"I beg your pardon. I go there so often myself, I forget it's not the kind of neighborhood a lady would frequent." His glance strayed to the outfit she'd given so much thought to that morning.

She wasn't quite sure his tone conveyed a compliment. "I should think not."

He considered a few seconds longer and finally answered, the words coming out slowly, as if he was reluctant to utter them. "If you'd like . . . I could accompany you there. Would late this afternoon be satisfactory? Your Miss Simms should really have some nursing help as soon as possible."

She nodded. "I will be at the theater this evening, but I don't have a rehearsal this afternoon."

"I can leave as soon as I finish with all my patients here."

"Very well. Do you have a carriage?"

He shook his head. "No, I don't keep a carriage."

"We can go in mine, if you think my coachman won't be beaten and robbed while he is waiting for us."

"He'll be quite all right, I assure you."

"Then I'll come by around three o'clock. Does that give you sufficient time?"

"Yes, that would be fine."

As she turned to go, his next words stopped her. "I believe I owe you an apology."

She turned around slowly.

"The other night, I mistook you for . . ."

Assuming her cockney, she filled in, "A doxy?"

She detected a slight flush on his cheeks. At his nod, she batted her hand coyly. "Gor! Think nothin' of it, guv'n'r. 'Appens all the time. I don't know wot it is about folks, but they're forever mistayken me for someone else. Sometimes even the Queen, poor old deah. I tell 'em 'I ain't such 'igh quolity.' " She finished with a hearty laugh. "But neither am I no judy, no, sir!"

He was giving her a bemused look, as if he didn't know what to make of her little performance. "You're an actress."

"Yes," she answered in her own accent. "You've never been to the Surrey — the Royal Circus now?"

"No."

"No? It's not far from here."

"I don't go to the theater."

Her eyes widened in disbelief. "Never?" The theater was one of the few places where everyone could meet and find enjoyment, from highest to lowest in society. "Are you a Quaker?"

He gave a slight smile. "No, I haven't the time for such amusement."

She remembered the packed waiting

room. "I can well believe that."

When he said nothing more, she knew it was time to make her exit. "I shall not keep you from those who need you more. Until three o'clock, then?"

"Until three o'clock."

Ian popped a few cardamom seeds into his mouth as he watched Mrs. Neville's chaise pull up at the curb of the dispensary. The actress was punctual, at least. He was still annoyed with himself that he'd committed to accompanying her to the mission. He had little time to spare for excursions like this. Still, the girl needed nursing. It was a miracle she was even alive.

The coachman opened the door and let down the steps. Ian climbed into the smart coach, nodding to Mrs. Neville and seating himself opposite her in its snug interior.

She glanced toward the dispensary before the carriage door shut behind him. "It looks deserted now. What a difference from this morning."

"Yes, every broken limb has been set, every wound bandaged."

As the carriage lumbered forward, she asked him, "Do you have such a roomful of patients every day?"

He smiled slightly. "No. Sometimes there

are more." He grinned at the horrified look in her eyes. "I'm only partially speaking in jest. The dispensary is only open four days a week. On the other days I do rounds at St. Thomas's Hospital a few streets down and hold an anatomy lecture for students there. I also tend the sick at the mission we're heading for. Then there are the days I pay house calls."

"When do you rest?"

"I honor the Lord's Day, unless I'm called for an emergency."

She nodded and looked out her window. Had he satisfied her interest with his answers and was she now back to thoughts of her own world?

What would occupy such a woman's thoughts? He found himself unable to draw his eyes away from her. For one thing, she had an exquisite profile. Her small-brimmed bonnet gave him an ample view. Her curls were sun-burnished wheat. Her forehead was high, her nose slim and only slightly uptilted, her lips like two soft cushions, her chin a smooth curve encased in a ruffled white collar.

But her most striking feature was those eyes. Pale silver rimmed by long, thick lashes a shade darker than her hair.

This afternoon she was dressed in a dark

blue jacket and white skirt, which looked very fashionable to his untrained eyes. He frowned, trying to remember if she had worn the same outfit earlier in the day. But he couldn't recall. It had been something dark, but he couldn't remember the shade. He'd been too dazzled by the shade of her eyes to notice much of anything else.

Chiding himself for acting like a school-boy, he tore his attention away from her and examined the interior of the coach. It had a comfortable, velvet-upholstered cabin, which looked too clean and new to be a hired vehicle. To keep such a carriage in London, with its pair of horses, was quite expensive.

He wondered how a mere actress could afford its upkeep. He glanced at her again, remembering Jem's high praises. She must indeed be a successful actress to be outfit-ted so well. Still, he doubted. He knew actresses usually had some titled gentleman setting them up in style.

But she went by *Mrs.* Neville.

"Your husband, is he an actor as well?" he found himself asking.

She turned to him. "There is no Mr. Nev-ille," she replied, her pale eyes looking soft and innocent in the light.

"I'm sorry," he answered immediately, assuming she was widowed.

She smiled, leaving him spellbound. The elegant beauty was now transformed into a lovely young girl. "You think I am a widow? I repeat, there is no, nor ever was, a Mr. Neville. It's merely a stage name."

It was his turn to be surprised. "You mean it's not your real name?" She must think him an unsophisticated country bumpkin.

She laughed a tinkling laugh. "I just liked the sound of Mrs. Eleanor Neville. It adds a sort of dignity, don't you think?"

"Yes, I suppose it does," he answered slowly, trying to adjust his notions of her. Curiosity got the better of him. "What was your . . . er . . . name before?"

The friendly look was gone, in its place cool disdain. "My previous name is of no account. It has been long dead and forgotten."

He felt the skin of his face burn and knew a telltale flush must be spreading across his cheeks, but Mrs. Neville had already turned back to her window. Despite her rebuke, he felt more intrigued than ever. Why would a person ever change her name? Was it a commonplace practice among theatrical people?

It was a long carriage ride, across the Thames and through the congested streets of the City. He spoke no more to her, preferring to concentrate his thoughts on the rest of the evening. He would probably stop at his uncle's apothecary shop to drop off several prescriptions and pick up the ones he'd had Jem leave earlier in the day. He needed to check on a few patients. That brought his thoughts back to the young woman who'd nearly killed herself.

"Did you have a chance to look in on — er — Miss Simms again, Mrs. Neville?"

Mrs. Neville. He couldn't get used to the name anymore. It made her sound matronly, completely at odds with the young ingenue looking at him.

"Yes, I stopped to see Betsy before I came to collect you. She had awakened. I fed her some broth and gave her the powder you left. She was still very weak although she didn't seem feverish."

He nodded, glad the danger was passing. "I'll go around tonight."

"She's very scared," Mrs. Neville added.

"She might well be. She almost killed herself."

"She doesn't think she had any other choice. If she'd been discovered in a family way, she would have lost her position. If that had happened, she'd have lost her room. She would have ended up in the street. What would she have done with a child then?"

Ian was well familiar with the scenario. He saw it played out countless times a day.

He began to feel a grudging admiration for the young actress. She had not abandoned her friend and was now going to some lengths to assure her full recuperation. He continued to observe her as the carriage trod the cobblestone streets. Beneath Mrs. Neville's fashionable appearance, there lay a woman very much aware of the grimmer realities of life.

The carriage drew up at the Methodist mission. Eleanor looked around her suspiciously as Mr. Russell helped her alight. The streets had grown narrower and smellier. She clutched her handkerchief to her nose as the doctor led her toward the entrance of the mission.

It at least had a welcoming appearance. A lamp stood at the door and the stoop was swept clean. They entered without knocking.

Eleanor breathed in the warm air before once more putting her handkerchief to her face, this time to mask the smell of cooked cabbage and lye soap.

Mr. Russell poked his head into a room and finding no one led her farther down the corridor.

"Good afternoon, Doctor," an older woman called out cheerfully as she emerged from another room. "We weren't expecting you today. What can I do for you?"

"Is Miss Breton in at the moment?"

"No, I'm sorry, sir, she had to step out."

"Who is in the infirmary?"

"Mrs. Smith."

"I shall go in and speak with her, then. Thank you."

Eleanor noticed the woman eyeing her as they walked by and entered a long room filled with beds. Every one was occupied, she noticed, and they all held children. She'd never seen a children's hospital before. She looked curiously at each bed as Mr. Russell led her toward a woman at the far end.

After brief introductions, she listened as the surgeon explained to the woman their need for a nurse. Eleanor only half paid attention, her interest drawn to the children in the room. A little girl in a nearby bed smiled at her, and she couldn't help smiling back. Slowly, she inched her way toward her. The child's dark hair and eyes reminded her of her own Sarah.

"Are you feeling poorly?" she asked the girl softly.

The child nodded. "I was, but now I'm

46

feeling much better. Nurse tells me I must stay in bed a while longer, though."

"Yes, you must get stronger." The child was so thin it was a wonder her illness hadn't done her in.

A young boy beside her called for her attention, and before long Eleanor found herself visiting each bed whose occupant was awake.

Mr. Russell approached her. "We're very fortunate. There is a lady who is available to spend part of the day with Miss Simms. We can go to her house now and make arrangements if you have time. She lives not far from here."

"Very well. Let's be off." She turned to the children around her and smiled. "I want to see you all well the next time I visit. If you promise, I'll bring you a treat."

"We promise!" they all chorused back.

CHAPTER THREE

After they'd visited the nurse, Mrs. Neville dropped Ian off, at his request, near London Bridge.

"Good night, Mr. Russell," she said, holding out her hand. "Thank you for accompanying me."

"You needn't thank me. It's part of my job," he replied, hesitating only a fraction of a second before taking her hand in his.

He felt a moment of union as her gloved hand slipped into his. For some reason, he was loath to let it go immediately. Repudiating the feeling, he disengaged his hand from hers. "Good night, Mrs. Neville."

Without another word, he opened the carriage door and descended into the dark street.

He quickly crossed the parapeted bridge, giving not a backward glance as he heard the rumble of the chaise continue on its way.

He breathed in the mild September air in

an effort to get the image of Mrs. Neville out of his mind. He had lived through too much and seen too much to let one pretty female face stir him.

Entering the neighborhood of Southwark, he walked the short distance to St. Thomas's Hospital. The new building was little more than a century old, a beautiful neoclassical design fronting Borough High Street. Instead of taking this main entrance, Ian continued on to the corner and turned down St. Thomas's Street toward the small church that formed part of the hospital's southern wall.

His uncle had been recently appointed the hospital's chief apothecary, and Ian was sure he would still be found in his herb garret under the church's roof.

Ian climbed the narrow circular stairs leading to the church's attic. The spicy aroma of drying herbs permeated the passageway. "Anybody here?" he called out when he reached a landing.

"I'm in the back." Jem's voice came from a side partition.

Ian poked his head through the curtained doorway and found Jem washing bottles. "Uncle Oliver in the garret?"

The younger man grinned. "Yes, he is."

Ian climbed the last section to the raftered

attic that served as his uncle's workshop. Sheaves of herbs hung from the roof. Bottles and jars lined the shelves set against the naked brick walls. One section held a cupboard full of small square drawers. A desiccated crocodile was suspended from the ceiling.

His uncle was hunched over a large glass globe that sat upon a squat brick kiln. As its contents bubbled and steam collected on the globe's interior surface, a slow drip ran down its narrow glass neck into a china bowl at the other end.

"Good evening, Uncle Oliver." Ian set down his medical case and leaned his elbows against the long, thick table that bisected the room.

His uncle twisted his gray head around. "Ah, good evening, Ian. Come for the prescriptions?" He resumed his watch on the distilling herbs as Ian replied, "Yes. I caught a ride across town."

"Is that so? How fortunate. Who was coming all this way at this hour? Someone coming to Guy's or St. Thomas's for an evening lecture?"

"No, just a —" He paused, at a loss to describe Mrs. Neville. "Friend of a patient's" sounded too complicated. "A lady —" Was an actress a lady? He doubted it.

"Someone in need of hiring a nurse. I took her to the mission to see if they could recommend someone."

"A lady? A young lady, an old lady?" His uncle stood and gave the bellows a few puffs to increase the flames of the fire in the kiln before turning away from the alembic and approaching the opposite side of the table.

"Give your uncle who rarely stirs nowadays from this garret a bit of color and detail to events outside the wards of St. Thomas's."

Ian smiled at his uncle's description of his life. "A young lady," he answered carefully, turning to fiddle with the brass scales in front of him.

"Well, I'm relieved she wasn't an old crone. Did you have a lively time?" Uncle Oliver went to the end of the table and brought forward some stoppered bottles.

Ian took the bottles from him. Digitalis against dropsy; essence of pennyroyal for hysteria; tincture of rhubarb as a purgative; crushed lavender flowers to use in a poultice; some comfrey powder to ease inflammation.

"I don't think one can describe a visit to the mission's infirmary as 'lively,' " he began, then stopped himself as he remembered the smiles and laughter of the children in the few moments Mrs. Neville had entertained them. "Have you ever heard of Eleanor Neville?"

"The actress?"

Ian looked in surprise that even his semisecluded uncle knew the actress's name. "I thought you knew nothing of the goings-on of the outside world."

Uncle Oliver smiled. "I do read the papers. I hear she's a hit in the latest comedy at the Royal Circus."

Ian began placing the bottles into his medical case.

"The Royal Circus," his uncle repeated with a fond smile, taking a seat on a high stool across from Ian. "My parents used to take me there as a boy when it was an amphitheater. It rivaled Astley's equestrian acts. It's not too far from here, on Surrey. Haven't you ever been?"

"No," Ian replied shortly. His uncle well knew he never went to the theater. He had little time for acrobats and tumblers.

His uncle rubbed his chin thoughtfully. "Now they put on melodramas and musical operas — *burlettas,* I think they call them. It was renamed the Surrey for a while under Elliston. Then Dibdin took over its management a few years ago and gave it back its original name."

"You sound quite the expert on the theatrical world."

"Oh, no, although I do enjoy a good comedy or drama now and then." His uncle gave him a keen look under his graying brows. "It wouldn't do you any harm to get out and enjoy some entertainment from time to time. You'll kill yourself working and found you've hardly made a dent in humanity's suffering."

"I'll tell that to the queue of patients waiting for me at the dispensary the next time."

Uncle Oliver chuckled. "Just send them over to me. Jem and I will fix them up."

"Most of them can't afford the hospital's fee."

"So, tell me more of Eleanor Neville. I imagine she is young and pretty."

Ian shut his case and set it on the floor. "Yes, you could describe her as young and pretty."

His uncle folded his hands in front of him and leaned toward Ian as if prepared for a lengthy discourse. "You are making me envious. To meet a renowned actress who is both young and pretty. What did the two of you find to talk about?"

Ian frowned. "What is that supposed to mean?"

"Well, I can't imagine your telling her

53

about your latest dissection, much less the doctrines of Methodism. And I feel you wouldn't want to hear too much about what goes on in the theater world."

"So, you think I have no conversation?" He took up the black marble mortar and pestle and began pounding at the chamomile flowers his uncle had left in it.

"Not at all. I'm just curious how you spent your afternoon with Miss Neville."

"She introduced herself as *Mrs.* Neville, but she explained later that she wasn't married, that it was merely a stage name." His pounding slowed as he thought about it again.

"Unmarried, eh? It gets more and more interesting. You know, Ian, I've told you before, you need to find yourself some female companionship. It's time you were married and settled in a real home and not just some rooms next door to your dispensary."

Ian couldn't help laughing. "When did we get from meeting an actress to settling down?"

His uncle didn't return the smile. "Perhaps when it's the only young woman I've heard you mention in I don't know how long. I'm grasping at the proverbial straw."

"Well, you can let it go. I met Mrs. Neville purely by chance and, I assure you, I'm unlikely to see her again, except in the course of my work, if our — er — mutual patient takes a turn for the worse." Ian began explaining the events that had led up to their meeting, in an effort to divert his uncle's attention from Mrs. Neville.

After Ian finished describing the night's struggle to save Miss Simms, his uncle got up from the stool and rummaged in his various drawers and Albarello jars, mixing together a variety of dried herbs. He came back with a small sack for Ian.

"Mix an infusion of this and have her drink it as often as possible throughout the course of the day. It should help with the bleeding."

Ian took it and put it with the other prescriptions. "Thank you."

"Speaking of your life," his uncle continued. "I've been thinking of talking with the board here at St. Thomas's. They could use another instructor in pathology. Why don't you curtail some of your patient load and take on additional teaching work? It would leave you more time for research."

Ian rubbed his temples. It was a familiar suggestion. "I am satisfied with my work as it is, as *you* well know."

"You would ultimately help more people

if you could continue working in the laboratory and at the dissection table."

Ian walked away from his uncle and stopped at the small dormer window overlooking the courtyard of the great hospital. He munched on a cardamom seed he took from the bag in his pocket as he watched a few students crisscrossing the courtyard's length on their way to an evening lecture.

It didn't help that his uncle knew Ian almost better than he knew himself. Uncle Oliver had become like a second father to Ian, when as a lad of thirteen Ian had begun his apprenticeship under him. Except for the war years and his time spent walking the wards at La Charité in Paris, Ian had been primarily under his uncle's tutelage since he'd left home.

He turned back to Uncle Oliver. "I must be going. I still have to look in on the young woman before calling it a day."

His uncle, as usual, knew when it was time to end a conversation. The two bid each other good night, and Ian descended the stairs. With a final wave to Jem, who was sweeping the floor before leaving for the evening, Ian exited the apothecary shop.

When he reached the main road, he saw the mist rising on the river in the distance.

He turned in the opposite direction and

continued walking but soon his steps slowed. If he turned down any one of the narrow streets on his right, they'd take him to Maid Lane. It would be less than a mile to New Surrey Street. There Mrs. Eleanor Neville was probably preparing to step onto the stage. He pictured the lights and raucous crowds. He imagined her cultured voice raised above the audience.

Giving his head a swift shake to dispel the images, he picked up his pace and headed on his way.

Life was full enough as it was. He had no need to go looking for trouble.

When Eleanor finally left her dressing room that night, exhausted yet exhilarated after her performance, she walked toward the rear entrance of the theater where she knew her carriage awaited her. She gave her coachman instructions to stop at Betsy's before going home.

She was afraid the landlady wouldn't open, but after several minutes, someone finally heeded her coachman's loud knocking.

"It's late to be paying calls," the woman snapped.

"I'm looking in on my friend."

"That Betsy Simms? She ought to be

thrown in the magdalen! This ain't no house of ill repute."

"I'm sure it isn't," Eleanor replied acidly, walking past the slovenly woman, who barely made room for her. She quickly climbed the foul-smelling, narrow stairs and opened Betsy's door without knocking. She found her friend awake.

"How are you feeling?" Eleanor asked softly, crouching by the bed.

"As if I'd been run over by a dray," she answered weakly.

"You might as well have been. Thank goodness that surgeon was nearby and came as soon as he was called. I had no idea what to do."

"He stopped by a little while ago."

"Did he?" A warm flood of gratitude rose in her that he'd kept his word.

Betsy gave a faint nod. "He said I was doing all right but that I needed to rest for several days. He told me how foolish I'd been." Tears started to well up in her eyes.

Eleanor pressed her lips together. Why couldn't his lecture have waited a few more days, at least until Betsy was a bit stronger? "Don't pay him any heed. He was just concerned about you."

"I tried to explain, but he didn't let me tire myself." She took a few seconds to gather her flagging strength. "He . . . told me you had already explained everything to him."

"That's right." Eleanor rose from her cramped position. "Now, don't concern yourself with any of that right now. Just think about getting well again." As she spoke she brought a glass of water she found by Betsy's bed. "Here, take a sip of this and then get back to sleep."

She cupped her hand under Betsy's head to raise it. The girl obediently took a few sips and then sagged against the pillow.

Eleanor set the glass on the bedside table and straightened. "I shall be off, then. A nurse is coming tomorrow, did Mr. Russell tell you that?"

Betsy nodded. "He was very kind."

Eleanor smoothed the bedcovers and adjusted the pillow beneath Betsy's head.

"What else could I have done?" Betsy asked. "I couldn't have the baby. The theater wouldn't have kept me on if they'd known —"

"Shh. Don't think about that now." Eleanor patted the girl's hand.

"But how do you manage it? Haven't you ever found yourself in such a situation?"

Eleanor hesitated, not wanting to upset Betsy further. But when she saw that the girl would not be quieted, she finally said, "Once . . . when I was very young — even younger than you."

"What did you do?"

"It doesn't matter now. It was long ago. What I learned since then is to be very careful. You mustn't let this happen to you again."

"But what do you do? You saw what happened. None of those potions did any good."

"You must prevent it from happening. You must be very careful with the kind of man you take up with. It's up to him. You must insist he take the necessary precautions."

"What kind of precautions?"

Eleanor looked at the pale young woman in pity. She had so much to learn. "You needn't concern yourself about that now. You have a long recovery ahead of you. But once you're well, we'll talk again. Because if you don't learn to be careful, you'd better stay away from men."

"But you laugh and flirt with them as much as the rest of us girls at the theater."

"It only looks that way. What those gentlemen offer must be very good before I'll allow them to come any nearer than arm's length."

The two were silent a few moments, each lost in thought. Finally Betsy sighed. "Mr.

Russell told me I wouldn't survive a second time. He said it was only by God's grace that I lived through this time."

"I don't know about God's grace, but I think you were lucky you had a competent surgeon. Now, don't think about it anymore for the moment. Get some rest and get yourself well. We all miss you at the theater. I've told the manager you have the grippe."

Again Betsy's eyes widened in fear. "Did he believe you?"

"He was just scared that we'd all get it. He told me you're to stay away until there is no danger of contagion. Now, get to sleep. I'll be by again tomorrow. I hope your new nurse isn't an ogre." With a laugh and a wave, she left the room.

As she sat in her carriage and resumed her ride home, she told herself to forget about Betsy's problems for the moment. She herself needed to get her beauty sleep. Tomorrow she would be having dinner with the Duke d'Alvergny. He had been very attentive at the theater for several weeks, and she had fobbed him off.

But she'd made some inquiries and discovered him to be extremely wealthy and influential.

She had spoken the truth to Betsy. Romantic attachments were dangerous, but a

61

gentleman with the right connections and a generous pocket was always worth a second look. Perhaps it was time to see what the duke had to offer.

"Come watch Punch and Judy! Watch Punch knock out Judy! Tuppence a show." The hawker's voice carried above the crowd. A young boy tugged on Ian's hand.

"Oh, may we watch?" The other children took up the chorus.

Ian turned to Jem as the children shouted their glee. "I guess Punch and Judy will be next." The two men shepherded the children they'd brought from the dispensary neighborhood toward the puppet theater.

Ian fished out his change and gave the money collector the fee.

As the hunchbacked Punch whacked his wife, Ian's attention wandered. His glance strayed to Jem. The youth seemed as entranced by the small puppet show as the children they'd brought to the street fair.

Leaving Jem laughing heartily at the high-pitched voice of Punch screaming at Baby, Ian looked over the crowd. The streets were packed with people for the annual Southwark Fair. It would be the last one until the winter carnivals.

His gaze was arrested by a small commotion about half a block down. As a few people shifted, providing an opening, he saw what held their attention.

Mrs. Eleanor Neville was holding court. There was no better way to describe the scene before him. Those around her fawned over her, as she graciously bestowed her favor to all and sundry. She smiled, offering her hand to men, women and children alike.

As if on cue, she moved on, ready to greet those farther on. The crowd parted, men doffing their high-crowned hats, women fluttering their handkerchiefs, children clamoring for a last-blown kiss.

She was with another young woman. As they came closer, her attention was drawn to the noise of the Punch and Judy show. Her face lit up and she turned to her companion. At that moment her glance crossed Ian's.

He thought she wouldn't recognize him in that crowd, but she raised an eyebrow and he inclined his head in acknowledgment. She said something to her companion and to his surprise, the two started walking toward him.

"Good afternoon, Mr. Russell. I'm surprised to see you at such an entertainment. Who is minding the dispensary?"

He smiled sheepishly, aware of the people

around them eyeing him curiously. "My partner."

She smiled. "I confess I find myself perplexed. You have no liking for the theater, yet here I find you at a fair." Her lips formed a pretty pout. Ian struggled to shift his focus away from them.

He nodded at the young children around him. "I've brought some of the children who usually spend their time in the streets around the dispensary." At that moment Jem turned around and his eyes grew wide at the sight of Mrs. Neville. He made his way to her side.

"Mrs. Neville! What a pl-pleasure," he said, holding out his hand, then drawing it back again as if unsure that was the proper thing to do.

Mrs. Neville laughed charmingly and held out her own hand. "The pleasure is mutual. It is good to see you again, Mr. Beverly, under more cheerful circumstances." She introduced them to her companion, a chorus member from the Royal Circus.

Ian, impatient with the curiosity of the crowd around them, said, "I think Punch is becoming angry with our drawing attention away from his show."

Mrs. Neville turned to the puppet stage. "I love Punch and Judy. I started out playing at street fairs, you know." She stood at his elbow, so close the sleeve of her dress brushed his arm, and it became even harder to keep his attention on the show than before.

When the show ended, somehow he found himself part of Mrs. Neville's entourage. She charmed the children, and their group moved along slowly through the jammed streets, stopping at the various stands.

She ended up walking at his side as Jem and the other actress moved in front of them with the children.

"What do you have there?" Mrs. Neville gestured to the bag in his hand.

"Cardamom seeds," he answered. He held out the bag to her, wondering if she would find the gesture unrefined.

Instead she removed her glove and took one. She chewed on it and smiled. "It's spicy."

He felt captivated by that smile, revealing such purity and sweetness. "I got in the habit of chewing on them when I was first apprenticed to my uncle. His apothecary was a treasure of spices and sweet-tasting lozenges for a kid. He told me to eat these instead of the sweets. Better for my teeth and breath, he advised.

"During the war, they helped alleviate the

boredom on long marches across the plains of Spain and fooled the stomach into thinking it had been fed."

"You were with the army?"

"As surgeon."

Jem stopped in front of a booth with a dartboard. The hawker immediately challenged them to try for the prizes. The children clamored for Jem and Ian to win them one.

Jem was unsuccessful after three attempts. Ian paid the man in charge and took his three darts. Like Jem's, his darts landed far from the bull's-eye. He turned to the children with a shrug. "Sorry, no prizes today."

Mrs. Neville gave him a coy smile. "I hope your stitches in surgery are better than your aim."

Her silvery-gray eyes were looking up at him in teasing challenge, and it occurred to him she was flirting with him.

He was accustomed to receiving unwanted attention from the many street women he attended in his practice, but they were derelict and only incited his pity. The heartfelt gratitude he received from other female patients or mothers of children he'd treated humbled him and made him all the more aware of the sacred trust between physician and patient. The only other women he dealt with were at the mission or chapel, modest and respectful in their comportment toward him.

Mrs. Neville's behavior was different. It was direct and demure at the same time, elegant and playful in one.

"Mr. Russell is the finest surgeon." Jem defended him immediately. "You wouldn't want anyone else if you were going under the knife."

She chuckled, a sound rich and charming like warm caramel. "I'll try to remember that when I need someone to cut me open and stitch me up. Now, I'll show you how to win a prize." She turned to the children. "Let's see, how many are there of you?" she asked the children as if she hadn't seen already. "Three only? That means one prize for each."

They yelled in excitement. Calmly, she turned to the man at the booth. "I shall need three darts, if you please." She gave him a coin and received her three darts.

The children began hopping up and down, pointing to the things they wanted to win.

"Now, you must hush." She put her finger to her lips and bent toward them. "Be very, very still so I can concentrate and win your prizes for you." Wide-eyed in wonder, they promptly fell silent. Ian couldn't help smiling at the immediate obedience Mrs. Neville's words invoked in the children. At the same time he wondered if it was wise getting their hopes up.

She turned to the dartboard and hefted the three darts in her hand, as if determining their weight. She chose one and brought it up level to her face, pointing it toward the round board. The crowds behind were forgotten as the attention of their party was focused on the black center of the dartboard.

Breaths held, they watched as, after an interminable few seconds, she threw the dart.

It arced, then descended and, with a soft thud, landed firmly within the bull's-eye. The children erupted in shouts of triumph.

She paid them no attention, as her hands once again toyed with the remaining darts.

"Beginner's luck! Beginner's luck!" the owner of the booth chanted. "Let's try for two in a row. Can't make two in a row."

Other patrons, waiting for their turn, took up the chant. The noise brought more people to the booth.

Mrs. Neville ignored them as she took aim again. The crowd fell silent as if collectively holding its breath.

Another tense few seconds went by, before

whoosh and bull's-eye.

The cheers were louder this time. Some of the children couldn't contain their excitement, but jumped higher, clutching at the railing of the booth. Ian glanced at the owner of the stand, who was the only one not looking pleased at the victory.

"Here, now, you watch it," warned the owner sternly to the boisterous children. "I don't want my stand comin' to pieces."

Ian gently held them back from the railing and told them to be still for the last turn.

Mrs. Neville moistened her lips briefly, the only sign that she was feeling anything other than perfectly calm. The last dart was held lightly in her fingertips. Slowly, it rose to eye level.

It flew through the empty space and landed at dead center, right between the other two darts.

The crowd shouted and applauded.

"I never seen such an aim. And a lady, too!"

"That's the actress, Eleanor Neville."

"She's a wonder."

"Amazing."

As if oblivious of the compliments being thrown around her, she bent down to the three children and asked them to tell her which toys they wanted. They pointed to

69

the desired objects. She turned to the stern-faced proprietor, who had taken out the darts and held them in his hand, and calmly told him her choice of prizes.

With a jerk, he took the toys off the shelf and slammed them on the counter, a Bartholomew baby doll for the girl, a wooden dog covered with patches of fur for one of the boys, and a yo-yo for the other.

The children grabbed them and chattered happily as they were led away by the adults.

"You've made a few children happy for the day," Ian remarked as they continued down the street.

"You say they hang about the dispensary."

"Yes. The whole neighborhood is full of children." She made no reply. "Mrs. Neville, where did you learn such an accurate aim?"

She smiled. "Oh, I've thrown a lot of darts in my life. I told you I started out my career at street fairs." She nodded up ahead. "See the acrobats? I was cutting capers and walking on ropes since I was fourteen. We traveled from village to village and town to town. There was ample time to play darts at taverns or just nail the board to a tree when we had to camp out on a meadow."

He listened, finding it hard to imagine such a fashionably dressed young lady up on a makeshift stage doing acrobatic tricks.

They ambled down the street, stopping frequently. The children watched in awe a juggler tossing balls in the air. Another player balanced a ball at the end of a stick.

"I've done it all. Even equestrian feats. That's how I started at the Surrey."

"And now?"

"Now? I have lead roles in the melodramas, only we mustn't call them melodramas, only burlettas, or we might lose our license. The royal theaters at Drury Lane and Covent Garden are the only ones permitted to put on straight dramatic works."

"I didn't think there was much difference," he said drily. He knew enough of the theater to know that in recent years the Drury Lane and Covent Garden were known to put on bigger and bigger extravaganzas instead of pure classical dramas.

"Strictly speaking, anything the minor theaters put on must be set to music, with no spoken lines permitted. But you're right, there is less and less distinction between the majors and minors. Still, we must watch how we bill our performances or we could be shut down."

A pastry vendor came by, swinging the tray suspended from his neck back and forth. "Tasty hot pasties. A ha'pence each,

71

penny for two. Come and have a meat pasty!"

Ian stopped the man and bought the children each a bulging meat pastry. He turned to Mrs. Neville. "Would you care for one?"

"No, thank you. I eat very little before a performance."

He eyed her critically. She seemed much too fragile to him. "You can't mean to say you starve yourself during the day."

"I have been recently following a regimen of only fruit and vegetables on a performance day and tea laced with honey and lemon for my throat. I only dine after the show."

"You certainly don't look as if you needed to follow such a strict regimen." He offered her his pastry.

"I shall only take a bite since it looks so tempting." She broke off a corner of the warm pastry he held out to her.

"Thank you, it's delicious," she told him after she'd swallowed it and daintily wiped her mouth with her lace-edged handkerchief. As she looked up at him, he was struck afresh by the color of her eyes. It was the clear gray of the mist hanging over the sea at dawn.

He cleared his throat, too dazed by his reaction to her to formulate any more compli-cated response than "You're welcome."

They stopped at another booth, this one selling all sorts of trinkets. After Jem had bought a pair of fans for the two ladies, he turned to present one to Mrs. Neville.

"I c-can't believe I'm really h-here walk-ing with a famous actress. How do you do such amazing things on the stage, from pretending you — you're a pirate to a princess —"

She laughed as she took the fan and opened it with a flourish. "Haven't you heard that 'all the world's a stage'? You live in one. Look around you. There are all kinds of dramas taking place right under your nose.

"Take that couple for instance." She motioned with her fan to a stout couple standing at the next booth. "You can tell by their gestures alone that he missed his target and now she is berating him for wasting his money and not getting her a prize."

"You're right," Jem told her in amaze-ment. He burst out laughing when the colorfully dressed woman turned to the man and scolded him for his clumsiness. "How did you notice them?"

She shrugged. "I take those things I see and use them on the stage — the irate wife, the distressed husband, the lost, frightened child." She stopped talking and, fixing her eyes on Ian, stared hard at him for a few seconds.

"Wot? Don't you see the draggle-tailed duck in front o' yous? Can't you 'it the bleatin' target? I didn't come to the fair so you could lose all our brass. What kind of a big looby are you?" She turned to Jem and the actress with a nod. "Gor, if it'd been my first 'usband, Alf, never a better man, if 'e'd ha been 'ere, 'e'd ha' knocked down a dozen ducks already."

Jem and the children were doubled over in laughter, and the younger actress was clapping her hands in glee. Ian couldn't help but smile. He was as captivated as Jem by Mrs. Neville's ability to capture the scene they'd witnessed only briefly at the next booth.

It struck him that this beautiful woman was as close an observer of human drama as he was of a sick body in order to diagnose it properly.

"Come, we'd better keep moving before they notice us," she said, once more in her natural tone. She placed her hand in the crook of his elbow, and Ian looked down at the kid glove, wondering at how natural it felt to have it resting there.

They walked along, following Jem and the children. Mrs. Neville's young friend had attached herself to Jem, and Ian watched in amusement as Jem blushed and stammered his replies to her.

A moment later Ian turned to an angry voice up ahead.

"They take away the food from a man's mouth. They make us fight for the king, then put us on the street when we come 'ome!" A dirty, disheveled man wearing an old army jacket, stood waving a crutch and shouting to the crowd. One foot ended in a filthy, wrapped stump.

Ian felt Mrs. Neville's hand tighten on his arm as she noticed the speaker. "Poor man," she murmured.

The speaker soon had a group gathered around him, raising their hands and shouting back in agreement.

They stood watching him for a couple of minutes, but then the mass of people attracted by the angry veteran began pressing uncomfortably around them.

"It sounds like a disgruntled soldier," he answered briefly. "It could get ugly. People have been drinking."

Mrs. Neville looked worried. "Perhaps we should turn around. The children —"

"Yes." Ian raised his voice to get Jem's attention. Unfortunately, the young man had been drawn to the excitement ahead, and Ian had to squeeze through the growing crowd to reach him.

"Jem, hold up."

"Yes? What — oh, it's you, Ian."

"I think we should leave this area."

By this time the voices had grown louder and angrier and people began jostling and pushing to get closer.

A rock flew over the crowd and glass shattered. As if a signal to erupt, the crowd took up whatever was at hand and began throwing things. Men swung their canes around, unmindful of who stood in the way. Women flung their handbags and umbrellas, children screamed.

In a matter of seconds, they were in the midst of a full-blown riot.

CHAPTER FOUR

The crowd took up rocks, clubs and sticks and directed the brunt of their violence at the booths and the shop windows around them.

"We've got to get the children out of here!" Ian shouted to Jem. The young actress clung to the apprentice, her eyes screwed tight. "Follow me."

Jem nodded his head and grabbed one of the children with his free arm. Ian grabbed the other two, who were crying. Mrs. Neville took the girl from him and sheltered her under an arm.

They fought against a wall of bodies. Ian picked up the child he had and swung him over his shoulder as he guided Mrs. Neville forward. Jem followed with the other actress, and the two muscled their way toward an alley.

They managed to reach a small area behind a booth.

"Jem, you take the children back to the dispensary. I'll escort the ladies to their carriage." He turned to them. "You have your carriage?" he asked Mrs. Neville.

"Yes, but it's quite a ways from here." She looked behind her in worry. "I don't think we can make it back."

In the few seconds they had been talking, the crowd had again surged forward. Angry men and women lunged at them, determined to break and smash everything around them. The children screamed, huddling into the adults' bodies.

"Take them away!" shouted Ian. "I've got to stay. There are bound to be injuries."

Jem nodded. "I'll get them to safety," he said, already making for the narrow alley.

Ian attempted to herd the women toward Jem, but at that moment they were separated by a mass of bodies. He was thrown against a wooden structure and felt the wind knocked out of him. Searing pain shot through his lower back.

When he looked up, he could no longer see Jem or the children.

"Are you all right?" Mrs. Neville leaned over him, shouting through cupped hands.

He nodded. "Where's your friend?"

"She's with Jem. He's gotten them out of the fray."

"You mustn't stay here. It's too dangerous." As he spoke, he attempted to rise. She took his arm to help him up.

He managed a few hobbling steps, ignoring the pain in his back. He put his arm around Mrs. Neville to shelter her as much as possible from the angry mob.

They were swept along by the crowd. All he could do was hope to shield Mrs. Neville from flying objects. Rocks were hurled without regard as to whether they hit building or human.

Inch by inch, Ian headed toward a doorway. When at last he reached it and pulled Mrs. Neville into its alcove, he stationed himself in front of her, creating a wall between her and the mob.

Glass shattered around them. The smell of smoke reached their nostrils. He prayed the fires wouldn't get out of control in this already poverty-stricken neighborhood.

"Down with the Regent!" the crowd yelled. Some had lit torches and with angry shouts, they struck them at the vendors' booths. The merchants yelled in fear and tried to protect their wares, but this only incited the crowd to attack them further. The merchants ran away in fear.

Dear Lord, guide Jem and the others safely out of here. . . .

■ ■ ■ ■

Eleanor heard the shouts of the crowd, the footsteps rushing past, but they were muffled now. She was safe, wrapped in a warm, shadowy cocoon.

Mr. Russell stood squarely in front of her, shielding her from the brunt of the mob. She stood on the step where he had placed her, unable to see what was going on but feeling strangely exhilarated by the circumstances, at risk yet protected.

She could make out the top edge of Mr. Russell's waistcoat above his coat. If she lifted her hand, she could trace the outline of the topmost button with her fingertip. Her bonnet touched his chin.

It was a nice feeling. A phrase drifted into her thoughts — *to love, honor and cherish* . . . Was this what it felt like to be "cherished"? The last part of the phrase came into her mind unbidden, *till death do us part.*

At that moment someone slammed against Mr. Russell's back. Although he braced his arms against the door behind her, he couldn't completely cushion the impact of the blow. Her face was crushed against his neck and her bonnet fell back. She smelled the fresh-laundered scent of his neck cloth.

As soon as he was able, he righted himself and drew away from her while still anchoring her between his arms. "I beg your pardon. Did I hurt you?"

His eyes roamed over her face as he spoke, examining it for injury.

Gingerly she touched the bridge of her nose with her gloved fingertips. "No. I'm quite all right." *Never better,* she realized. "Are you?" He had taken the brunt of the impact.

"Yes, I'm fine." His perusal over, his brown eyes fastened on hers.

She stood spellbound. For the first time in her life she had the sensation of being safeguarded by a man, and not safeguarding herself from one.

They stood several minutes in the alcove of the doorway as the crowds pushed by them, wreaking destruction everywhere. Eleanor stood content, sure nothing could happen to her in the shelter of Mr. Russell's arms.

She didn't notice when the shouts eventually diminished, but felt the immediate absence of Mr. Russell's body when he took a step away from her. Sunshine fell back on her face. He looked away from her. "They've moved on down the street. Toward the

Thames, I expect."

"I hope they don't set fire to the theater."

"There's no telling with the mood they're in." He turned around and surveyed the area. She wrapped her arms around herself, feeling abandoned.

Everything lay in chaos. Overturned and charred vending stalls, shattered glass, refuse and merchandise scattered everywhere. Here and there they heard moans.

He swiveled suddenly back to her. "Are you sure you're all right? I didn't hurt you when I pulled you in here?"

Still standing on the stoop, she was about eye level to him. Although his words were clipped, almost sharp, she couldn't help a bemused smile at his insistence. "No, you didn't hurt me."

Once again, he had been rapidly surveying her. Now he stopped and looked as if he was doubting her word. Although she couldn't read what was in the chocolaty-brown depths of his eyes, again, she felt a deep, unspoken connection.

Abruptly he turned away and tugged at his waistcoat. "Good." He moved farther into the street and looked up and down it. "I must attend to the injured."

She stepped down and joined him in surveying the wreckage. Before he could say anything more, she placed her arm in his. "I'll go with you."

He frowned down at her. "You most certainly will not. I shall first escort you to your chaise and then I'll return to the dispensary to get some supplies. Now, if you will be so good as to lead us to it."

She planted her feet firmly in place. "There's no danger now. I can assist you." She motioned around her. "Can't you hear them? There are many who need our help. We can use my carriage to get your things. It will save time. I've left it at the Bull and Horn."

When he made no reply, merely set his mouth in a firm line, she tugged on his arm. "Come on. There's no time to waste."

"Very well, but only back to the dispensary. I'll leave you there and return here."

That's what you think, she thought as she hurried down the street.

Eleanor regretted her rash impulse to assist Mr. Russell as she knelt by his side, watching him wash out bloody gashes and sew them up. She brought him pitchers of water, helped bind up wounds with the rolls of bandages, tried to hand him whichever instrument he called for from his large square bag.

She struggled to keep from fainting each time she encountered a serious wound or fracture.

How could anyone bear such pain? she cried inwardly, trying her best to hold a patient still as Mr. Russell dealt with a deep cut or an ugly-looking laceration.

She focused instead on the steadiness of Mr. Russell's nerves as he set broken bones, stitched up wounds and soothed crying children.

Those were the worst to behold. Eleanor could hardly stand their cries as, in their mothers' arms, they writhed in pain, from the injuries inflicted on them by the angry mob. But Mr. Russell's hands were so sure and capable. Gentle yet strong, never hesitating to use force when needed, but able to manage the most minute, even stitches across someone's brow in record time.

Even when bloody, his hands managed to look pale and clean.

She poured water over them between patients and gave him a clean cloth to wipe them dry.

"Thank you," he told her each time, his eyes scrutinizing her as if he wanted to make sure she was holding up.

His assistant Jem finally arrived when they were nearing the end. It had taken him a while to get the children back and then escort the other actress home.

Finally it was over. No more pitiful cries, no more victims to be pried from beneath a stall or cart. She wiped the perspiration from her brow, feeling light-headed all of a sudden. She closed her eyes, willing the sensation to pass.

"Let me get you to your carriage." She heard Mr. Russell's voice as if from far away as he supported her by the elbow. "You look done in."

She shook her head and took a deep breath. "It's nothing. I just felt dizzy all of a sudden."

His eyes narrowed. "I'll warrant it's because you haven't eaten anything." He turned to Jem. "You'd better get back to the apothecary."

Without giving Eleanor a chance to interrupt, he began walking and she was forced to follow him as he hadn't let go of her arm. "There's a coffee shop near the dispensary. I'll get you a cup of tea."

A cup of tea. "That would be lovely," she said with a grateful smile.

He didn't even glance her way, but helped her into the chaise and gave the coachman instructions.

Eleanor leaned against the back of the seat

and closed her eyes. It probably had been foolish of her not to eat the meat pastry he'd offered her earlier. But she'd never dreamed how her afternoon was going to end.

She didn't speak during the ride. She kept her eyes shut and tried to recover her strength. Mr. Russell was going to think she was a ninny. So much for her valiant show of stalwart nurse.

When they arrived at the coffee shop, Mr. Russell sat opposite her at a small, round table and ordered a pot of tea and a plate of sandwiches.

He poured her a cup and laced it with milk and sugar without asking her how she took it.

She made no protest but held it in her hands a moment, breathing in its delicate aroma as she surveyed the doctor over the rim. He placed a couple of the sandwich quarters on a small plate and moved it toward her.

"There, have those with your tea and the faintness should pass."

"Yes, Doctor." She began at first to nibble at one corner of the roast beef sandwich, but soon found she was famished despite — or because of — all she'd experienced in the past few hours.

"Here, have some more. You could use

them," he said as he put the platter close to her.

She stared at him in surprise. "Aren't you having any?"

"You forget, I ate earlier."

"So you did." She continued eyeing him until he looked away. She detected a faint coloring across his cheeks and wondered at it. Had her scrutiny made him uncomfortable?

She tapped her fingernail against the tea mug, pondering as she watched him sip his tea.

"How do you stand it, day after day?" she asked after a few moments when it seemed as if he was unaware she was even there. She was not used to being ignored.

"Stand what? Ah . . . the blood, you mean?" he asked.

She nodded. "All of it. The screams of agony. The exposed —" She shuddered in memory. "I even saw someone's bone."

He toyed with a spoon. "You get used to it." He grinned at her, revealing a dimple in one cheek, and she marveled at how young he suddenly looked. "That wasn't always the case. I got quite sick the first few times I watched my uncle perform an operation."

"Your uncle. He's an apothecary?"

"Yes. More of a surgeon-apothecary. I apprenticed with him a few years before going to Guy's training hospital. By then I felt quite the veteran among the first-year students. You could always tell the novices. They would faint around the operating table their first time."

"The medical profession runs in your family?"

"Not entirely. Only my uncle and myself. My father was a Methodist lay preacher."

She nodded, envisioning some man preaching in the open air. "Are you also a surgeon-apothecary?" she asked. The little bit of history he offered her made her suddenly hungry to know more about him. He hadn't hesitated to risk his life to stay and take care of the injured during the riot.

"Strictly speaking, I am a surgeon, since I am a member of the Royal College of Surgeons, which conferred the license on me, and who frown on any dilution of medical practices.

"Even helping your young friend the other night would not come under a surgeon's duties, even though I performed a surgical procedure on her."

"Then whom should she have called upon?" Eleanor asked, horrified at the notion that a man of the medical profession wouldn't attend someone during an emergency because it didn't fall under his purview.

"A midwife or an accoucheur, if a man had been required."

"But you came. Why?"

"Because in actual practice I am a surgeon-apothecary-midwife, as you have been able to witness over the last few occasions. On the days I lecture or operate at St. Thomas's, I am strictly a surgeon. When I open my doors at the dispensary, or am called on an emergency, I treat anyone who comes along, whether the illness is internal or external."

"And whether they can pay you or not," she stated with quiet irony.

He shrugged. "Those are the ones who most need my attention. I earn enough as a lecturer and resident surgeon at St. Thomas's to make up for any shortfall."

She smiled. "Your profession is somewhat like mine."

He raised an eyebrow.

"We stretch the narrow definition of the burletta — the only dramatic form we're licensed to perform — until we are doing the same sorts of performances you would see at the royal theaters, only we mustn't let on to the fact."

He returned her smile. "I suppose the

parallel is a just one. I never would have seen the connection."

She stirred her tea. "You could also say we both deal with healing. You take care of the physical injuries. I attempt to bring respite to people through a few hours of laughter."

His smile disappeared, leaving an uncomfortable silence. Had her second comparison displeased him?

"You've ruined your outfit," he said softly.

She followed his gaze down to her gown. He was right. The front was hopelessly soiled with blood and dirt.

"It's the second time you've ruined a gown when you've been in my company."

"So it is," she said, realizing it was the second time she'd assisted him in doctoring. What a strange turn of events. "You must ruin a good many shirts and neck cloths."

"That's why I don't dress in the finest."

She studied the cut of his coat. "No . . . I can see that. What a pity. You are not a bad-looking man, but as they say, clothes make the man."

She caught that slight flush on his cheeks again. "Have I put you to the blush?" she asked, feeling inexplicably pleased. "Forgive me if I've been indelicate. We're very frank about our looks in the theater. It is part of our livelihood.

"My physician is always tailored by Weston," she continued. "He's particularly proud of the knot of his cravat. Dr. Elliot, do you know him?"

"I know of him," he answered. "He has quite a reputation."

She could read nothing from his tone, and was left wondering how to interpret his remark.

"Thankfully, I'm usually as healthy as a horse, but Dr. Elliot does give me drafts for my throat to keep my voice at its best."

Mr. Russell felt in his waistcoat pocket, then frowned.

"What is it?"

"I keep looking for my watch, before remembering I have no watch. It was stolen from me last week."

"How dreadful. The streets are being overrun by cutpurses these days." Quickly she drew out her own watch and snapped it open. "It's just past four."

"I need to be getting back to the dispensary. May I escort you to your carriage?"

She nodded and began to collect her things.

When she dropped him off at the dispensary, he turned to her. "I wish to thank you for your able assistance this afternoon. I did need your help."

She lowered her lashes. "It is I who must thank you for your protection and for making me eat when I felt faint."

"Think nothing of it."

She felt a sense of regret when he stepped down from the chaise. After so many hours in his company, in danger and working side by side with him, she felt a bond with the dedicated young surgeon who smiled all too infrequently.

"Well, I must be off." He stepped away from the carriage and lifted his hat.

As her carriage drove away, she glanced back. Mr. Russell stood watching her. She raised her hand in a wave, but he didn't return the wave. Instead, he wheeled about and entered the dispensary.

CHAPTER FIVE

Ian dipped his pen into the inkstand.

Under the heading Respiratory Disorders, he wrote "Consumption and Phthisis." Beside it he jotted the number three, the total number of cases he had seen that day. Next he wrote "Pleurisy and Pleuritic fever." One case. "Catarrh." Two cases.

Thankfully, the weather was still warm, so the dispensary hadn't yet seen many respiratory cases. That would soon change as late summer gave way to autumn.

The next category was gastrointestinal. Several cases of colic, diarrhea, and worms among the infants and children. Two deaths. The columns grew. Ian pushed away from the desk in frustration. Too many children were dying.

His uncle had taught him the importance of meticulous record keeping. Although many times the number of fatalities was discouraging, Ian knew in the long run the only way to convince officials of the need for decent living conditions was to show them hard numbers.

At least more and more parents were bringing in their sick children. When he'd first opened the dispensary, the only children he'd seen were the ones on his visits to people's homes. The people were used to hospitals and physicians refusing to treat children, claiming they were too hard to diagnose. He had found the opposite true. By paying close attention, he had found that many times their symptoms were actually more evident than in their adult counterparts.

He continued to record the day's cases. Surgical treatments included ten broken bones set; eleven bruises; two head injuries; five tumors, of which three were untreatable, the other two possibly operable; six toothaches, with two ending in extraction; four leg ulcers; two abscesses.

He had scheduled one amputation tomorrow. A man had smashed his hand in a doorway, and now gangrene had set in and the arm begun to turn black. Even though amputation was always used as a last resort, in this case there was no help for it, if the patient's life was to be spared.

He finished recording the day's patient

histories, scattered some pounce over the writing and dusted it off. He eased the kinks in his shoulders as he placed the pen back in the standish.

Taking a few moments to massage the back of his neck, he found his thoughts straying once again to Mrs. Neville.

Over the past few days since meeting her, her pretty face kept floating into his thoughts at odd moments of the day. No, not pretty, he corrected himself. Beautiful. She was the most exquisitely formed creature he'd ever beheld. Each time she looked at him, he was startled afresh by her silvery eyes, her delicate features, her golden hair.

Her figure was slim and dainty. Everything was pleasing to the eye. Even when tired and disheveled after assisting him, she still managed to look fresh and appealing.

He rubbed a hand over his jaw, knowing he had to get his thoughts under control. It did no good daydreaming about an actress. She might look pure and innocent, but he knew how deceptive the image was. Actresses were little better than prostitutes he reminded himself for the countless time.

But try as he might, he couldn't seem to block her image from his mind.

Thankfully, he hadn't run into her since the street riot, although he'd been to check on Miss Simms a few times. He'd had to stifle the sense of disappointment, for he knew she visited because Miss Simms waxed eloquent over how kind and generous "Eleanor" had been to her, coming to see her each day. It seemed most of her visits were reserved for late evening after a show or early afternoon before she went to the theater.

"Halloa!" a voice called from the doorway.

Ian looked up to see his friend's tall frame leaning against the doorway.

"You looked so deep in thought I was afraid to disturb you, lest you be on the verge of discovering a new surgical technique that might aid all of humanity."

Ian made an effort to chuckle. "Nothing of the kind. I've just finished up with the records for today. Come in, Henry, don't stand there."

Lord Cumberland eased away from the doorpost and maneuvered himself over to a chair in the cramped room that passed for an office. He sank down with a contented sigh as if the few moments standing had tired him out.

"Too many hours spent doing nothing?" Ian teased, eyeing Henry's evening clothes. He was about Ian's age with short-cropped hair cut in the latest fashion.

Henry grinned back shamelessly. "Doing nothing is an art form. Didn't Byron say that? If he didn't, he ought to have."

"I keep telling you to find a useful occupation."

Henry sighed. "And I keep telling you if you'll only let me introduce you into society, I'd have a Herculean job on my hands." He rubbed his hands together. "It would offer me just the challenge I need since the battlefield."

Ian closed the ledger and set it aside, refusing to rise to the familiar bait. He leaned back in his chair. "So, what brings you to these humble surroundings this evening?"

"I come to invite you to a gathering of intellectuals, artists, and the pink of the ton."

Ian yawned, used to these invitations, which he invariably turned down. It was a game between them by now, he supposed. "Let me guess. It's being held at the home of the Duchess of Longworth, and she's simply dying to meet a lowborn surgeon from St. Thomas's."

Henry snorted. "Lowborn, indeed. My wealthy and titled friends and acquaintances would love nothing better than to listen to an eminent surgeon who has not only trained on the battlefield but has been to Paris and brought back the latest techniques. They are agog at the thought of all those postmortems performed at the great teaching hospitals. I keep telling you, anatomy and pathology are all the rage. Bring some of your wax models and let the layman understand the mysteries of the human anatomy."

When Ian said nothing, Henry continued. "There'll be quite a crowd. It's being held at Somerset House. You've never been there. We can cross over the new Waterloo Bridge. You'll see the house in all its splendor, its colonnaded facade lit up over the Thames.

"It's a rare opportunity. I wouldn't be surprised if Prinny himself showed up. Come on, old boy, you know you'll never get the funds you need for your children's hospital if you refuse to go where the money is."

"I doubt I'll make much of an impression if I stand among them to lecture. They'd be bored silly."

"Don't be totty-headed! You know yours are some of the most popular lectures at St. Thomas's."

Ian was tempted, more than he'd ever been. After two years back from the Continent, he was finally willing to concede that public awareness had to be raised to the overcrowded condition of the poor if change was to come to the city.

"By the by, I read your article in the *Medical Journal*," Henry remarked. "You might not think so, but many of these aristos read such journals. This is your opportunity to be among them, answer their questions, let them see you not as a fanatic, but as the dedicated surgeon you are."

They argued good-naturedly for a while longer. Finally Ian rose with another yawn. "I'm sorry, but not this evening. Perhaps another time. I still have some work to do at home before I turn in."

Henry stood as well, his look eager. "You mean that? I shall stop pestering you if you give me your word you'll accompany me the next time I invite you to a social event."

Ian looked at Henry a moment. What did he have to lose, anyway? Another evening's work? But what might he gain? He gave Henry a brief nod. "Very well. The next time I'll go wherever you say."

Henry clapped him on the back. "That's the way, old man. You won't regret it. After all, I'm building your reputation each time I'm among the ton."

Ian extinguished the lamps and locked the dispensary behind him. He felt for his watch and once again remembered it was gone. It must be near nine in the evening.

He bid Henry good-night, refusing his offer of a ride. He lived only a few doors down.

His neighborhood was one of the most gin-soaked in the city. Prostitutes and men headed in or out of the taverns. Many would end up in the roundhouse by evening's end. Some children called out to Ian and waved.

He returned their waves. "Time for you to head home to bed," he told them.

"Aw, Doctor, it's too early for bed."

He said nothing more, knowing that some had no home to turn in to, and the ones who did never knew what they would find there.

He picked up his pace, thankful the nights were still mild. Soon, the autumn chill would seep into bones, bringing with it coughs and fevers.

When he entered his house, he greeted Mrs. Duff, his housekeeper.

"I've put a snack for you in the study," the plump, cheery-voiced woman told him as she helped him off with his coat. "If that will be all, I'll be leaving."

"Yes, thank you. I won't be needing anything further." He bent over and scratched the cat who was rubbing himself against his leg.

"Hello there, Plato." The tabby, which had been a stray, immediately began to purr as Ian scratched behind its ears. "Had a long day? Any mice for dinner?"

The two continued enjoying each other's company for a few minutes before Ian straightened and proceeded up the stairs. After washing up, he went to his study.

As he ate the bread and cheese and munched on the apple left out for him, he read the latest medical journal. As soon as he'd finished, he turned eagerly to the package that had been delivered in the mail. It was postmarked France.

He still corresponded with a doctor he'd met at La Charité, one of the largest, most successfully run hospitals on the Continent if not the entire world. He clipped the strings of the oblong box and slit the wrappings with a penknife. He opened the box and drew away the wadded-up tissue paper. Carefully he took out the long cylindrical instrument, which resembled a flute. He turned it over in his hands, studying it curiously. Could it be a musical instrument?

After examining it a few moments, he dug around the box and found a letter. In it, his friend described an exciting new invention by the great physician Laennec. Ian had met him in Paris and observed his care and skill with the wounded French soldiers at Salpetriere Hospital.

The instrument was to aid in "auscultation," a term created by the physician to describe the process of interpreting the sounds emanating from the body cavities, especially the lungs. Laennec called the new instrument the stethoscope, an "observer of the chest."

Ian held up the instrument with a new sense of awe. He placed it to his ear as his friend described. How he wished he had a patient with him at that moment. His gaze fell on Plato, who was curled up on his desk, breathing in and out rhythmically.

Ian placed the other end of the long tube, which his friend said the French were calling *le baton,* at Plato's chest. The cat stirred and stretched. This gave Ian better access to his chest cavity.

Sure enough, the sounds of heartbeat and breath became magnified, greater than Ian had ever imagined from the current method of putting one's ear to a patient's chest, which respect for modesty many times prevented.

His thoughts raced ahead, imagining the possibilities between the relatively new technique of percussion — tapping one's fingertips against a patient's chest wall — and now this incredible little baton-shaped object that could increase the interior sounds of a human body.

He reread his colleague's letter. Nothing had yet been published on the stethoscope. Laennec hadn't even given any public lectures. But those who worked with him were amazed at the range of diagnostics available with the use of the baton. He described the differences being distinguished in the various diseases of the chest. The lungs of a consumptive had their own distinctive sounds, those of a pneumonic another.

Ian placed the instrument carefully back in its wrappings. Tomorrow he would take it with him on his rounds after surgery.

After he'd cleared off his desk, he headed to the other side of his study and lit the lamps in that area.

Sitting down at his microscope, he began examining the different cultures he'd brought home with him from the dispensary.

Gangrenous matter, ulcerous tissue, a rotted tooth, a slice of a tumor he had cut out and preserved in alcohol. He stared at the tiny orbs moving about under the lens, the different striations, the tiny world brought to visibility under the specially ground lens.

He stared fascinated, carefully describing each sample in the notebook at his side.

How did the tissues form abnormalities, the illness attack the healthy organs? These questions challenged the best physicians and surgeons of his day. He compared the healthy tissue to the diseased; he read every journal with the discoveries of his colleagues across the Channel. He thought back to the years he'd spent in France, visiting the large teaching hospitals, studying the effect of spacious wards and good ventilation.

He compared the diseases of the poor in the City with those of the wealthy.

He could only come to one conclusion. The filth and squalor of the living conditions of the poor contributed much to their illnesses and mortality rates.

As the clock struck midnight, Ian finally rose and stretched, realizing how little he knew — how little any of them knew.

When he'd put everything away, burning the putrid matter and washing his slides, he sat back down at his desk and drew forward his Bible.

He opened it to where he'd left off the previous evening and continued reading. The stories of Jesus' earthly ministry never failed to fascinate him. A pastor, physician, teacher, exhorter, prophet — all in one man.

The part of Ian that yearned to preach to the masses the way his father had, rescuing souls from eternal damnation, met the physician in him who wished to cure every bodily illness that caused such human suffering and premature death in the world.

"And the whole multitude sought to touch Him: for there went virtue out of Him, and He healed them all."

Ian gazed at his own hands. Would that virtue flowed out of them to heal all he ministered to. Where had that healing power gone to since the days Jesus walked the Earth?

Despite the excitement of the new inventions, how paltry they seemed in light of the healing power of God. These instruments served to better illuminate disease, but they did nothing to hasten a remedy.

What had happened to the church in the intervening centuries that had caused the disappearance of the miracles of Jesus' ministry?

Ian sighed as he closed his Bible. He had surgery tomorrow and must be up early. He needed to get some sleep.

First, though, he bowed his head and clasped his hands atop the black cover of his Bible.

Dear God, I thank You for Your hand on my

life. Please continue guiding me in Your perfect will. His prayers turned to the more pressing cases he'd attended to that day and he prayed for each patient.

Another face kept intruding.

Dear Lord, I don't know the state of Mrs. Neville's soul. I don't know why I keep thinking of her. Ian rested his head on his clasped hands. *If it's wrong, take the thought of her from me. Purify my thoughts of her. Let me see her as another soul that needs to know of Your goodness and mercy. Oh, God, make Yourself real to her. Bring her to repentance and salvation in Your dear Son, Jesus', name.*

Though his prayer had ended, thoughts of Mrs. Neville persisted for quite some time before he eventually fell asleep.

Eleanor and her daughter passed the fields at a brisk clip. The top of the carriage was pushed down to receive the afternoon sun. The two had just enjoyed an ice at a confectionary shop at the nearby village.

Eleanor gazed at her ten-year-old daughter in admiration. Sarah looked fetching in the new bonnet and parasol Eleanor had brought her. They matched Eleanor's exactly.

Sarah had thought that stupendous. Now she twirled the parasol around, laughing in delight each time they passed a farmer in his field. She waved at all they rode by, human and animal alike.

The leaves on the poplars shading the lane were just beginning to fade from green to yellow.

"Oh, Aunt Eleanor, may we stop here for a moment," she cried, pointing to a lovely willow-lined pond.

"Of course we may." Eleanor immediately bade the coachman to pull over.

They descended the coach and waded through the tall grasses until reaching the pond. They found a dry bank to sit upon and watch the ducks swimming lazily across the dark water.

"Tell me again about my mama and papa," Sarah said in the soft tone she always used when speaking of her real parents.

Eleanor looked down at the dark-eyed, dark-haired girl with the dimpled smile. How Eleanor loved that smile. She didn't know whom Sarah took after, but she was eternally grateful she had nothing of her natural father's looks — ugly, lecherous knave that he was.

Eleanor put her arm around the girl, who never tired of hearing the tale. "Well, let's see . . . your mother, she was the most beautiful lady I ever met — even prettier than the most fashionable lady of the ton. She had your hair and eyes. How they sparkled when she smiled, just like yours." She squeezed Sarah's shoulders.

"More importantly, she was lovely inside, too, where it matters most."

"And you were her best friend?" asked Sarah the way she always did at that point.

"Yes. Although she was about five years older than I, we became fast friends from the day we met. We told each other every-thing, just the way you and I do now. She was married when I first met her. She'd made the most brilliant match, a true love match. Why, it was more romantic even than Princess Charlotte's to Prince Leopold."

She could feel Sarah shiver beneath her arm. "Ooh! How romantic! How did they meet?"

"It's funny, because in a way it was the same as the princess met the prince. Your father, too, came from a far-off land similar to Coburg. Transylvania, deep in the Carpa-thian Mountains."

"Transylvania," breathed Sarah. The very syllables sounded romantic.

"Count Otto von Ausberg from Transylva-nia was tall, dark and handsome. He had the bearing of a prince. Oh, did he look handsome in his gold-braided uniform, just like we saw Prince Leopold when he first came over to court Princess Charlotte!"

They smiled at the memory of seeing him beside Princess Charlotte, waving at the crowds from a balcony at Carlton House, when he was the Prince Regent's special guest.

Eleanor sighed to heighten the drama of the tale. "Alas, your papa was a poor, impoverished nobleman like Prince Leopold when he first came to London.

"Your mama's parents, on the other hand, were ever so rich. They disapproved of a match between your parents. But your mama and papa were so very much in love. Finally, they were forced to run away together. They were poor, but so happy together.

"I never saw a couple as happy as they — until they had you!" She turned to Sarah. "You can't imagine any more joy, but there it was. When you arrived, they were even more full of joy."

Sarah's smile disappeared. "But then came the sad part."

"Yes, my dear, then came the sad part. They both died from an awful outbreak of fever that year. Your mother first then, within a week, your father. I had taken you away at the first sign of illness. Your mother begged me to. She didn't want you catching it, you were such a wee baby."

"Why didn't you keep me as your own?"

"Oh, my dear, how I wish I could have, but I was just a girl myself. I had no husband. So I did the next best thing I could. I found a couple for you to stay with. Mama and Papa Thornton could offer you a nice home and family until someday you would be grown up enough to come and live with me. Since the day I brought you here, I've come and visited you every week."

"Yes. I do so love your visits." Sarah played with the tassel at the end of her parasol. "What about Mama's family?"

"Her parents had died after your mama ran away. They had no other children, so there was no help from anyone on that side. You were all alone in the world." She wondered if Sarah would still believe every detail of this story as she got older. Eleanor hoped that with the repetition, each fact would become so engrained in Sarah's memory, it would be impossible to question the veracity of the tale.

She patted her knees. "Well, we'd best continue back. Mama and Papa Thornton will wonder what's keeping us. We don't want to be late for tea."

Sarah scurried up and gave Eleanor a

hand. The two dusted the grass off each other's skirts, then headed back to the carriage.

When they arrived at the prosperous farmhouse where Sarah lived, they were greeted by a married daughter of the Thorntons who had come by for a visit. Sarah ran off to show the woman's two daughters her new parasol. Eleanor followed Mrs. Thornton and her daughter to the large kitchen in the back.

Mrs. Thornton poured them each a cup of tea. "Eleanor, you mustn't bring Sarah so many fancy gifts each time you come to visit her. Her wardrobe can scarcely contain the gowns she has."

"Oh, Louisa, I can't help it. I see something pretty and I immediately think of Sarah."

"It's not right," Mrs. Thornton said with a shake of her head. "She needs to live at her station. Look at my daughter Lydia's children. They're not poor by any means. They're well dressed, clean and proper behaved. You couldn't ask for anything more. But they're not rich and they don't go acting as if they are."

Lydia nodded in agreement.

Eleanor pursed her lips. This subject had come up more than once of late. She looked forward to the day she could take Sarah away for good to live with her. Soon.

"Well, in another year or two, Sarah will be going away to Miss Hillary's Academy for Young Ladies," Eleanor replied in her most soothing tone. "There she will be on an equal footing with all the young ladies."

"Humph," was all Mrs. Thornton said. But she didn't remain silent long. After a sip of tea, she added, "What good will it do Sarah to study amongst all those lords' and ladies' daughters, when she don't come from the same world? When they have their come-outs, where will Sarah be? Right back in this village but with notions way above her station. She won't be able to follow her new friends from the young ladies' academy. They certainly won't welcome her into their circle when they know her humble parentage. No high-and-mighty lord will have her for his wife."

"There are plenty of respectable young gentlemen she can marry," countered Eleanor, who had given her daughter's future lots of thought over the years. "She could marry a solicitor or a — a — doctor —" A fleeting image of the one she had recently met invaded her thoughts. "There are many men who are not of the ton, but who are gentlemen nonetheless."

"But will she have them if her head has been filled up with such notions of society, starting with all these tales of her own ma and dad? I've been saying it for years, dear Eleanor, you haven't done her any good telling her those Banbury tales."

Eleanor gave a careless laugh. "Louisa, you worry too much. I have it all figured out. Sarah will go to Miss Hillary's school and she'll move to London with me. By then I shall have a nice place in Mayfair. When it's time for her come-out, I shall put out discreet inquiries and I'm sure we'll meet several eligible young bachelors."

"Who'll be wanting to know the amount of her dowry."

Eleanor sat up straighter in the ladder-back chair. "I have been putting money away for her since she was an infant. She'll have her dowry."

Once again Mrs. Thornton harrumphed, but said no more.

CHAPTER SIX

Ian walked into the operating theater at St. Thomas's promptly at ten o'clock the next morning. The semicircular, amphitheater-style viewing area known as the "standings" was already crammed. Students, fellow surgeons, interns, some physicians and apothecaries stood leaning against the wooden railings on each of the five tiers rising from the operating floor.

The front row was reserved for the dressers of the other surgeons. His own, as well as his apprentices, already stood around the operating table, a plain, stout deal table half-covered in a sheet of oilcloth.

He glanced at its end. Good, no outside visitors today. Usually these special guests of his colleagues sat in chairs at one end of the operating table, but today they stood empty.

The hum of voices diminished only somewhat as he walked to the wooden pegs by the entrance. He removed his coat and rolled up his sleeves. Then he donned the coat hanging by the door. It was stiff with dried blood. He turned up its collar to protect his neck cloth. Over the coat he tied on a grocer's bib and apron, then proceeded to wash his hands in the basin. Most surgeons laughed at this last step, but Ian's fastidious nature demanded this measure both before and after surgery.

Ian walked to the table for his inspection. Sunlight streamed in from the skylight above, giving good natural light for the operation.

"Good morning, gentlemen," he greeted his assistants.

"Good morning, Mr. Russell," they replied, standing at attention.

The wooden box beneath the table had been filled with fresh sawdust. The tables beside the operating table were covered with green baize cloth and the instruments neatly laid out. Ligatures of various sizes; tourniquet and tape; knives and saws; tenacula, scissors, needles, and pins; rolls of lint and bandages.

On another table were basins of water, pledgets and sponges.

"Very good," he told his assistants. For months after he'd arrived, he'd had to fight for adequate instruments and hygiene. After observing the conditions of La Charité, and the high standards of cleanliness maintained by the sisters who looked after the patients in the wards, he'd striven to institute such standards here, but it had been a steady uphill battle.

The patient was brought in and told to sit on the wooden table. Ian shook his left hand, the other lying in his lap inert.

"Good morning, Mr. Halliday. Are you ready?" At least the man looked strong and healthy. There was a good chance he would survive.

"Guess I'm ready as I'll ever be. Make it quick, Doc."

"It'll be over in a few minutes."

As Ian moved to his instrument tray, his assistant gave the patient the "physician's stick" to bite on.

As soon as his assistants were ready, one supporting the man's back and tying his good arm behind him, the other holding his thighs, Ian said a short, silent prayer and turned to his instrument table.

Another assistant drew up the skin of the man's upper arm tightly and tied a tourniquet around it. A dresser bound a tape below this. Taking up a knife, Ian made a quick, clean incision, ignoring the patient's sudden cry and involuntary jerk backward. The assistants held him firm. Ian took up one of the heavy, square-edged saws and bore down hard, sawing through the bone and sinew. Blood spurted out, spattering his apron, falling into the sawdust.

Ian took the needle and catgut held out to him by the dresser and secured the artery and some of the other vessels together.

His assistant loosened the tourniquet and the dresser cleaned the stump with one of the sponges. Ian drew the flaps of skin down over the stump and covered them with the lint. The dresser wrapped a damp pledget over this and then bound the stump with bandages.

It was over quickly, as Ian had promised the man. As those in the amphitheater shouted and applauded, two of Ian's assistants carried the patient out of the theater and into an awaiting bed, where they would give him a draft to quiet him and take turns keeping the arm raised to prevent the ligatures being pulled off with the pressure.

Ian turned to wash his hands and oversee the washing of his instruments. The next operation involved a lithotomy, or removing a bladder stone.

The patient was a man in his seventies. He'd been given quite a quantity of barley water to drink to inflate his bladder. He was trembling with fear and Ian did the best to assure him the entire procedure would take under half a minute.

Ian finished his rounds at St. Thomas's. Thursdays were grueling, beginning with surgery in the operating theater, followed by checking on patients in the eight different wards.

He removed his soiled jacket and put on a clean one he kept on a hook in one of the lecture halls. Tomorrow would be his weekly anatomy lecture, followed by dissecting and pathology as they cut open and analyzed the cadavers of those patients who had died the night before.

There had been much resistance to dissecting the bodies of deceased patients, but now they were gradually following the French model begun under the great Corvisart. Hypotheses based on unfounded theories of the four different humors of the bodies were no longer acceptable, but only those findings based upon detailed observation and repeated experimentation.

Whatever else the French Revolution and the Napoleonic empire had wrought, one positive development had been the reorganization and formation of the medical schools and teaching hospitals in France. The two years Ian had spent in the city after the allies had entered Paris until the final defeat of Napoleon at Waterloo had been among the most illuminating of his career. He'd seen the success rate in the large, airy wards of La Charité, where he'd followed the French physicians with their coterie of students going from the patients' wards to the dissecting rooms. They rigorously compared the symptoms of the sick with the condition of their organs after death.

Since his return to England, Ian had tried to acquaint his colleagues with all he'd learned both through surgery on the battlefield and at the great Parisian hospitals. But change was resisted by the very boards — the Royal College of Physicians and the Royal College of Surgeons — whose purpose it was to maintain the highest standards among the medical community.

With his limbs aching from weariness, Ian left the hospital. Some days felt more draining than others. The surgeries had gone well, but the next few days would be critical. So many of the patients developed erysipelas, and then it remained to be seen whether gangrene would set in.

He exited the hospital and turned up his collar. September was almost over and the evening had a distinct chill to it. He picked up his pace, looking forward to a warm fire and a pot of tea in his rooms.

"Get your copy of *The Times.* Two pence. Latest news," a newsboy shouted, holding a paper aloft. Ian slowed his steps as he fished in his pocket for a coin and handed it to the boy. While he waited to receive a folded copy of the paper, his eyes strayed to the playbills glued to the wall behind the boy.

The Parson's Peccadillo. Under it was a list of names and characters, but the name that stood out in bold, black letters was *Mrs. Eleanor Neville as Marianna.* The piece was described as a burletta in three acts. Printed at the bottom of the poster was the name of the theater and time of the show. The Royal Circus — Surrey Theatre.

He felt something thrust at him. "What —" The boy handed him his newspaper. "Oh — thank you." He automatically felt in his pocket for his watch as he turned away, wondering what time it was. It had been close to seven when he'd left the hospital.

The show would be starting soon.

He tried to ignore that fact, but as he continued down the street, it persisted. He pictured Mrs. Neville standing on a stage. What would she sound like up there above the crowds? He remembered her uncanny

120

ability at mimicry and didn't doubt she had some talent. Still, he viewed with distaste a woman exhibiting herself onstage.

He had almost reached Marshelsea Prison when he stopped at the corner of Union Street. Ignoring the warnings in his head, he found himself turning away from the road that led home and crossing the street. He headed down Union, a street that would cut across to Southwark.

With each passing step, the voice in his head diminished, until he reached New Surrey. As he drew closer to the Thames, the well-lit street revealed the imposing arched front of the theater. Small groups of people loitered at its shallow steps. Many of the women he recognized clearly as streetwalkers, their dresses only to mid-calf, their looks provocative. Carriages drew up to deposit their better dressed occupants at the front entrance.

Ian slowed down as he reached the steps, acutely aware he was about to enter Mrs. Neville's world. Although her world and his were only a short distance apart geographically, a vast gulf existed between them. He'd never been to any type of musical comedy. His family had brought him up to believe the theater was evil. During his apprenticeship, his uncle had taken him to see a

Shakespeare play a few times at the Drury.

"You're an 'andsome gent-cove," a female voice said, as the woman sidled up to him. "Whad'ya say to a little entertainment tonight?"

He pushed himself gently aside. "No, thanks."

She gave him a sly smile. "A quid to a'a'penny I can entertain you better'n what's inside there." She jerked her head toward the theater. "Come on, duck, whad'ya say?"

He stepped away from her toward the lobby doors. "I say you're wasting your time with me."

"Oh, you're one o'them highty-tighty gents." Her voice turned scornful. He heard no more as he entered the lobby and headed to the ticket window.

He purchased his ticket and headed across the lobby toward the red-carpeted saloon. Here again, many prostitutes loitered. One or two eyed him boldly but left him alone. He could see they were interested in more lucrative quarry — the well-dressed youngbloods and dandies milling about, parleying innuendos.

He could hear muffled sounds from beyond the saloon, so he knew the play had already started. He opened one of the doors leading to the lower tier of boxes.

The interior of the theater was well lit and he had no trouble locating his box, which was toward the rear. The theater was only half full.

He recognized Eleanor's voice before he saw her on the stage. Though she spoke in a theatrical tone, his heartbeat quickened at the mere sound of it.

Ian turned his gaze stageward and fumbled in his pocket for his spectacles. Since he'd returned to London, he'd begun having to wear spectacles to see at a distance. Too many years of book study were undoubtedly taking their toll on his eyesight.

He stared at the stage, which now came into sharp focus. The backdrop was a painted scene of a country landscape with rolling hills and blue sky and plumy clouds.

Eleanor wore a pretty frock full of frills and lace, her hair dressed in ringlets. Her voice came across strong and clear as she began to sing.

The plot soon became clear to him. It featured a lecherous old man who played the part of a country parson. Mrs. Neville played the innocent young maid. The audience burst into laughter at the words sung by each.

Ian knew he shouldn't have come. The

mockery and disrespectful allusions to the "Evangelicals" was patently clear. While the parson preached hellfire and brimstone from a field, the people swarmed to him, crying in repentance. No sooner had his preaching ended than he went in search of the young maid.

The play ended with the young maid at his mercy. At the last minute she was rescued by the young hero, a poor man who had been ridiculed by the parson and exorcised from the community.

True love triumphed, and the young man's integrity was restored, as the old parson was run out of town.

As the actors took their bows, the audience yelled their approval.

The actors exited by the side doors at each end of the stage. The painted backdrops were lowered through the floor as the stagehands prepared for the next performance, a short pantomime.

Ian had looked down at his program, deciding he wouldn't stay for it, when an attendant opened the door to the box and handed him a folded note.

Ian opened it and read,

Mr. Russell,
I'm so glad you found time for the

theater this evening. Please join me in the greenroom backstage after the performance.

Respectfully,
Eleanor Neville

He wrestled with himself. It would do no good to see her again. Tonight had clearly shown how far apart their worlds were. But still he sat, unable to forget the young woman who had stood so close to him he could breathe in her soft perfume as the angry crowds rioted all around them. The same young woman who had labored tirelessly at his side afterward, seeming to anticipate his every need before he voiced it.

Who was the real Eleanor Neville?

Something in him yearned to discover the answer.

So he sat back, waiting impatiently through the pantomime. Mrs. Neville wasn't in it, and he cared nothing for the ludicrous antics of the players.

As soon as it was over he exited the box and asked directions to the greenroom from an attendant busy trimming the wicks of the candles in the wall sconces. Ian walked down the corridor and through a door leading backstage. Laughter came through the doorway as he followed a pair of men entering the same room. It resembled a comfortable sitting room.

He regretted coming as soon as he saw the crowd.

Well-dressed dandies young and old flocked around the pretty young actresses and dancers. Disgust flooded him as he contemplated the scene. Vultures circling their prey, he thought. The young women hadn't heeded the message of the play very well. They ridiculed a man of God, but didn't see the lecherous intentions of the wealthy men of the city right in front of them.

Before he could make a move, Mrs. Neville spotted him. Leaving the men surrounding her, she came toward him with a smile.

"Mr. Russell, what a nice surprise to see you here this evening."

He bowed over her hand. She still wore the heavy white makeup and rouge she'd had onstage. Close up it looked thick and unnatural.

"Come and sit here." She took him to the group of gentlemen, who eyed him with scarcely disguised scorn.

One of the young bucks snickered.

"May I present Mr. Russell, a surgeon from St. Thomas's? He saved our poor dear

Betsy's life when she was very nearly off the hooks."

One of the young men rose and offered his hand. "Well, 'pon my honor, why didn't you say so in the first place? We thought you were one of those dull Methodist coves."

The other young gentlemen burst into rude laughter.

The young man let his hand go. "We're much obliged to you, Doctor. We miss Betsy sorely. When will she be back on the boards?"

"Not for a while," he answered curtly. Was this perhaps the young man responsible for Miss Simms's plight? Or perhaps one of the others? His gaze traveled over the lot.

"You must excuse me a moment, Mr. Russell, while I change."

"I can't stay," he told Mrs. Neville. "I merely wanted to pay my respects."

"How did you like the show?" she asked eagerly.

"The show itself was a piece of rubbish, but your individual talent rises above it. You have a very nice singing voice."

From dismay at his first remark to pleasure at his compliment at the end, her face underwent a variety of expressions. He felt pleased that he could somehow put together some kind of compliment from something he had been thoroughly disgusted with.

"I hope the piece didn't offend you."

"You should rather hope it didn't offend your Maker."

She looked askance. "It was all in good fun. That's what burlettas are — they poke fun at everyone and everything." She shrugged. "At any rate, it's an old piece. I don't know why Mr. Dibdin decided to revive it. Wait until you hear what we will be doing next." Her eyes shone. "It will be a brand-new piece."

He looked down at his folded hands. It was a mistake to have come. "I really must be off."

She looked crestfallen. "So soon? I wanted to invite you to dinner. Not only to share my good news." She lowered her voice. "I wanted to thank you for all you've done for Betsy. You truly saved her life."

He felt his resolve weakening at the softness in her tone.

"Besides, if you don't take me, I'm at the Duke d'Alvergny's mercy, and I find him quite tiresome tonight."

Ian followed the direction of her gaze to the gentleman who sat eyeing them. Ian judged him to be about a decade older than himself, at least in his forties. He was dressed in black evening clothes, making Ian's black frock coat look shabby. Pomade darkened his blond hair. His neck cloth held a diamond stud pin and his face had a ruddy, well-fed look where his shirt points met his clean-shaven jaw. He'd probably suffer from gout or a bilious liver in another ten years.

The man sat back in the chair, resting one ankle on his knee. He studied Ian coolly as he dangled his quizzing glass from its silk ribbon from one hand. It swung back and forth, tapping against the shiny black half boot. Something in the expression of his eyes challenged Ian.

"Very well," Ian replied, turning his attention back to Mrs. Neville. "I'll wait here while you change."

"You are a dear." She gave him a sweet smile. At the protest of the lounging dandies, she blew them a kiss and exited the room.

Ian walked away from the group and stood near the entrance. He watched the antics of the other actresses with the wealthy young men. One by one he could see arrangements being made. D'Alvergny ignored the other young women. After a moment he unfolded himself from his chair and stood, and Ian could appreciate what a large man he was.

He exited through the door Mrs. Neville had taken. Ian tensed, tempted to follow him out.

He stopped himself. What business was it of his? Mrs. Neville was an actress, he reminded himself. She'd doubtless had many liaisons with these society men.

Disgusted at his own weakness for accepting Mrs. Neville's invitation, he turned his back on the company and studied a playbill on the wall. He was no better than any of those men present, he told himself. Why had he come tonight?

When Mrs. Neville returned, Ian looked at her closely, to determine if d'Alvergny had addressed her. He could discern nothing from her features, but he was relieved to find she had washed all the makeup from her face. The ringlets were gone, and her hair was gathered simply beneath her bonnet.

"Come, my carriage is at the rear." She put her hand in the crook of his arm and directed him out the back. They walked down a shadowy corridor directly behind the stage. Discarded scenery lay stacked against the wall, and stagehands were busy putting things away.

"Good night, Eleanor," said several workers, and she bade each one good-night.

"Have you ever been on a stage?" she asked him.

He shook his head.

Before he knew what she was about, she led him through an arch and he found himself at the rear of the stage. She walked forward with him.

"Watch your step. There are trapdoors and grooves for the scene flats."

He looked down and saw what she meant. There were large slits in the floor where scene backdrops were raised and lowered.

She took him to the forestage where the actors habitually stood. It thrust out with columned doors at either side. In front of it lay the orchestra pit, with the galleries and boxes surrounding them at either side.

Although the seats were empty, he felt the sensation of being exposed to many eyes.

"What does it feel like addressing a crowd?" he asked.

"Tonight was nothing. We're almost at the end of our run. But when the theater is full, as on an opening night, it is quite heady." She let his arm go and took a step forward, facing the nonexistent audience. Clearing her throat, she began:

This Comic Story, or this Tragic jest,

May make you laugh, or cry, as you like
  best;
May exercise your good, or your ill-nature,
Move with distress, or tickle you with sat-
  ire.

Her voice was rich and carried easily across the auditorium. With a flourish, she turned to him and smiled.

He couldn't help smiling back, beginning to understand the draw she held for the audience. "What was that from?"

"Gay's *The What D'ye Call It,* an early burlesque comedy."

"Is that what you were doing this evening — making the audience laugh?"

"Or moving them to distress," she added significantly. "I'm sorry if you were displeased."

He shook aside the apology, preferring to forget the play. "Shall we go and dine?"

"Yes, I'm famished!" she replied with another captivating smile.

He followed her out, amazed at how easily his scruples disappeared when he was in her company. All it took was one smile from her, and he was willing to be led anywhere.

They sat in a noisy oyster house on the Strand. "I so adore oysters, don't you?" she asked after they had placed their order and the waiter left them.

He smiled at her enthusiasm. "If they are fresh, and the place is a reputable one."

"Oh, these are very fresh. And this eatery has been here as long as I can remember. You shall see, they make the best oyster pie in puff pastry."

They sat at a window side table overlooking the busy street. Many late-night theatergoers sat at the surrounding tables.

"I haven't received your bills yet for Betsy's care," she said after a moment. "Please send them to Ten Bedford Place, right off Bloomsbury Square."

He shrugged. "I hadn't planned on billing Miss Simms, since she won't be able to earn her living for some time."

Her eyes widened in astonishment. "You saved her life, she owes you a great deal."

"I simply did what I was called to do. The Lord saved her life."

"I shall not refine too much upon the matter, but I do insist on paying her medical bills. It's the least I can do after all you did for her."

Ian made no reply as the hot pastries and tankards of porter were set before them. As soon as the waiter left them again, he bowed his head to ask a silent blessing over the food.

"You are a pious man," Mrs. Neville remarked as he was unfolding his napkin.

"I was raised by some very pious people and I work with others at the mission. As for myself . . ." He shrugged. "I don't think of myself as pious, only as God-fearing."

"I have little time for piety." She lifted her tankard. "Tonight is a night of celebration for me."

"So you mentioned," he said, going along with her change of topic. "What is the occasion?"

"I have been offered the part of Leporello in Dibdin's new burletta of *Don Giovanni, or The Spectre on Horseback.*"

"*Don Giovanni,* isn't that an Italian opera?"

Her laughter tinkled over the sound of cutlery. "A travesty of the opera. In this play, Don Giovanni kills Donna Anna's father and must escape to London. He ends up falling into the Thames and is rescued by some fishermen, at which point he immediately tries to woo their wives, whose names are Shrimperina and Lobsteretta."

Her laughter died when she noticed he hadn't joined in her amusement. "Don't you think that's funny?"

"It sounds ridiculous."

"It is. Don't you see? The humor is found in the rhymed couplets we sing. The story itself is a silly version of the Don Giovanni story, but it's Dibdin's libretto and our rendition of the lines that bring amusement to the audience.

"The Don pursues every woman he meets before being caught in the end. It's all quite droll. I read a bit of the script earlier today, when the manager told me about the piece. In this version, Donna Anna is bent on revenge, but another part of her wants Don Giovanni for herself even though she is engaged to another."

He frowned. "Isn't that a bit capricious?"

She shrugged. "It's a better role than many. Most of the heroines in today's melodramas and burlesques are such simpering fools, always needing to be rescued as you could see from tonight's piece. Donna Anna is another stamp altogether."

She took a healthy bite of her oyster pastry and washed it down with a swallow from her tankard. Then she laughed afresh, and he could see nothing he said could dampen her spirits.

"We shall be rehearsing next week to open in a fortnight," she continued. "I hope you come on opening night."

"After what I saw tonight, I think I was

right in staying away from the theater."

She drew herself up. "What do you mean?"

"I was brought up to believe the theater was devoid of morals. What I saw tonight has not disabused me of this notion."

She flicked aside a flake of pastry from the tablecloth. "Morality is for those who have the blunt."

"Your young Miss Simms might have saved herself a lot of trouble if she'd had a higher moral standard."

"Betsy is young and ignorant. She'll learn the ways of the world soon enough."

"If the conduct of those young actresses backstage tonight is any indication, they haven't learned from their mistakes. They seem to believe they may have any man they please with no consequences."

"Any man who can make it worth their while," she countered in a hard voice.

"What is the difference between that and one of the lightskirts hanging about the theater entrance?" he asked, his tone matching hers.

"Between a common streetwalker and a woman who knows how to secure herself a tidy nest egg for her old age? There is a vast difference, Mr. Russell — the difference between ending up dead in some alleyway

136

or living out one's years in a comfortable house in a respectable part of town."

He swallowed, shaken by her convictions despite himself. "Is that what you have done?"

"That is an impertinent question, Mr. Russell."

"You are right, Mrs. Neville. My apologies."

"Don't use that disapproving tone with me. Come," she said, her tone softening, "it is all very well for a young woman who has a father to defend her virtue. What happens to the one whose stepfather strips her of her virtue before she has scarcely entered womanhood?"

"Is that what happened to Miss Simms?"

She shrugged and looked away. "Who knows? 'Tis often enough the case."

She leaned her head back and stared at him through half-closed lids, looking in that moment dangerously seductive. His glance strayed down her slim white throat, and he felt his own throat go dry.

"What about your morality, Mr. Russell? Dining late in the evening with a common actress, while your wife sits at home with the little ones? Does she wait up for you? Is she sitting by the fireside? Does she believe you are on a medical call?" Her soft, sultry words mocked him.

"I am not married," he answered steadily.

"I am sorry." She leaned forward, immediately contrite, the image of seductress vanished with the speed of a snuffed candle. "Have you been widowed long?"

"I am neither wed nor widowed."

Her gray eyes opened wide. "I can scarcely credit what you say. You look old enough to have long since wed."

"The fact remains I have never entered into the state of matrimony."

"Excuse my impudence, but how old are you, Mr. Russell?"

"Two-and-thirty this past summer," he answered stiffly.

She raised her eyebrows. "Why haven't you married? Are you waiting for a woman who satisfies your high moral caliber?"

" 'Who can find a virtuous woman? For her price is far above rubies,' " he quoted softly.

She made an inelegant sound. "That's because she probably doesn't exist except as a figment of your imagination."

He ignored the mockery in her tone. "I am waiting for the Lord's choice for me. Up to now, He hasn't made it clear. And, yes, she will be a virtuous woman."

She gave him a pitying look. "You are so

sure about that. Women can be very crafty about their purity, you know. I have an acquaintance who has feigned virginity a half-dozen times."

"I know that my future wife will serve God, and her purity of spirit will shine through her."

"And how will you know she is the one God has chosen for you? Will He beat a drum when this virtuous woman appears and you will know you are to wed?"

"I don't know how He'll let me know. I only know that He will."

"And what about you? Will you be as pure as you expect your future bride to be?"

He could feel himself reddening in the face, but he refused to back down. "I have kept myself pure for my future wife."

He could see the incredulity in her eyes, and it irked him.

"You must be a lonely man." Before he had a chance to negate the charge, she answered for him, "No, of course you aren't. You have your work. You don't have time to be lonely. You wouldn't have time for a wife. Where would you ever fit one in?"

She gave a mirthless laugh. "We have that in common. I have little time for amorous entanglements. I work half the night like you, and sleep half the morning."

He shrugged, feigning an insouciance he was far from feeling. "You can believe what you like. It makes little difference to me. I care only for the Lord's good opinion."

"You are serious, aren't you? Aren't you afraid you will grow old before having tasted the delights of the flesh?" The question teased him.

"A Christian is more concerned with eternity than with the temporal of this world."

"Don't you like women?"

The outspoken question took him aback, and when he understood her meaning, he felt his face flush again, this time in anger. "I like them well enough," he answered shortly.

She sighed, as if the conversation were completely beyond her ken. "What happens if God withholds your future bride for another ten years? Aren't you afraid you'll be a little old to be enjoying matrimonial bliss?"

"Then He will redeem the time for us," he answered. Her words weighed on him despite his confident tone. What would happen if he were obliged to wait another decade?

"I have seen too much of the fruit of worldly vice," he answered after a moment.

"Every day I treat poxed men and women. I see too many die on the streets. No, I have no desire to compromise my trust in God's way. He has ordained *holy* matrimony between a man and a woman. I am content to wait for that union."

"So you will keep yourself virtuous and unspotted until that blessed day?"

"I plan to continue so, yes."

"You poor gull." Her tone dripped with pity, and Ian knew he had been a fool to come with her tonight. He deserved her derision.

He pushed away from the table. "I may be so in your eyes, but since I am not concerned with the approbation of the theatrical world, I may rest easy."

When she had dropped him off, Eleanor sat a moment in her dark carriage, watching Mr. Russell reach his door. The evening had ended badly, and she was sorry she had teased him. But his high-toned morality had irritated her and she had merely wanted to knock him off his pedestal a bit.

She hadn't succeeded. Instead, she'd been made to feel as soiled as a girl from a flash house.

She tapped on the panel to signal her driver to go.

As the carriage rattled over the cobble-stones, her mind went over the evening's conversation.

Could the good surgeon truly be faithful to some far-off hope of a divinely appointed bride?

Eleanor couldn't credit that such a man existed on the face of the earth. Every man of her acquaintance was susceptible to a female's charms.

Undoubtedly, Mr. Russell was no different. He just hadn't been tested by the right set of circumstances.

It would be amusing to discover how high his moral standards truly were.

Eleanor decided at that moment to make it a game to test the righteous surgeon. Let him dare to judge the likes of Betsy and herself then.

It would be interesting to find out what type of woman he preferred. She could play the part soft and demure like a debutante in her first season, or bold and alluring like a siren, singing her seductive song. She could even play the role elegant and lady-like.

Or perhaps none of these. Perhaps she'd already discovered the key — a helpmate in his work. She remembered the mission. She could visit it again and offer some assistance.

She laughed inwardly. How long could Mr. Russell resist her charms? She had seen many lesser men fall. There had been something in his eyes the day of the street riot. Under all that disapproval lay a man like any other. He was no better than d'Alvergny with his offers of jewelry and other as-yet-unnamed favors.

It would be amusing to toy with the good doctor, she decided, her thoughts returning to Mr. Russell. She would carry out a little wager with herself. She wouldn't let it go too far. No one would be hurt. After all, she had bigger fish to fry, and had no possible interest in an entanglement with a low-paid surgeon.

It would serve Mr. Russell right to be brought down a peg or two.

Ian entered his quiet house and hung up his coat. As he was making his way down the corridor, his cat appeared at the top of the stairs and sat staring at him.

"Hello there, Plato. Did I wake you up?" he asked.

As he entered his bedroom, the cat followed him.

Mrs. Neville's mocking tone and looks came back to him as he stroked his cat and felt its purring beneath his fingertips.

Was he a normal man? He felt like the rarest oddity in her eyes.

But oh, yes, he was very much a normal man. If she only knew the very natural reaction he experienced every time she stood near him and he smelled her perfume or she slid her hand into the crook of his arm.

His fingers clenched into fists. He forced himself to abandon the path his thoughts and feelings were taking.

She was *not* the one for him. He must be patient and wait, trusting in God for the eventual choice of helpmate for him.

His future wife would be as pure as the driven snow. He'd been waiting for her for a long, long time, and he wouldn't compromise now.

CHAPTER SEVEN

"Oh, look, isn't that Lord Halford?"

Eleanor followed Betsy's gaze. "Where?"

"Over there on the bay."

"Yes, I see him."

Betsy looked around Hyde Park enthusiastically, like a child at a fair. "All the ton seem to be out driving today! It's so funny to see the same gentlemen I see in the theater now riding in the park in such stately processions with their ladies."

Eleanor agreed. She glanced over at Betsy seated beside her in her carriage, to make sure the girl wasn't tiring. It was her first outing since that awful night.

"How are you feeling, my dear?" she asked, adjusting the carriage blanket around her friend's legs.

"Oh, I'm fine. Really. I just wish I didn't feel so weak all the time."

"You have to be patient. Each day you'll get stronger if you follow Mr. Russell's advice." Her stomach fluttered when she said his name. "Has he been by to see you lately?" she asked casually.

Betsy nodded. "Yes, just a few days ago. He said I was vastly improved."

Eleanor nodded. She had not seen him since the dinner, almost a fortnight since.

"Tell me again about the new show." Betsy's voice interrupted her thoughts.

"Oh, it will be a true extravaganza, as Mr. Dibdin is billing it. 'A specter on horseback, a comic, heroic, operatic, tragic, panto-mimic, burletta spectacular extravaganza!' How is that for hyperbole?"

Betsy laughed in appreciation. "How I wish I were in it. You are so lucky!"

"Yes, but I've been walking the boards much longer than you have."

Their carriage continued down the con-gested row. The October day was mild enough to have the top removed, and the turning leaves formed a canopy overhead.

"Just think, it will only open a few months after Mozart's production at Covent Gar-den. You'll be following Kemble's act," Betsy said in exaggerated terror. "It will be interesting to see how the crowds react to such a different production of the Don!"

"Oh, I think the two pieces are nothing alike. Dibdin's is pure amusement. Besides,

Mr. Dibdin is a genius when it comes to upstaging his competitors. I think he's even planning on a live horse onstage in the finale."

Betsy eyed her in wonder. "I shall so miss being part of the cast. Perhaps I may come to the rehearsals?"

"Of course, as long as you feel up to it."

"Eleanor?"

"Hmm?" she answered, continuing to scan the carriage crowd around them.

"Do you . . . think I did wrong to . . . do . . . what I did?" she said in a low voice that ended in a whisper.

Eleanor turned to her, knowing immediately what she was referring to. She had dreaded this question. The topic was not an easy one for her. She knew so well the terror of finding herself in Betsy's predicament. And yet, would she have ever done anything differently? Her love for Sarah was so all-consuming that she could not imagine having rid herself of her unborn daughter. But Betsy hadn't had any place to go. Eleanor knew nothing of the man responsible for Betsy's predicament.

She took her friend's hand in her own. "You mustn't even think about it. Just put it behind you, and think of the future. You'll soon be back at the theater. You're fortunate

Dibdin loves you," she said with a face. "I seem to have run-ins with him all the time. I suppose I'm too outspoken for his taste."

Betsy fidgeted with her gloves. "The gentleman . . . well, the one . . . I was seeing," she explained, her voice hushed. "He has never come to see me." Her lower lip trembled. "I was so foolish . . . I th-thought he loved me."

"Don't cry, Betsy." Eleanor patted her clasped hands, knowing well that scenario. Once, she had been just as foolish, believing a gentleman's avowals of love.

"Just forget him. He's a scoundrel, and that's all there is to it. Think about the theater. Someday you'll get a lead role like I did. You'll see."

Betsy sighed. "Yes, I suppose so. Sometimes, though, it's hard to forget." She pressed her lips together, visibly trying to hold back her tears. "It helps when Mr. Russell and Jem come." She gave a watery giggle. "Jem makes me laugh."

Eleanor smiled. "That's the best medicine you could have, I'm sure of it."

"Mr. Russell has been so kind." She stared off into space. "That's the kind of gentleman I wish I could meet someday. If I'd known someone like him, I never would have . . . you know . . ."

"Oh, nonsense, don't let your head be turned by a man like Mr. Russell," Eleanor scoffed to hide her dismay at the younger girl's words. Betsy saw Mr. Russell practically every day. How cozy were they getting?

"A poor surgeon, who gets called at all hours of the night," she continued, "whose life is never his own. What kind of husband would he be? You'd be left all alone most of the time. He'd never let you back on the stage, and where would you be when he tired of you? High and dry."

"Oh." Betsy's voice was small, and she looked down at her folded hands. "I was just being foolish." She sighed.

Eleanor stifled an impatient remark. Why had Betsy's harmless infatuation gotten her so out of countenance? It was an absurd notion — Mr. Russell with Betsy! The irony was certainly not lost on her. If only poor Betsy knew how high Mr. Russell's standards were.

"Good afternoon, ladies." A familiar male voice intruded upon her thoughts.

She turned to find the Duke d'Alvergny tipping his high-crowned beaver to them from atop his white stallion. She acknowledged his greeting.

"Your Grace, how delightful," she said,

feigning pleasure. In truth, she found the man impossibly conceited.

"The delight in finding two such lovely young ladies abroad is all mine."

Betsy blushed and thanked him for the compliment.

D'Alvergny sidled his horse up to Eleanor's side of the carriage. "Did you find my gift last night to your liking?" His gaze strayed to her unadorned neck.

"It was a pretty bauble," she replied, referring to the necklace of garnets entwined in a gold-filigreed design.

"But not pretty enough to sport this afternoon?"

"I've placed it in my jewel case . . . sandwiched between my diamonds," she added with a sidelong look at him. Men like him needed to be put in their proper place.

"You prefer diamonds," he answered smoothly. "If I send you diamonds, I shall expect something tangible in return."

"Jewels don't tempt me. I have enough to please me."

"What does tempt you?" he asked, his gloved hands resting across the pommel, the riding crop held between them.

She pursed her lips, as if seriously considering his question. "An invitation to a fashionable party of the ton?"

"Your wish is my command."

She gave him a mocking smile. "It must be truly fashionable. Nothing in some gentlemen's club. No lightskirts present."

He bowed over her hand. "You will see the power I wield."

"We shall see." If he were able to bring this about, he might be worth a small favor of hers in return.

The next day after rehearsals, Eleanor dressed in her plainest gown and directed her carriage to Whitechapel. Thankfully, her coachman remembered the way to the mission.

When she expressed her desire to help in the work, she was introduced to a woman about her own age named Miss Breton.

"Good day," she said, offering her hand. "I came by the other day with the surgeon, Mr. Russell."

Miss Breton looked at her with a pleasant smile. "Oh, yes. I heard you kept the children quite entertained. I'm sorry I wasn't here to meet you then. Would you care for a tour?"

"Yes. I was very impressed with the work, although I only saw the infirmary with the sick children."

"Well, we also have a few classrooms, and

a dining hall, a chapel next door . . ." As she spoke, Miss Breton escorted her down the long corridor.

After they had poked into the various rooms she mentioned, they came to the infirmary.

Eleanor glanced around. There were only a few children in the beds. "There were more the other day," she commented in a low tone.

Miss Breton nodded solemnly. "Two have passed away, and three have recovered. Thankfully, there have been no more outbreaks of illness. These warm days are a blessing."

Eleanor noticed a couple of the children looking her way in recognition. As soon as she smiled at them, they smiled back. With a look to Miss Breton, who nodded encouragement, Eleanor approached their beds.

"You came back," one of the young girls said.

"Yes, indeed."

The girl's smile disappeared. "You said you'd bring us a treat if we promised to be well. I'm sorry I'm not better." She hung her head in disappointment.

"Ah, but you are looking much better to my eyes." She tilted the little girl's chin with her fingertip and examined her face. "Yes, I detect a definite improvement. What do you think, Miss Breton?"

"Oh, yes. Alice is much improved. She'll be back at home in no time."

"What about me, Miss Breton?" the little boy piped up. "Aren't I much improved, too?"

Eleanor turned and surveyed him critically before breaking into a wide smile. "Very much improved."

The children's eyes widened. "Does that mean — ?"

Eleanor rummaged in the capacious reticule she had brought with her. From it she extracted two hand puppets, then removed her gloves and replaced them with the puppets.

"I should like to introduce you to Mr. Bashful and Mr. True Heart, two of the most comical individuals you are ever sure to meet."

The children laughed and clapped their hands.

Eleanor turned to Miss Breton. "Perhaps if we could get a makeshift theater together? All I need is somewhere to kneel behind."

Miss Breton looked around. "I know! We'll overturn this table . . ." Quickly the two women cleared off the table and placed it on its side, in view of the children. Eleanor sat behind it and began her show.

"I will present to you a farce of major proportion. It involves the story of my friend Mr. Bashful. Hark! Here he comes now. . . ."

Ian stepped into the infirmary. He was late coming by for his weekly visit, but he knew there were not many patients there, and none of them in grave danger.

He stopped in the doorway. The sound of children's laughter drew him to the scene at the end of the room. Their thin bodies were turned to the puppet show being enacted from over the edge of a table.

"You are a coxcomb and a wastrel, Sir Livermore."

"Hold your tongue, True Heart. If ever there was a reason to call a body out, it would be now. By Jove, I shall have satisfaction. Anthony! Anthony! My sword case. Where are you, my man?" The puppet twisted around, looking for his manservant.

Ian leaned against the doorpost, watching a few moments. Had Althea found someone to entertain the children? He didn't recognize the voice, which changed with each puppet. But when a female puppet appeared, he recognized Mrs. Neville's voice immediately, although it was shrill and shrewish.

Mrs. Neville. The very timbre of her voice gave him a pang. Whatever was she doing at the mission? He was sure he had seen the last of her the other night at dinner. He'd gone home disappointed in her and disgusted with himself for wanting her to be someone she was not. He was long past the age of being taken in by a mere pretty face.

Since that evening in her company he'd kept repeating the Scripture he'd recited to her, as well as an equally familiar one to him:

"For the lips of a strange woman drop as a honeycomb, and her mouth is smoother than oil: but her end is bitter as wormwood, sharp as a two-edged sword . . . Remove thy way far from her . . ."

There was no misunderstanding the warning, and he was no callow youth to seek temptation. Why, then, must he run into her here, of all places, when he'd resolved for himself that to see her anymore was dangerous?

The puppet show ended, and the children clapped heartily, shouting for more. Althea seemed equally entranced.

Mrs. Neville did not comply, however. The puppets made their final bows, and then she emerged from her crouched position. To silence the children's protests, she gave them the puppets to examine up close. Seeing him, she smiled above the children's heads. Ian resented her knowing look, as if she understood his struggle and reveled in it.

"Good afternoon, Mrs. Neville," he addressed her curtly as he approached the children. "I see you've met Miss Breton. Hello, Althea," he said, his tone softening.

"Yes, we've met," Althea answered. "I told Mrs. Neville how sorry I was that I wasn't here the other day, but now I am doubly sorry, when I see how talented she is. I hope this is not to be the last time we see a performance. The children clearly love it."

Mrs. Neville smiled demurely, looking down.

Why did she have to look so beautiful? His heart ached from standing in such close proximity to her and knowing she was not what she appeared to be.

Eleanor stayed around the mission while Ian examined the children. Other parents brought their sick children to him, knowing he would be at the mission on that day. She accepted a cup of tea from Miss Breton, whom she was soon calling Althea, and sat in a small room off the infirmary.

When Mr. Russell came to let Althea

know he was finished, he seemed surprised to see Eleanor still with her. The three walked out together, where Althea bid them farewell.

Eleanor stood on the front steps of the mission. As the doctor turned to take his leave of her, she said, "Where shall I drop you — the dispensary?"

"There's no need. I'll hail a hack at the corner." His tone was brusque.

What was the matter with him? Was he still offended from the other evening? "Nonsense," she replied, trying to remember what she'd said that night. "I'm just on my way home. My coachman has the rest of the afternoon free."

"I thank you, but no."

Realizing he was going to walk away from her, she knew she had to do something. She put a hand to her brow and pretended to stumble.

Immediately, the doctor's hand came to her elbow. "Are you all right, Mrs. Neville?"

"Yes," she breathed. "Just a sudden faintness. My carriage — if you could help me to my carriage . . ." She leaned heavily against him.

"Yes, of course." He turned and called to her coachman who already had the door open for her.

The next thing Eleanor knew, the good doctor swept her up in his arms and was carrying her to her awaiting coach.

Perfect. Better than she could have asked for. She didn't dare open her eyes, but felt him lay her down along the seat and arrange the squabs beneath her neck.

"My salts . . . I have them in my . . . reticule," she mumbled.

"I have some as well in my bag." She heard him rummage in his medical bag and then the sharp whiff of ammonia brought her eyes open.

"Thank you," she gasped. "I don't know what came over me."

"Starving yourself again," he concluded. "Although I should think that tea you had would have restored you."

"Yes, it should have," she answered innocently.

"When you get home, you'd better see your physician if these spells continue." His tone remained businesslike.

"Yes . . . yes, I shall." She rested her head back against the cushions and closed her eyes as if it was too much effort to keep them open. "Could you please tell McGinnis to take me home?"

"Of course." He knocked on the panel with his stick, and when the coachman's face appeared in the small opening, he gave the instructions.

Eleanor settled back comfortably when she saw that Mr. Russell made no move to depart the carriage. When he didn't speak but sat with his attention fixed out the window, she finally said, "Two of the children at the mission passed away. They must have been among the ones I met the first time I was here."

"Undoubtedly," he answered shortly. "Hundreds perish each day in London, and no one takes it amiss."

"I'm sorry," she said softly.

When he made no reply, she ventured, "Do you have a case on your mind?"

"What — er?" He turned to her, and his eyes locked on hers.

She let the seconds linger, doing her best to keep her own eyes trusting and childlike. At last she spoke as if nothing had passed between them during that interval. "You at least are trying your best to keep some children from perishing."

He took a deep breath. "It sometimes seems that my efforts are in vain. What can one — or even a few individuals — do against so much poverty and squalor?" He gestured futilely at the window.

"Perhaps if more people were aware of the

plight of the children, more would be done."

"They have but to open their eyes and look around them," he replied in a bitter tone.

"Not everyone has your courage to venture to these parts of London."

"These parts of London are everywhere. All you have to do is walk but a few blocks from the City and you are in St. Giles or Clerkenwell."

She shuddered. "I know it well." She closed her eyes again.

"Are you quite all right?"

"Yes. I must have slept too little. I shall be fine."

When they arrived at her street, a quiet, narrow little street between two squares, the coachman opened the door, and Dr. Russell eyed her. "Do you think you can stand?"

"I'll try." She attempted to sit, and the doctor helped her slowly to her feet. He preceded her out of the carriage and spanned her waist with his hands to carry her down. She leaned against him as the two walked up the neat pavement to her door.

"Oh, Mrs. Neville, are you all right?" Mrs. Wilson, her housekeeper, asked as soon as she saw her.

"Yes, I just felt a little faint. This is Mr.

Russell, a surgeon. He has been so kind as to see me home."

The older woman looked nervously from her to Mr. Russell. "Are you sure she is all right?"

"Not completely sure, without an examination. But for the moment the best thing is for Mrs. Neville to lie down."

"Oh, yes, sir, indeed. Let me show you to the sitting room and get a nice pot of tea."

"Yes, that would be lovely. You will stay for a cup, Mr. Russell? You didn't have any at the mission."

She looked up into his eyes as she leaned against his arm. She felt like a master fisherman, playing with the fish on her line. He wouldn't be loosed so easily.

"Very well," he answered slowly.

She was pleased with her little sitting room. It was fashionably furnished, with gold-and-green-striped upholstery on the chairs, light-colored wood paneling, and a tasteful wallpaper above the wainscoting. A few landscapes by Turner hung on the walls.

The doctor helped her to a chaise longue. He cleared his throat. "I think you should loosen your spencer."

"Yes." She began with the top button but dropped her hands to her sides after the first button as if exhausted with the effort. "I'm afraid I must ask your assistance."

She watched him as he leaned over her. His hands were clean and strong looking, the nails neatly clipped. His lean fingers took the button and silk and, after only a momentary fumble, loosened each button in turn. She took a deep breath as if freed from a terrible constriction. At the sound he took an immediate step back.

He was terrified of her. The realization came to her in a flash. Mr. Russell, serious, morally upright surgeon, was frightened of the loose-moraled actress, Eleanor Neville. Oh, it was too rich! She managed to keep her expression properly demure as she waved him to a seat near the chaise.

"Thank you. That has helped immensely."

"You'd better have your maid loosen your stays," he said, a telltale flush tinting his cheeks.

"Yes, I certainly shall." She continued to look at him, caressing him with her eyes.

At that moment, Mrs. Wilson brought in the tea tray. Mr. Russell went immediately to help her carry it.

"No need to bestir yourself, sir. I manage this all the time." The woman set the tray down on a low table, then bustled about, pouring the tea. She helped Eleanor sit up and placed a cup in her hands. "There, I'm sure that'll put you to rights."

"Thank you, Mrs. Wilson," she murmured.

The housekeeper asked the doctor how he took his tea. Eleanor listened idly to their murmurs as she considered the next move of her game.

When the housekeeper had gone, she sipped her tea, her eyes on the doctor. She noticed he kept his attention on the cup in his hands.

"Have you always lived in London?" she asked, growing tired of the silence.

"No. I only came here for my apprenticeship."

"Oh. Where did you grow up?"

"In a small village on the road north. It's only about an hour's ride from here."

"Do you still have family there?"

He smiled slightly. "Oh, yes, both my parents are still living there, as well as several brothers and sisters."

"How many are there of you?" she asked, feeling a small pang, as she always did when she thought of her own family.

"Eight, all still living, God be praised."

"That's a large family. Are you the oldest?" She could easily picture him in the role of the responsible older brother.

He shook his head with another smile.

"No, the youngest. That was perhaps the reason I was able to come to London to commence my medical studies. By then, all of my older siblings were settled."

"What do you think you would have done if you hadn't been able to study medicine?" She was unable to picture him as anything but a dedicated doctor.

"Probably studied for the church. My home saw many great preachers in the years I was growing up. Berridge, Romaine, Newton, and many others whose names have been forgotten, but whose labors have not perished." His features softened in recollection. "My father even took me to hear Wesley preach one of his last sermons at The Foundry in Moorfields when I was but four. They were all great men of God, but they always had time to address a word to a young lad."

She felt a stab at his fond memories of childhood. "What about you?" he asked her before she could respond. "Did you grow up in London?"

"London born and bred," she replied, hoping he wouldn't ask for details of her childhood.

"Your father and mother?"

"I've no idea," she answered, looking away. "I never knew who my father was, and

164

I left my mother when I was fourteen and haven't seen her since."

"I'm sorry. She must have missed you."

"I don't know about that. I had plenty of brothers and sisters. Unlike you, I was the oldest."

"Why did you leave home?" Mr. Russell asked softly.

The direct question caught her off guard. She licked her lips, deciding how much to relate. As he waited for her reply, she resolved to tell him a portion of it. She was curious to see his reaction.

"When I was twelve and my mother great with another child, my stepfather decided I was woman enough to substitute for her. Actually, I don't know if he had ever married my mother, but he certainly fathered enough children with her."

The room was still except for the ticking of the clock and the sound of an occasional carriage in the street. She stirred her tea, telling herself to end the story there.

"Your stepfather took advantage of a child." Mr. Russell's words stated the fact for her.

"I had a pretty face and already a womanly figure," she explained. "I endured it as long as I could. I had nowhere to go, you see."

She risked a look at his face. All she saw

was compassion in his brown eyes. "Finally, I could stand no more and ran away."

"How did you manage that?"

"Waiting till my stepda was plenty drunk. I knew he had just been paid. That's when he'd get drunkest. As soon as I heard him snoring, I stole his purse. I've never been so scared in my life. I knew he would kill me if he found me."

She hadn't brought up the memories in many years, and telling them now brought back the terror of that night. She set the teacup down, afraid she'd spill it.

"I gave the money it contained to my next youngest brother — my favorite — and told him if he valued his life, he'd hide it and use it when there was nothing to eat. I took only a sovereign for myself and ran off that night."

"Where did you go?" Mr. Russell's low voice prompted her to go on.

She gave a deep sigh. "I had been to see a traveling troupe of players earlier that week. When I saw them act, I decided that's what I wanted to do. So I went back to them. They were packing up to leave. I asked for a job." She stopped, reluctant to recall what happened next.

"Did they hire you?"

"They laughed at me and tried to run me

off. But I persisted until I finally got to see the owner."

"How did he receive you?"

"I had a lot to learn of the ways of the world. He made it clear to me there was only one condition if he hired me."

She gauged his reaction, but his serious features gave nothing away except that he was listening intently.

"I agreed in return for work on the stage." She paused. "Do I shock you, Mr. Russell?"

He sighed. "Unfortunately, no. I see all too frequently around me the degradation of women of your class."

Women of her class! The words burned her. He lumped her together with the lowest dregs of fallen women. It hadn't been compassion she'd read in his eyes but pity.

She decided to lay it on thick then. "The owner was a horrid-looking, middle-aged man," she described slowly. "I found him as hideous as my stepfather, but at least he kept his part of the bargain.

"He only gave me bit parts at first, but I did anything required of me. I learned acrobatics, singing, juggling, whatever I saw others do, as long as it put me in front of an audience.

"It was a tawdry little company," she admitted with a flick of her fingers at a piece of lint on her skirt. "It could barely keep itself together from town to town, but by the time I left, I was a lead player.

"I stayed four years, learning everything I could. When we returned to London on one occasion, I came to the Surrey, as it was called then, and auditioned for a part. They hired me and I never went back to the other."

Only the muted sounds of the street below penetrated the curtained windows.

"You never saw your brother again?"

"None of them. The troupe traveled all over the country, and by the time I came back, they were gone. Who knows, an epidemic could have taken them all."

"I'm sorry."

She stared at him, angry at the pity she read in his eyes. "You needn't be. It happened long ago." She waved a hand around her sitting room. "You see me now. I'm quite happy with the way things turned out."

He made no reply. They finished their tea, and she changed the subject, asking him about his work at the hospital.

When Mr. Russell left, he was tender and solicitous with her. He took her pulse before leaving and told her to be sure to have something to eat and see her own physician.

She could have wept. Why had she told him anything of her past? Instead of shocking him, she had only been made to feel shame, a shame she had thought buried from those long-ago days.

That evening, Ian sat once again in his study, but his mind could not focus on his specimens. He got up from the microscope and paced the confines of the room, coming finally to the dormer window. He looked out the dark panes, seeing again a young, helpless girl, at the mercy of who knows how many lecherous men in her past.

He felt again her frail frame beneath his arms as he settled her in her carriage; he smelled again her soft fragrance; he looked again into those clear eyes exuding only innocence.

But she wasn't innocent. She was a woman used by men, and who'd learned to use them to her advantage by the looks of her comfortable apartment.

He turned from the window and walked to his desk. Opening his Bible to Genesis, he reread the story he'd been hearing since he was a boy, the story his father had read to him of how the Lord had chosen a wife for Isaac.

Ian went to the beginning of the chapter.

When Abraham was old and knowing his time was drawing near, he made his servant swear that he would not take a wife for his son of the daughters of Canaan, but would go back to his country and choose one.

Several verses down, when the servant had arrived and prayed for this divine appointment, Rebekah appeared.

"And the damsel was very fair to look upon, a virgin, neither had any man known her: and she went down to the well, and filled her pitcher, and came up."

A virgin. Neither had any man known her.

Ian lowered his head in his hands. It seemed as if all his life he'd been waiting for his Rebekah. He'd kept himself pure for her.

Why, then, did he feel a pull toward this other woman, a woman used by men, a woman who might show an external beauty, but who knew nothing of the beauty of holiness?

It was only a fixation, an obsession, which he vowed to conquer. He returned to the passage. At the end of the chapter, the future groom, Isaac, was meditating in the field at eventide when Rebekah appeared. He lifted his eyes and beheld his future wife, riding toward him on a camel.

Isaac had been praying, spending time in

the evening with his God, alone in the open field.

Ian's father and mother had both instilled in him the notion that God would choose his helpmate. They had counseled him to wait on the Lord, confident that the day would come.

But he'd been waiting years now.

What if he'd missed her? What if she'd been one of the women he'd worked with at the mission or sat near at Sunday chapel services and simply not seen? Once he'd thought it might be Althea Breton. She possessed every quality he sought in a helpmate: zeal for the Lord, strength and dedication in His work. She was an attractive, intelligent young woman with a warm heart. She would have made an ideal companion.

But somehow, nothing had ever materialized. They were each busy in their own labors. Then she'd taken a leave from the mission for most of the past year to nurse a child in Mayfair. Since she'd been back, he'd sensed a change in her, a preoccupation that he could only attribute to her experience in the household where she'd been nursing. Her charge, a young girl, had passed away, and Ian knew she must be grieving.

Ian bowed his head and prayed, *Lord, give*

*me a sign when my bride comes. Let me be
as Isaac. Let me be praying and when I look
up, let me behold her.*

Chapter Eight

Eleanor descended from her coach and approached the neat, thatched farmhouse where Sarah lived. Every week she looked forward to this day, and yearned for the time when she could have her daughter with her permanently. But she knew she must be patient. Her daughter had a good, stable life with the Thorntons, and she must consider Sarah's best interests.

As soon as she'd knocked and been greeted by the maid, she knew something was not right.

"Oh, Mrs. Neville, you've come at last!" The young maid wrung her hands. "Poor Sarah's been feelin' poorly."

Eleanor untied her bonnet ribbons. "Dear me, what ails her?" Already, she was heading for the stairs to Sarah's room.

"Mrs. Thornton thinks it be a marsh fever, mum."

Eleanor quickened her steps at the

dreaded words. Every summer many were felled by the fevers. She'd thought it too late in the year for it to strike anyone now.

She met Louisa at the door to Sarah's room.

"Oh, 'tis you come to see poor Sarah. She'll be glad of it, but I don't know as you should go near her."

"Of course I shall go to her," Eleanor said, attempting to get past her in the doorway.

"Now, now, don't fret. The girl is resting. Mr. Allerby has been to see her twice already, once yesterday and now this morning."

"What about a physician, shouldn't she see a proper physician?"

"Why, Mr. Allerby has been treating this family for nigh on ten years, from broken bones to the croup. There's no physician better than our apothecary. He brought his cupping jar and has already bled her. Left her Dr. James's Fever Powder to drink. She'll be better in no time, I'm sure."

Eleanor forced herself to remain calm. "Tell me how it started."

"Well, let's see." Louisa tapped her jaw with a finger, thinking back. "Sarah began complaining of a megrim yesterday after she'd been out in her pony cart. I thought to myself, she's taken too much sun. It's all

I can do to get her to take her parasol. By teatime she was feeling so poorly she went to lie down. That's when I felt her forehead and saw she had a fever. Well, o' course I sent for Mr. Allerby.

"He was delivering Hannah's baby. She's been due for over two weeks now. But as soon as he was through, he come by. That was nigh on eight o'clock yester evening. He immediately bled our little Sarah and she rested easier after that."

Eleanor finally managed to squeeze past Louisa and enter Sarah's room. She hurried to the bed and bent over her daughter's flushed face. "Hello there, sweeting. What is this I hear that you've gone and gotten sick?"

"Hello, Aunt Eleanor. I'm sorry, I wish we could go riding today. I had so much to tell you."

"Well, that's quite all right. I didn't feel much like riding today, anyway. Today shall be a reading day, how's that?"

Sarah gave a weak smile. "Oh, that would be lovely. Only my head still hurts so."

Eleanor touched her forehead gingerly. It felt hot. She looked around and seeing the basin of water, took the cloth Louisa had left hanging over its edge and wet it and wrung it out, then laid it on Sarah's forehead.

"There, that will cool you off."

"Yes . . . that feels better," the girl mumbled, her eyes fluttering closed.

Eleanor brought over a rocking chair and sat down, feeling helpless. What could she do to make her daughter well?

She sang a soft melody, but afraid she would disturb her daughter with the sound, she fell silent. She spent a few more moments changing the compress on Sarah's forehead and worrying her bottom lip, wondering what else she could do. When she determined that Sarah slept, she walked out softly, searching once again for Louisa.

She found her in the kitchen, helping the maid with the week's baking.

"I really think we should send for a physician," Eleanor told the older woman.

Louisa looked at her in consternation.

"I can send my coachman for a physician," she insisted when the older woman said nothing.

"Well, you know there's nobody nearby but Mr. Allerby. Nearest physician is two towns over."

"We must send for him, then."

She looked doubtful. "He's new and I don't know anything about him. Let's see . . . there's two surgeons in Dartford, but they only set bones, as far as I know . . . and none o' them is as trusted as our Mr. Allerby."

At the word "surgeons" Eleanor's mind went immediately to Mr. Russell. Eleanor couldn't think of anyone she'd trust more to doctor Sarah than Mr. Russell. But where might he be now? Perhaps it would be better to send her man to seek out these others than make him go all the way back to London and search from the dispensary to the mission to who knows where?

"Where is McGinnis, my coachman?"

"He's gone out back to the stable, ma'am," the maid answered promptly. "He'll be in shortly for some refreshment."

"I must see him," Eleanor said, already hurrying out the back door.

"But, Eleanor —" Louisa's voice was lost to Eleanor as she left the kitchen.

Ian was examining a patient at the dispensary when Jem handed him a note from a "fella in livery."

Dear Mr. Russell,

I have a very feverish little girl who needs your help. Could you please come? My coachman will bring you. I am about

177

an hour's ride out of London in Surrey. Please come.

Eleanor

He looked at Jem. "This was just delivered?"

"Yes, the man's in the waiting room."

"Finish up here," he instructed Jem, knowing the lad was capable of applying the poultice.

Ian stepped outside and spied Mrs. Neville's coachman. They exchanged a few words and then Ian excused himself to get his bag.

As he rode southward, Eleanor's plea reverberated in his mind. Finally he pulled out the note and read it again.

Please come. Eleanor.

What seemed hours later, but was little more than one, Mr. Russell entered Sarah's room. Eleanor immediately stood from the rocker and came to him. "Oh, thank goodness my coachman found you. Thank you for coming."

He nodded only briefly to her and approached the bed. She watched him remove his gloves and feel her daughter's forehead.

"She's only been feverish since yesterday afternoon, I'm told. She was out riding and came back with a headache. We've been bathing her with vinegar water every few minutes. She's been bled . . ." Eleanor realized her words were tumbling out in a rush, but she couldn't help herself.

Mr. Russell's attention remained fixed on Sarah. After taking her pulse, he opened his medical bag and extracted two long cylinders, which he screwed together. After lowering the bedcovers, he placed one end on Sarah's chest, and the other to his ear, bending over to listen.

Eleanor stared, fascinated.

He continued his examination, feeling and palpating other parts of her body.

Finally, he straightened. "Her lungs are clear. She seems to have a mild intermittent fever, not uncommon here near the fens. It's late for this time of year, but with the unseasonably warm weather we've been having, it's not unheard-of. Do you know if she has been given any Peruvian bark to drink?"

"I don't know . . . I don't think so. Let me ask Louisa."

After they'd ascertained that the apothecary had not prescribed any Cinchona bark, Ian got a packet from his bag.

"Boil this in water and make a tea. Give it to her every hour or so."

179

Louisa hurried out to comply with the order.

He turned to Eleanor. "You should see some improvement in a few days. She'll be uncomfortable until then, but she should be all right."

Eleanor closed her eyes in relief, not realizing how much she had been holding in her fear until that moment. She felt the tears welling over her lids.

She turned away from the doctor and brought a hand up to her eyes to wipe at them.

"You care a great deal for the girl," he said softly, handing her a handkerchief from behind.

She dabbed beneath her eyes, only nodding in reply. The handkerchief was a thick folded square. It smelled clean, like his neck cloth the day she'd collided with him. She breathed in the fresh scent, feeling the relief swell through her anew that he'd come. How many other patients had he had to leave to come to her? But he'd done so.

"Thank you, Mr. Russell," she said. "I'm sorry. I was so worried about Sarah . . . She's usually such a healthy girl, and when I saw her so pale and fretful, I didn't know what to do. I . . . couldn't bear if anything happened to her."

"Is she a relative of yours?" he asked, still standing behind her.

Feeling composed enough to turn around, she finally faced him. "In a manner of speaking. She was a foundling. Someone left her with us when I was with the traveling players, and we all adopted her. Mr. and Mrs. Thornton, who were with us then eventually took over her upbringing."

She held out the handkerchief to him. "Thank you for coming so quickly, Mr. Russell. I hope I didn't take you away from another patient."

He shook away her apology. "Think nothing of it. It's good that my partner and apprentices are with me at the dispensary. I was able to leave at once."

"That's two lives I'm indebted to you for now," she said softly, realizing it as she spoke the words. "The second one is infinitely more precious to me, I'll confess."

"I'm not God, Mrs. Neville," he replied equally softly, a slight smile playing across his lips.

"You're the closest thing I've known to Him, then," she whispered in reply.

The next fortnight passed in a whirlwind for Eleanor. She divided her time nursing Sarah at the farmhouse in the mornings and going to the rehearsals in town in the afternoons. In the evenings she returned to the farmhouse.

She saw no more of Mr. Russell for a few days and debated sending for him again, wanting his reassurance that Sarah was truly all right. Over and over she pondered how quickly he had come when she'd summoned him. Would he do so again? Had he done it out of a mere sense of duty? Or was it out of pity? she asked herself, remembering his manner toward her after she'd confessed her past to him.

Not all her past, she admitted. She hadn't told him the truth about Sarah. She didn't trust anyone with that secret. What would the upright surgeon think of an illegitimate daughter? She didn't care for her own reputation, but she didn't want any slurs cast upon Sarah's name.

Just when she had decided to stop by the dispensary at the end of the day, she spied Mr. Russell entering the theater one afternoon during a rehearsal.

She missed her cue and the orchestra had to begin the music anew. Taking a deep breath to begin her song, she watched Mr. Russell take a seat in the rear of the pit. What was he doing here? Hadn't he as much as said he'd never come to the theater again?

Her heart beat wildly for the rest of the song, and she waited impatiently for the break. When the director finally called for one, Eleanor wiped her face with a handkerchief. Aware she was not looking her best in an old pair of men's breeches, she made her way down the row of benches to where the surgeon sat.

He rose as she approached. "Good afternoon, Mrs. Neville," he began, fiddling with the hat in his hands. His voice seemed stiff and the eager smile she had for him waned.

"What is it?"

"Nothing. I merely stopped in to inquire after the young girl. How is she? Would you like me to look in on her again?"

Eleanor smiled widely in relief. "Oh, she is much better! I can never thank you enough for coming so quickly that day. I was out of my mind with worry."

"It's understandable. I'm glad I could come."

"I can't believe how quickly she improved after taking the tea. You did wonders for her."

"It's a well-known remedy. I don't know why your physician hadn't already recommended it to her."

"I haven't any idea. Mrs. Thornton uses the apothecary who's treated people in the village all his life. He's getting on in years. But yes, if you have time, I would appreciate your coming by and seeing for yourself that Sarah is truly better."

"Very well." He hadn't smiled during their interchange and his manner had been so subdued that she was on the brink of asking him if something was the matter, when she realized the direction of his gaze and understood. The breeches! He disapproved of her outfit.

Feeling lighthearted with relief that it was only that, Eleanor took a step back and twirled around. "This isn't the final costume, but what do you think? Do I look like a proper Leporello to you?" She put her hands on her hips and assumed a manly posture.

He cleared his throat and looked away from her. "I must get on with my rounds. I'll stop by the farmhouse tomorrow afternoon if that is convenient with you."

"Yes, of course. I shall be there around six in the evening."

He gave a final nod and, after placing his hat back on his head, he turned and left her. She remained standing looking at his departing figure. What a strange man. How dare he censure her outfit? Then she giggled. There was something strangely pleasurable in shocking him, so much more stimulating than dealing with those jaded society men whose only goal was so transparent.

Several nights later, Henry waylaid Ian as the latter was on his way down a corridor in St. Thomas's.

"Tonight's the night."

"Yes? For what, a lecture?"

Henry's teeth gleamed. "Better. A stimulating few hours among the ton at Devonshire House. D'you have a set of evening clothes?" He eyed Ian's jacket critically.

Ian frowned. "No."

"P'raps Southey has something that will fit you. You're about his size." He gave Ian a slap on the shoulder. "Come along with me to my rooms. We'll have you looking like a gent in no time."

Ian's steps slowed. "Wait a moment. What are you talking about? I'm due to lecture here at eight."

Henry shrugged. "No matter. We can still arrive by ten. The party will be just commencing. I'll meet you here at nine and we'll go to my place."

Ian stifled a sigh. "Not tonight."

"You gave your word, my good man. Have

you already forgotten?"

Ian stared at him as the foggy memory finally came to the surface. "And you mean to exact fulfillment this evening?"

Henry smiled. "As soon as your lecture is over."

Ian nodded wearily. "Very well. I'll be here."

Eleanor fanned herself in the warm press of people. She had never been among such a brilliant gathering. She recognized many figures of the ton from their theater boxes, but had met very few in person, except, of course, for some of the gentlemen, when they hadn't been with their spouses. Most of those pretended not to see her tonight.

The thought didn't perturb her. She understood how the game was played. She looked sidelong at her escort. At least His Grace, d'Alvergny, had been as good as his word. Her invitation had arrived by post a few days after her meeting with him in the park.

She had been surrounded by young bucks since they'd arrived. Since the opening of *Don Giovanni, The Spectre,* her renown had grown. The piece was a smashing success. Every night the theater was filled to capacity.

"Would you do me the honor of dancing with me?" A handsome young man, whose name she couldn't remember, stood before her as a new set was starting up.

"I would be delighted," she replied. As they lined up to dance, she felt a sense of awe that she was ranged along with the gentle ladies of the ton. None had yet addressed her, but here she was in their midst. Someday they wouldn't ignore her.

The orchestra began to play the notes of the piece, and Eleanor moved through the formal steps. Those hours of private dance lessons were finally paying off.

What a splendid company of people. Eleanor's gaze swept across the immense ballroom. The light from a dozen chandeliers glittered off the mirrored and marbled surfaces, sparkled off the diamonds in women's hair and around their pale necks, and shone from the fuller's white of the men's cravats.

She knew she had nothing to be ashamed of in her own appearance. Even the jaded d'Alvergny had given a low whistle when he'd come to collect her.

Eleanor promenaded hand in hand with her partner before separating from him at the end of the line. As she pivoted back into place, she caught sight of a familiar face.

Her stomach did a flip-flop and she almost missed her step. It couldn't be! She couldn't turn around at that moment to see if she'd been mistaken. It had certainly looked like Mr. Russell. She wouldn't mistake the fiery luster of his hair anywhere.

But what would he be doing in such an exalted assembly? She had missed his second visit to the farmhouse and had wondered when she might see him again.

She bit her lip, impatient for the end of the set. The piece seemed interminable. When the music finally died down, her partner began with some pleasantries, but she ignored them and led him back to d'Alvergny. Her heart sank, wishing now she were not obligated to remain with him the entire evening. Her joy at coming to this exalted assembly suddenly decreased as she realized the price.

D'Alvergny smiled benignly at her and she repressed a shudder. Overfed, aging dandy. But she smiled sweetly.

"Enjoying yourself?" he asked.

"Immensely." She flicked open her fan to hide her expression.

He nodded. "As you see, I deliver on my promises."

She inclined her head but made no rejoinder. Did he expect her to be his exclusively on the basis of one favor? If so, he had a lot to learn.

"Let me introduce you to some more people," he said after a few moments.

"Delightful." All the while her mind raced, looking for a way to excuse herself for a while.

As they walked around the ballroom, she was able to scan the other side of the room.

Her eyes hadn't fooled her. It *was* Mr. Russell, stuck against one gold-embossed wall, looking as if he was at Newgate awaiting sentencing rather than surrounded by a company of the first stare at a splendid gala. Whatever would he be doing at a gathering like this? she asked herself again.

Another man, who looked far more at ease, turned to address Mr. Russell.

She waited until the duke had made some introductions and was deep in conversation before placing her hand on his sleeve. "Excuse me, Your Grace. I am going to retire for a bit."

He bowed over her hand, and Eleanor left the duke chatting with some people. She made her way around the room to the salon set aside for the ladies' use. It wasn't until she returned that she looked for Mr. Russell, glancing around first to seek d'Alvergny. Good. He was nowhere to be seen. Probably gone to the card room.

She wended her way toward Russell.

He didn't notice her until she stood directly in front of him and tapped his arm with the tip of her ivory fan.

The frown on his face transformed to one of surprise. His dark eyes scanned her appearance for a few seconds, from the white ostrich plumes in her piled hair to the silvery-gray crape of her gown.

"What a pleasure to see you here," she said, her heart dancing wildly. He looked incredibly handsome in his black coat, his auburn hair combed back to reveal his wide, strong forehead.

"Good evening, Mrs. Neville. I didn't expect to see you here."

She smiled coyly, fluttering her fan to mask her nervous state. "Pray, why ever not?"

He seemed at a loss how to answer.

"I do beg an introduction," the gentleman at his side broke in then. "Ian, you mustn't be selfish keeping the identity of this beautiful lady all to yourself."

"Mrs. Neville, may I present my friend, Lord Cumberland? Henry, the actress, Mrs. Neville. I'm sure you are familiar with her work."

The man's eyes widened. " 'Pon my

honor, of course! Mrs. Neville, I've seen you many times on the stage, but never had the dream of meeting you in person. May I salute your prodigious talent?" He bowed deeply over her hand.

She curtsied. "Thank you for the kind compliments."

"Your portrayal of Leporello is absolutely brilliant. I've never laughed so hard."

"Well, Mr. Dibdin's libretto is partially responsible for that."

"To be sure, but your singing and execution of the lines are what bring the audience to such riotous applause." He turned to Ian. "Don't you think so?"

Mr. Russell cleared his throat. "I haven't as yet been to see the show."

"You haven't? You must. It's all the talk of the town right now. Why, the score pokes fun at everything from melodramatic tragedies to the state of matrimony." Cumberland frowned at him. "However did you come to meet Mrs. Neville if you haven't seen her on the stage?"

He turned to her. "Ian never goes to the theater or mingles with the ton." He gave the surgeon a friendly jab. "You sly fox, keeping your acquaintance with Mrs. Neville all to yourself."

"Actually it was on a medical call, Lord

Cumberland," Eleanor replied when all Russell did was scowl at his friend.

Cumberland looked dumbfounded. "A medical call? You didn't break any bones, I trust?"

She chuckled. "No. A fellow actress needed attention, and Mr. Russell rushed to the scene."

"That's Ian for you. Always on duty. Well, I am glad to know you at last. What a crush tonight. May I get you some refreshment?"

"No, thank you. I'm quite all right."

"I had to drag Ian here tonight, and to think how narrowly I missed your acquaintance."

"Indeed?" She raised an eyebrow at Mr. Russell. *Ian,* she repeated to herself silently, storing away the information. "What finally induced him?"

"Well, I keep explaining to my slow-top friend here that the only way to get people of influence aware of the plight of the other half of the city is to rub shoulders with them and tell them they can help. It's all a matter of opening their eyes."

She looked with interest at the two. "Do you really think they'll care?"

"Undoubtedly," Lord Cumberland replied. "But we must bring it to their level. For example —"

"If they don't begin to care about the filthy living conditions of half this city, the typhus will not stay within the boundaries of the East End," Mr. Russell cut in. "They'll find it is no respecter of persons."

She widened her eyes at his harsh tone. "You mean to frighten them?"

"Unfortunately, Ian is a bit extreme in his methods. I am trying to tell him that charm goes further than fear tactics."

She smiled mischievously at Ian. "Yes, indeed, I agree wholeheartedly."

"Did you know Ian dreams of opening up a children's hospital?" Cumberland went on.

She turned with even more interest to the surgeon. "Is that so?"

"Oh, yes," his lordship answered for his friend. "Our hospitals currently don't admit children. Unless it's a case of a broken bone to be set, we turn away children with illnesses."

"Most doctors are intimidated by children," Ian said. "They somehow think because children's bodies are smaller, they will be more difficult to diagnose."

Eleanor's hand went to her heart as she thought of Sarah. "I didn't realize . . . I thought it was because most families didn't have the money to pay for a doctor to attend their children."

"That's also the case," Ian conceded. "Between the two, few children in the East End, and even in the more prosperous parts of London, receive any medical care."

"How do you propose to change that?"

Mr. Russell spent the next several minutes explaining his idea for a hospital primarily for children, but also as a place to educate mothers. He said most of the existing books — the few there were — were full of remedies centuries' old.

Eleanor was amazed at the animation that took hold of his features as he warmed to his subject. His brown eyes lit up with passion for the defenseless members of society. His long fingers jabbed through his hair in frustration at the slow-moving bureaucracy of medical institutions and government agencies. His words painted eloquent and vividly graphic images.

Suddenly, he broke off with a disconcerted look at the two of them. "I beg your pardon. I didn't mean to monopolize the conversation. I'm sure you are not interested in listening to me discourse at length —"

Eleanor and Cumberland both began to speak at once, Cumberland with a laughing retort, but he immediately stopped, gesturing to Eleanor. "Let the lady speak. Is my friend boring you to distraction or not?"

"Mr. Russell may be a lot of things, but he is never boring." With an enigmatic look at him, she continued. "I admire his commitment to the least fortunate members of our city and I wish him all success with his endeavors."

With regret, she took a step back, knowing that d'Alvergny would be looking for her. He could be most persistent. "I must rejoin my party, gentlemen, but I have enjoyed the conversation immensely. It was a pleasure, Lord Cumberland."

"Oh, must you go when we've only just met?" he asked with exaggerated regret.

"Oh, I'm sure we'll run into each other again this evening." She granted him a lavish smile and held out her hand.

She turned to Mr. Russell and offered her hand. He took it in his and the two gazed at each other a long moment.

What was going through his mind? she asked herself. Did she have the same effect on him that he had on her? Did his blood stir at the touch of their two hands, the way hers did?

She let his hand go reluctantly and turned away.

It was several moments later before she located d'Alvergny. He was talking with a heavy, florid gentleman she recognized as the very wealthy Mr. Digsby. *Digsby the old wigsby,* she recited to herself, because he still clung to the old fashion of wearing a powdered wig.

D'Alvergny turned to her. "Ah, Mrs. Neville, there you are. Digsby has been regaling me with tales of your show last night. Is it true the horse was a bit restive?"

Eleanor laughed, trying to recapture her mood of earlier in the evening, when she'd been so dazzled by the gathering. Why did it now seem dull and drawn out? "Yes, we weren't sure for a moment whether Don Guzman's statue would be able to get it under control, or whether the poor beast would go dashing over the orchestra and into the pit."

Mr. Digsby bowed over her hand. His dark little eyes lingered on her décolletage and Eleanor had the urge to slap his jowled cheek. But she knew how important it was to keep the admiration of men like Digsby. Digsby himself was a banker and a generous patron of the arts.

As other gentlemen joined them, their conversation turned to financial matters, then to politics. Many voiced their concern over the growing riots since the end of the war. They all feared an uprising among the masses.

Eleanor compared their conversation to Mr. Russell's. She looked across the large ballroom. Russell and his friend were still where she had left them. Cumberland was in a lively conversation with a lady, but the surgeon remained standing stiffly, his expression severe.

He certainly wasn't going to catch any backers that way.

Eleanor turned with her most persuasive smile to Digsby, and placed her hand on his arm. He looked at it, then back at her, his expression immediately warm and interested.

"There is someone you must absolutely meet." She turned to d'Alvergny. "Your Grace, we shall return shortly."

D'Alvergny bowed in her direction and continued the conversation he was in. His focus lingered on her and she gave him a smile full of promise.

She led Digsby through the crowd of people until they came to Mr. Russell and his friend. Mr. Russell's eyes widened to see her again. He looked from her to Digsby as she introduced them.

"My dear sir, you must have heard of the

eminent surgeon, Mr. Ian Russell. He is over at St. Thomas's."

"Is that so?" The fat banker gave Ian a sharp look.

Ian inclined his head, wondering why Mrs. Neville had brought him over.

"Mr. Russell is doing great work in Southwark with the poor masses. If anyone succeeds in calming their anger, it is people like him." She began to describe the day they had been caught in the middle of the riot. The banker's eyes widened in consternation and he began to eye Ian with more interest.

"All these people seem to want are jobs and food on the table. And you should have seen the children that day." Her voice almost broke. "Do you realize how many are without homes? Many live in overcrowded conditions in buildings not fit for animals. They are underfed and lack the most basic necessities. I know it must tear at your heart to think of such things, but isn't it wonderful that there are individuals willing to help the needy? Mr. Russell has a plan to provide medical care to many of these children. Mr. Russell —" she turned to him with an encouraging smile "— you must tell Mr. Digsby of this noble undertaking."

She immediately began asking him detailed questions, and Ian marveled at how skillfully she used the information he had imparted to her in their previous conversation to ask the right questions now.

"And what happens to these children in the winter months?"

"Many live in little better than hovels, with no heat, no supply of clean water. They huddle together for warmth. There are always outbreaks of fevers and other epidemics. Typhus, measles, dysentery — you don't see massive outbreaks of these maladies in this part of town. We isolate the infectious, give the patient the proper care, and the illness is prevented from spreading, except perhaps to the most immediate family."

The banker nodded thoughtfully.

"I can only see the problems growing and eventually spreading as more and more people come to the city. Since the end of the war, the population has grown. In and around the borough of Southwark, there is probably a gin shop on every corner, but a great number of women and children go hungry.

"Children are left on church doorsteps and at foundling homes. Many are stiff and blue by the time they are discovered."

As Digsby began asking him questions, Ian warmed to his subject, seeing real interest in the man's eyes. By the end of their conversation, the banker had invited him to address his private club in a week's time.

Ian watched Mrs. Neville as she and the banker walked away. Why had she done this for him? What had motivated her? His heart sank when he saw the group she returned to.

All men.

What was she doing among a group of middle-aged, obviously wealthy men?

There was only one possible reason.

He turned away from the sight, feeling a bleakness in his soul that not even his work could relieve.

CHAPTER NINE

The next night Ian went to the mission for one of its weekly street preachings. He usually assisted with handing out tracts and praying for people.

"Lord, as we Thy Name profess, may our hearts Thy love confess And in all our praise of Thee, may our lips and lives agree . . ."

As the hymn rang out across the cobbled streets, Ian's mind wandered as he thought again about the evening among the city's elite. All day he'd been remembering Eleanor's dazzling appearance and how nimbly she'd hooked the financier's interest in the plight of the children.

When everyone around him began to pray, Ian bowed his head and tried to concentrate on the reason he was there. He prayed for souls to be saved that night.

A special preacher was expected from a western county that evening. Ian had been particularly interested in hearing him preach. It was said he had a healing ministry. Ian looked out across the sea of faces, many smudged and unwashed. Already the preacher's fame had spread. People had brought many who were clearly ill. Mothers held young children. Older people sat huddled in chairs. Some even lay on litters.

As the fiery words began to ring out through the area, people stood transfixed.

" 'For the word of God is quick, and powerful, piercing even to the dividing asunder of soul and spirit, and of the joints and marrow, and is a discerner of the thoughts and intents of the heart.

" 'Neither is there any creature that is not manifest in His sight. But all things are naked and opened unto the eyes of Him with whom we have to do.' "

The pastor scanned the crowd. "How many of you here would care to have your thoughts and intents visible to all to see?"

His words rent the air, and Ian felt the convicting power of truth invade the recesses of his heart. He knew his thoughts had been dwelling too much on Eleanor Neville in a way that was not proper. He must rid himself of this obsession he was developing.

The pastor's arm waved in the night sky, encompassing them all. "And if any man

202

sin, we have an advocate with the Father, Jesus Christ the righteous . . ."

From the conviction of sin, the preacher turned to the hope found in the gospel message.

"If by one man sin entered the world, and death by sin," he said, quoting the Scriptures, "therefore, it is clear that disease — the precursor of death — entered the world by sin. Therefore, its ultimate cure must be found in the redemption of Christ."

He explained how disease that has gone beyond the ability of the body to fight it, beyond the knowledge of medicine to heal it, and beyond even the ability of the afflicted to pray for, only the sovereign power of God could reverse. This required confession and repentance. It required the atoning work of the cross.

"Only by the substitutionary work of the cross can the curse be removed," he exhorted them.

As Ian listened, he forgot everything else for the moment, caught by the notion of healing in the atonement. The preacher described the examples of atonement in the Old Testament, from the Passover lamb to the slaying of the bullock, the mercy seat of the tabernacle sprinkled with its blood on the Day of Atonement preceding the blessings of the year of jubilee.

"The Israelites were healed when they looked up at the brazen serpent, a type of the Atonement, which removed the curse of the plague . . ."

Ian marked his Bible with the passages the pastor gave. He noted the seven redemptive names of God, paying particular note to Jehovah-Rapha, "I am the Lord that healeth thee."

"The Lord is our physician!" the preacher exclaimed. "Come unto me, all ye that labor and are heavy laden!" As he marched back and forth in front of them, his words urging them to reach out in faith and believe, the murmurs of the crowd grew. Ian could feel a momentum growing. He compared it to the day of the riot. Here, it was the sound of hope and expectation instead of rage and frustration.

As the sermon ended, the preacher called forward the sick. He called the elders of the church to come and "lay hands on the sick and anoint them with oil." Ian followed the others from the mission, adding his prayers to the others, but feeling more an observer than a man of faith praying for the sick.

Suddenly one woman gave a shriek.

"It's gone! It's gone! The lump I had on the side of my neck — it's gone!" The crowd went wild, everyone shrieking, those around the woman clamoring to see.

The preacher, after talking with the woman and her neighbors, who testified that she indeed had suffered from a growth at the side of her neck, turned to the crowd. "We must praise God for this miracle. Come, lift your voices in worship."

One of the members of the mission began singing a joyous song, and soon all joined in.

Ian pushed his way through the singing mass of people, eager to see for himself the woman who'd claimed to be healed. He'd heard of such healings in the early days of the revival that had swept the British Isles in his father's day.

When he reached her, he examined her neck, but it looked and felt perfectly normal.

"Suddenly I felt a heat all up and down the side of it," she told him, putting her hand to her neck, "and the next thing I know, I feel it like this, and I notice it's flat." She began to cry afresh.

"God be praised," he murmured, his heart aching with doubt. Why did he find it so hard to accept this miracle? He had certainly witnessed miraculous recoveries after surgery on the battlefield, but he'd never witnessed an instantaneous one as this purportedly had been.

It was probably because he'd never seen the woman prior to this evening and could therefore not be fully certain of her previous condition. He felt like doubting Thomas and thought of the gentle rebuke Jesus had given his disciple. *Blessed are they which have not seen, and yet have believed.*

Althea approached him at the end of the meeting. "Wasn't it glorious?" she asked, her eyes shining.

He nodded.

"How many were healed?" she asked. "I counted ten."

"Yes, I examined ten. Unfortunately, I was only familiar with one case previously, so it's difficult to ascertain which are genuine miracles."

Althea frowned. "What do you mean? Do you doubt that the Lord was healing tonight?"

"We've never seen such a —" He stopped, at a loss to describe the sight he'd seen tonight. "A manifestation. I've seen plenty of charlatanry, on the other hand."

"I see. I can understand your hesitancy. It's not the kind of preaching we hear of much. I must confess, however, to having diligently studied God's Word concerning healing before tonight, and I could find no fault with Parson Riley's preaching."

He nodded. "That is reassuring," he said, trusting her judgment on religious matters. He helped her collect the hymnals and unused tracts. "I have not ever really delved into it."

She looked at him. "That surprises me. I would think having been raised as you have been with your father and then entering into the medical profession, you would have turned to God's Word to guide you in the healing arts."

"Oh, I have prayed for His guidance and wisdom whenever I treat anyone. I also pray for His mercy to heal. It's not that I haven't seen His mercy at work — I have, many times. It's that I have seen death steal away a person's life more often."

"It must have been hard on the battlefield," she said softly.

"It was. Seeing young men cut down in their prime. Men devise newer and ever crueler ways to hack at each other, and we surgeons are left to try to piece them together as they cry out in agony." He placed the remaining hymnals in the carriage.

"And yet, since I've returned, it is sometimes even harder to watch the people around me. We're a city at peace, the great-

207

est in the world according to many, with ever more poverty and illness, much of which could be conquered through decent nutrition and living conditions. I'm convinced half the deaths could be eradicated by these simple means.

"Look at the mission," he went on. "Your rate of success is twice that of the hospital, and I'm sure it is due to wholesome conditions."

Althea nodded, sympathy in her eyes. "You haven't made much headway at the hospital?"

"No, they mainly laugh and criticize me behind my back with names like 'spick-and-span' Russell or 'old housewife.' "

Althea laughed. "How horrid of them. I wish you could just come and be our doctor full-time."

He nodded. "Maybe I will someday."

"Unfortunately, we can't pay you much, if at all."

"And I need my salary to support my other work."

"Yes, and how we do appreciate all you give us both in time and materials."

They parted company, Althea encouraging him to read the Scriptures on healing.

Ian nodded absently, doubting he'd find the time. He had enough trouble stretching the hours in the day to reach all the sick who needed attention.

Tonight's preaching, if not convincing him fully of a preacher's ability to heal the sick, had certainly convicted him of harboring sinful thoughts in his heart. He renewed his determination not to let his thoughts turn to one silvery-eyed actress who beguiled him every time they met.

"We will begin by examining the upper portion of the forearm." Ian pointed to the extremity in question on the skeleton hanging on a stand beside him in the lecture theater. "The ulna. It is a long bone, its shape prismatic, and it lies parallel with the bone beside it, the radius."

Ian addressed the group of pupils who attended his weekly anatomy lecture. The hall was the same as the operating theater, which doubled as lecture hall on the days it wasn't used for surgery.

"The ulna is the larger and longer of the two bones composing the forearm. It is located on the inner side." He lifted the elbow of the skeleton slightly. "You can observe it is quite thick and strong at its upper extremity. This is the portion to which much of the articulation of the elbow joint is due —"

As he was moving the forearm back and forth to demonstrate, he was interrupted by the sound of whispers and rustles from the top end of the standings, where the students were crowded together. He looked up in irritation. His students knew better than to be late to a lecture.

He stared in disbelief.

Making her way between the packed students was Mrs. Neville, dressed in a bright red cloak and white skirt — colors that stood out all the more against the sober bottle-greens, navy-blues, and black of the men's jackets and pantaloons.

His surprise deepened when he saw who was squeezing in right behind her. That man — he struggled a moment and then remembered him from the society event Henry had dragged him to. Dillon . . . Doherty . . . no . . . Digsby was the man's name.

What were they doing here?

He gathered his scattered thoughts and turned back to the skeleton. He cleared his throat. "Uh, to proceed, the ulna is thickest at the top and then decreases downward toward the wrist."

The rustlings above continued, and he had to focus on his next words. The woman had the temerity to come marching into a medical lecture hall! Whoever heard of a woman attending an anatomy lecture at St. Thomas's? And an actress at that! After he'd vowed to put her out of his thoughts — his life — once and for all.

"The wrist end is quite small in comparison to the upper extremity."

At least she hadn't come unattended. That would have been too much.

He pointed to the skeleton's forearm. "Here at the top are two curved processes, the olecranon and the coronoid process, and two concave, articular cavities, the greater and lesser sigmoid cavities." He paused, hearing the muffled whispers circulating through the lecture hall.

This would not do! He'd lost his students' attention. He turned around, searching for what he knew was the distraction. She wasn't hard to find. All eyes were turned to her. There she was, in the middle of the standings, her red outfit like a beacon, bestowing that charming smile to all the men around her.

Her attention fell on him. He ignored her smile and turned away.

He squared his shoulders. "First, to the olecranon process. It is a projection at the upper, rear side of the ulna. It is curved at the top to fit into the depression of the coronoid rossa of the humerus during flexion of the forearm." He demonstrated with his own arm.

He stopped speaking as he observed a student beside Mrs. Neville whispering to her in an animated fashion.

"Mr. Morton, I suggest you turn your attention back to Octavius if you hope to master the intricacies of the forearm before next week."

The young man jerked around with a guilty look. "Yes, Mr. Russell."

Ian walked to his lectern and glanced at his notes, searching for his place. As he resumed his discourse, he was aware of Mrs. Neville watching him attentively. Each time his glance skimmed past her, there she was, her chin propped in her hand, following his every move.

He felt he was speaking a language he himself didn't understand. The terms came forth, but only because of years of memory — greater sigmoid cavity . . . lesser sigmoid cavity . . . shaft . . . anterior border . . . posterior border . . . interosseous border — but he himself didn't know what he was saying.

Finally, it was over. Ian took out his handkerchief and mopped his forehead.

Clattering footsteps reverberated throughout the theater as most of the students rushed to other lectures, but a few came down to the platform to ask a question or to examine the skeleton more closely.

Although he wasn't looking directly at her, he knew Mrs. Neville was surrounded by young men. He heard her infectious laughter floating down to him from above.

He knew the exact moment she began to descend the steps leading down to the platform.

Against his will, he raised his eyes and watched her.

She walked slowly, and he marveled at her presence, even now, away from the theater. Was every locale a stage for her? Mr. Digsby puffed behind her.

A subtle, flowery fragrance reached his nostrils as she came to stand before him. "Good morning, Mr. Russell."

Why was it every time he came so near her, she managed to take his breath away? Her skin was flawless as an eggshell's, the cheeks with the barest tint of pink, her irises quicksilver.

"What are you doing here?" he finally managed.

Her brow furrowed. "Mr. Russell, do you mean to frighten me with that tone of voice and that ferocious scowl? I might remind you I am not one of these green boys who must cower at the sound of your stern reprimand."

Not awaiting his answer, she turned to Digsby. "My dear sir, isn't Mr. Russell simply brilliant?" As the man nodded, she held up her arm. "To think I have so many bones in this one small portion of my arm." She walked over to the skeleton.

"So, this is Octavius. How do you do, Octavius?" she asked with a curtsy. "Wherever did you come up with him?"

"He was a patient at Guy's across the street."

She turned to Ian and shivered. "How gruesome."

"Cadaver stealing?" Digsby asked. "I've read that's a problem among you medical men."

"It has been a problem, but it's being alleviated somewhat as we are permitted more and more the dissection of patients who expire and leave no instructions for the disposal of their — er — corpses. There are no family members to claim the bodies, and they would end up in a pauper's grave." He approached the skeleton, his confidence returning as Mrs. Neville's attention was fixed on it.

"That's how I obtained Octavius here. Octavius Skinner was a patient of mine several years ago, an 'incurable' whom Guy's took in. He had no family. In gratitude, when he knew he was going to die, he told me I could have his body to dissect." He shrugged. "After using it, I was left with the skeleton."

Mrs. Neville listened. He now recognized the expression in her eyes that indicated she was spellbound.

"It sounds more fantastic than one of my melodramas, Mr. Digsby." She turned to Ian. "I invited Mr. Digsby to come along with me today. I thought he might like to see you at work. Perhaps you could give him a tour, show him the dispensary?"

He weighed her suggestion, remembering Henry's advice. The banker had made time to come to him; the least he could do was spare a few moments and show him the area.

"Certainly. Allow me to lock Octavius away in his closet." He turned to Digsby. "Authentic skeletons are still at a premium, and I wouldn't want to lose this one. If you will excuse me, I shall be right with you."

He nodded and, turning to the hanging skeleton, he tipped him on his side and rolled him toward the cupboard door at the end of the theater.

When he returned to them, he said, "I

shall give you a short tour of one of the wards, and then we can proceed on foot, or if you have your carriage . . ." he inquired of Mrs. Neville.

"Mr. Digsby has brought his carriage. We shall be more comfortable in that," she replied.

"Very well. Shall we go?"

Eleanor walked with Digsby as they followed Mr. Russell out of the lecture theater and into the female ward. They strolled the length of it, Ian stopping from time to time to talk with a patient or explain her condition. She observed his gentle manner with the patients and marveled that by no hint did he indicate the least aversion to the person's ailment or condition.

They descended to the ground floor and crossed one of the large courtyards within the hospital compound.

"This block of the hospital dates from about a hundred years ago, although St. Thomas's has been here since medieval times." He motioned toward the east. "There are six more wings down that way. It is quite extensive. But since it's a chilly day, I suggest we go to your carriage and I'll take you to the dispensary."

He led them from the courtyard through

the main arched entrance onto Borough High Street. "It is only a few blocks from here to my dispensary."

"Why is a dispensary necessary, with the hospital so close by?" Digsby asked.

"The hospital doesn't admit every patient, and not all can afford to be admitted. Many don't require an overnight stay. There is also the question of mortality rates. We find a higher mortality rate among patients admitted to a hospital than those taken care of in their own homes. This is probably due in some degree to the proximity of sick patients to one another."

Digsby nodded at the information and proceeded to ask him more questions.

When they arrived at the dispensary, Mr. Russell motioned to the crowded sidewalk. "As you'll notice, the area is teeming with children. Most have nowhere to go.

"There is a growing problem of children left to fend for themselves in this city. More children are born to women unable or sometimes unwilling to take care of them. The foundling homes receive so many, and as far as I'm concerned, many of those are immediate death sentences to the infants left on their doorsteps."

"What do you mean?" Digsby asked sharply, as they made their way past the line

217

of people waiting outside the dispensary.

"It's one way of curbing the population. Starve them, expose them to the elements, and few newborn infants will survive."

Eleanor felt sick at heart at the thought. How close her own daughter could have come to such an end.

"Many philanthropists in the city give to these foundling homes," Digsby argued.

"But do they ever bother to see how they are run?"

The banker fell silent, glancing at Eleanor. "Are you all right, my dear? You're as pale as a bleached rag."

"Ye-es," she replied faintly, wishing she could dispel the image of so many unwanted infants.

"Are you sure?" Mr. Russell asked. "I have smelling salts inside."

She nodded, wanting only to get past the sick people crammed around the entrance. The surgeon held the door open for her as she clutched Digsby's arm.

They entered the crowded waiting room.

"What do they do when you're not available?" Digsby asked with a look of surprise around the room.

"I have a partner, an apothecary, who is just as skilled as I in performing certain surgeries. We also have a couple of apprentices."

He directed himself to the crowd. "Excuse us, please. Make way for the lady." He opened a passage for them to the examination rooms at the rear of the waiting area.

"Good morning, Albert." Mr. Russell nodded to his partner and to the apprentices.

"Hello there, Ian. Done so soon at the hospital?"

"I'll go by later. I brought a few guests to see our work here." He introduced them to the young apothecary-surgeon.

"What is wrong with our patient here?" he asked Denton, with a nod to the man sitting at the examination table.

"Mr. Jenkins has an ulcerated throat. It's quite severe. He's had it for three weeks now, haven't you?"

The man nodded without speaking.

"What you need most," the apothecary told him, "is bed rest. But as I know you are not able to follow this advice, I shall give you a prescription for a draft made of liquorice, marshmallow, and meadow sweet, three herbs to aid in reducing the inflammation. In the meantime, keep your throat well wrapped."

After he'd escorted the man out, Mr. Russell's partner shook his head sadly.

"Without proper rest and care, I don't know how he can expect to get well."

"Why doesn't he stay home, then?" Digsby asked.

"Afraid he'll lose his job," Mr. Russell replied. "Jobs are scarce these days."

After he had answered Digsby's questions concerning the number of patients and types of illnesses they most treated at the dispensary, Mr. Russell asked them if they wouldn't like to accompany him on some of his rounds.

Eleanor tried to gauge Digsby's reaction. She sincerely hoped he'd been moved by all he'd witnessed so far to support the surgeon's work.

"Despite what you see here, many sick people don't go anywhere to be treated," Mr. Russell was saying to the banker. "Many can't afford the fee. Although we accept anyone who comes to our door, there are many who are suspicious of doctors. They prefer to buy some remedy from an empiric hawking a tonic at the nearest corner."

Digsby agreed to convey the surgeon to the vicinity of the mission in the East End. The three of them returned to his carriage. They crossed the Thames and passed Great Fire Memorial, before turning down Gracechurch Street. Ian rode up with the coach-man and instructed him. Eleanor glanced out the window as the coach entered a warren of narrow streets. The houses were crammed together, many leaning precariously outward over the street as if squeezed from the pressure of the buildings at each side.

The appearance was all too depressingly familiar from her childhood.

The carriage stopped frequently as Mr. Russell paid calls on the sick. Eleanor and Digsby followed him, trudging up dark, smelly staircases, picking their way past loiterers whose smudged, sullen faces stared at them. She edged closer to Digsby's comforting bulk, her lacy handkerchief to her nostrils.

Most of the patients were bedridden with coughs and congested lungs. Mr. Russell told those parents with sick children to bring them to the mission. Those with toothaches he sent to the dispensary.

As they reemerged into the murky light of a narrow street, a woman in a calf-length skirt approached and clutched at Mr. Russell's arm. "Give us a farthing, luv."

Eleanor stared at the woman's face. Her skin was covered with ugly nodules and bumps. But the surgeon seemed not to

221

notice. He rummaged in his pocket and brought out a few pennies. "There you go, Celia."

"You're a good man." She looked past him to Eleanor and Digsby. "Who're the swells with you? Find yourself a lady at last, Doc? You deserve a good woman . . ." Her words were slurred and she turned away from Ian, weaving her way into a refuse-strewn alley.

"What was wrong with her?" Eleanor came up close to him as they resumed walking.

"The skin lesions and ulcers, you mean?"

She nodded.

"Secondary stage of syphilis."

"The pox!" She stepped back in horror.

"She won't come in for treatment, and I'm afraid it will soon be too late."

They walked in silence and arrived at a squalid flat, where he checked on a young boy who lay on the floor with a high fever. The dwelling was cold and only a thin blanket covered the child on his dirty pallet.

Mr. Russell turned to Mr. Digsby. "This boy had only a runny nose last week," he explained in a grave voice. "I'm going to take him to the mission. We're not far from it. There's clearly no heat in these rooms, and this child has no chance if he stays here."

"Feverish is he?"

"Yes. I would ask your favor in allowing me to transport the child in your carriage."

He waited for Digsby's assent.

The man looked left and right, clearly nervous at the idea. "Isn't it contagious?"

"There is always a risk," the surgeon answered. "I could go down and seek a hack. But it's a very short ride to the mission. We were heading that way."

Sensing the urgency of the matter, Eleanor approached Digsby and cooed in her softest tones, "Come, Mr. Digsby, we'll sit the child far from you, and air out the carriage afterward."

Leaving them to work it out, Mr. Russell crouched back down at the child's side.

"Will my boy be awright?"

Ian looked up at the woman. "Do you have any other blankets or a cloak?" he asked the mother. The mother, a woman so emaciated her bones seemed to jut out from her skin, from her drawn cheeks to the knobby wrists protruding from the threadbare sleeves. Her black hair grew straight and stiff like a scarecrow's hay stuffing.

"Nothin' I can spare. There're the other young ones to think o', you see." She took the moth-eaten shawl from around her scrawny shoulders. "Here, take this. It's all I have."

He pushed it back toward her. "No, keep your shawl. I'll wrap the child with what we have."

Eleanor's heart squeezed painfully. "I'm sure there's a carriage blanket down below," she said. "Let me fetch it." Before Digsby could object, she hurried from the room.

In a few minutes she was back, panting from her quick climb up and down the stairs.

"Thank you," Mr. Russell told her with a grateful smile. She felt her cheeks grow warm at his regard. He knelt back down by the boy, whom Eleanor estimated to be between seven and eight years old. After wrapping him in his own blanket, the surgeon spread out the much thicker, woolen throw she had brought up. He laid the child in this and wrapped him up like a cocoon.

The next instant he lifted up the bundle and turned to Digsby. "Well?"

"Come along," the older man said, as if resigned to his fate. "The sooner we get him out of this cold, the better."

The boy's mother clutched Mr. Russell's arm. "Take care o' him, Doctor. I can't pay ye anything."

"Don't worry yourself about it. I'm taking him to a Methodist mission nearby." He gave her the directions, and they descended back to the street.

Mr. Russell laid the boy on the coach seat. Digsby sat as far from him as he could on the opposite side of the roomy vehicle. Eleanor stroked the boy's hot forehead. *Poor lamb.* He reminded her of Sarah a scant few weeks ago.

In a few minutes they arrived at the mission. Eleanor followed Mr. Russell, who carried the child directly to the infirmary, where a nurse came up to them immediately.

"A wee sick one?" she asked. "Come along, then, we have an empty bed over here.

"Oh, dear me, let's get these filthy things off him. I'll fetch a clean nightshirt."

Another woman came to assist, and they soon had the boy in a warm bed.

Mr. Russell turned to the banker when they stood once more in the corridor of the mission. "Thank you, Mr. Digsby."

He grunted. "If I come down with anything, I hope you'll be by to treat me."

The surgeon grinned. "Just send someone to fetch me. I'll come any time of the day or night."

"Don't worry yourself, Mr. Digsby," Eleanor reassured him, "Mr. Russell is very good at treating fevers."

He harrumphed and led them back out to his awaiting carriage, grumbling about airing it out and burning the blanket.

Mr. Russell turned to Eleanor with a look of concern. "We're in the heart of Whitechapel. Do you have the stamina to go on a few more visits in the neighborhood?"

She realized how useful she'd felt in the past few moments. "Only if you'll allow us to take you someplace for dinner afterward. I think you'll have earned a good meal by then."

"This from the lady who faints from self-starvation?"

She returned his smile with a lighthearted laugh. "I have no performance tonight. I can eat like a horse."

He was looking at her so cordially she felt herself blush. She, who was so used to manipulating men's emotions while keeping her own under strict control, found herself time and again in Mr. Russell's company giving way to reactions and feelings she had no command of.

Where would it lead? She could see no simple ending to the script.

CHAPTER TEN

Henry did nothing but rave about Mrs. Neville for the rest of the week. He told Ian they must take her everywhere to promote the idea of a children's hospital.

After he'd gone to see *The Spectre* for a second time, he said to Ian, "You must go. Mrs. Neville is adorable as the fainthearted Leporello. The audience is wild about her. They predict the show will run over a hundred days."

Ian ignored his friend, but when he left the dispensary, he was once again tempted to turn his footsteps toward the theater. The same argument that had waged in his mind since the party at Somerset House began again.

He owed Mrs. Neville something for what she had done that evening. Digsby's visit had proven invaluable. He'd corroborated everything Ian had said during his talk at the gentlemen's club. The men were interested in a constructive plan to stem the rising tide of illness and debauchery in the city. Riots were on the rise among both mill workers and unemployed. They vilified the Prince Regent, who was almost afraid to ride his carriage in the streets.

After Ian's talk, another gentleman approached him saying he'd read a paper Ian had published on a surgery technique. The man had then invited him to address the Royal Society on the subject. This was the most prestigious gathering of scientists, philanthropists and intellectuals of the day.

All this because Mrs. Neville had introduced him to Digsby. The least Ian could do was go see her in her new show. He owed her that much. It was such an insignificant action, but one that would best demonstrate his gratitude. Why his reluctance?

Because the rational part of him knew he mustn't keep seeing her. The more he did, the more drawn he felt to her. It had gone beyond her beauty, he realized. He had seen a genuine distress and caring in her when she'd visited the sick. He could no longer dismiss her as a mere actress concerned only with rising to fame in her narrow world.

He had heard from Althea that Mrs. Neville had been visiting the mission a few mornings a week. Sometimes it seemed he couldn't escape her name. Like a spider's thread, the more he sought to evade it, the more entangled he became. He *would* go, he finally resolved. He'd go and be done with it! At least it would silence Henry for a few days.

The decision made, Ian turned the corner toward the Royal Circus. When he arrived, the entrance was once again filled with loitering prostitutes and merchants peddling food, flower girls selling their bouquets, and ticket sellers announcing the plays.

"Five shillings a box, two shillings the pit! Sellout crowd! See Mr. Moreland as Don Giovanni, Mrs. Neville as Leporello! Come and get your ticket before they sell out."

Ian climbed the steps to the lobby with a heavy heart, feeling dragged to his destruction. Why had he no strength of will when it came to the actress? This was madness, he told himself as he purchased a box seat and made his way to his place.

The orchestra began to play and soon the actors appeared on the stage from the side doors. Ian put on his spectacles and sat back, prepared for a piece he would certainly disapprove of.

The crowd loved the bawdy lyrics, hooting and calling out. Mrs. Neville winked at them several times as she delivered her lines. She strutted around the stage in her long coat and knee breeches and powdered wig.

He had to admire her talent. Her voice wasn't dainty or refined; it was warm and lusty.

How had God given to one so much talent to squander among such a lowly audience — men shouting their lewd remarks, women talking and laughing among themselves whenever they wished?

The longer he watched her perform, the more his admiration grew. He recalled what she had come out of and her fight to rise above her beginnings. She'd achieved much in her young life. These realizations only deepened his sorrow that she could never be the one for him.

Mrs. Neville reached one end of the stage and swiveled about it, her hands on her hips, belting out a song. Ian remembered the sensation of standing on the stage. How it must feel tonight with a crowd applauding her.

She took a step forward in the middle of a syllable, and the next second she disappeared.

Ian leaned forward, wondering for a second at this trick. He remembered the trapdoors on the floor. Why would they have her go down one now? A bloodcurdling scream rent the air, eerily echoing from the chamber below.

Ian leaped to his feet before anyone could react and ran out to find a way onstage. That had been no act. His heart pounded as he jerked open the stage door. Pandemonium broke out, actors shouting and running to the open trapdoor, their panic spreading to the audience.

Ian pushed his way through actors and audience members who had managed to climb onto the stage. He reached the gaping trapdoor and knelt at its edge. "How far does it descend?" he asked an actor beside him.

"About ten feet, but there's all kinds of equipment down there she could have fallen on," the man answered in fear.

"Get some light! Someone get some light!" Ian shouted.

Soon a stagehand was shining a lantern down below.

Ian's heart constricted seeing Eleanor lying deadly still, her body splayed like a rag doll's. A large metal contraption of wheels and pulleys sat right below the trapdoor. It was clear she must have hit that before falling onto the floor to one side.

"Is she dead?"

"She doesn't look like she's breathing to me."

"She must've broke her skull falling on that machinery."

Ian ignored their cries and rushed to the back of the stage, grabbing a stagehand who was just entering. "Show me how to get down there. She needs medical attention. Hurry, man! I'm a doctor."

At that, the man's eyes widened and he came to life. "This way. There's a staircase at the rear. Wait, we'll need a light." He grabbed a candle from a wall sconce and continued to the back of the stage, behind the scenic backdrops.

They ran down the stairs, their shoes clattering against the steps. It seemed an eternity before they reached Eleanor.

Ian knelt beside her and immediately felt for her pulse.

"Is she alive? Is she breathing?" came the shouts from above their heads.

As soon as he heard the steady throbbing of her vein, Ian bowed his head. *Thank You, Lord.*

"Yes, she's alive," he told the stagehand. He proceeded to check her for any broken bones.

Her eyelids fluttered open. "Where — what happened?" Her voice sounded faint.

As she took a breath, she gasped in pain.

"Where does it hurt?"

"My . . . side," she whispered, making a faint motion with her hand but flinching as she moved. "Oh . . . it even hurts . . . to bre . . . athe . . ."

As she moaned softly, he opened the heavy jacket she wore and touched her rib cage gingerly.

She cringed when he touched the middle sternal ribs. "It hurts awfully."

"Do you remember what happened?" he asked as he continued his probing, his fingers running along each ridge, his eyes flicking back and forth from her torso to her face, watching for the least reaction.

"I turned . . . and the next thing I knew . . . I was falling into the dark. I smashed into something . . . I don't remember anything more until now."

Satisfied that no bones seemed to be broken, he shifted to her head and touched her scalp. A large lump was beginning to form at one side of her skull, the same side as her injured ribs. "Your head hit a piece of equipment, probably your ribs as well in your fall. Can you move your legs?"

"Yes," she replied after a second.

He moved down to her legs and felt the length of them. "Any pain?" he asked her, his fingers pressing her ankles.

"No, just at my side."

He looked at the stagehand. "We need to get her somewhere that I can examine her properly."

At that moment a man entered the basement room. "How is she? I'm the stage manager."

"She has sustained some damage to her ribs, and likely a concussion to her head. But I need to get her somewhere to examine her."

"Her dressing room is right on the ground floor, up just one flight of stairs."

Ian picked up Eleanor's hand. "We need to move you. I'm going to try and carry you, but if that hurts too much let me know and we'll fashion a litter."

She looked at him, fear in her eyes. "Just don't drop me . . . please," she begged.

He gave her hand a gentle squeeze before releasing it. "I won't, I promise you."

Eleanor cried out at the pain when he first reached down and slid his hands under her arms and knees.

"It's all right," Ian crooned. "You'll soon be more comfortable. Just bear with us a little." He tried his best not to hold her too tightly as he climbed the winding stairs, but still she whimpered at each jostle.

"I feel as if I'm in my own melodrama," she muttered, clasping her arms around his neck, "except the pain isn't going to stop when I get offstage."

"I'll give you something to ease it soon."

"I'm going to tell that orchestra to begin playing or we'll have a riot on our hands," said the stage manager. "I'll be up to see Mrs. Neville as soon as I can."

Ian and the stagehand made their slow progress up the winding stairs. When they finally arrived at Eleanor's dressing room, the wardrobe mistress had a couch prepared. "Just lay her down here," the woman told him. "I've spread out a blanket."

Eleanor winced as Ian lowered her onto the couch. The wardrobe mistress placed a cushion under her head.

"It's almost over," Ian told Eleanor, wishing he could take away her pain. He motioned with his head to the mistress. "We've got to remove her coat."

She came immediately to his side and began working at a sleeve.

Eleanor cried out.

"Just one more, ma'am, we're almost through . . . there we go," the wardrobe mistress said, slipping off the other sleeve and taking the heavy coat away.

She came back to the couch with another

blanket over her arm. "The doctor'll have you right in no time, isn't that right, sir?"

Ian made no response but nodded to the stagehand. "Thank you for your quick help. If you'll leave us now, I'll examine Mrs. Neville."

The man nodded. "Just let us know how she is. Good night, Eleanor. We're so sorry this happened. Can't understand how a trapdoor could give way like that." He shook his head, muttering in disbelief as he shut the door behind him.

Eleanor closed her eyes again, her head sinking back on the pillow. She looked deathly pale, and Ian's heart constricted.

Before he could request it, the wardrobe mistress began unbuttoning the vest and shirt. "I hope that's all right, Doc. I'm an expert at helping them dress and undress."

"That's fine, thank you. You'd better remove her shoes as well and cover her with the blanket."

Eleanor made no protest as her shirt and vest were slipped off, but Ian noticed her biting down on her lip to keep from crying out. She was left in only a pair of men's breeches, a thin camisole, and stays. Quickly the mistress loosened the stays and removed them.

For the sake of her modesty, Ian left the

camisole on, but he lifted it above her waist and once again probed the area of pain, which had begun to swell.

"Tell me when it hurts." He turned Eleanor's body slightly so he could examine her vertebral ribs. She only nodded her head, her eyes still closed.

"Good, it looks as if the only injury is to the sternal portion of your rib cage, most likely pulled or torn ligaments."

Satisfied, he covered her with the blanket.

"What does that mean?" she asked in a voice laced with pain.

"It means it doesn't look as if you have broken any bones, but it does mean you've torn tissues, and that is what is causing you so much discomfort."

Eleanor seemed to be in too much distress to take in what he was saying. He turned to the wardrobe mistress. "I'm going to bind her ribs to prevent further injury when she moves. I would recommend giving her some willow bark tea to ease the pain. We could send a boy around to the apothecary at St. Thomas's. I know he'll still be there."

"Very good, sir. I'll fetch an errand boy."

"In the meantime, I'll need some cold compresses to apply to her head and ribs, as well as some long strips to bind her rib cage with."

"Very well, I'll get them straightaway."

As the woman hurried out to carry out his instructions, he sat in a chair beside Eleanor. He pushed her fallen tresses away from her forehead, feeling a tenderness well up inside him.

"Are you still here?" she asked after a moment. "I thought you'd gone."

"I'm still here. How are you feeling?"

"Like I've been stretched out on the rack."

He smiled. "Sounds like an accurate description."

"I wish I could stop breathing until the pain goes away."

"As soon as we get the remedy from the apothecary, the pain will lessen . . . at least enough to breathe."

"So, what is the diagnosis?"

"A sprain, I would say. It's difficult to tell how severe. You had quite a fall."

"Have you ever had a sprained rib?"

"No, but I have broken an arm."

She opened her eyes at last and glanced at him. "Really? I thought a doctor wasn't supposed to get sick or injured."

He smiled ruefully. "We suffer the same debilities as anyone else."

"Tell me how it happened," she asked, her face grimacing with her own pain.

"When I was a lad. I disobeyed my father

and climbed up into the hayloft with some friends. We dared each other to jump down onto the ground. They came away unscathed. I broke an arm. I don't know which was worse — the pain of the break or the pain in seeing the disappointment in my father's eyes."

The wardrobe mistress returned at that moment, her arms laden with her commissions. "How are you, luv?"

Ian took the materials from the older woman and went to work with the compresses. Eleanor sucked in her breath as he gently pressed the cold compress against her bare rib cage.

He lifted her head just enough to set another on the lump. He and Mrs. Baldwin, the wardrobe mistress, changed these frequently.

"All right, I'm going to bind this tightly," he warned Eleanor as he removed the last compress from her ribs. "I'm going to need you to sit up for a moment. It will hurt at first because I need to pull it tightly, but then I think you'll find it more comfortable."

Mrs. Baldwin helped Eleanor sit up.

"Hold up her camisole," he instructed the woman, keeping his voice as impersonal as possible while he desperately tried to ignore what lay beneath the sheer cotton. Instead, he concentrated on the long strips of sheet in his hand. Working quickly and efficiently, he wound them around her torso.

"This is worse than my stays," Eleanor gasped.

"I'm almost finished. There," he added, as he tied the final knot. "Thank you, Mrs. Baldwin. You can let her lie down."

The woman covered Eleanor with the blanket once again. Eleanor looked on the verge of fainting. Ian's heart went out to her, wishing once again he could bear her pain.

"I think a sip of brandy might be called for," he told the wardrobe mistress.

"Yes, of course, I should have thought of it sooner." She bustled to the dressing table and poured some liquid in a tumbler.

"Here, you go, dearie," she said, lifting Eleanor's head enough for her to take a few sips.

When Eleanor was resting quietly, Ian motioned Mrs. Baldwin to the door. "She needs to be transported home and put to bed. She shouldn't be left alone during the ride. With that knock she took on the head, she really needs to have a close eye kept on her."

The woman looked doubtful. "I don't

know, Doctor. I have my family I've got to get home to."

"Perhaps one of the other actresses?"

"I'll inquire."

Ian didn't want to go near Eleanor again. He had kept his professional detachment, but seeing her now lying on the settee, he was afraid he'd betray himself.

He wandered instead to her dressing table. It was a sturdy square wooden table with lots of drawers up each side. There was a large mirror facing him, and the surface of the table was covered with all manner of pots of paints, powders, feathers, combs and brushes, and an assortment of jewels made of paste.

A world of make-believe, he thought, fingering a paintbrush.

"Oh, Mr. Russell, no one's available," Mrs. Baldwin announced sorrowfully, entering the room again.

Ian frowned. "Very well. I shall accompany her to her house. Could you be so good as to call for her carriage?"

"Very well, Doctor."

Ian was loath to leave Eleanor after he'd carried her up to her bedchamber. Her maid and housekeeper were there, and they promised to look after her during the night, rousing her at intervals, but he felt pity that she had no family member to stay with her.

She was resting more tranquilly since he'd given her the bark tea. But still he lingered, needing to have one last look at her. He took her slim wrist in his hand and checked her pulse.

She looked so pale and helpless. How he wanted to bend over and place a kiss on her brow, but he could only play the serious doctor.

With a sigh he laid her arm down gently on the green coverlet. The bed was a mass of frills and lace. He glanced around the room before leaving it. It was everything feminine with its pastel wallpaper and white-and-gilt furnishings. A subtle hint of perfume pervaded it.

When he left her town house, Ian had to walk several blocks before he found a hack stand. One lone coach stood there, its horses bent down in repose.

As he rode through the dark streets, he threw his head back against the squabs and closed his eyes. Despite his weariness, he couldn't dispel the image that haunted his mind. Eleanor Neville was the loveliest creature he'd ever beheld. Her torso was as perfect as marble statuary, her skin as soft as a vestal virgin's.

Ian clenched his fist. What a deceptive image. She'd probably been used by more men than he could number.

As soon as he got home, instead of collapsing in bed, he headed to his study and sat down at the desk with his Bible.

He turned to a psalm he had been reading the night before.

"Judge me, O Lord; for I have walked in mine integrity; I have trusted also in the Lord; therefore I shall not slide.

Examine me, O Lord, and prove me; try my reins and my heart . . . I have walked in Thy truth. I have not sat with vain persons . . . and will not sit with the wicked."

Instead of meditating on those passages, he found himself flipping several pages forward to Song of Solomon.

". . . thy navel is like a round goblet, which wanteth not liquor; thy belly is like a heap of wheat set about with lilies. Thy two breasts are like two young roes that are twins . . ."

No, he mustn't read these words! They only inflamed him. He turned to the gospel of Matthew, looking for the Sermon on the Mount. His forefinger ran down the page. Yes, there it was.

"But I say unto you, That whosoever looketh on a woman to lust after her hath committed adultery with her already in his heart.

And if thy right eye offend thee, pluck it out, and cast it from thee . . ."

He felt the weight of condemnation fall heavily upon him.

Another verse he'd heard often from the pulpit came to him: "Know ye not that the unrighteous shall not inherit the kingdom of God? Be not deceived: neither fornicators, nor idolaters, nor adulterers . . ."

He need read no more. He knew what the Word of God said on the subject of lust.

His head fell into his hands. All these years, he'd kept himself pure, and now here he was sinking deep into the pit of lust. Even as he admitted all these things, visions of Eleanor Neville's body rose before him, haunting him, drawing him.

He wanted her as he'd never wanted a woman before.

Was he lost?

CHAPTER ELEVEN

Early the next afternoon Eleanor, after a restless night, sat in her dressing gown in her upstairs sitting room, sipping a cup of hot chocolate.

No position felt comfortable. Everything hurt, from her head — she didn't even want to think about her ribs — down to her calves.

How could this have happened? One moment, starring in a hit comedy, and the next, feeling as if every bone in her body had been broken.

She wanted to weep. How cruel could fate be?

"Excuse me, ma'am." Her young maid popped her head in the door. "The surgeon, Mr. Russell, is here to see you."

Her heart quickened at the memory of last evening. He'd been so kind, so protective of her.

"Show him up," she told Clara.

Before she had a chance to do more than place her cup down and smooth her hair, there was a knock on the door.

Mr. Russell, looking well groomed and very much dressed in contrast to her dishabille, followed the maid into the room.

His eyes barely met hers as he said, "Good morning."

He set down his medical bag and stood stiffly while the maid asked if she could bring him anything. Receiving a negative reply, she left the two of them.

"How are you feeling this morning?" he asked Eleanor, approaching her settee, his eyes not meeting hers but fixed somewhere near her chin.

"I'm feeling awful. I can hardly breathe, and you've got me trussed up like a fowl ready for a spit. How can I bathe this morning?"

At the word *bathe,* she immediately noticed the flush rise in his cheeks.

What was he uncomfortable about? She was the one who looked and felt terrible. It couldn't be her state of dress — or undress. He was, after all, a doctor; he must see women all the time.

She took a deep breath and immediately regretted it.

"We'll take off the bindings and I'll show

your maid how to put them back on," he was saying. "I've brought some better ones anyway." He pulled up a chair close to the settee. "Has the pain abated at all?"

"No," she said with a pout. "I could scarcely sleep last night. Mrs. Wilson kept waking me every time I managed to fall asleep."

"That's entirely my fault. I instructed her to rouse you throughout the night to ensure you didn't fall into a coma. It was a nasty blow to your head."

She touched it gingerly. It felt sore and tender. "How long will my convalescence last, anyway?"

"Hopefully not more than about six or eight weeks."

Her mouth fell open. "You are funning me!"

His brown eyes finally met hers fully, their expression serious. "Unfortunately not. Whether sprains or fractures, they take their time to heal. You will aid in the process if you continue to rest —"

"Rest? What about my show?" Her voice rose and she held her side at the sudden jab of pain.

He immediately leaned forward, steadying her. "You must calm yourself. Any sudden movement, as you see, will only aggravate the condition."

"I can see that," she said through gritted teeth, torn between feeling comforted by his concern and ready to throw a tantrum by his cool manner in telling her she must sit still for six weeks!

"Here, lie back," he urged, his tone gentle as he helped ease her against the cushions the maid had set behind her.

"Mr. Russell, I don't think you fully understand the enormity of what you're telling me. I have just opened with a show that is proving a success. Do you know how many shows close after only one week, because the audience tires of them?

"We've had a packed house every night for the last fortnight. I am one of the leads in this show. I cannot afford to be off the stage right now."

"You must be thankful you've come off with only some sprained ribs. It was a miracle you didn't break your neck after a fall like that."

"It couldn't possibly be worse. Six weeks off the boards, I might as well have broken my neck. In six weeks no one will remember who Eleanor Neville is."

"I sympathize with what you're saying. I'm not responsible for your injured rib cage. The fall did that. I'm merely telling you from experience what has happened and how long it will take your body to mend. If you rush this, you will only find yourself in a graver situation."

She hated that calm, condescending tone, as if he were speaking to an ill-tempered child. "Do you know how long I've waited for a part like this?"

He sat back and folded his arms across his chest.

"I've been walking the boards since I was fourteen. I shall be five-and-twenty in a few months. Do you know what that means?"

"That you are a young woman with many more years ahead of her . . . if you don't go falling down trapdoors."

She snorted at the last remark, then flinched. "It means I am a *mature* woman on the stage. I have another five years before I'll be playing nothing but old dowager roles. This show was my break. Don't you see, a hit show, the kind of show to attract the managers and owners of Covent Garden or Drury Lane?"

"I am truly sorry for your unfortunate accident —"

"What would you know about it?" She turned away from him, her voice catching, despair engulfing her.

They sat in silence a few moments, Eleanor feeling more and more miserable as the minutes ticked by on the clock sitting on her mantel. She sat with her chin in her hand. Her eyes filled with tears, until finally able to stand it no longer, she brought her hand to her eyes and wiped them away.

"I'm sorry," she gulped. "I just feel so awful . . . and I can't believe you're telling me I'm going to feel this awful for the next six weeks . . . and why now? Of all the possible times for this calamity, why did it have to be now?" The tears were flowing freely, but she didn't care.

Where was Betsy when she needed her? She needed someone's sympathy, not censure. She felt a handkerchief pressed against her face, and blindly she took it with her other hand, recognizing the familiar scent of soap.

"I am truly sorry. I wish I could tell you this will go away tomorrow. It may prove just a light sprain and in a fortnight, you'll only feel a twinge of pain."

She wiped her nose, refusing to look at him. Her face must look a downright mess. "Even a fortnight is too long," she sniffed. "By then my replacement will have the part down to perfection and the audience will have forgotten me."

"I'm sure that's not so. You were brilliant

in the piece."

She looked at him. His eyes were no longer looking so aloof. "You're just saying that to be kind."

"Indeed I am not. I saw you last night for the first time in your new role. You were truly magnificent, albeit in a man's costume."

She heard the last words in astonishment, remembering his disapproval at her men's breeches. "Even the critics who've hated these burlettas in the past praised me in this role."

"Rightly so. There will be other shows, you'll see."

She toyed with the damp handkerchief in her hand. "It won't be the same. I'm not exaggerating. I've waited a long time for a role like this, and my time is running out."

"They're fools if they don't offer you another good role."

She had to smile at that. How little he knew of the theater! "Do you know how many younger, more beautiful women there are knocking on the manager's door each day?"

He was looking at her so kindly, she expected him to disagree. Instead, he cleared his throat and motioned to her rib cage. "Let me see how you're doing since yesterday."

Swallowing her disappointment, she replied, "If you can get through all the swathing you've wrapped me in."

She loosened her dressing gown and let it lie open. As on the night before, he gently lifted her camisole only as far as necessary and asked her to hold it up.

His look and tone again took on that impersonal professional quality. Deftly, his fingers loosened the knot of the binding. She wondered if he would ask her to remove her dressing gown to make it easier to remove the tape, but he didn't. Although it was an awkward maneuver, he unrolled the tape from her body, his arms loosely spanning her torso.

Then his cool fingers were touching her skin and she felt it down to her toes. She remembered he'd done the same the night before. Then the pain had clouded her to all else, but this morning, she was supremely conscious of the feel of his fingers on her bare skin.

"Does this hurt?"

"A little."

"This?"

"Yes."

"Here?"

She shied away. "Yes."

His head was bent so she could lift her hand and touch his hair. The reddish hue was more apparent this close up. The light bounced off the thick waves of deep burnished copper.

He ought to have freckles, she thought, but she couldn't detect any from her angle. But then he pushed back from her and she could see his face.

There was a faint shadow of freckles, as if they were under his pale skin. "The area is still swollen," he said, seemingly unaware of her close scrutiny. He rose and went to his bag. He came back with a white cloth roll in his hand.

"This will work like the binding we used last night, but it will be easier to get on and off." As he spoke, he put it around her. It had a couple of tapes on one side, which he tied up tightly.

"It feels snug, but not as if it will cut off my breathing," she said when he had stepped back.

"You may close up your dressing gown."

"Oh, yes." She'd forgotten she still held her camisole up.

He turned away and went back to his bag. "I've brought you some laudanum if you have trouble sleeping at night. Also, some more willow bark tea, to take during the day if you are in discomfort. For the rest, you must try to move as little as possible, at least for several days."

"When can I begin to walk about?"

"You'll see. As the pain diminishes, you'll be able to do more. Just don't overdo things at the first sign, or you'll injure the muscles and ligaments once again and be in more pain than before."

"Yes, Doctor," she answered meekly. *We'll see about that,* she added silently. She could not accept the fact that she'd be out of commission for six to eight weeks.

"Would you like some tea or coffee?" she asked him.

"No, I really must be going. I have patients to check on."

"Of course," she replied immediately, wondering at the sense of loss she felt. "Thank you for stopping in to see me."

"There's no need to thank me." He seemed to hesitate. "You might want to call your regular physician."

"Dr. Elliot?" She hadn't given him a thought. "Is that necessary?"

"Strictly speaking, no. A sprained rib falls in my domain. Still, he might want to know what's happened to you and what treatment you are following."

"Very well. But won't you . . ." She hesitated in turn, not wanting to appear that she needed him. "Be stopping in anymore yourself?"

"Yes, if you don't mind, I'd like to measure your progress."

She smiled in relief. "Of course not. You were the one there last night. You saw exactly what happened."

"Have you heard anything more about how that trapdoor came to be opened? Is that usual?"

"No! I've never heard of such an accident. Occasionally an actor will fall from a swinging position from above, but never through the stage floor. Betsy has gone round to the theater to see what they've discovered."

"I'm glad to hear it." He took up his bag. "Well, I must be on my way. Other rounds." He came up to her and held out his hand. "Good day, Mrs. Neville. I'm sorry about the interruption in your work, but things could have been much worse."

She took his hand in hers and smiled wanly. "Good day, Mr. Russell. I look forward to your next visit."

When he'd left, she pondered the visit. She didn't know what to make of Mr. Russell. He seemed so professional in his capacity of doctor, his manner aloof and impersonal, his hands so gentle, his voice soothing and calm. And yet, when she'd broken down in front of him, he'd truly seemed to care.

But he'd never crossed the bounds of modesty. She'd never experienced that degree of respect in a man. Usually they were undressing her with their eyes, even if their words were decorous. This man had been the soul of propriety.

What had he been thinking as he'd looked at her?

She remembered his story from last night. He'd disobeyed his father and paid the consequences with a broken bone. She tried to imagine him as a disobedient little boy — a boy even at a young age conscientious enough to feel bad at a wrongdoing.

She lived in a world where a person was always scheming to get the advantage over another. Could Mr. Russell be a "good" man? She'd never met such a person. In her experience every man could be bought. Since she'd been a small girl, all she'd known was that survival drove people.

Whatever drove the good surgeon, the man was an enigma to her, and she looked forward to his next visit more than she cared to admit.

"Oh, Eleanor, are you feeling any better

today?" Betsy asked as she hurried into the room, untying her bonnet as she approached the settee.

"Only slightly better since drinking that vile willow bark tea the doctor left," she replied, eager to hear Betsy's news from the theater.

"Everyone sends their well-wishes," Betsy began, sitting in the chair Mr. Russell had vacated earlier. "They were so shaken by seeing you toppling down that awful hole last night. Half the audience thought it was part of the show."

"It would have been comical if it didn't have such tragic results for me. The doctor says I must rest for several weeks."

"Oh, you poor dear. But you must do as he says."

"Did you find out how that trapdoor gave way?"

"No." Betsy's blue eyes looked troubled. "No one can figure it out. For some reason, the hooks weren't fixed tight. When you stepped on it, as near as they can figure out, it must have given way. The stagehands have been instructed to check each trapdoor before the show tonight.

"The stage manager has questioned everyone. But no one knows anything. He can only think it was an oversight on someone's part."

Eleanor frowned. Someone's oversight was going to cost her career dearly. "Did Mr. Dibdin say anything?" she asked.

"Oh, yes, he offers his heartfelt wishes for your speedy recovery. He told me he'd be by to visit you later in the week when you're feeling better."

Eleanor sat back, mollified. At least he hadn't forgotten her. She wondered when he'd be by. She needed to assure herself that he still recognized her importance to the company.

Later that day Eleanor began to receive cards and flowers from many well-wishers. The vast majority were from gentlemen who were used to seeing her perform. She read the notes with pleasure, glad at least that some people already missed her. She read the accounts of her accident in the various newspapers.

A large box of bonbons from one of the finest chocolate confectioneries in the city was delivered. Eleanor opened the accompanying note.

I am desolate at your terrible misfortune and beg leave to come and see for myself that you are truly all right.

Your servant,
Gustave Marivaux, Duc d'Alvergny

What a distinguished name. Eleanor considered the note, bringing the folded paper to her chin. She repeated the name to herself. The son of émigrés, d'Alvergny had amassed a fortune in the decades of the war. There must be a way to make use of his friendship, especially during her misfortune.

The next afternoon Mr. Russell came by for his visit. Eleanor knew she looked much better than the day before. Her hair was down, artfully arranged around her shoulders.

"Good afternoon, Mrs. Neville," he said, bowing briefly over the hand she held up to him.

"Good afternoon, Mr. Russell," she answered coyly, enjoying the way color stained his cheeks, blotting out the faint freckles.

"I trust you're feeling the slightest bit better?"

"The slightest," she replied with a smile. "I slept tolerably last night with the help of the laudanum. And despite its vile taste, the willow bark tea seems to alleviate the hurt. I can actually breathe without stabbing pain."

"I'm glad to hear that." He held out a parcel to her. "I brought you something to help pass the time while you mend."

"Oh, what's this? More presents?" she asked eagerly, taking the package from him.

"*More* presents?"

She waved a hand around the room. "Dozens of notes and bouquets."

"I see. I should have realized you'd have a surfeit of gifts." His tone was light as he surveyed every tabletop adorned with a vase filled with a colorful array of flowers.

"Oh, but I'm sure yours is much more original than those," she hastened to assure him.

"Don't be too sure."

She unwrapped the package eagerly and looked with interest at the stack of books, all new and obviously just purchased.

"I thought you might enjoy *Rob Roy*," he began. He cleared his throat. "You might have already read it."

She looked up at him with a smile. "No, I haven't. I look forward to reading it," she answered softly, wanting to let him know his gift had touched her.

"I've also brought you an edition of *Emma*. This latest work is dedicated to the Regent."

"There's all sorts of speculation about 'the lady' who has written these delightful novels," she said, opening the edition of *Emma* and reading the dedication. "I shall certainly have plenty of time for reading."

"That's what I thought."

She looked at the next book. "What's this?" She read from the front cover. "*Romances and Gothic Tales, Containing 'The Ruins of the Abbey of Fitz-Martin,' 'The Castle on the Beach,' 'The Mysterious Monk.'*" She raised an eyebrow. "A gothic horror from the good Methodist?"

He looked embarrassed. "I didn't know your reading tastes, so I brought along a wide selection."

She flipped to the next book. "*Practical Piety, The Influence of the Religion of the Heart on the Conduct of the Life* by Hannah More." Her mouth turned downward as she read the title. "That's more what I would expect from you, but I fear to disappoint you if you think I shall be able to get through something written by someone who writes religious tracts . . ." Eleanor wrinkled her nose and laid the book aside.

"Well, I thought it might make for edifying reading while you are housebound."

She was no longer listening as she sat looking at the last book. "The Holy Bible?"

He cleared his throat as his fingers curved around the arm of his chair. "It's the source of all comfort when one is enduring a trial . . ."

"Are you trying to turn me into an evangelical?" she asked in amusement.

"Have you never read it?"

The question took her aback. "No," she answered, glancing back down at the leather-bound volume as she searched her memory. "Churchgoing never formed part of my upbringing."

"There are some good things in that book."

She looked back down at the Bible in her lap. "Are there?"

"Permit me." He reached across and took it from her.

He opened it up to a marker and began to read, " 'Delight thyself also in the Lord; and He shall give thee the desires of thine heart.' "

" 'The desires of my heart'? I can't imagine God caring about what I want. I thought the Bible was all hell-fire and brimstone."

He smiled. "No, there's much more to the Bible than that. It takes a lifetime to plumb its depths."

"I don't know if I'll be able to understand anything in it. Would you mark the place you read?"

"Of course. That was Psalm Thirty-seven.

The psalms are a good place to start. I think you'll find some pleasing things in them." He replaced the ribbon between the pages he'd been reading and shut the book.

"I shall attempt it," she said, wanting to please him for his thoughtfulness. "But I can't promise you I'll understand anything I read. I do thank you for the lovely books, though."

She turned away with a sigh, thinking again of the reason she would have so much time to read.

"What is it?"

"I just remembered. Tomorrow is the day I usually go to visit Sarah, the girl who was ill with the fever."

"She doesn't yet know about your accident?"

She shook her head. "I didn't have the heart to tell her I couldn't come. She looks forward to my weekly visits. As I do." She bit her lip. "I must send word, that's all there is to it."

"I can inform her."

"Oh, but that's quite out of your way."

"I've meant to pay her a visit, to see how she has recovered."

"She was doing extraordinarily well when I visited her last week. You did wonders for her with that cinchona bark. You are the man of 'bark,' " she teased.

"I did nothing unusual. I'm just glad I could come when you called me."

She could feel her cheeks grow warm under his steady regard. She looked down, clutching the dressing gown to her neck. "Aren't you going to . . . examine me today?" she asked, her mind going to the reason for his visit.

He cleared his throat. "No, not today. There's no need, unless you feel something differently today from yesterday."

"No," she whispered, wondering whether to feel relieved or disappointed.

"Well, I'd better be off, then." He rose.

"Thank you for stopping by," she told him, wishing he weren't leaving so soon. "Thank you for the lovely books."

He returned the Bible to her. "Think nothing of it. It was my pleasure."

"You'll see Sarah, then? You'll tell her why I can't come tomorrow?"

"Yes."

"You won't say anything to worry her, will you?" she asked.

"No, of course not. Trust me," he reassured her.

"Yes, all right." As a doctor, he would know the right thing to say. "Well, I'm very grateful." She held out her hand.

His own reached out and enveloped hers and she was overwhelmed by the sense of security it gave her.

The next day Eleanor felt worse than ever. Usually she spent the day with Sarah. The effects of the willow bark tea had worn off, and she felt a throbbing pain in her side with each breath.

The owner of the theater had stopped by, but his commiserations hadn't totally re-assured her. She'd have to ask someone like Betsy to see how the show was being re-ceived with her replacement.

Clara popped her head around the door-way. She was beaming. "You have visitors."

"Yes, who?" She strained to look beyond her and was rewarded with a sharp pain.

"Mr. Russell with a couple and a young girl."

She opened her eyes wide. *A young girl?* Could it be? "Show them up, please."

A few minutes later Sarah came bounding in the room. "Aunt Eleanor, are you sur-prised to see me?"

"I am indeed," she replied, trying her best to sit up.

Sarah knelt down beside the settee. "Does it hurt very much?"

She smiled amidst the pain. "Only a little

when I move."

Mr. Russell stood over her. "Permit me," he said, putting his arms around her and helping her prop herself against the pillows.

"That's better," she said, resting her head back. She placed her hand on his forearm as he was about to move away. "Did *you* bring her here?" she asked, searching his eyes.

He shrugged, looking away. "They insisted on coming along."

"Thank you," she whispered, squeezing his arm. She wished she could show him how much this meant to her.

"There's nothing to thank me for," he replied, drawing away from her gently.

Louisa and her husband came up then. "What horrors are these the good surgeon is telling us about? Falling through trapdoors?" Jacob Thornton demanded.

Eleanor tried to laugh but stopped herself with a grimace. "I wish I knew myself. I feel very clumsy."

"Oh, my dear Eleanor, you should have sent for us. We would have come instantly," Louisa wrung her hands, scolding, as she bent to examine her. "You look so pale. Are you eating properly? What have you given her, Doctor?" She turned to Mr. Russell.

"I'm being perfectly well taken care of,"

Eleanor reassured the older woman, "so please leave poor Mr. Russell be and give me a proper greeting." She held out her hand to Louisa. "I thank you so much for coming today. I needed to see a friendly face." Her eyes went to Sarah. "Two —" she amended, then glanced at Mr. Thornton. "Three friendly faces . . ." Finally her attention rested on Mr. Russell, standing in the background, and she added softly, "Four . . ." Her glance lingered on him. Why had he been so kind and thoughtful to her since the accident? Did he treat all his patients so attentively?

"I couldn't bear to be so long away from you," Sarah exclaimed. "Mama Thornton has promised we may stay three whole days with you!"

"Is it so?" At the other woman's wide smile and vigorous nod, Eleanor brought her hands up to her cheeks. "Oh, that is wonderful. I didn't know either how I was going to bear being away from my little Sarah so long."

Once again her glance strayed over Sarah's head to the surgeon. Had he suggested the visit? Before she could voice her question, he approached her settee. "Now that you are well accompanied, I will excuse myself and leave you to enjoy your visitors."

"You've only just arrived," she said. "Must you go so quickly?"

He didn't quite meet her eyes. "Yes, I fear I must."

She held out her hand. As his joined with hers, she asked, "Tell me truly. Was it your idea to bring the Thorntons back with you?"

Instead of replying, he only gave Eleanor's hand a brief squeeze before disengaging his own. "I trust their company will help lift your spirits."

He turned to the others, giving her no chance to probe further. "I wish you a pleasant stay in London."

They all protested, but he was adamant. Soon, Sarah demanded Eleanor's attention, and all she could do was give the doctor a final wave of her hand and a silent thank you with her eyes. Amidst Sarah's chatter, Eleanor's thoughts lingered on the doctor's looks and words. He had told her more by what he hadn't said than by what he had, and she felt a deep satisfaction and gratitude at how thoughtful he had shown himself since her accident.

She wondered how long it would be before the good surgeon declared his feelings for her.

And what her response would be . . .

CHAPTER TWELVE

The three days passed all too swiftly. Louisa fussed over Eleanor, preparing possets, syllabubs and cordials to drink. Sarah read to her, and Eleanor marveled at how their roles were reversed. Suddenly she saw how grownup Sarah was becoming. In another few years she would be as old as Eleanor had been when she'd had her.

She pushed the thought aside. Too close behind it lay the question, where would she be in another five years?

Ian stopped by his uncle's garret a few days later.

"He's over in his garden," Jem told him.

"Thanks. I'll look for him there."

Ian left the herb garret and walked down St. Thomas Street, the length of the hospital. Across the street, a few blocks down, was its sister hospital, Guy's, where he had trained. Ian continued a little farther on and entered through an arch that led to a grassy courtyard, hidden away within the large hospital compound.

Ian followed the brickwalk that divided the different garden beds laid out inside the courtyard. Dying plant stalks stood brown and bent, their seed pods dry and full. Ian picked off a poppy bulb and upended it, watching the hundreds of tiny gray seeds scatter over the soil.

He spied his uncle at the far end, kneeling beside a flower bed. Before he had reached him, his uncle heard his footsteps and turned. "Ian, what can I do for you, lad?"

"Nothing terribly urgent. I dropped off some prescriptions with Jem, but I'll come round tomorrow to collect them. I just thought I'd visit a few moments before I return to the dispensary."

"Well, I'm glad you did, my boy. You see me gathering my herbs and seeds before the first frost."

"Yes, it won't be long now."

His uncle clipped the stalks off the bushy herbs and laid them in his basket. Soon they would hang from the rafters of his garret drying before being chopped and macerated into pills and tinctures.

"Pennyroyal for gastric upsets and nausea. Spearmint soothes the stomach, too." *Clip,*

clip went his shears. "Ah, my chamomile, I must get plenty of that." Uncle Oliver stood and moved down the herb bed to the lacy-leafed plant with the tiny, daisylike heads.

Ian helped him break off the yellow flower heads and tossed them into his uncle's sack when he'd collected a handful. They had a pleasant odor and he inhaled the fragrance lingering on the palm of his hand.

A visit to this garden always soothed him. Even though it showed the decay of autumn, it was still an attractive, well-kept garden. Above and surrounding it, the windows of the furthest wards of the hospital overlooked it. These were the wards of the "incurables," those not admitted to the other hospitals. Among them lay the blind and deformed, the asthmatics, those diagnosed with consumption and cancer, and those simply suffering from old age. Then there was the "foul" ward beside it, which contained the many patients who came to them to be treated for venereal diseases.

Ian always hoped a glimpse at this little square of green in summer or white in winter with its bare spindly tree branches set sparsely in the geometrical layout would ease their suffering.

"Some ground ivy . . ." Uncle Oliver tugged at the stubborn vine and clipped several long shoots. "And some wormwood, the age-old cure-all." Once again he stood and moved to another bed.

"There, that's all I can carry in my basket. Help me gather some seed pods into these sacks and we're done for the day."

They walked around the rectangular beds, plucking dried flower heads as they went. When he was satisfied, Uncle Oliver led Ian to a wrought-iron bench, one of two set at opposite ends of the courtyard garden.

"Sit a spell and visit with me. It's not too cold for you, is it?"

"Not at all," Ian assured him as he took a seat beside his uncle.

"Where have you been keeping yourself the past few days?"

"Here and there. I haven't had a chance to come up to the herb garret."

"Well, I've missed you. I read about your actress."

"What did you read?" he asked, refusing to rise to his uncle's use of the possessive pronoun.

"Why, about the accident. It sounded frightening. How is the young woman?"

"She's blessed to be alive. It was quite a nasty fall. It's a wonder she sustained only some painful sprains and no fractures."

His uncle's eyes twinkled. "Mayhap she

was fortunate there was a surgeon in the house. The news account said a surgeon rushed to her aid."

Ian shrugged and looked ahead at the faded garden bed. "Yes, well, I happened to be there that night."

"How timely . . ." his uncle said, his voice sounding amused.

Ian rubbed the back of his neck. "I thought I'd see for myself what all the commotion over this musical 'burletta extravaganza' was about."

"So, tell me what you made of it. What about Mrs. Neville? Is she as talented as they say?"

Ian shrugged. "Yes — no —" He struggled to find an adequate response. "I mean yes, she has some natural ability and raw talent. But . . ." He shook his head in disgust. "The medium! She makes herself a spectacle in front of an unruly audience singing to a cheap imitation of Mozart's opera, the lyrics crude and simplistic. The men come there to gape at the chorus girls."

"But you do find her talented?"

"Yes," he finally answered with a grim sigh.

"What about you? Are you interested?"

Ian turned to look at his uncle. "What do you mean?" he asked carefully.

"You know what I mean. As a man, are you interested in the young actress? From all accounts I've heard she's a beauty."

Ian stood and took a few steps along the brick path, too restless to sit still any longer. "Why would you ever think I'd be interested in someone like Eleanor Neville?" He strove for a tone of amazement even as his conscience pricked him, reminding him how often he'd been to see her since her accident.

"Apart from the obvious — her beauty and talent — there's your part in the rescue. It takes a strong man to resist the role of rescuer to a damsel in distress."

Ian gave a bark of laughter. "You spend too many hours up in your garret. Your imagination is taking flight."

His uncle stared at him, which only served to irritate Ian more. He kicked at the uneven bricks with the toe of his boot. "What kind of a woman would an actress make for a — a — wife?" There he'd said it, astounding himself more than anyone. "An actress's morals are as loose as a courtesan's. A man would never know when he's being cuckolded."

"There is that. Is Mrs. Neville as bad as all that?"

Ian blew out a frustrated breath. "How

should I know? On the surface she seems as innocent as a child, but her art is impersonation. One moment she's a great lady, the next a villain on the stage. How does a man know who the real person is?"

"Funny, but I haven't read any scandals concerning her. Her name isn't linked to anyone's in the gossip sheets."

Ian refrained from commenting on his uncle's habit of reading the gossip sheets. He turned and walked the length of the garden bed. When he returned, he said, "I vowed long ago I would wait for my helpmate and soul mate, a woman pure and set apart from worldly vanity. I will not settle for second best."

His uncle regarded him it seemed almost sadly for a moment before nodding. "You've waited a long time," he ended softly.

"That's funny coming from someone who never married." Ian matched his tone to his uncle, giving him a rueful smile. "Why did you never marry?" he asked, taking his seat once more.

It was his uncle's turn to look off into the distance. "I would have . . . once upon a time."

Ian couldn't imagine his confirmed bachelor uncle comfortably settled with a wife and children before the hearth. "What happened?"

"She died."

Still less could Ian imagine his staid uncle young and passionately in love. "I'm sorry. What was she like?"

"Nothing special to anyone outside her own small circle of friends and family." His uncle shrugged. "Young, sweet and pretty. What more can a young man want?" He chuckled. "I was besotted. A young apothecary, fresh from his apprenticeship, just come to London, and I met her in the market." He shook his head in reminiscence.

"We were making plans to marry, but a typhus epidemic came and swept her away almost overnight. None of my pills or tonics could do anything for her."

He turned to Ian with a bittersweet smile. "The Lord giveth and the Lord taketh away. Isn't that what Job said?"

His uncle always refused to consider the goodness of God. He saw only a capricious, vengeful creator. Perhaps this was the reason.

"You never met anyone else?"

"I discovered after the first waves of grief had passed that I preferred being alone amongst my herbs and plants."

The thought brought Ian no comfort. He could see himself going the way of his uncle, alone and dedicated to his work in the years ahead.

Eleanor realized she actually felt better. It wasn't just the fact that she'd bathed with very little pain, but that she was dressed to go out for the first time in weeks. She couldn't wear any stays, but still, the walking dress flattered her, she decided, inspecting herself in the long glass. It was a pretty pelisse of gray kerseymere wool trimmed in a wide band of ruby velvet down the front and around its hem and cuffs. The wide bonnet was similarly trimmed and was crowned with a high plume of ostrich feathers.

She touched the side of her rib cage gingerly. It really did feel better. Each day had been such an effort in controlling her movements to avoid pain that she'd hardly noticed it had indeed been diminishing. The weeks had gone by. Soon she would be able to resume her acting.

Mr. Russell had been very attentive, stopping in to see her almost every day. He never stayed above a quarter of an hour. The purported reason for his visits was to check on his patient, but Eleanor wasn't fooled. She knew the good surgeon was smitten.

She smiled at her image in the mirror. He was a dear man; she enjoyed teasing him. She'd had a few other visitors. Althea from the mission, some fellow actors, including the lead in *The Spectre,* who'd done nothing but hint how well her replacement was being received. She knew he was only peeved because she'd spurned his attentions for some time. Fool if he thought she'd give herself to someone like him.

Her other gentlemen admirers stopped in occasionally, but less frequently as the weeks went by. If it hadn't been for Russell and d'Alvergny, she would have been put out indeed.

But d'Alvergny had proved as faithful an attendant as Russell. He came by every few days, but his visits were longer. He always brought her a gift. She smoothed the expensive cashmere scarf she wore now against the bitter November cold. That had been a particularly thoughtful gift.

Perfumes, flowers, chocolates, or the newest naughty print by Cruikshank, which they would laugh over together. He brought her the latest *on dits* from court, described how the Prince was spending more and more time at Brighton, the lavish dinners hosted there, and his increasing girth, which hardly permitted him to leave the pavilion.

The day young Princess Charlotte died giving birth to her first child, D'Alvergny arrived solemn and wearing a crepe armband. He comforted Eleanor as she wept for Prince Leopold's sudden bereavement and the tragedy of their too brief marriage.

D'Alvergny lent Eleanor a black-edged handkerchief of the finest lawn, embroidered with his initials and smelling faintly of his cologne. It brought to mind the other handkerchief she had held to her nose.

Although she laughed with d'Alvergny, she mimicked him behind his back to Betsy. He really was a pompous man. Yet, conversely, she found his visits stimulating. For one thing, she could practice her acting skills on him, telling herself it was good to keep her hand in.

One day she would pout over an imagined slight, and she would watch in amusement as he strove to assure her that he'd never intended to offend her. The next day he would give her an elaborate gift by way of atonement. Another day she was cool and aloof, showing him she belonged to no man, regardless of how many gifts she received from him. After toying with him this way, she would be warm and amusing, as if to reward him for his constancy.

He remained unflappable and attentive

throughout. She could never manage to irritate him or drive him away. It was as if he knew her game and was content to bide his time, plying her with expensive baubles as tokens of greater gifts to come.

She laughed inwardly. Little did he know she had been promised such things before and wouldn't be fooled so easily.

How different from the good surgeon. He presented a much greater challenge. All decorum and reserve, but oh, how she delighted to excite the telltale flush on his cheeks when she'd said something outrageous or moved too close. It gave her odd shivers of delight. Between the doctor's visits, she would devise ways of bringing it about.

It became more difficult all the time. Mr. Russell was the soul of circumspection. He never even examined her anymore. She had to be subtle. It wouldn't do to have the high-minded doctor suspect her of anything but the purest motives.

The other day as he'd taken his leave, she'd held his hand a few seconds longer than necessary and looked deeply into his eyes.

Another day she'd winced particularly violently as she'd made a sudden movement. In truth her pain had been a vast deal less than her features had conveyed. But he'd rushed immediately to her. She'd placed his hand on her side to indicate where the pain was, forcing him to do a cursory examination.

She giggled at the memory. She'd watched his features the entire time — only a few moments in all, but she hadn't miscalculated his reaction. As his hands had palpated her rib cage through her gown, the flush had stained his cheeks, covering that pale skin and masking the subcutaneous layer of milky freckles.

She'd felt such a sense of her own power, proud of her ability to read men. Mr. Russell had moved away from her quickly, but she'd eyed him triumphantly for the rest of the visit, secure in the knowledge he was hers whenever she beckoned.

Still, she was grateful to him for all he'd done for her, particularly his attentions to Sarah. She'd never forget how he'd brought Sarah to her. After the Thorntons had departed with Sarah, Eleanor had had a fit of the dismals for a few days. So much so that she'd even attempted reading the Bible Ian had given her. Louisa had read it to her a few times during her visit — only the nice parts, Eleanor had insisted.

But she hadn't gotten very far on her own.

And that edifying work by Hannah More! Dry as powder. Eleanor shuddered. How could a woman who'd been born with no particular pretensions of family or wealth yet who'd managed to achieve a measure of success in playwriting and notoriety in the bluestocking set give that up to write tracts and sermonizing works?

"Mr. Russell is below," her maid informed her now.

"Thank you, Clara. Tell him I shall be down."

Giving herself a final examination in the full-length mirror, with a slight adjustment to her bonnet and a tug to the lace at her collar, she prepared to see the good surgeon.

Her convalescence was becoming long and tedious. Mr. Russell had invited her to a chapel service as soon as she was well enough to go out, and that day had finally arrived.

A chapel service — the idea was daunting, but she was willing to go anywhere after three weeks at home.

"Good morning, Mr. Russell."

Ian turned to see Mrs. Neville in the doorway of the sitting room. He drew in his breath at her elegant appearance. Just when he'd begun to grow used to her dressing gowns and, more recently, morning gowns, here she stood, silhouetted by the door frame, as if knowing how attractive she looked in her fashionable street clothes. She stepped slowly into the room, her soft gray gown rustling slightly.

He breathed a sigh of relief at the subdued elegance of the gown and bonnet. He hadn't dared hope. He'd already debated with himself so many times about his decision to invite her to chapel.

"Good morning, Mrs. Neville. I trust you are feeling up to this outing today?"

"I am feeling almost my old self except for an occasional twinge."

"Shall we be on our way?" he asked.

"I'm all anticipation." She gave him that saucy look which was impossible to decipher. Was she making fun of him, or just displaying high spirits?

When they arrived at the chapel, he took her first to the Sabbath school for children.

"How do you get so many children to a Sunday school like this?" she asked in amazement, looking at the children of all ages seated on the long benches, listening to their teacher.

"It's modeled on the Sabbath schools established by Robert Raikes in Gloucester about thirty years ago. Since then the concept has spread and you find them everywhere now."

She watched a little boy stand and recite one of the Ten Commandments, followed in turn by other children.

"They are very well behaved, though they appear to be nothing more than street urchins," she said.

"For the most part they are. They know they'll get something hot to eat early in the morning. It used to entice them in, but now, you see, they enjoy the lessons themselves."

She shook her head in amazement as they turned to enter the chapel. "I never knew of such things when I was a girl."

"Would you have attended one?"

"For a hot meal, very likely I would have." She gave a bemused smile. "Whether it would have helped me otherwise, I cannot say. Very likely not."

She fell silent, and he thought of the horrors she must have endured in her childhood. The infamy of her stepfather sickened him every time he allowed himself to remember it.

The chapel was already full, and they were obliged to squeeze into a pew at the very back. Ian located the hymn for her and handed her a hymnbook.

During the singing, he glanced down at her, amazed at the beauty of her voice up close. He had heard it on the stage, but having her right beside him, singing the lyrics of a song glorifying God, sent a thrill through him. How could such an angelic voice and countenance belong to a woman who used the same gifts for the bawdy songs of the stage, and her charm to attract men? For a few moments he allowed himself to imagine the type of woman she would be if the circumstances of her life had been different . . . if she had had the benefit of the teachings he'd received growing up.

He turned away from these thoughts with regret. They could only cause pain and unfulfilled longing in him.

The preacher spoke on the second verse of the twelfth chapter of the Book of Romans, "be not conformed to the world: but be ye transformed by the renewing of your mind . . ."

As he exhorted the congregation to stay away from all worldliness, Ian felt strong conviction come upon him. Every lustful thought he'd had was anathema to his Lord and Savior. He dared not even look at Mrs. Neville standing beside him, for fear of flooding his mind again with impure thoughts.

When he'd given his life over to the Lord, he'd turned his back on living for himself. There were eternal implications to every decision he took. He vowed anew that he wouldn't let his flesh dictate his actions.

After the service, Althea came over to greet Mrs. Neville. "How nice that you could come to one of our services."

"It's my first time out since the accident."

"Oh, then we are doubly thankful to have you with us. I'm glad you are feeling better. May I introduce you around?"

Ian felt relieved when Althea led Eleanor away, questioning his own motives in bringing her today. Had it been a mistake? Was his attraction to her overshadowing the more important matter of the redemption of her soul?

He looked over the crowd. Mrs. Neville stood out in her fashionable outfit. But she seemed to charm the people at chapel just as she had the children at the mission.

After the service, he took her to the mission for lunch, and Ian was surprised at how well Eleanor adapted herself. She modeled her conversation to theirs, and no mention was made of the theater. Ian could almost believe a transformation had taken place in her after one service.

By the time he escorted her home, the

conviction of the morning's sermon had faded, and he was feeling optimistic that she had indeed been touched by her time among the church brethren. He turned to her as the hackney he had hired neared her town house. "How was your first outing?"

"Most pleasurable. It was good to be outside the confines of my house if only for a few hours."

Her words stirred a wave of compassion in him. She had been shut up in her house for a long time, and her first outing had been to hear a strong sermon. Yet she'd made no complaint. Perhaps she deserved some amusement.

"How about another outing tomorrow or whenever you feel up to it?" he suggested before he could talk himself out of it.

"Where to?" she asked, her eyes alive with interest.

"Have you heard of laughing gas?"

"I've read about it. Will you take me to see a demonstration?"

"That's what I had in mind. We could go to Faraday's Laboratory on Albemarle Street."

She clapped her hands, as happy as a child. "I'd love to go. It's all the rage. So many of the ton have tried it. Is it safe?"

"Yes, I believe so. It doesn't last too long.

I am interested in observing the effects from a scientific point of view."

"Let's go tomorrow, then."

He agreed to come round the next afternoon. By the time he arrived home, he was once again debating the decision to himself. Why was it he forgot all his resolve when he was in Eleanor Neville's presence?

CHAPTER THIRTEEN

Eleanor was finishing her morning coffee, leisurely perusing the theater reviews in the *Morning Post* and *The Examiner,* when her housekeeper brought up Mr. Dibdin's card.

Eleanor put aside the paper, tired of reading how well the show had continued to do without her. "Send him in. How do I look?" she asked.

"Oh, very fetching, ma'am. That shade of blue suits you admirably."

Eleanor rearranged her skirts on the chair and smoothed her hair. Thomas would see how well she looked, ready to return to the stage.

"Good morning, Eleanor, I hope this isn't too early to pay a call," Mr. Dibdin began as soon as he entered the room.

Thomas Dibdin was a fashionably dressed, middle-aged man. His hair was cut in the latest style of a dandy, with its high-swept graying curls falling over his forehead.

His neck was encased to the jaw in a cravat, and he wore a tight-fitting, navy-blue, double-breasted coat.

"Of course not, Thomas. How kind of you to come and see me. Please have a seat. Would you like some refreshment? Coffee? Cocoa?" she asked in a lighthearted tone, indicating the tray in front of her. "I can ring for a fresh pot of coffee."

He waved aside the offer. "Don't trouble yourself, my dear, I mustn't stay. You know how busy things can be this time of year."

After kissing her hand, he settled himself across the room, crossing his legs and sitting back with a sigh. When he made no effort to initiate the conversation, she held up the paper.

"I was reading about Miss Byrnes's first appearance on the London stage in *The Haunted Tower* at the Drury Lane. Have you seen it?"

"Yes, when it first opened."

Seeing he made no other comment, she explained, "I'm reading the old papers, trying to catch up on theater news, since I haven't been out until now. She seems to have made a hit at the Drury."

She read from *The Examiner,* " 'She is young; and is of a prepossessing appearance, with fine dark eyes and hair and a little ladylike figure. Indeed, we think we have not seen an actress for a long time so genteel in her air and natural deportment.' " She looked across at Dibdin. "What did you think when you saw her?"

"Oh, a fine young actress indeed. Very nice voice, too," he said in a distracted tone.

"At least the paper didn't pan our *Spectre on Horseback*. Leigh Hunt has not been known to deal kindly with your librettos."

"No, he's merely ignored it," he answered sourly.

"Theatergoers haven't seemed to notice the snub. I read the show is packed every night."

"Oh, yes. It is indeed."

He didn't look as happy as he should be. Perhaps it was because he thought she'd be sensitive to the fact that she wasn't in it. Well, she would reassure him.

"I'm just about completely recuperated, you see?" she asked, stretching her arms wide. "No pain."

"That's wonderful, my dear. Terrible thing that accident." He was looking around him.

"Thomas, I am well enough to come back in a week or so, not above a fortnight, my doctor assures me."

He cleared his throat again. "That's what I came to talk to you about today."

"Oh, really! Why, the two of us must have been thinking along the same lines. I was ready to stop by the theater —"

"I want you to take all the time you need," he continued as if she hadn't spoken. "As you know, our season will end in another month. We may run a bit longer this year with the success of *Spectre.* Don Giovanni seems to be all the rage these days. I've heard of other productions at the other minors —"

"But that's all the better. It will give me a chance to get back into my part and do it justice."

He was rubbing his hand against his face. "Well, you see . . . Miss Smith . . . you know . . . she's been doing so well as Leporello . . . wouldn't like to change horses in midstream . . . confuse the audience and all that, you know."

She could hardly distinguish his words, which were coming out mumbled against his hand.

"What are you saying, Tom?" she asked in clipped syllables.

His eyes met hers and she read a plea in them. "I just . . . well . . . with its being almost the end of the season . . . well . . ." His voice trailed off.

"You just said you were not going to close

so soon."

"The truth is, Eleanor, the crowd loves Miss Smith. I'm afraid the audience, if they were to see you again so soon, well, you know, all they might think of is the trapdoor. And that might prove distracting."

It was as if he had screwed up all the courage he'd had to say it all at once, and now finished, he had nothing more to add. The silence rang in her ears like the thunderous applause at the end of the final act.

Only this wasn't applause. She hadn't received any applause in almost six weeks. And if Thomas had his way, she wouldn't be hearing any applause for another half a year.

No, this was monstrous. Not to be borne.

She rose and began to pace. "You can't do this to me. You know the audience loved me."

"I'm sorry, Eleanor. Of course I don't want to do any such thing to you. But come, my dear, the convalescence will do you good. There'll be other shows in the spring —"

She turned on him. "Spring! We won't open until June. What am I supposed to do until then? Sit home and knit?"

"You'll travel with us when we tour. Come, Eleanor, it's not as bad as all that.

There's Bath and Bristol, York . . ."

"As what? Donna Anna's maid?" she asked bitterly.

"There are several other shows we'll be performing on the road. There's your old role in *The Parson's Peccadillo.*"

She turned away from Dibdin, no longer listening. "I'm feeling a bit fatigued. If you'll excuse me, Thomas, I think I shall retire for a bit."

He was up in a flash. "Of course, my dear. So sorry, didn't want to disturb you. You mustn't overdo. I'll just see myself out . . . I'll let you know what we have lined up for the spring . . ."

When he'd left, Eleanor fisted her hand and pounded it into her palm. With any luck at all, Thomas Dibdin wouldn't find her in the spring. The next time he came calling, she simply wouldn't be available.

She had to find a way to get on the majors! She'd have to finagle an audition at the Drury or Covent Garden; even the Little Haymarket would do.

Ian came by that afternoon. They had arranged to take Mrs. Neville's carriage to Faraday's Laboratory and it was waiting at the curb when he arrived.

They drove down Shaftesbury Avenue

through Soho. When they reached Piccadilly Circus, the coach slowed with the congested traffic heading toward Mayfair. The rumble of heavy drays and delivery wagons, angry shouts between their drivers and the gentry's coachmen, came through the closed window of their chaise.

"Are you feeling quite all right?" he asked in concern. Mrs. Neville sat unusually quiet opposite him.

"What? Just a bit blue-deviled is all," she replied. "Nothing the laughing gas won't fix."

He studied her more closely. She looked well enough. More than well in her plum-colored outfit with its narrow fur ruff and pert bonnet. Her cheeks were tinged pink from the chilly air. But he sensed something was wrong.

He didn't press her, hoping that eventually he would be able to get at what was troubling her.

Once again he questioned whether he was doing the right thing in inviting her today. He'd argued back and forth since the spontaneous invitation yesterday. The poor woman had hardly stirred from her house in six weeks. She deserved a treat. He didn't know if this visit would be a "treat," but it should amuse her for a few hours at any rate.

When they arrived at the brick town house, Ian helped her descend and gave the coachman instructions to come for them in about an hour. That should give them sufficient time to observe all there was to observe. He offered Mrs. Neville his arm, and the two proceeded up the brick walk.

Once inside, they could hear sounds of laughter in the room beyond. They were shown into a large, tastefully furnished drawing room, where several well-dressed people wandered or sat about. Mrs. Neville looked around her at the strange behavior of the individuals. Ian had already been once, so he knew what to expect.

Some of the people were laughing for no apparent reason. Others were sprawled in armchairs, their expressions vacuous. One woman was dancing about the room with no partner.

"I feel as if I'm floating," she declared, her arms held wide. "Oh, this is delicious."

At one corner of the room, a man stood next to some barrels, a line of people standing in front of them.

"Is that where we receive the laughing gas?" Mrs. Neville asked him.

"Yes, that's where the nitrous oxide is

dispensed," he explained. "One inhales it and soon a most pleasurable sensation is experienced. Afterward, there is an insensitivity to pain."

They walked farther into the room and began promenading around it to observe the different people and their conditions. "A colleague of mine inhaled some when he was suffering from a toothache and it took away the pain."

"I wish I had been able to take some after my fall."

He nodded. "It is possible it would have alleviated the pain. But the effect wears off rather quickly, within an hour or so, and then the pain returns."

"They all look as if they're having such fun, yet there is nothing indecorous," she noted.

"I can dance! I can dance!" a portly gentleman exclaimed, twirling about the room.

Most of the people were merely laughing with abandon. They would fall silent and then all of a sudden start up again.

"Is that the main effect — laughter?" she asked, smiling at the hilarity around her.

"Yes, that's why they call it 'laughing gas' — another reason it wouldn't have been wholly beneficial for you. Too much laughter would have strained the ligaments in your rib cage further."

"I see. Yes, the slightest movement was excruciating. I'm glad you stuck to your willow bark."

He noted the amusement in her silvery eyes, and was gratified he'd managed to bring her out of whatever had preoccupied her.

"Oh, they do so look like they're having such fun!" She clasped her hands together. "Mightn't I try some?"

"Are you sure? I don't want you to strain yourself."

"I'm perfectly recuperated, I assure you. I feel no pain whatsoever! Truly!"

It might do her good to laugh, he conceded. "Very well. I'll make sure you come to no harm."

"Will you?" she asked softly, her eyes looking at him with such wonder and trust that it made him feel giddier than any dose of nitrous oxide.

He cleared his throat and looked away, using the pretext of steering her toward the laughing gas dispenser to ignore her question. Why was it every time she looked at him like that, he felt incapable of refusing her anything? If he let himself go, he would resemble that portly man, dancing about the room, spinning out of control.

"Ready for a dose of laughing gas?" the gentleman at the barrel asked them when they had arrived at the head of the line.

"Yes, I'm ready to forget my cares and troubles and laugh at all the world," Mrs. Neville replied.

"You've come to just the right place. Now, take a deep breath from here," he said, indicating the wide hose, "when I open this valve."

Just before doing so, she turned to Ian. "You are, too, aren't you?"

"Not this time. I have tried it before — purely for medical research," he added quickly.

"Why not do it today purely for fun?" Her eyes challenged him.

"Today I must act in the capacity of your surgeon, which means forswearing amusement to ensure you come to no harm."

"A pity you cannot manage both."

He watched her inhale the gas.

She turned to him. "I feel so strange." She put her hands up to her cheek. "There is a luscious warmth all over my body." As she stared at him in wonder, she began to laugh.

He smiled back at her. "What is so funny?"

"You are. You are hilarious." Soon she had to clutch his arm to remain upright. Every time she looked at him, she burst out laughing all over again.

"Oh, I don't know what is so funny — but it's all so funny." She giggled at the people around her. "They're all so fu-unny!

"I am floating." She closed her eyes and began swaying against him.

He led her gently to a vacated settee.

"I wish I were like this all the time." She hummed a tune, then began laughing again.

He sat beside her, noting her reactions until the effect wore off. She had only had a small dose, so he knew it wouldn't last long. In the meanwhile, he took out a small notebook and pencil and jotted down some observations. The gas seemed to bring on feelings of euphoria and a heightened desire to laugh; at the same time it deadened sensations of pain.

Afterward, they listened to a lecture on the properties of the gas. Many of the attendees were only interested in getting a second dose of the gas, but there were others like himself who were interested in it from a scientific point of view.

When the lecture ended, Mrs. Neville looked longingly at the people lined up for more laughing gas. "It would be lovely to feel the effects one more time."

"I think you've had enough for today.

Don't forget, you still are recuperating."

"Must you be such a stickler?" she asked although her smile took away the sting of her words.

In order to appease her, he suggested a trip to Gunter's.

"Tea and crumpets — a poor substitute, but tempting nonetheless." She sighed. "Very well."

They drove the few blocks to Berkeley Square and the famous confectioner's.

When they were seated at a small dainty table, Mrs. Neville looked around her at the other patrons. "This place is veritably patronized by the *haut ton.* Isn't that Princess Lieven?" she indicated with a slight lift of her chin.

Ian didn't bother to turn around. "I wouldn't have a clue, never having met the lady. I merely find they make good pastry."

She smiled at him. "You will insist on being unmoved by the distinguished company in your midst. That is all very well for you operating on all and sundry down in Southwark. But for a poor actress, patronage goes a long way." She nodded toward another table. "That is the Marquis of Salisbury. He is a subscriber of the Royal Theater at Haymarket. Those are the kinds of gentlemen who have power over who does and who doesn't get an audition with the manager."

"As long as you don't have to sell your soul in the bargain," he commented.

"A soul isn't worth very much if it's starving in the gutter."

"Jesus would argue that it's worth every bit as much as one of these ladies' or gentlemen's."

"Tell that to a starving person."

"Many of these people are starving and don't even know it."

"Let us not argue on this fine day, Mr. Russell. Tell me instead more about this laughing gas. How did it come to be discovered?"

"Actually, it was a nonconformist minister who first identified the gas over forty years ago."

"A clergyman? That is certainly amazing."

"Not entirely. The Bible tells us wisdom is found in God. Many of history's greatest scientists have also been its most devout men."

When she made no comment, he went on to explain how the gas was isolated at the turn of the century by some medical men at Bristol. "Humphry Davy is perhaps the best known of them since he has become a director at the Royal Institution here in London. It was he who began experimenting the way we saw today with some of society's leading figures like Coleridge and Southey. The notoriety has helped achieve a social phenomenon, but it hasn't really advanced the scientific investigations. There has been little serious experimentation although the potential for its uses is great."

"Goodness, yes. What I felt today was astounding."

"The implications for numbing pain could be revolutionary."

"Yes! Just think, for surgery —" Her eyes sparkled.

"Unfortunately, it seems to increase the pressure of blood circulating through the vessels, so for surgery, that would be counterproductive, indeed dangerous."

"You mean, someone might bleed to death?"

"Precisely," he said, pleased with her quick understanding.

The waiter brought them their tea and lemon tarts.

"I must have gained a stone with all this convalescing. I am growing fat and lazy," she said, eyeing the tarts.

It was on the tip of his tongue to disagree and tell her she looked lovelier than ever, but he stopped himself. He must never forget he was merely a medical attendant to her, nothing more.

"These are delicious, I confess," she told him when she'd eaten one. "I concede your opinion that Gunter's primary attraction is its pastries and not the company that frequents it."

"I'm glad the laughing gas succeeded in lifting you out of the doldrums. I sensed something was on your mind when I first came by this afternoon."

"You are very discerning."

He waited to see if she would volunteer anything.

She took another pastry and stirred her tea, but after a while he was rewarded.

"I had a somewhat — unpleasant — visit this morning before you came by."

Ian waited patiently, preferring to feast his eyes on her than sample the pastries. Everything about her was feminine and graceful, from the way she held her teacup to the way she dabbed at the corner of her mouth with the edge of the napkin. It was difficult to believe she had arisen from the depths of poverty. Where had she learned to be a lady?

Her words startled him out of his speculation. "The owner of the Royal Circus came by. I was naive enough to think he was coming to see how soon I would be back."

"And?"

She looked away from him. "He merely wanted to tell me not to bother coming back until next season. Oh, he couched it in very pretty terms. I must take my time to fully recuperate, and so on and so forth."

"Is that such a terrible thing? Maybe he is concerned for your welfare."

She gave him a pitying look. "He no more cares for my health than that waiter over there does."

"So, what is the real reason?"

"The real reason is that my stand-in has proved popular in the role, and Mr. Dibdin doesn't find it in his interest to remove her from the part at this point in time." She dusted away the crumbs from the tablecloth. "For all I know he is smitten with her, and doesn't want to upset her."

"I'm sorry," he said, knowing the words were inadequate and, worse, probably insincere, but feeling she had been dealt an unfair blow.

She gave him a twisted smile, which affected him more deeply than he cared to acknowledge. "Thank you."

"What will you do now?"

"I am going to look for a part in a new theater," she said with a note of determination underlying her dulcet tones.

"You shouldn't have any problems after

the success you enjoyed before the accident."

"That success hasn't come easy. I've had to fight for every role." She sighed. "It is true I have achieved a certain amount of success. I don't believe there will be great difficulty securing a position with a company at one of the other minors. But I want a role at one of the licensed theaters this time. I feel my time has come."

"You mean Drury Lane or Covent Garden?"

"I mean precisely that. And those are coveted roles." She leaned her chin in her hand. "Oh, to act beside Kean," she said in a dreamy voice. "Now, there is an actor."

"Even *I* have heard of him," Ian said in amusement.

"It's said he's a bear to work with . . . exacting, demanding all attention. Poor man, he was born for greatness and yet, he can only act in the tragic roles."

"Why is that?"

"He is short and ugly."

"Is that what a man is judged by on the stage?"

"If he wants to play a leading man. So poor Edmund must be content to play twisted Iago or evil Richard the Third. He is brilliant in those roles, but I think a part of him wishes to punish those who can play the handsome leading roles."

"You are one of the fortunate ones, then," he said lightly.

She met his gaze and he could feel his face redden.

"Why, Mr. Russell, is that a compliment?"

"It is merely a statement of fact."

"I see. Ever the exacting man of science. Yes, I'm thankful for my passable looks. They would be much more dramatic onstage if I were dark. Thankfully, there are wigs and blacking for brows."

Ian coughed to keep himself from commenting on that. "Is Kean playing in anything currently?"

"I've heard he just opened at the Drury in *Richard, Duke of York*. I'd like to go see him. The Drury has recently been redecorated. It is the only theater with gas lighting." Her voice sounded wistful.

"Why don't you go?"

"It isn't so easy going to the theater as a woman alone. And to go with an escort . . . that requires care in the selection. It wouldn't do to have my name linked with just anyone's." She caught his frown.

"That surprises you? I do not seek to have my name in the scandal sheets, contrary to what you may think of actresses." When he said nothing, she looked at him steadily. "I am not a promiscuous woman. There has only been one man in my life whom I have cared about."

Ian could feel himself grow cold with the admission.

She continued, unaware of how the words were affecting him. "The only man I have allowed in my life — the first being forced upon me, and the second being a matter of survival — the only man I ever allowed in my life was a gentleman. He is the one who taught me all the refinements of the fashionable world. Because of him you needn't be ashamed of being seen with someone like me at a place like this. I know how to hold my spoon and sip my tea, thanks to him."

The tea turned acrid in his stomach. He should have guessed it had been a man who had taught her how to be a lady. For long moments at a time, he allowed himself to believe in the illusion of her persona — such pure, innocent looks, such a stage presence, such convivial company. But she was nothing better than a prostitute, picking and choosing her lovers. She might be a high-paid one in contrast to those he came across every day in the streets around his practice, but a prostitute nonetheless.

He was almost relieved when he heard a

voice beside them say, "Good afternoon, Eleanor. What a pleasure to see you out and about again."

His relief evaporated when he recognized who it was.

Beside the table stood the same gentleman who had followed Mrs. Neville out of the greenroom the first time he'd gone to the theater. Ian hadn't missed the fact that he'd addressed her by her given name. The knife twisted further in his gut.

"Your Grace," she replied with a slight smile, which to her credit was neither effusive nor displeased. Or was it merely calculating?

The Duke didn't even spare a glance in Ian's direction.

"Lady Holland is holding her salon this Thursday evening. She is sending you an invitation."

"To Holland House? How lovely." She looked genuinely pleased. As pleased as when Ian had invited her to Faraday's? "I look forward to receiving the invitation."

With that, d'Alvergny bowed and retreated. Mrs. Neville watched him until he'd left the restaurant. Then she returned her attention to Ian as if just remembering his presence. "He was awfully rude to ignore you," she observed.

"He'd notice me quickly enough if he had a sudden attack of gallstones."

Mrs. Neville laughed heartily. Ian stared at her slim neck, wondering how he could be so drawn and repelled by one person at the same time.

"You've made me laugh almost as much as the laughing gas did," she said, wiping her eyes. Despite his anguish, he felt himself soften toward her.

"You're not appreciated until people need medical attention, is that it?" she asked sympathetically.

He shrugged. "I met many young men of high birth on the battlefield. I was not gentleman enough to be noticed by them when they were hale and hearty, but they screamed out to me when their bodies were broken and bleeding after a battle. All thoughts of their lineage and breeding were forgotten then." He sighed. "So few of them made it. That's how I met Lord Cumberland."

"He was in the army?"

"Yes. He's sold his commission since then. He's the only one who has kept up our friendship since he's returned to England. The rest have gone back to their Mayfair existence and scarce remember mine."

"How horrible," she said softly.

"It's no different in civilian life. The moment a person receives a sentence of death, he'll look to his surgeon or physician for succor. Unfortunately, there is little a medical man can do in many cases."

"You see much death?"

"It's all part of the practice."

"Doesn't it disturb you?"

"I believe in eternal life. When a man or woman has lived the full extent of his years on this earth and has made his peace with God, I feel it a privilege to be there at the end to shut their eyes."

His jaw hardened. "But those occasions are fairly rare. Much more common is to see death and destruction among the young and those who've scarcely begun to live their lives. I fight death then with every tool I have. It angers me exceedingly."

"I cannot imagine you angry. You always seem so scientifically detached."

"You little know me, Mrs. Neville."

"That is undoubtedly true, Mr. Russell. Do you let anyone know you to that extent?"

He looked away, uncomfortable with the direction of the conversation.

"So, do you rail at your God when you lose a young patient?" she asked softly.

"No. I hate the Devil even more on those occasions."

"The Devil?" she asked in a puzzled tone.

"Yes, with each premature death, I feel Satan has scored another victory."

"The Devil . . ." she mused. "I always pictured him as that little goblinlike figure with a pitchfork and long, pointed tail. Is he really so dangerous?"

"He is only concerned with destroying God's creation."

She shivered, and he didn't know whether she was mocking him or really feeling frightened. "He sounds like a very evil fellow."

"He is evil personified."

"Well, then let's talk about someone or something else, shall we?" She brightened. "I have a stupendous idea."

"What is that?" he asked, wary at her sudden switch.

"Why don't you take me to the Drury to see Kean? Have you ever seen him act?"

He shook his head cautiously.

"Oh, you needn't fear what I said earlier of my being seen with you. You are merely my surgeon. There would be no impropriety."

Before he knew what was happening, he had agreed to escort her to the play. What was worse, he went as far as feeling pique that she didn't even consider him as worthy of causing gossip.

On the wings of that thought came the question, was d'Alvergny suitable fodder for the gossip mill? The notion disturbed Ian greatly.

Eleanor took her second cup of cocoa over to her window seat and sipped it slowly. She wanted to savor the events of the previous evening.

It had been truly a magical night.

She had felt attractive again after so many weeks shut in. No more tight binding around her ribs, her hair dressed in curls with glittering jewels threaded through it, her evening dress a latest French creation.

The redecorated Drury Lane was a suitable backdrop. It was one of the biggest theaters now. The foyer was a marvel, decorated *à la chinoise.* Chinese lanterns hung along the walls, and a row of pagodas ranging in ascending size ran down the middle of the long room and ended at a Chinese tearoom. "A miniature copy of the pavilion at Brighton!" she had exclaimed upon seeing it all.

But the most spectacular change was the gas lighting. The improvement to the stage from candlelight and oil lamps was incomparable. Encased in glass globes on the stage floor, and hidden from view by props and side scenes, the gaslights illuminated the cavernous stage like daylight.

Mr. Russell had purchased a box near the stage, as she had advised him. With such a large theater, the actors' words were lost to those sitting in the rear half.

Eleanor savored her chocolate, remembering how distinguished Mr. Russell had looked in his evening clothes. She smiled, remembering how, just as the play was ready to begin, he had pulled on a pair of spectacles and she had teased him, telling him he looked like an eminent physician with them. He hadn't responded to the humor. Instead he had replied seriously that it seemed he already needed a new pair, because one lens wasn't focusing properly. Too many nights studying specimens under a microscope was taking its toll on his sight, he'd explained.

Just then the houselights had dimmed — another vast improvement over other theaters. Unlike traditional candlelight, the gaslights could be lowered, leaving the audience in shadow, and bringing the stage into bright relief.

The show itself had been wonderful and Kean's performance riveting. She'd stolen peeks at Mr. Russell and was gratified to note he was as engrossed as she in the story unfolding onstage.

During the intermission, a few young gentlemen who recognized her from the Royal Circus stopped by the box to greet her while Mr. Russell went to fetch her a refreshment from the Chinese tearoom. At least she hadn't been completely consigned to oblivion in the weeks she'd been absent from the stage.

When the show recommenced, her mind wandered. Now, looking back on it, she realized last evening had marked a turning point of sorts in her life.

For the first time since achieving success as an actress, she had felt *respectable.* Despite her material achievements, she had never felt an equal to the society ladies sitting in their theater boxes. But seated there beside Mr. Russell, she had let her imagination take flight to a place where she was a proper member of society out for the evening with her distinguished husband. Their daughter, Sarah, lay asleep at home in their nice town house in Mayfair. Perhaps not even Mayfair, but Kensington or Chelsea. It needn't be anything too grand, just respectable.

Eleanor leaned back against the window embrasure with a contented sigh. The disappointment over not getting her role back in *The Spectre* didn't seem so catastrophic anymore.

She would begin inquiring about openings with the other companies. Perhaps at the Lyceum or the Sans Pareil. She tapped her finger to her lips. Elliston was manager at the Olympic. He used to manage the Surrey. There were rumors they were going to do a version of *Don Giovanni* to open after Christmas. Perhaps Elliston would be happy to steal her away from Dibdin. At least until she could find a way into the Drury or Covent Garden.

In the meantime she felt truly grateful to Ian Russell. He had given her a magical evening, probably without even realizing it. He was such a dear man. She wanted to thank him in some way.

Perhaps she would begin attending chapel. She smiled. That would surprise him. She'd love to see the look on his face if she turned up at the chapel on Sunday morning on her own.

Now that she was better, maybe she'd pay another visit to the mission as well. She frowned. Would they allow her if they knew she was an actress?

If she was attending chapel services regularly, they couldn't object to her offering her help at the mission. And, technically, she wasn't acting on the stage at present.

She took another sip of her now tepid cocoa. Life was taking an interesting turn. . . .

Ian tossed and turned, castigating himself for having taken Eleanor to the theater. It was bad enough he'd escorted her to chapel, but to make a public spectacle, first at Gunter's and then at the theater. It was true, no one knew him at those locales, but Eleanor had a certain amount of notoriety. He did not want his name paired with hers. All it needed was for Henry to see them together and word would be all over the hospital — and after that, the mission.

He kept coming back to her confession about her gentleman lover. Even her manners had been taught to her by a lover. The thought galled him.

He punched his pillow and turned onto his other side. But no matter what position he assumed, all Ian could think about was a phantom gentleman from Mrs. Neville's past. His imagination conjured up visions of this man escorting her to the theater as he himself had done, driving in the park, sharing a pastry at Gunter's.

Had he been the one to set her up in the

neat town house in Bloomsbury?

Ian stared at the dark ceiling, his soul hitting a new low in its contemplation of Eleanor Neville.

CHAPTER FOURTEEN

December 1817

"All right, children, let's go over it one more time." Eleanor took a deep breath, regathering her energy.

Amidst the protests, she marshaled the children behind the makeshift stage and convinced them to go over the play again.

"We need Joseph at the stable and Mary beside him."

"I'm coming, Mrs. Neville," Peter, the little boy elected to play Joseph, told her. "I just had to look outside the window."

"How does it look?" she asked with a glance outside. The snow had begun to fall about an hour ago.

"It looks all white. I wish we could go out and play."

"We will, as soon as we finish here," she promised.

The children shouted with joy, and she had to struggle once again to get them to their places.

She was feeling a pressure at her temples, and all she really wanted to do was get home and lie down. The last thing she needed was to go and frolic in the snow. Perhaps she could get someone else at the mission to take over, and she would excuse herself early.

As she listened to the children stumble over their simple lines, she knew she was merely out of sorts because she was feeling hagged that afternoon. In the fortnight she had been coming to the mission, she had truly enjoyed helping out.

When she had suggested putting on a skit for Christmas, the children had all jumped in with ideas. They had decided on the nativity story, as befitting the holiday season.

Eleanor had never actually read the account in the Bible, and it had been a revelation for her. She'd never realized, for one thing, that the same story was told four different times, with varying details in four different books of the Bible.

When the rehearsal finally came to an end, Eleanor applauded loudly, even though there were still so many rough spots her perfectionist eye could see. "Come, let's put on our warm wraps and go out of doors for a bit."

The dozen children whooped and ran out to the cloakroom. Eleanor followed more slowly, wishing she was in a nice warm chair by the fire.

"Hello, Mrs. Neville," Mr. Russell's friendly voice greeted her. "What are you doing here so late?"

"Attempting the impossible."

He looked after the running children. "Tame the wild herd?"

"Indeed. Except today I'm not feeling up to the task."

He turned immediately to study her features. She felt the same curious anticipation whenever he did that, which wasn't often; he usually was very brisk and businesslike when they ran into each other at the mission, and if she didn't come and help nurse the sick children, she wondered sometimes whether she would ever see him, except at Sunday chapel services. She missed his daily visits to her house.

"You do look a bit peaked. How do you feel?"

"Overtired, I suppose. A bit of a headache, but I sometimes get those when it's gray and overcast."

"Well, you certainly have reason today. I'll stop by later and see if you feel any worse, if you like."

"There's no need," she said quickly, not wanting him to come by if it was only in a professional capacity. The closeness she'd felt growing between them during her convalescence had gradually faded since her recovery, even though she had made such an effort to go to chapel and help at the mission. "I think early to bed and I will be fine in the morning."

"As you wish," he said. With a brief nod, he turned and headed toward the infirmary.

Shaking away the sense of abandonment, she followed the children's shouts down the corridor.

That evening, she regretted not having asked Mr. Russell to stop by. She felt feverish and the headache had certainly grown worse. She debated whether to have her housekeeper send for her regular physician, but since she'd been seeing Mr. Russell, she hadn't called him.

Finally, taking a hot toddy her housekeeper prepared for her, she decided simply to go to bed and hope for improvement in the morning. But her sleep was fitful and she woke up frequently, feeling chilled to the bone. Her head continued to ache, and her throat became parched and sore. In the wee hours of the morning, she was throwing up the little she had eaten the evening before.

She groaned in pain, not able to deny any longer that she had caught what had afflicted some of the children she had nursed the week before at the mission.

"Shall I send for your physician or for the good Mr. Russell?" Mrs. Wilson asked her after the maid had come in to make up her fire and rushed out again to fetch the housekeeper.

"Anyone, no one . . . I don't care . . . just let me die in peace . . ." she mumbled into the pillow.

"Oh, madam, you mustn't speak that way. I'll get you a good warm broth and that will make you feel better."

Eleanor didn't know how much time had passed, but suddenly she felt a hand on her forehead. She'd been dreaming, but she couldn't remember what the dream had been.

"Who — ?" she asked groggily, cracking her eyes painfully open against the light. Mr. Russell stood over her.

"Why didn't you tell me you were feeling so poorly yesterday?" He sounded angry.

"I wasn't . . . then . . ." she croaked.

"Don't try to talk anymore." He continued examining her, feeling the sides of her neck, listening to her lungs, and examining her skin. "You haven't experienced this in the recent past?"

She shook her head, feeling the pain reverberate from one side of her head to the other as she did so.

"It just came on all of a sudden yesterday?"

"Well, I . . . just started to feel so . . . listless . . . no energy . . . I thought I was just tired . . ."

He nodded as he felt her pulse. "Any vomiting?"

She looked away and nodded.

"Thirst?"

"Very much."

"Appetite?"

"I have none."

"Your pulse is elevated and you are quite feverish. But you have no rashes, and thus far I don't detect any inflammation. Your lungs appear to be clear, and for that you can be thankful. You must stay in bed. I will give your housekeeper instructions for your care. Is there anyone who can look after you for the next fortnight?"

She closed her eyes, unable to think that far ahead. There was too much for her to do to be abed for a fortnight. Hadn't she just played a variation of this scene scarcely a month ago? What was happening to her?

Sarah! What about Sarah? Once again thoughts of her daughter were uppermost in her mind. She reopened her eyes and frantically felt for Mr. Russell's arm. When she found it she clutched it. "You must tell Sarah —"

"Take it easy. You mustn't upset yourself."

She gripped him tighter. "Don— don't let Sarah come here!"

He nodded. "I will send word to her parents to keep her away from here for at least a fortnight."

"Thank you," she gasped, sinking back on the pillow and letting his arm go. "I don't want her . . . getting . . . sick . . . again."

"Yes, I agree. She shouldn't be exposed to this. You undoubtedly contracted one of the infectious fevers going on around the infirmary. You shouldn't have been entering there."

She grimaced, keeping her eyes closed. "And you should?"

"It's my calling. Now, if you will excuse me, I shall talk with your housekeeper."

She didn't bother to answer anymore, feeling too weary to formulate any thoughts, much less words.

■ ■ ■ ■

Ian found Mrs. Wilson waiting in the corridor.

"Oh, Mr. Russell, how is she?"

"I'm afraid it's an acute fever. It will likely intensify before the night is out." He looked at her steadily. "It can be quite dangerous. She must be kept isolated."

"Oh, Doctor, what must we do?"

"Is there anyone — any family member — who might be willing to come and nurse her?"

The housekeeper furrowed her brow, thinking. "She has no family . . . none that I know of. There is the little girl, Sarah, and her parents, but I don't think they're any relation."

"The child shouldn't come here on any account. Can you send someone to inform them of the situation?"

"Yes, I'll send a boy this morning." She tut-tutted. "There's no one else I can think of . . . unless . . ."

"Yes?" Ian prompted her.

"What about the young woman — the dancer who comes to visit quite frequently — Miss Simms?"

Ian nodded slowly. "She might do. Let me

stop in and see her. In the meantime, you must ensure that on no account does Mrs. Neville try to get up. If her breathing seems labored, she can sit up for short intervals.

"If she doesn't break out soon in perspiration, you must give her plenty of liquids to provoke it. Bathe her feet and legs in warm water. Keep the room warm but not stuffy. A little air circulation is good. Just keep the fire going at all times."

"Very good, sir."

"She can have water gruel, oatmeal tea, barley water, clear whey, apple tea, anything light and watery. Give them to her warm. See if she can keep them down, but if she vomits them up, that is all right. It means her body is expelling the poisons invading it. Give her a little balm tea or weak chamomile tea then. I shall be by this evening to see how she progresses. Send someone for me at the dispensary if she should take a turn for the worse before then."

Ian left Eleanor's town house with a heavy heart. He shouldn't have let her be exposed to the sicknesses prevalent at the mission this time of year. She had seemed so willing to help and she was so good with the children. She'd shown a real interest in the work at the mission, and she'd been to chapel every Sunday. Sometimes he'd let himself imagine that she was not an actress — or that she'd never go back to the stage.

Now his thoughts turned to the dangers of the fever. Already some of the children at the infirmary had died from it. Every winter it was the same. Fevers took so many lives.

With proper care, Eleanor might survive. He hoped her constitution was stronger than her frail appearance indicated.

Dear God, grant her Your grace. Bring her through this. I — He paused, trying to formulate his next thoughts. *I don't ask for my sake, but for hers. Grant her life. Grant her the chance to know You. Don't take her prematurely. God, grant her Your salvation through Your dear Son, Jesus. Oh, Lord, have mercy on her . . .*

Desperation seized him and he quickened his pace through the chilly streets. What would he do if — ? No! He wouldn't think it. She would be well. She must be well!

By evening the fever was high enough to warrant bleeding Eleanor. Ian removed the lancets from their cloth roll and took the cupping jar from its suede pouch. He was not a believer in frequent bloodletting as some physicians were, but he had seen the merit with certain high fevers.

He inverted the glass cupping jar upon

the pale, tender flesh of her inside forearm. Jem lit the wick on the burner and brought it to him. Ian lifted the glass just enough to insert the burning wick and held the flame under the glass for a couple of seconds to exhaust the air.As soon as he removed the wick, he pressed the cup firmly against Eleanor's skin and watched as her skin slowly rose into the vacuum created within the jar until it was half-filled with her skin. He waited a minute longer.

Meanwhile, Jem had been warming the scarificator with its movable lancet blades. When Ian was ready, Jem handed him the knife. Ian quickly removed the glass and made an incision through the tumefied skin. Immediately the blood from her vein flowed freely and fell into the metal basin Jem held under her arm.

After removing about a pint of blood — he didn't want to take more, considering her size and constitution — she rested easier and the fever lessened somewhat.

The next day, however, her skin was burning once again. Reluctantly Ian repeated the procedure every twenty-four hours over the following days until he had let blood three times. He was afraid to weaken her further, but knew it gave her a modicum of relief from the fever in the intervals.

■ ■ ■ ■

Ian rubbed his forehead wearily. Eight days had passed and Eleanor was worse. He knew it was the natural course of the fever, but it was terrifying to feel so helpless in the face of it. All his medical knowledge — all the poultices and infusions he and his uncle knew about — had done nothing to break the fever.

He leaned his elbows on his knees and observed her sleep. Her hair was pushed away from her forehead in damp streaks from the frequent compresses against her forehead.

Her white muslin nightgown was loosened at the neck to allow repeated bathing with cooling washcloths. Her color was still un-naturally high and her lips had that rough, chapped look of the feverish. Her skin was dry and hot to the touch like seasoned wood sitting too close to the fire.

She had been delirious off and on, her words slurred and unintelligible.

He knew her fever had to break soon. If it didn't by the tenth or twelfth day, and he knew the ominous signs, the slowing pulse, the labored breathing, the trembling in the limbs, the starting in the tendons — then the prognosis was almost hopeless.

If there was no improvement in a day or two, he'd begin applying blistering plasters on portions of her body. His uncle had already prepared the gummy substance concocted of Venice turpentine, yellow wax, powdered Spanish fly beetle and mustard.

He had seen many a person with a greater constitution succumb in this many days to similar fevers. For someone who looked so fragile, she amazed him with her strength. But even the toughest constitution was worn down with each passing day of fever and chills.

He'd come every day and evening to check on her. After the first day, he'd despaired of finding an adequate person to nurse her, and had been prepared to drop everything and nurse her himself, but by the next morning, Betsy Simms had shown up.

"Oh, the poor dear," she cried. "Of course I'll stay with her. I owe her everything!"

Betsy entered the room softly now. "Oh, Doctor, you must go home and get some rest," she whispered to him. "You know we're taking the best care of her possible."

"Yes, I know you are," he said, giving her a grateful look. Betsy had been a godsend, and he thanked the Lord every day for her. It was amazing how one found help in the oddest places. If he hadn't been summoned to her that night . . . she would probably have died . . . and he'd probably never have met Eleanor . . . and she wouldn't be lying here with such a deathly pallor.

The thoughts went round and round — from fear to crying prayers to self-reproach. If not for him, she wouldn't be lying here near death . . .

Betsy wrung out a rag in the cool water in the basin and placed it on Eleanor's forehead. Eleanor made no movement.

None of Ian's knowledge aided her. It was up to the body to fight the infection or succumb to it. He buried his head in his hands. *Oh, God, grant her Your grace. Bring her through this. Please . . . please don't take her . . .*

When he finally left Eleanor's town house, it was past midnight. He knew he had to get some sleep. He had other patients to see in the morning. Thankfully, his partner was willing to take a lot of his load at the dispensary, and his uncle was lending Jem whenever they were shorthanded.

On top of everything else, Ian was feeling poorly himself. He could no longer ignore the blurring of his vision in his left eye. It was not the lens of his glasses. He'd already been to see an oculist. Added to the blurring was an increasing incidence of head-aches. Sometimes he thought his head would explode with the dull pressure building inside his skull.

As he negotiated the dark cobblestones, keeping his eye out for a hackney bringing someone home from a late evening out, he stubbed his toe against a cobblestone and went flying headlong. His arms shot out for balance and he managed to right himself.

He didn't know what was wrong, but knew he was becoming increasingly clumsy. In the darkest recesses of his mind lurked the growing fear that his hour had come. Too long he'd dealt with human illnesses, remaining immune himself. A part of him felt the time of reckoning was here. Somewhere in the distance as a church clock tolled the hour, he felt a death knell.

There at last, a lone hackney coach turned the corner. Ian picked up his pace, hailing the driver. He just needed more sleep. That's what it was. As soon as this crisis was over — *please, God, heal Eleanor, please* — he would be able to get some decent rest, and he would be fine again.

Eleanor opened her eyes. For the first time in so many days, the bright sunshine didn't hurt her eyes. Her head no longer hurt. Following this discovery came thoughts of Sarah.

Where was she? How was she? How many days had it been since she'd seen her? Her mind couldn't grasp the sense of days. She'd awakened off and on, always in pain, feeling chilled to the bone or as if she couldn't breathe. The last time she'd awoken she'd been bathed in sweat. Betsy and Mr. Russell had been leaning over her, he feeling her forehead, Betsy crying.

Now she let her gaze wander beyond her bed. Was there anyone in the room? Yes, there was Mr. Russell . . . Ian, she'd called him that in her dreams, standing by the window, his head bowed. What a dear man he was. He'd stayed with her throughout.

She must have made a sound, because he turned toward her. Immediately he was at her side. "Good morning," he said.

She smiled at him, and he smiled back, and she thought what a beautiful smile he had.

She reached out her hand, realizing how weak she was, but he saw the motion and met her halfway, clasping her limp hand in his warm, strong one.

"Welcome back," he said softly.

"Have I been away long?" she asked.

"About a fortnight."

"It seems forever and as if not a day has passed."

He nodded. "Don't tire yourself with talking. You've had a strong fever but it broke last night."

She digested this information, closing her eyes as the lassitude came over her again. She would just take another short nap and then ask him about Sarah. . . .

Ian looked at their joined hands, continuing to hold hers in his until her steady breathing indicated she was asleep again. She looked so wan and fragile. The blue shadows beneath her eyes and the thinness of her arm frightened him, but they didn't take away the gratitude he felt for her survival.

She would be many days rebuilding her strength. A relapse was an ever-present danger, but with the proper care, she should grow strong again.

He returned to thanking God for His deliverance of her. His forehead sank onto the bed as he knelt there, continuing to praise Him. *Your mercy and grace endureth forever.*

That evening after her first meal of something other than watery gruels, Eleanor pushed away from the spout of the posset cup, which Betsy held for her.

"You still have some of the whey left," her friend said.

"I've had enough for the moment."

"Would you like me to spoon the curds for you?" Betsy asked.

She nodded and Betsy gave her a spoonful of the sweetened custardlike curds.

"That's all I can manage for now," she told her after a few spoonfuls.

"Well, no matter. Perhaps some more a little later?" Betsy asked hopefully. "We've got to restore your bloom."

"Do I look so terrible?" she asked. Although her maid and Betsy had washed her earlier in the day and dressed her hair, she hadn't seen herself in a mirror yet.

"No, dear, just a bit thin," she replied, taking the napkin from under Eleanor's chin and wiping her mouth.

"Well, I must eat all my curds, I suppose," she answered drowsily, still feeling too tired to care much about anything beyond the thought of sleep.

As Betsy was tidying up, Eleanor thought of what her friend had done for her. Betsy and Mr. Russell both. He had never even billed her for attending her sprained ribs, and now two weeks of a fever. She remembered how he'd come to Sarah's aid when

Eleanor had called for him. As the gratitude flooded her, she felt a stirring in her heart. She had never known a man to do so much for her without asking for something in return.

What did Mr. Russell want of her?

She'd think about it tomorrow. Tomorrow, when she'd feel a little more alert than she did today.

The first time she saw herself in the mirror, Eleanor almost fainted. She looked like a witch. She eyed the pasty skin, the fair hair that hung as limp as seaweed, the wrists sticking out of her nightgown like sticks.

She shivered in distaste and turned away from the mirror. She didn't want anyone to see her like this.

Mr. Russell — she stopped, realizing how much he had seen. Feverish, probably delirious, wretching, sweating like a hog, and worse. She groaned. How could she ever appear beautiful in his eyes again? The desire she had read in them was surely gone for good. If she tried to flirt with him now, she'd appear ridiculous. Shame burned her cheeks.

She reasoned with herself that he was a doctor; he was accustomed to seeing people in all states of sickness and distress, but it didn't help. She had read desire in his eyes once; how could she ever bear to read disgust in them?

In the ensuing days, she diligently ate and drank whatever Betsy or Mrs. Wilson brought her. She allowed them to wash her and dress her until gradually her energy returned and she could begin to do some of it for herself.

When Sarah was finally allowed to visit, Eleanor's spirits lifted. But at Sarah's first words, "Oh, Aunt Eleanor, you look so skinny!" Eleanor's spirits plummeted and she had to fight to put up a cheerful appearance before Sarah and the Thorntons.

Mr. Russell stopped by frequently, although his visits were brief in those first few days, but soon they became fewer.

She hadn't realized how much she'd come to rely on him until two days went by and he didn't appear at all. Every time her maid or Betsy came into the room, Eleanor started up, ready to smile, thinking it would be Ian.

She sank into depression each time she saw herself in the mirror. It was because she was no longer attractive to him that he avoided coming by. Once she'd been sure of her allure. Now she shuddered at the thought of his seeing her bony frame.

She was shaken out of her gloom by the faint sound of music outside her window. As she lay there listening to it, wondering if she had the strength to stand on her own and go to the window, Clara entered the room.

"Oh, miss, you must come see who is here!" The maid's smiling face beamed at her.

"Who?" she asked, distracted from the Christmas carols.

"Let me help you over to the window, and you shall see."

"That music! Does that have something to do with it?" she asked as the young woman began to draw off the bedcovers and help her sit up.

Clara only smiled.

Intrigued, Eleanor tried her best to stand and make her way across the room. Her legs still felt like jelly, but Clara held her firmly under the arm.

From the window, Eleanor looked down into the street. Puzzled at first, she surveyed the group of children standing below. They were all looking toward her window, their faces red with the cold, their cheeks straining with singing. Her maid pushed the window up an inch, and the sound of Christmas tunes was clearer.

" 'Hark, the herald angels sing!' "

"Let me get your wrap so you don't get chilled."

When she'd donned her dressing gown and a warm shawl Clara brought her, Eleanor listened, enjoying the music. Mr. Russell stood beside the children and Althea on the other side of them. Eleanor smiled and waved down at them.

Strains of "Joy to the World" came up to her in childish voices, then "O Come, All Ye Faithful." She felt her throat swelling for a moment and her eyes threatening to fill with tears. They hadn't forgotten her!

She had missed all the holiday festivities, including the Christmas pageant. All that work for nothing, but now hearing the children's voices, she felt a welter of emotion struggling within her. Gratitude for Mr. Russell predominated, for she was sure it had been he who had brought the children.

When the caroling was over, Eleanor sent the maid down to invite the children in for cups of hot chocolate and cakes. She had Clara distribute the small parcels she had prepared for Christmas before she had fallen ill.

As the children were enjoying this downstairs, Mr. Russell and Althea came up to greet her.

"What a wonderful surprise," she told them, sitting up in bed now. "It's just what I needed to cheer me up."

"The children wanted to show you how much they have practiced their songs," Althea said eagerly.

"It's a shame about the play," Eleanor began. "I'm sorry I couldn't finish what I began with them."

Althea smiled at her, making her pale features come alive. "Oh, but your labor wasn't in vain. The children put on their play Christmas Eve. Everyone enjoyed it immensely. We were only sorry you couldn't be there to see it."

"They did?" Eleanor shook her head in amazement. "I can scarcely believe it. They hardly seemed ready that last afternoon I rehearsed with them."

"Oh, but I think they were so sorry to hear you'd fallen ill — particularly that you could have contracted this fever from the mission infirmary — that they wanted to practice as much as possible and put on the show for you."

"How lovely of them." She glanced at Mr. Russell, who hadn't said much of anything at all since entering the room. "I have some gifts for each of you, gifts I'd purchased before succumbing to the fever."

"You didn't have to think of getting us gifts," Althea began.

Eleanor fumbled with the bedcover, suddenly shy. What if they didn't like what she'd bought? "I know I didn't have to, but you've welcomed me without . . ." How could she explain it? "Well, you know . . . without knowing much about me . . ."

"We all have our past," Althea said softly, and held out her hand to her.

Eleanor reached over to her night table to the two parcels her maid had placed there. "I hope you like what I got. It's not much, but anyway, happy Christmas, though it's a little late in coming." She struggled with the words as she presented each gift.

The surgeon approached the bed slowly, almost reluctantly, or was she being overly sensitive?

"Oh, they're beautiful," Althea exclaimed, touching the embroidered handkerchiefs Eleanor had purchased in a fashionable shop on Piccadilly.

Mr. Russell took longer unwrapping his small parcel. When it was opened, he said nothing at first, but then sensing the others were waiting, he looked up. "I — I don't know what to say."

He took the pocket watch from the surrounding tissue paper and held it up.

Althea broke the awkward silence. "Oh, Ian, it's just what you've needed."

His first name upon her lips was like a reproach to Eleanor, making her painfully aware there were women closer to him who had the right to call him by his given name, a right she was not entitled to. For the first time she wondered what the relationship between the surgeon and the director of the mission was.

"I —" Again Mr. Russell hesitated, holding the silver watch as if not knowing what to do with it.

"I'm tired of your being late to your appointments," Eleanor replied carelessly. Why was he behaving so strangely? "Truly, I sometimes wonder how more of your patients don't expire as they're waiting for you to appear."

Althea laughed at the remark, but Mr. Russell only gave a pained smile. "Thank you," he said at last, placing the watch carefully back into the tissue paper and reclosing the box. Eleanor breathed a sigh of relief that he hadn't rejected it on some moral high ground. Was that the reason?

After the doctor and Althea had departed with the children, Eleanor fell back into a low mood. She felt helpless. Never had she been out of work so long, and now it would be weeks before she was once again her normal self. Helpless anger engulfed her. What a mistake it had been to spend all that time visiting the mission. What had it accomplished but almost kill her?

It seemed she had ended in a deeper pit than when she'd first begun her acting career.

She pounded her fists against the bedclothes, but even that gesture mocked her, as the effort left her exhausted.

Life was a bitter struggle. As long as she could remember, she'd been up to the fight. Was she getting too old and weary now to do anything more but fall down and let herself be trampled?

CHAPTER FIFTEEN

Despite her bouts of depression, each day Eleanor felt herself grow stronger. After a fortnight, she could get dressed and go downstairs. She felt almost recovered, even though her dresses still hung on her, and her hair still hadn't yet regained its former luster and bounce. She'd had to resort to a little rouge on her cheeks to give them their former bloom.

Was it more than the ravages of the fever? Or was it that she was growing old? Soon she would be five-and-twenty. She frowned at the mirror over the mantelpiece, examining around her eyes and mouth for any signs of lines. She didn't like the shadows that still lingered under her eyes. She knew they were evidence of her sleeplessness at night when she lay awake thinking of her bleak future.

"Mr. Russell is here."

"Thank you, Wilson, send him in," she

replied to her housekeeper. Was he finally come to check on his patient? she thought bitterly. Since she'd given him the watch, she hadn't seen him and had tried in vain to put him out of her mind. It was only because her circle was so reduced that his visits had come to mean so much, she told herself.

But she couldn't stop the thudding of her heart, as she waited for him to come up. When he did enter the room, she felt her mouth go dry. He looked fresh and full of vigor, probably from walking all over town. Really, she'd probably have to buy him a carriage — or horse, at least — someday as a gift. Every successful physician kept his own carriage, or at least a mount, these days.

"Good morning, Mrs. Neville. How are you feeling?"

"As you can see, I'm up and dressed," she answered with false brightness, holding her arms out from her sides.

"Yes, you look quite well," he said, taking his glance off her as soon as he'd uttered the words.

His tone sounded stiff and formal. Couldn't he at least *pretend* to be glad to see her? He made her feel as if all her efforts this morning to dress in a pretty frock and do her hair had been in vain.

She hid her dissatisfaction and pasted a smile on her face. "Please, have a seat. I haven't seen you lately. How is everything at the mission?"

"Much fever and influenza are going around right now. The infirmary is overflowing with sick children. Mr. Denton and I are out every day visiting patients too ill to come to the dispensary."

"You must be exhausted," she said, immediately contrite at her selfish thoughts.

He rubbed a hand across his jaw. "No rest for the weary at this time of the year."

Compassion welled up in her and gave her courage. "You've done so much for me."

He waved aside her remark.

"No, I really am grateful," she began again, too restless to sit. She took a step toward him and saw the alarm in his eyes. It almost made her laugh, except she was feeling too unsure of herself.

She looked down at her hands. "Ever since my fall at the theater, you've come to my rescue, taking care of Sarah . . . and now this fever."

"I only did what any physician or apothecary would do." His voice sounded strained.

She gave a choked laugh. "You haven't even billed me for any of this! How can I not feel beholden to you?" She reached out an arm, but he was too far from her to reach him, and it dropped back to her side.

His tone softened. "You mustn't feel that way. I'm just grateful to God that you are better. That's enough for me to feel repaid."

She took a step closer, emboldened by his gentle words. "I want to give you something in return."

"I don't want anything," he said sharply. As she stared at him in shock, his tone softened. "I mean — you've already given enough . . . the watch. I really meant to tell you it wasn't necessary."

"Don't you like it?" she asked in a hurt tone.

"Yes — no . . . I mean it's a fine watch, but it's too good for me." He'd stood and now ran a hand through his hair, as if uncomfortable with the whole topic.

She pressed her lips together, to keep from crying. He was rejecting her gift. She'd known she was no longer attractive to him. Had all the longing she'd seen in his eyes left forever? She had to know. She gave a gasp and clutched her chest.

He was immediately alert. "What is it?"

"Nothing," she murmured.

"Are you sure you're all right?" He'd moved closer at least.

"I feel . . . palpitations," she said softly. "I haven't been sleeping well at night." At least that much was true.

When he said nothing, nor came closer, she grew desperate, remembering the days when he hadn't hesitated to examine her. Had she lost all appeal to him that he couldn't bear to touch her?

"That stick you have . . . that baton, the listening device." She struggled for the right word. "Why don't you use that?"

"The stethoscope . . ." Even his tone sounded reluctant.

"Yes," she whispered, desperately playing her last card.

She heard him open his medical case and take out the instrument. She waited quietly, her hands clasped in her lap, her heart thudding till it reverberated in her ears.

He finally approached the settee and sat down beside her, the black baton held loosely in his hands. She turned to face him, making it easier.

When he placed it against her chest, she waited, willing herself to remain still and not reach out and touch his hair.

"What do you hear?" she asked in a low voice.

"Your heartbeat."

"Do you hear how hard it beats when you

come near?" she whispered, her hand no longer able to remain still.

He retreated from the touch of her hand on his and put a space between them on the couch.

She looked deeply into his eyes and found only wariness. "You've been so good to me. I don't know how I can ever repay you." She glanced down at her hands, trying to remember the words she'd rehearsed during the waking hours of the night. "I haven't much to offer now." She swallowed, determined to go on. "But what little I have I want to give you."

He seemed frozen, staring at her. Thinking he didn't understand, she went on. "I have only myself to give."

The silence grew long in the room. Did he still not understand? She put a hand to the neckline of her dress.

This time he came to life, springing away from her and off the settee. He coughed. "You need say no more, Mrs. Neville. As I said, you owe me nothing for my services. If it makes you feel better, I will send around a bill —"

It was her turn to stare. Her worst fear had been realized. He no longer wanted her! As the fact penetrated her numbed brain, she clutched at the cloth of her gown, seeking support.

He was refusing her offer. She had to repeat it to herself to fully grasp the fact. She had truly lost all physical appeal. Of course he no longer wanted her. She felt more than mere wounded vanity. She knew she hadn't misread the desire in his eyes all those weeks, nay, months, as she'd dangled her attractions before him. No, what stared her in the face now was her future. A woman with no physical appeal had very little future anywhere.

She rose from the settee. "Don't trouble yourself. I understand perfectly. You are no different than any other man. I'm thin and ugly now, so you can scorn me. I no longer have anything attractive to offer. I have been out of work for longer than I care to think. The public has forgotten me, so I have no allurements left."

She turned away, bitterness suffocating her. She was finished, her beauty gone, her acting career in ruins.

His words broke the stillness. "You are wrong."

"I don't think so," she said with a short laugh.

"I am not like those other men."

She wiped at a tear that had begun to fall down her cheek. She wouldn't give him the satisfaction of knowing he'd brought her to tears.

"And it has nothing to do with your fame on the stage or lack of it."

"It's because I'm ugly now —"

"How little you know. Free of the artifice of the stage, you are as flawless as a diamond. You are the most beautiful woman I've ever known."

She could have wept with relief. She swiped at the rouge on her cheeks as she slowly turned to him. Could he be speaking the truth? She needed reassurance. "Am I really?"

It was his turn to expel an impatient laugh. "Can't you see that I speak the truth, Eleanor?"

Her name on his lips was more thrilling than anything she'd imagined. As she stood there, saying nothing, he must have read the lingering doubt in her mind.

Instead of saying anything more, he took a step toward her. That step seemed to activate hers, and without quite knowing how it had happened, she found herself face-to-face with him. He was looking at her so seriously that she almost doubted she had heard his words correctly.

And then he was leaning down toward her, and she leaning up to him. When his lips touched hers, she felt the same sensation she had the day of her fall through the trapdoor on the stage. Suddenly the floor gave way beneath her and she was free-falling. She clutched the lapels of his coat, not wanting the moment ever to end.

He held her lightly by the elbows as she drank of him.

She'd wondered an eternity how those lips would feel against hers. They were warm and slightly full for a man, oddly sensuous for such a serious man. His breath was sweet and spicy like the cardamom seeds he was always chewing on.

The moment was enchantment itself, completely stopped in time. She had never known such a thing. In her experience, men's kisses were always a prelude she must endure. She, who'd never enjoyed their damp intrusion, now found herself craving more.

Only with William — Lord Eaton — had she come close to letting herself go, and then he'd left her. And she'd vowed never to be vulnerable to someone again.

Now she found herself forgetting the past in the pure touch of Ian's lips against hers.

Before their bodies could draw closer, he disengaged his lips slightly from hers. "There, you may laugh at my inexpert attempts at kissing you," he said in a low tone, his breath brushing her.

In reply, she grasped his face in the palms of her hands and brought it down to hers, and began to kiss him deeply, giving herself to him in that kiss, holding back nothing of herself, as she had always done with others.

She could feel his yearning in the way he returned her kiss, in the way his hands came up to embrace her. And then all she felt were the barriers crumbling inside her. Emotions too long pent up behind her defenses began to build and crest until the walls buckled.

Before she had a chance to explore the kaleidoscope of sensations he was producing in her, before she had a chance to do more than rest her hands on his shoulders, before she'd even had a chance to whisper his name, Ian broke the contact of his lips against hers. Gently but firmly, he grasped her by the wrists and set her away from him.

"I cannot!" he whispered.

She was so stunned by the abrupt end to the kiss, she would have fallen forward if he hadn't been holding her. He returned her to the settee and strode away from her as soon as she was seated.

He reached the window and leaned against the sill.

"I will not give in to this!" The words seemed to burst forth from him. "I haven't kept myself for so long to give myself to one such as you!" The words spoken in soft vehemence exploded in the silent room, like glass falling against a stone.

They found her with all her defenses down. Not a shred of pride or anger or resentment covered that naked organ of her heart. Tender and defenseless, it lay exposed to the stiletto sharpness of those deadly shards.

She brought her hands to her chest, as if to cover her heart from his words. But it was too late! He'd found her laid bare.

"Get thee behind me, Satan," he ground out, his back still to her.

Satan! He was calling her Satan! The words succeeded in bringing her out of her stupor. No! It wasn't too late to defend herself.

He turned at last and came toward her. "Please forgive me, Mrs. Neville. My conduct was unforgivable. You have been under my professional care, and I had no right to . . . touch —" he stumbled over the word "— you in any way like that. I'm sorry. Good day, madam." Already he was turning away, leaving her destroyed.

How dare he be the one to leave?

She stood as regally as Mrs. Siddons in her last performance.

"You can't even say the word," she hissed. "Is it because you daren't call such an inept, fumbling attempt a kiss? A man who has never been with a woman." She looked down her nose at him. "At your age — it's not natural. What kind of a man are you?"

His jaw clenched, and she knew the barb had hit home. She was hurting his manhood, and she took great pleasure in it.

"What did you hope? To bed Eleanor Neville? Not many men have had that privilege, I can promise you that!" She gave a harsh laugh. "I must thank you for your refusal if your moral sensibilities stopped you in time.

"For what could *you* possibly offer me? A penniless surgeon who squanders all his talent on the miserable rabble of London?"

His throat worked but still he said nothing, and her satisfaction deepened. She was a great actress, and he'd never realize how great.

"Do you honestly imagine all your noble self-sacrifice is doing any good? Have all those years of self-denial pleased your God to any discernible degree?" She looked him up and down with scorn, knowing she must not overplay the scene. "At least my antics on the stage make the poor fools laugh for a few hours, so they can forget their pain and squalor. What do you do but cut them open and cause them more pain? Most of them end up dying anyway, don't they?

"What have you done for them, in the end?" she taunted him. "Hastened them to their Maker?

"Yes, go ahead and save yourself for some pious evangelical bride — it might be a long wait. I may be Satan's spawn, but at least I shall have some enjoyment from my short duration upon this stage. What shall you end up with, Mr. Russell? If you don't shrivel up and grow old waiting, you'll die prematurely contracting some foul disease from one of your wretched patients."

When he said nothing, his face pale and set, she smiled. "If you were in the theater, Mr. Russell, you would realize this is your cue to exit the stage."

As if the words prodded him awake, he bowed formally and said, "Good day, Mrs. Neville. I shall not trouble you further, I promise you."

"Good day to you, Mr. Russell. You know the way out."

It wasn't until she heard the door close behind him that she allowed herself to collapse on the settee.

She felt sick, and she wondered if she

would have a relapse of the fever. She leaned forward, her head between her knees, her breath coming in gasps.

She was not acting now. She felt as if she couldn't get enough air into her lungs. Oh, God! she cried to that unseen deity Ian worshipped. Help me!

Gradually the spasms passed and her breathing returned to normal. She lay back against the couch, wondering at the numbness that was already encasing her heart.

She hadn't thought it would ever be awakened by a man again, not after Lord Eaton had nearly destroyed it.

What a young fool she'd been then, recently arrived in London and landing her first real acting job after that miserable stint with the traveling troupe. Lord Eaton had seen her on the stage and declared himself smitten. She'd been overwhelmed by the handsome young lord. He'd set her up in her town house, lavished her with gifts, promised her the world.

She'd been at his beck and call for four years, until her heart had been caught, and she'd secretly yearned for him to offer marriage. But the day had arrived when he'd tired of her. Oh, he'd been generous enough, making sure she didn't lack materially. It was shortly after he'd ended things that she'd read in the papers of his engagement to a young lady enjoying her first season. Miss Beatrice Farnsworth. Eleanor had never forgotten the name.

She came back to the present. Why after so many years had she let herself believe in a man's sincerity? She crossed her arms over her chest, rocking back and forth, despising herself for her gullibility.

She was a mature woman of four-and-twenty who could no longer blame youthful folly. She must look out for herself and her daughter. That's all she had.

Ian was probably right. He was a good man, and she was tarnished.

But why must it always come down to this: destroy or be destroyed? She had almost been destroyed once before and had sworn it would never happen again.

Ian walked and walked. He had no idea how long or in what direction. All he heard were Eleanor's words.

What kind of a man are you?

A man who has never been with a woman at your age.

Do you honestly imagine all your noble self-sacrifice is doing any good?

What do you do but cut them open and cause them more pain? Most of them end up dying anyway, don't they?

What have you done for them, in the end? Hastened them to their Maker?

The accusations swirled round and round through his mind, spreading like poison until they touched and contaminated every hope and dream he'd ever had.

He ended up on Blackfriars Bridge with no recollection of how he'd gotten there. Oblivious of the cold, to the sights and sounds around him on the busy waterway, he stood looking down at the murky green water. The denunciations against his manhood were bad enough, but worse were the ones leveled against his work.

What had he accomplished in all his years of practicing medicine? Eleanor's mocking tone lashed at him over and over, her scornful eyes belittling him.

"Hey, there, get a move on! Don't you see we've got a dray coming through?"

Ian started at the angry shout, and resumed his aimless walk, crossing the bridge and entering Southwark. He didn't miss the irony as he found himself across from the theater. The familiar women selling their favors strolled along the pavement in front of it. Others plied the more honest trades of hawking flowers or sweetmeats.

Was Eleanor right? he asked himself as he

looked at the brightly-lit theater. Did the brief pleasure these tawdry actors afford the crowds compensate for the audience's miserably short existence? He stared at the classical facade, already feeling the familiar pressure building inside his head.

Would Eleanor's words prove prophetic?

You, what shall you end up with? If you don't shrivel up and grow old waiting, you'll die prematurely contracting some foul disease from one of your wretched patients.

God, where are You in all this? Had he sinned so grievously in his thoughts that he could no longer hear his Lord's voice? He remembered the verse about the heaven over his head being brass. He glanced up now at the leaden sky, feeling completely and utterly defeated.

Had his lust for a fallen woman led him to this place . . . or had it begun earlier? Had he become so wrapped up in his desire to heal the wounds of mankind that he had neglected his Lord? Had he missed the call to preach the gospel?

As he resumed his aimless walk down New Surrey Street, he felt a sudden strange sensation in his legs, as if they no longer belonged to him. He pushed out his arms to keep his balance, but the movements were disjointed.

The next thing he knew he was falling . . .

When he awoke, Ian had no idea where he was. He could hear a murmur of voices around him and felt the warmth from a fireplace to one side. He was lying on something hard. He put a hand against it and then he remembered the last time he tried to use his limbs how disconnected they had felt.

His eyelids flew open, panic gripping him. He found himself staring at a smoke- and water-stained ceiling lit only by the flickering light of the fire. At least his hand was behaving normally now. He seemed to be on a wooden bench.

"You're awake," a woman said. Then her face appeared over him, a worn and deeply lined one.

"Where am I?" he asked, his voice coming out a rough whisper.

She gave a deep chortle, revealing crooked teeth, the few that remained. "At my ken. 'Ere, take a sip o' this. It'll put you to rights." Before he could refuse, she lifted his head and brought a tankard to his lips. He drank automatically and almost choked on the gin burning a path down his throat.

That made her laugh the louder. "Not used to max, are ye?"

He struggled to get up, his legs encased in a thin blanket. The woman helped him to a sitting position. He looked around him at the small room, and started when he saw a man sitting nearby on the other side of the fireplace.

Ian nodded his head and the man did the same, saying nothing.

"I —" He cleared his throat and began again. "I'm not sure what happened. How did I get here? What time is it?" He patted his waistcoat for his new pocket watch, but feeling it brought remembrance afresh, and his hand went limp. He didn't think he could look on that watch face right now and cope with all that it would bring up until he sorted out where and how he was.

"You fell flat on your face," the woman said, smacking her lips on the remains of the gin in the tankard. "We thought you was jug-bitten. Didn't we, Abner?" She turned to the man.

The man grunted as he continued to stare at Ian. He looked familiar to Ian, but he couldn't seem to get his thoughts straightened out enough to remember.

"My Abner 'ere, 'e picked you right up, slung ye over 'is shoulder like a sack o' rye and carried ye right on up 'ere. Ain't it so?" She had a strong lower jaw, which made her lower lip protrude beyond the top one.

Abner grunted assent.

"I thank you . . ." Ian spoke the words slowly, still unsure his words would follow his thoughts properly. All he was certain of was he felt exhausted. "How long . . . have I been here?"

She rubbed her lips with grimy fingers. "Couple o' hours, I reckon, wouldn't you?" Again she turned to Abner.

Ian waited for the grunt.

He didn't let on how much what he was hearing shocked him. A couple of hours out cold! Had he experienced a fit? A seizure? He had no recollection at all, and that terrified him.

He straightened his jacket and smoothed his tangled hair with his fingers. "I must be going," he said, finally feeling confident enough to stand. "I'm grateful you picked me up off the street."

"Abner'll take you 'ome. You don't look none too steady on your stampers."

"That's quite all right —" Ian began, but Abner had approached him. He was a large man, with a rotund belly and arms like plump rolls of bread.

"You cured 'im once," the woman explained. " 'Is leg was broke from a cargo fallen off a ship. You set it right back in place and tended him till he could walk again."

The memory came back to him like a puzzle piece falling into place, and he felt profound relief that not everything was gone from his memory. "You're a dock-worker at Wapping."

"You didn't charge 'im none, brought him 'is tonics, even victuals till 'e could go back to work. 'E'll see ye 'ome now."

Without a word Abner turned and the two left the flat. When they reached a steep, dark stairwell, Abner put his hand on Ian's elbow and stayed at his side until they reached the bottom. Once on the street, Ian tried to get his bearings, but before he could make out much in the evening light, Abner began walking.

"I assume you know where I live?" he asked, finding it an effort to keep pace with the large man.

Another grunt, but this time it was followed by some speech. "Most everyone 'round 'ere does."

After that Ian said no more, preferring to leave the navigation to more capable hands. His legs threatened to collapse from exhaustion at any moment, but at least now they felt like his own.

He didn't want to think any more about his spell, not right then, but his surgeon's mind couldn't help drawing conclusions. It was clearly some type of fit. It could be apoplectic. In that case, he was lucky to be even alive right now, much less walking. It could be epileptic. He breathed out slowly, hating all the conclusions. As long as he could keep his deepest fear at bay . . .

But as they neared the dark building housing the dispensary and his living quarters a few doors down, he could feel the fear coiling around the pit of his stomach, ready to strike as soon as he was alone.

They heard the watch call out the hour. "Ten o'clock and all is well!" The voice resonated from down Borough High Street.

All is well. Was it, indeed?

Ian thanked Abner and turned to his own door. A dim light still shone within.

As he fumbled with the door, finally closing it and pulling the bolt across, he heard footsteps behind him.

"Oh, Mr. Russell, at last you're home. I wondered when you didn't come home for dinner, and Mr. Jem came by, looking for you. I thought you'd be at the dispensary, but he said they hadn't seen you all afternoon."

"Yes, I'm home at last." He turned to her, not sure what he was going to say.

"Are you all right?" she asked, peering up

at his face.

"Yes, quite. Why, what is it?"

"You look awfully pale, that's all. May I get you something? A hot tea or toddy?"

"No." He stretched his lips into a smile. "I'm fine, I assure you. Why don't you go on home for the evening?"

She gave him one last doubtful look before nodding. "Very well, sir. I'll bid you good-night, then."

"Yes, good night, Mrs. Duff." He waited until she had left before taking the lamp and climbing slowly up the stairs.

"Hello, Plato." The cat appeared out of the dark and followed at his heels. Once he'd closed the study door behind him, Ian leaned against it, feeling a great sense of relief in having reached this room. He set the lamp down and brought up his hand to wipe his brow. Despite the cold outside, he felt a sheen of perspiration on his skin.

How many lifetimes had he lived since early this afternoon when he'd visited Eleanor?

The name threatened to open up a monstrous wound that was only being held shut by a very tenuous thread. What kind of surgeon was he, to have done such a shoddy job sewing up the incision?

But not even thoughts of Eleanor could

distract him for long from the fear waiting for him in the shadows.

Something was growing inside his head. He could no longer deny it. The throbbing pain that refused to go away, the fuzziness in his left eye, the clumsiness, and now the spasmodic movements in his hands and legs before he'd lost consciousness this afternoon.

The symptoms culminated in one conclusion: a painful, very imminent death.

He knew as sure as he knew that he was standing in his study that his prognosis was utterly hopeless. He'd dissected enough cadavers to have seen the kinds of tumorous growths possible in every organ of the human body. Sometimes they were operable, but more often they were not, since the operation would kill the patient faster than the tumor.

He pressed his head together in his hands. In his case, it was most certainly inoperable. He shuddered thinking of the only known surgical procedure to the skull. Trepanation. The very word filled him with dread.

He'd seen it done only a few times during his student days. It required boring open a hole in a person's head, plunging the end of the drill in cold water every few minutes because it became so hot from the friction of metal on bone. The procedure was used to cure fits or violent behavior in mental patients, but the results were questionable.

Ian walked across the room, terror flooding him, threatening to cut off his ability to breathe. He collapsed in his chair and reached for his only weapon, his beloved Bible, already reciting the passages he knew by heart.

"The Lord is My Shepherd, I shall not want . . . yea, though I walk through the valley of the shadow of death, I will fear no evil: for thou art with me; thy rod and thy staff they comfort me."

His fingers shook as he flipped the pages from Psalm 23 to Psalm 91. "He that dwelleth in the secret place of the most High shall abide under the shadow of the Almighty. I will say of the Lord, He is my refuge and my fortress: my God; in him will I trust."

He read the next verse eagerly: "Surely He shall deliver thee from the snare of the fowler, and from the noisome pestilence." Hadn't God delivered him all these years from every foul disease he'd treated?

"He shall cover thee with His feathers and under His wings shalt thou trust: his truth shall be thy shield and buckler." Yes, now for the crux of it: "Thou shalt not be afraid for the terror by night; nor for the arrow that flieth by day; Nor for the pestilence that walketh in darkness; nor for the destruction that wasteth at noonday . . ."

He continued reading, drawing strength and solace from the words, and finding peace at last. The fear receded to the edges of the room, and he sat in the circle of light, filled with the power of the words.

Was the Lord calling him home? Was his labor on this earth finished? These thoughts no longer wrenched at him. There was still so much work to be done, and he felt he had only touched the surface, not only in his medical practice, but as a servant of God. How many souls had he won into the kingdom?

Was it too late? Would he stand before the Lord someday having little to show with the talents he'd been given? Ian prayed, seeking the Lord for the answers. Had he strayed in some way that the Lord was displeased with him and must now cut short the length of his days?

His thoughts turned again to Eleanor Neville. Had these months of lusting after her finally reaped this destruction in his life? He cried out the words of David. "Oh, God,

cast me not away from Thy presence; and
take not Thy Holy Spirit from me."

Chapter Sixteen

"Dr. Elliot, you must have something more effective than that tonic you gave me last week," Eleanor said peevishly, eyeing the offending bottle as if it contained arsenic.

"But, madam, Salvator Winter's Elixir Vitae is the best restorative available today. It says here plainly." He took the bottle from her and read through the half-moons of his spectacles. " 'An excellent Life-Preserving Remedy, so speedy a Reviver of the Spirits and Restorer of Decayed Nature.' " He looked at her as if it was her fault the tonic had done nothing for her.

"Well, give me something stronger. I'm not sleeping at night, my nerves are delicate."

"In that case we shall try Rose's Balsamic Elixir. It will sweeten the blood and correct all imperfections of the digestion. You shall see, your bloom will return in no time at all."

She glanced dubiously at the new bottle he held out to her. She took off the stopper and sniffed. It had an agreeable odor, more like a cordial than a medicine. "Very well, I shall try it. And some sleeping powders."

"Of course, Mrs. Neville." Quickly he wrote out a prescription. "I shall leave you a sample here, and you can get more at the apothecary's."

She took it, only somewhat satisfied. The man was certainly charging her enough; the least he could do was leave her a sufficient dose to get her through the week.

"You should have called me when you first fell ill." The physician recommenced the scolding he'd begun after he walked in. "There are too many quacks about nowadays. I can't say you are looking at all the thing. I would also recommend Godbold's Vegetable Balsam and Vandour's Nervous Pills."

"Very well. Write them down." She handed the prescription back to him. The top of her vanity was already full of bottles and pillboxes, but there was always the possibility she hadn't found the right one yet.

After her physician had left, Eleanor paced the length of her sitting room. It was too cold and dreary to go out on this January day. She jerked to a stop every time she heard a carriage go by. Perhaps today she'd hear if she'd gotten the part in Moncrieff's new production of *Don Giovanni* at the Olympic.

She smiled, momentarily distracted by the thought of the new show. In this one, the part of Don Giovanni was going to a female. Madame Vestris was already a hit in a similar production at the Sans Pareil.

Eleanor held her breath as a coach rumbled down the street. She glanced toward it and recognized d'Alvergny's gold-and-blue crest decorating the door panel. She sighed wearily. At least he would distract her. He'd resumed his frequent visits since she'd recovered from the fever.

"Good afternoon, Eleanor," he said, bending over her hand after he'd been shown into her sitting room.

"Are you here to amuse me? Because I warn you, I am in dire need of amusement," she told him.

"I shall endeavor my best. Shall I tell you the latest *on dits* from court?"

"Court sounds like a dreary place since Princess Charlotte died."

"There is still amusement to be had if one knows the right people."

"I wish you knew some of the right theater people," she said as she turned away from

374

him with a bored sigh.

"Perhaps I do."

"Robert Elliston?"

"I know him."

"I'm trying out for the don's part in Moncrieff's new production at the Olympic."

"Ah," he said with a smooth smile. "From Leporello to the don."

"I think it would be amusing to play Don Giovanni this time. In this production, he comes back from the dead and ends up in London. It's called *Giovanni in London, or the Libertine Reclaimed.*" She laughed. "Tell me, have you ever seen a libertine reclaimed?"

He answered with an enigmatic smile. "Why not try out instead for *A New Way to Pay Old Debts*? They are reviving Philip Massinger's old play at the Drury Lane."

She made a doubtful face. "If I could get an audition."

"Kemble is manager." He shrugged. "I'm on their committee. Say the word and I'll arrange an audition."

"You do, and I'll be your slave for life," she half joked.

"Would you? That's a very attractive offer."

Her smile evaporated as she realized he was deadly serious. Leaning back in her chair, she considered. "I don't like the term 'slave.' "

"What term would you prefer?" he asked smoothly.

She returned his look steadily. Although she'd been stringing him along nicely for several months, she'd never seriously considered him for a lover. But now circumstances had changed. Drastically so. "Can you guarantee me a leading role at the Drury?"

"I can guarantee you an audition for a leading part. Your talent will do the rest."

She assumed a nonchalant air, although she was feeling far from calm. "Fair enough. But I owe you nothing unless I land the part."

He inclined his head in assent. "Naturally not."

"And if I do land the part —" She left the sentence for him to finish.

"I think you know what I want . . . have been wanting for a long time."

"A liaison?"

He bowed his head in reply.

She said nothing for a moment, feeling as if her life hung in a balance. One word and her destiny would be forever altered. "If I got a plum role, and that's still an *if,* I would expect more in return for my . . . favor."

He made a careless motion with his hand. "Name it."

She moistened her lips. "A Mayfair address."

"Naturally."

She looked down at her manicured nails, wondering at how easily that had been accomplished. She met his gaze again, this time naming a yearly stipend. It wouldn't hurt to continue investing in the three-percents for the day she would no longer find acting work.

He shrugged. "A trifle."

She sat back and let out the breath she hadn't realized she'd been holding. "Well, let us see how that audition goes."

He smiled. "I am all anticipation."

After he'd left, she considered what she'd done. What matter if he used her body? It had been used before and survived. He could never have her heart; there was certainly no danger of that. Her body was merely a tool, available for whatever advancement she could procure from its use. Her time was running out; she couldn't afford to wait any longer.

A week went by and Ian felt himself growing worse, but he confided in no one. Like a boat bobbing against the tide, he didn't know what his secrecy would accomplish, but he couldn't bring himself to let anyone know his condition. Was it because there was no sorrier sight than a sick physician? He thought of the proverb Jesus had quoted — "Physician, heal thyself."

Well, he hadn't the power to do so.

He lived in terror lest he lose consciousness again. What if it happened during an operation?

He swallowed, pushing the terror back down his throat, knowing the effort was only momentary, dependent on the strength of his will.

Even if he managed to stay on his feet during surgery, could he get his hands to obey him? Would a spasm strike him and prevent him from holding the surgical instruments in his hands? And what of his eyesight?

He remembered the words of the eminent surgeon, Astley Cooper of Guy's Hospital: "A surgeon must have the eye of an eagle, heart of a lion, hand of a woman, and mind of a scholar."

Was he losing two of these critical faculties — his sight and steadiness of his hand?

He had told his uncle nothing. The previous week he had asked him for a powder to take for his headache. His uncle had asked him if he was suffering any other symptoms, but Ian had brushed him off with something about feeling mental fatigue. His uncle had said no more but given him a bolus to be swallowed when he felt the pain coming on. He hadn't dared ask for any more, afraid to arouse his astute uncle's suspicions that something was worse.

It was during his weekly rounds at the mission that he stumbled as he was going from one patient's bed to another. Althea, who was following behind him, grasped his elbow.

"Are you all right?" she asked in concern.

He shoved her hand away. "I'm fine," he snapped.

"Forgive me."

"I'm sorry," he said, immediately contrite. "Just clumsy, that's all."

She gave him a close look but said nothing more.

After he had finished his rounds and gone into the small alcove used as his office when he was there, he busied himself cleaning and putting away his instruments. Thankfully, he'd felt nothing more than a momentary loss of control.

But he felt weary. He let the instruments drop onto the table and collapsed into the wooden chair behind him. Resting his head in his hand, he felt despair overwhelm him.

He started up as he heard a soft knock on the partially opened door. Althea stood in the doorway. "I'm sorry, Ian. I didn't mean to disturb you." He expected her to excuse herself and leave him, but she remained there. "May I come in?" she asked when he said nothing.

"Yes, of course," he finally replied, straightening.

She brought up another chair close to his. "Ian, is there nothing I can do to help?"

He looked at her gentle eyes, debating what to say or not say, but finally the need to unburden himself became greater than he could bear. He felt a sense of relief as he nodded. "Yes, something is very wrong."

"What is it?" she asked when he didn't continue.

He swallowed and looked away, not knowing how or where to begin. He rubbed his hand over his eyes. "Oh, Althea . . . Althea . . . I'm in trouble, and there's nothing you or anyone can do."

She leaned closer, grasping his hand. "Tell me what's wrong, Ian. It can't be as hopeless as you make it sound."

"I'm dying."

Her hand stilled on his. "Tell me," she repeated quietly.

He removed his hand from hers and

bowed his head in his hands, resting his elbows on his knees. Slowly, he began to speak, describing his symptoms and how long he'd had them. She had been a nurse long enough to understand his medical rundown.

When he'd finished speaking, the room was still.

"Let me pray for you."

He glanced up at her from under his brows. "What? So God can heal me of this? Or so He'll give me peace to leave this life gracefully?"

"So that He may heal you," she answered simply.

He laughed sadly. "Oh, Althea, the day of miracles is over."

"Is it?"

She had such a calm look in her eye that it made him feel a spark of hope. It was gone as quickly as it had come, his rational mind firmly in control.

"I appreciate your wanting to help me, but I'm afraid I've seen too many others fall to this kind of cancerous growth to doubt my end."

" 'But unto you that fear my name shall the Sun of righteousness arise with healing in His wings,' " she quoted softly.

"Will some Scriptures change what is

growing inside me?"

"For 'the Word of God is quick and powerful and sharper than any two-edged sword,' " she replied.

"What about the little girl you were nursing? Didn't she succumb to her malady?" he asked, referring to the private patient she had cared for the previous autumn.

She looked down at her hands. "She did. It doesn't change the fact that God is our healer and that His Son purchased our healing for us through the cross."

The words stirred him. He remembered the preacher who had preached a similar thing a few months back.

"The Scriptures say Jesus bore our sins in His own body on the tree so that 'we being dead to sins, should live unto righteousness, by whose stripes we were healed.' "

He wanted to believe, but he didn't dare. He knew his prognosis better than anyone.

Instead of saying anything more, Althea stood and gently laid her hands on his head, covering his forehead with one and placing the other one atop his head. For a brief second, his thoughts went to Eleanor, remembering the touch of her hands.

He squelched those thoughts. What was wrong with him? That blunder of his life was over. Soon, his whole life would be over.

Gradually Althea's words penetrated his understanding. The prayer was composed more of Scripture than of her own words, and he marveled at how well versed she was in God's Word. Scripture after Scripture dealing with healing washed over him, and he felt revived. When she said the final "amen," he was able to smile at her and say a heartfelt thank-you.

"I will continue praying for you," she replied, then pressed her lips together as if preparing to say more. He waited as she clasped her hands together. "I felt in my spirit as I prayed that God *has* healed you —"

He couldn't help the hope that arose in him.

"But," she continued, looking at him earnestly out of her grayish-green eyes — so different from the shade of gray of Eleanor's, "now it's a matter of walking in faith."

Faith. The word resounded in the stillness. Did he know what faith was? He'd been hearing the word for as long as he could remember. He'd grown up with the concept, heard his father and many an eminent preacher preach about it, but did he know what it was? "How do I do that?" he asked, feeling humbled at the prospect.

Once again she quoted Scripture. " 'Faith

comes by hearing and hearing by the Word of God.' "

"In other words, I must apply myself to hearing God's Word?"

She nodded. "Consider it an apprenticeship in faith."

"My experience with apprenticeships is that they are long and arduous."

"Patience is a virtue," she replied.

"I don't know if I have been given the luxury of time."

"Then use what you have to the fullest." She took his hands in both of her smaller ones. "No one can rob you of your life. Only God can take it when you have finished your course on this earth."

When he left her, he felt he had a new purpose. That night, he began to pore over the Scriptures, with his *Cruden's Concordance* at his side, looking up every Scripture dealing with sickness and health. Those Scriptures led to others, and as gray began to tinge the skies, he had filled a sheaf of papers with notations.

Eleanor stood with Edmund Kean and the line of lesser actors on the forestage and took the final bow. The pit went wild, standing and applauding them. Her eyes roamed the circle of boxes above the crowd. A more illustrious crowd sat in them, and they applauded more sedately, yet nevertheless enthusiastically.

The show was a hit. She could feel it, sense it in the very marrow of her bones. With a slight sidelong glance at Kean beside her, she bent and curtsied once more, realizing much of the success of the show was due to his performance of the evil Sir Giles Overreach.

He had been a preening, egotistical man to work with, but the result had been well worth it. This show had been a testing for her, and she knew she had passed.

She could still scarcely believe she was standing on the same stage as the great Kean. The man might be half mad, and drunk the other half, but when he was onstage portraying a greedy, malevolent creature, he was brilliant. His deep-set dark eyes glared at the audience, his mobile face exuded malice, his voice rose and fell like an orchestral movement.

Eleanor's own role had not been a bad one, although she played the older woman. She glanced to her other side at the young actress who played the young heroine. Miss Stephens was only seventeen. She was a passable actress, Eleanor conceded grudgingly, but owed her presence upon the

Drury Lane stage more to the fact that her father was a veteran actor than to any excessive talent.

As she rose from her final curtsy, Eleanor swept the packed house one last time with her eyes, feeling the staggering absence of one individual whose presence would have made her success complete.

She was being silly. Mr. Russell would have found nothing different in her role on this stage from the one at the Royal Circus. Both would have been degrading and lacking in common decency in his eyes, she reminded herself. This was her moment and she would let no thought ruin it for her.

The actors exited by the two side doors at either end of the proscenium. Congratulating each other on a good performance, they separated to their dressing rooms.

After she'd cleaned off her makeup and removed the seventeenth-century-style gown she wore, she dressed in her own dress and pelisse, wrapped herself in a warm, fur-lined cloak, and went to the side rear exit of the theater. Although much of the cast were going to a nearby tavern to celebrate their triumph, Eleanor felt no such desire. She was a veteran actress, and for the first time all she longed for was her quiet house and cozy room.

Her house. Her heartbeat quickened at the thought of her new abode. A very tidy brick town house on Jermyn Street, in the heart of the fashionable world, only a short ride from Drury Lane, and a mere block from St. James's and Piccadilly. D'Alvergny had chosen well.

She descended the coach with a satisfied sigh, her earlier moment of melancholy having passed. Tonight was her peak and she would savor it. No one could take it away from her.

"Good evening, madam," her new housekeeper greeted her at the door. D'Alvergny had generously insisted on hiring a whole houseful of new servants for her. Mrs. Wilson had stayed at her old house with its new tenants. "How was everything?"

"Wonderful, thank you," she said, as the woman helped her off with the cloak. She handed over her bonnet and gloves, missing her old housekeeper. She hadn't yet warmed up to this woman, who seemed severe and humorless in contrast.

Eleanor turned away from the woman and gave a quick look in the mirror. Her color was high from the cold winter air, and her pupils were large, matching the rims of her irises and making her eyes look dark and frightened. She dismissed the silly notion and patted her locks.

"The duke is here. I've put His Grace in the drawing room."

Eleanor met her housekeeper's impassive gaze in the mirror. "The duke?" she repeated, feeling her windpipe constricting.

"Yes, ma'am. I told him I didn't expect you until late, but he said he was willing to wait. I took him a tray of hot water and scotch whiskey."

"Thank you. You did well." She managed the words in a composed tone. "That will be all, Hanson. I'll bid you go-good-night."

"Very well, madam, good night."

When the woman had disappeared down the darkened corridor, Eleanor looked at her reflection once again. She dampened her lips and pressed them together, then took a deep breath and straightened her shoulders.

Time to pay the piper, it seemed. Why then was she so reluctant? She had known it was coming. She had made a bargain, and she certainly intended to keep it. Why this sudden dread?

Was it because she'd been her own person, independent and comfortably well-off for so long? How could she now voluntarily cede her independence to a man she had no regard for? It was a business transaction, like signing a contract with a theater troupe, she insisted to her reflection.

Or was it the memory of one searing kiss with a man who was pure and wholesome and everything she was not? She put her hand to her mouth, willing the thoughts to oblivion.

She removed her hand and straightened her shoulders. Best to get it over with. She practiced a careless smile, a toss of her curls. She was an actress after all. Tonight had proved that.

Each day Ian felt strengthened by God's Word, but each day's end brought defeat in some way, whether it was more blurred vision, a spasmodic jerk of a limb, or simply blanking out of something he'd just done or said. Each night, he doggedly got back into God's Word, and felt like a man clinging to the only source of sanity he knew.

"He was wounded for our transgressions, He was bruised for our iniquities: the chastisement of our peace was upon Him; and with His stripes we are healed." Jesus had paid the price for Ian's healing.

Each week as he stood in the operating theater, he called upon God's grace to get him through, to prevent him from blacking out, to steady his hands. He clung to the verse from his beloved Psalms, "I will guide thee with mine eye," so that if his eyesight should fail, God would see him through.

He stood at the operating table one wintry February morning, prepared to perform one of the operations he was renowned for, a lithotomy, otherwise known as "removing the stone." The best surgeons could do it in less than thirty seconds. Ian averaged it in twenty-five seconds.

He took the round-edged knife held out to him by his assistant and made the incision next to the patient's os pubis and through the integuments. Quickly, he took the next knife and widened the wound. A third knife was handed to him, the one he called the "crooked knife," which he used to cut through to the bladder wall. He slit downward, and a second later, the water that had been injected into it with a large syringe gushed out and with it the bladder stone that had caused the man so much pain.

Ian straightened, glad the stone had been expelled so easily so that he wouldn't have to use the gorget to dislodge it from the bladder wall.

Just then one of Ian's legs buckled under him. He managed to grab the chair behind him, falling away from the patient. His last view was of his young assistant's pale face over him, shouting, "Mr. Russell, are you all right?" and then everything went black.

When Ian awoke, he felt that same torpor weighing down his limbs that he'd felt every time he'd lost consciousness.

He was lying down. Looking toward his feet, he realized he was in one of the ward's beds, but he wasn't in one of the large wards, because he seemed to be by himself. He tried to move his head to get a better look at his surroundings.

"Ah, you've come to."

Ian recognized his uncle's voice and then saw him as the man moved into his field of vision and sat upon a chair beside the bed.

"Where am I?"

"In the room adjacent to the operating theater. They moved you here when you collapsed and sent for me immediately. I told them to keep you here for the time being. More private than one of the wards."

"The operation —" Memory was returning and with it the horror of what had happened.

"It's all right. Jensen was right there and he was able to take over. The patient is already in the ward."

What had he done? He'd almost killed a

man. How could he have even thought of operating when the possibility of losing consciousness loomed over him? Ian felt himself suffocating with the enormity of what he'd done.

"What happened, Ian?" His uncle's voice came from far off.

How could he reply to that? He was little better than a murderer.

"One of your apprentices rushed to the garret telling me you'd keeled over right in the middle of an operation."

Ian pushed the hair off his forehead, his hand feeling like a leaded keel. "Everything went black. One of my legs felt numb and the next thing — nothing."

"Is this the first time you've experienced this?"

He looked away from his uncle's concerned face and shook his head.

"How many times?"

"A few." He'd lost count.

"Why didn't you tell me?"

"I didn't want you to worry." No, that wasn't true. He hadn't wanted to have his own diagnosis confirmed in the eyes of another medical man.

His uncle made an impatient sound. "What else have you felt?"

Ian looked up at the ceiling. "Head-

392

aches . . . blurring of vision in my left eye . . . clumsiness . . ."

"How do you feel right now?"

"Tired . . . as if I'd been swimming against the Thames."

His uncle was quiet a few moments and Ian stole a look at him. He appeared deep in thought, his head bent, his chin in his hand, the way he'd hunch over his worktable when he was contemplating the best remedy for a patient.

"How long have you experienced these symptoms?"

Ian let out a gust of breath. "Too long . . . several weeks . . . I don't remember when the headaches first began, a few months ago probably. They've gotten worse."

"Everyone is most concerned. They want Harold to examine you when you come to. I told them I'd look you over first," he said with a faint smile.

"He'll probably poke and prod me no end and then suggest trepanation," Ian said of the hospital's head surgeon.

"I wish you'd told me sooner."

"Why? What could you have done? When I die, you and Stemple and Cridley and all the others can open me up and find out what is growing in my brain."

"Don't talk nonsense."

"Why not? I've done enough dissections to know what ugly things can start growing inside a body." He shoved off the blanket and attempted to sit up.

"You stay put —"

Ian succeeded in standing. "No, thank you. I'm not waiting for the entourage. If anyone needs me, they can find me at the dispensary."

"Ian, you can't just take off after what happened." Uncle Oliver looked frightened. Ian had never seen him like that.

"Don't fret. I'm merely going home. There's nothing anyone here can do for me."

"What are you going to do?" his uncle asked, a bleak look appearing for the first time in his eyes.

Ian gave him an uneven smile. "I'm going to pray. That's all that's left for me to do."

CHAPTER SEVENTEEN

In the quiet of his room, Ian's head sank down on his desk.

Oh, God, what am I to do? I read that You're my healer, and yet I'm not getting better, only worse. He paused, not even sure how to pray anymore. What did he want?

His desires had so long been subsumed to the greater notions of good, that he wasn't even sure he could articulate them.

God, I've never asked for healing for myself, only for others. He felt his own helplessness at having to ask. Was it pride . . . or fear? Fear of refusal. Had he been serving God all these years out of a need for approbation, and had never learned how to receive?

God didn't need his services. Had Ian been currying favor with God in order to mask his own lack of an experience with Him? For so many years his medical training had taught him to accept nothing that couldn't be seen, felt, touched, smelled. Is that why he stood like a rigid statue while others were weeping or shouting for joy at the services?

Whatever the reasons, Ian knew there was only one source of help. He slid down from his desk chair and knelt beside it. *I ask You now, Lord. Would You heal me?* Even as he prayed the words, he realized his own lack of faith. He didn't really believe in his heart that God could — or would — heal him of this . . . tumor. There, he'd said it. He whispered the ugly word in the silent room.

He remembered the leper's plea. *"Lord, if thou wilt, Thou canst make me clean."* That was the crux of it, did he truly believe God was willing?

Jesus had answered without hesitation: "I will: be thou clean."

Lord God, I need Your healing. I'm asking you the impossible. I know You've done the impossible. You healed the leper. You raised Lazarus from the dead. Tears wet his fingers as he sobbed the plea.

He thought of the father of the son possessed by a demon spirit. He had come to Jesus seeking help for his son, and Jesus had answered him, "If thou canst believe, all things are possible to him that believeth."

The father had cried out to him, "I believe; help thou mine unbelief." Ian was in the same predicament. He needed God's grace even to believe. *Help thou mine unbelief,* he prayed. *Grant me the grace to believe, to believe with every fiber of my being.*

In the stillness he felt a quietness in his soul, as if Jesus Himself had said "Peace, be still" to the turbulence and fear raging within him.

When he finally arose, his muscles felt stiff. Looking out the window, he saw it was dark already, although when he glanced at the clock, he saw it was only half-past six.

Feeling a need of air, he went to his bedroom to change his shirt and wash his face. When he emerged into the corridor, his hat and greatcoat in his hands, he encountered his housekeeper.

"Are — are you going out, sir?"

"Yes."

"Should you —"

Hearing the hesitation in her voice, he asked with a trace of impatience, "Should I what?"

She cleared her throat, twisting her hands in her apron. "Should you go out alone, sir? After what happened this afternoon?"

He rubbed his hand over his mouth in annoyance. His uncle had insisted on having Jem accompany him home this afternoon, so of course, his housekeeper had been apprised of everything.

"I shall be fine," he said more calmly. "You needn't trouble yourself."

"But — but where will you be?"

"Out on the town," he answered shortly. Regretting the sarcastic words as soon as they'd been spoken, he added more gently, reaching a hand out to cover hers, "Forgive me. It's hard to be watched when one is used to going where one pleases. I shall just take a short stroll. I assure you I'll be all right. My life is in God's hands now."

Mrs. Duff just pressed her lips together, her eyes showing a brightness of unshed tears, but she said no more.

He let himself out of his house, feeling as if he'd escaped. From what? The danger was within him. Without making a conscious decision he turned the corner and headed down Union Street for the theater.

When he stood outside the Royal Circus, nothing had changed from the last time. Hawkers stood outside the entrance advertising the evening's billing. Prostitutes continued strolling along the pavement, eyeing the gentlemen descending from their curricles. The lobby doors stood wide-open, revealing a glimpse of the rich, lit interior, promising a slice of magic for the evening.

Nothing had changed except this time he

didn't have a hope of meeting one of the theater's principal actresses after the show for supper. What conceit! What a blind, conceited fool he'd been for a space of time.

He shook his head and was about to turn away, wondering why he had come but finding himself still unable to leave. He walked closer to the entrance, telling himself he would simply see what the evening's fare was.

He could no longer find any sign of the Don Giovanni production Mrs. Neville had appeared in. Instead, all the playbills announced a show called A Tale of Mystery, a "comedy set to music in two acts." He scanned a poster for Mrs. Neville's name and frowned, not seeing her in any of the casts of characters. It was as if she'd never formed a major attraction at the theater.

He walked over to the box office.

"Two shillings the pit, four for a box," the ticket woman told him in a bored tone before he had a chance to open his mouth.

"Excuse me, but is Mrs. Eleanor Neville in any of this week's performances?"

"Mrs. Neville? She ain't been with this company in over a month," she said, disdainful of his ignorance.

"Not with this company?" Had she really lost her place since her illness, or had she left them?

The woman looked beyond him to the next person in line. "Excuse me, sir, but I got tickets to sell. Show starts at seven sharp." As he turned to go, she said, "You might try the Drury Lane if you want to see Mrs. Neville. Heard she was over there."

The Drury Lane? What a slow-top he must appear, repeating everything he heard. He stood at the corner, uncertain, but feeling a pull across the river. He reached the corner and, seeing a hack stand, he hailed a jarvey.

"The Drury Lane," he told him, climbing inside the coach.

A quarter of an hour later he descended the cab and paid his fare in front of the magnificent theater building. It had only recently been rebuilt after a fire. He couldn't help thinking of the last time he'd been there. He walked slowly up the shallow steps leading to the lobby. Spying a playbill, he went closer and read it. He scrolled down the list of players, recognizing only Edmund Kean's. There at the bottom of the list of dramatis personae were the only two female characters, one played by Mrs. Eleanor Neville, the other by a name unknown to him.

He turned toward the box office and

requested a box. Paying, he received his ivory ticket check.

When he was seated inside, he scrutinized the program.

Theatre Royal, Drury Lane
A New Way to Pay Old Debts

There followed the list of characters and the actors who played them. He skimmed these, not caring who played what, until he came to her name. *Lady Allworth . . . Mrs. Neville.*

So, she had achieved her goal. A pity he couldn't congratulate her. He sat back, covering his eyes from the gaslights with one hand, not interested in his ornate surroundings or in the celebrated company around him. Why was he here? To punish himself? He had no answer.

When the play began, Ian found himself caught up in the story unfolding on the stage. The piece was a comedy, the actors were good, and unlike the pieces Eleanor had played previously, this one was not set to music.

His attention was truly captured when Kean came onstage. The man played an unscrupulous character, using his daughter Margaret for his greedy ends.

Ian's breath caught when Eleanor came onstage. She was more beautiful than ever. She might never have suffered the ravages of fever. She played an elegant lady, desperate to stop the evil Sir Giles Overreach.

Ian forgot everything but the story unfolding on the stage. Only once did he glance toward the pit, his attention drawn by the crowd's laughter. It was then he noticed the packed house, and that the audience was clearly enjoying the play.

Eleanor must be happy, knowing the play was a success. He wondered how she had gotten the part. Not that she didn't deserve it: her acting was superb, an understated dignity the perfect foil to Kean's evil genius.

He found himself wondering who the real Eleanor Neville was. He could easily believe the role she played onstage now. But there had been that other role, the innocent young maiden seduced by the lecherous parson. And how about the kindly lady entertaining the young children at the mission?

He swallowed, the memories digging at him. What about the woman who had offered herself to him so artlessly, and then kissed him with such passionate abandon?

He rubbed his mouth with his palm, unable to forget her touch. The pain intensified as he thought of her next incarnation, the scornful woman belittling his inexpert lovemaking. Which had been the real Eleanor Neville?

He remembered something she'd told him long ago — that even her name was an invention. Had any of her words to him been sincere? Was everything about her artifice?

During the intermission, Ian idly watched the people below him milling about. He felt no desire to go in search of refreshment in the coffee room. As he skimmed the box seats opposite him, he froze, recognizing the gentleman who rose from his seat and exited his box.

The Duke d'Alvergny. Distaste curled in the pit of Ian's stomach. Still following Eleanor about. Ian wondered how she was handling him these days. As if it were any of his concern, he told himself bitterly.

He found it hard to concentrate on the remaining acts when the play resumed. His glance kept straying to d'Alvergny's box. The man seemed as at ease as if he owned the theater.

When the show ended and the actors took their bows, Ian clapped along with the enthusiastic crowd, although his heart was no longer in it. Eleanor deserved the applause, but he felt only a dull aching melancholy in his heart.

He rose to leave, not interested in seeing the pantomime that was to follow the play. He couldn't help glancing one last time at d'Alvergny's box, but the man had already left. Where? Ian thought of the greenroom with its lounging dandies, men in wait of their prey. Was d'Alvergny among them or was he admitted to her dressing room?

Pursued by these thoughts, Ian left the theater. Once outside, he hesitated, still unwilling to return to his lonely house. But it was too cold to linger outside, so he began walking with no clear destination in mind. The streets were packed with theatergoers, prostitutes, and late-night diners. He headed to Covent Garden and wandered around the booths, wondering how long he would be able to stand and walk as he was doing.

Feeling tired and cold, he reached the Strand and continued his aimless promenade, jostled by pedestrians. He passed the Sans Pareil Theater, where more theatergoers were exiting. Men shouted for their coaches, laughter mingled with conversation as people discussed their evening plans. Farther down he passed the Lyceum. More crowds to press through. He should have stayed home, safe within his study. The side of his head throbbed with a familiar pain.

Gazing across the street, he glimpsed Waterloo Bridge in the distance. He could call a hack and be on his way home. Instead he plodded doggedly on, not knowing what he was searching for. To recapture the recent past? That was finished.

He ended back up near the Drury Lane, a futile circle. A boisterous group burst forth from a door in front of him. He looked up at the swaying sign, The Craven Arms. Through the thick mullioned windows, he saw a merry crowd seated inside the cozy-looking tavern. Before the door swung shut again, Ian stepped inside.

At least it would be warm. He'd have a bite to eat and something hot to drink and then he'd return home, a pilgrim on an unsuccessful journey.

There didn't seem to be any table available, but the brawny waitress squeezed him into a dark corner. He gave his order, no longer feeling hungry for anything. At least he wouldn't be noticed in this shadowy nook. No one here knew of him and his disgraceful collapse in the operating theater today. He could imagine the headlines — Surgeon of Repute Imperils Life of Patient When He Falls into a Swoon During Operation.

Cridley would probably call him in on the

morrow. Ian would tender his resignation, of course. Cridley could call it a "leave," but in any case, they would both know it to be permanent. Ian sat sipping his tankard, the pasty on his pewter plate forgotten as he went over the recent events of his life, everything seeming to unravel in a few short weeks . . . months.

A gust of fresh, cold air pushed the smoke farther into the room each time people entered or exited the tavern. Ian glanced toward the door, watching the latest entrants. His tankard stopped before it reached his lips, as he watched Eleanor come in, followed by the Duke d'Alvergny.

The tankard never reached his lips. He heard its thud on the wooden tabletop, not noticing the contents spilling over it until they splashed his hand. Without conscious thought, he removed his hand, his eyes all the while on the woman who retained the power to slice him open and disembowel him with excruciating finesse.

She handed her cloak to d'Alvergny with a practiced smoothness and followed the waitress. Despite the crowded tavern, the two had no trouble procuring a choice table by a window. Ian remembered his first evening with her, in just such a place. Her back was to him, so there was no danger of his being seen.

He needn't have worried. She seemed completely engrossed with her present companion. Ian watched her profile as she turned a moment to consult the waitress. She was breathtakingly lovely as always. His scientific mind went over every detail with meticulous thoroughness.

Finally, when he could bear it no longer, he rose slowly, the ale curdling in his stomach, and threw down some coins. He'd just endured the most agonizing few minutes of his life.

He left the smoke-filled tavern, the woman he'd given his heart to as unaware of his presence as if he'd been a fly on the wall.

Eleanor dug into her plate of beef and vegetables with relish, always famished after a performance. It also gave her a good excuse to ignore d'Alvergny. What a bore he was becoming, monopolizing her company. Just because he'd set her up in a wonderful house on Jermyn Street didn't mean he owned her.

"Mrs. Neville, you were simply magnificent tonight!" A tall young gentleman stopped by their table, boyish enthusiasm coloring his voice.

She smiled graciously. "You flatter me."

"Not at all, you are a goddess among women. You make Lady Allworth sound sublime."

"You are too kind. Who is your friend?" she asked with a glance at the dark-haired gentleman behind him.

"This is Rupert, Viscount Stanley. He is half in love with you, too, but is too shy to own up to it."

"Why don't you two join us?" she asked with an inviting smile, throwing a careless look d'Alvergny's way.

The two gentlemen accepted immediately and hailed the waitress to bring some chairs. Soon, Eleanor found herself regaling them with tales of what it was like to work with Kean. Seeing the younger man, Stanley, hardly able to say a word to her without blushing, she paid especial attention to him, drawing him out with consummate skill.

"I think it's time we were leaving," d'Alvergny said once their dinner dishes were cleared away.

"It's early yet," she replied, sparing him only a glance.

"It's past twelve," he replied, flipping open his watch.

"I'm sure you don't retire till dawn," she told Stanley, who blushed and stammered a reply.

"Nevertheless, it's time to depart," the duke insisted, standing. The other gentlemen rose immediately, each reaching into his pocket to withdraw money.

She waved their intention away. "His Grace will cover it." She threw him a smile. He said nothing, but tossed some sovereigns onto the table.

In his carriage, the two were silent. She wondered whether this was what a couple who'd been married for years felt like.

At her door, she turned to him, putting a hand to her forehead. "I'm tired tonight. Perhaps you'll call round tomorrow."

"A pity, you didn't seem tired at all at the restaurant." He descended the carriage and held out his hand for her. She had no choice but to follow him, her heart sinking.

Once inside, she asked him if he cared for any refreshment but he declined. "Well, I'm off to bed, then," she said with false brightness. "I shall see you in the morning."

He took her arm as she passed him. "You'll see me tonight."

"I beg your pardon?" she asked in haughty disdain.

"I think you need reminding of who is master in this arrangement of ours."

"Don't be tiresome, d'Alvergny." She refused to ever call him by his given name.

Before she could evade him, he kissed her in a bruising, punishing kiss that held no warmth or tenderness. She struggled to break free but his grip was like iron.

"Now that we have taken care of the preliminaries, I expect your full cooperation tonight."

"And if I refuse?" she asked coldly, hating the very sight of his cleanly shaven, well-fed look.

"Then I shall take great pleasure in demonstrating my superior strength."

The next instant he took her by the arm and threw her away from him with such force she went flying backward, hitting an end table and landing on the floor. She stared at him, her mind refusing to believe what he'd just done.

He smiled down from his great height. "Don't think of screaming. I pay those servants of yours, and they know who is in charge. In future, you will never presume to treat me like one of your lackeys. You kept me dangling for months, but now you're mine, bought and paid for dearly. Do I make myself understood?"

She struggled to stand and he offered her no aid. "I belong to no man."

In reply, he walked over to an umbrella stand and removed his riding crop. Slapping it rhythmically against his leg, he returned to her. Despite her urge to take a step back, she stood her ground.

"Next time, it will be that pretty face of yours, and you won't be fit to be seen on the stage." He smiled, a smile so sinister she put her hand to her mouth to keep from screaming. "I put you on that stage, and I have the power to take you down again, do you understand?"

She nodded, terror immobilizing her.

He laughed, a deep, self-satisfied sound. "Who do you think engineered your last accident?"

"Wha-what do you mean?" she asked, her mind going to the only accident she'd had on the stage.

"The faulty trapdoor," he reminded her softly, the smile still playing along his fleshy lips.

"How . . . how could you . . ." She stared in horror, her mind refusing to grasp the implications of what he was saying. "I don't believe you."

He laughed. "Money can buy anything, including trapdoors that unhinge at the most inconvenient or — shall we say convenient — times?"

What kind of monster was he? "I could have been killed."

He shrugged. "Then no other man would have ever known you. As it is, I am the only man who can have you!" With those words, he raised the riding crop and brought it smartly against her bare arm. She flinched at the stinging pain.

He touched her cheek with the handle. "Remember, not a word or your pretty face will be maimed beyond recognition."

CHAPTER EIGHTEEN

Ian slept fitfully that night, waking time and again with the wisp of a dream he couldn't quite regain. He felt the blackest despair he'd ever experienced in his life — greater than after the bloodiest battle on the Peninsula. There he'd fought against death, too busy rescuing life to have time to dwell on it. He hadn't been responsible for taking men's lives, only in trying to save them, so the panorama of the battlefield had only confirmed to him the fallen nature of humanity and the need for a redemptive savior.

Now it was not only his own imminent end he faced, but also the betrayal of a woman, the only woman he'd ever given his heart to. Oh, the perfidy of woman! For this he'd saved himself? In vain, all in vain. The bitterest pill was the fact that he still wanted her. Her kiss still haunted him.

He fell asleep again from sheer exhaustion, only to awake again. This time he remembered the last fragment of his dream.

Search the Scriptures. A voice had been telling him to search the Scriptures. What did it mean? He had been searching and studying the Scriptures diligently. What more could he do?

Wearily he lit his candle, knowing he'd get little more sleep that night. His clock read four in the morning. Rubbing the gritty fatigue from his eyes, he sat up in his bed and reached for his Bible.

It opened to his marker. His eyes fell on the twenty-first verse of Mark 11: ". . . behold, the fig tree which thou cursedst is withered away." Ian felt a stillness permeate his being. His eyes scanned the verses above it. He'd read them only yesterday, but they hadn't held any particular significance for him then. Now he scrutinized them carefully. The verses recounted how Jesus when he'd passed a fig tree the day before had cursed it because it hadn't contained any fruit. The following day the disciples, passing by it again, noticed that it had dried and withered to its very roots.

Ian continued reading. "And Jesus answering saith unto them, Have faith in God . . . whosoever shall say unto this mountain, Be thou removed, and be thou cast into the sea; and shall not doubt in his heart, but shall believe that those things which he saith shall come to pass; he shall have whatsoever he saith.

"Therefore I say unto you, What things soever ye desire, when ye pray, believe that ye receive them, and ye shall have them."

Whosoever. That meant anyone. Whosoever meant Ian Russell. And the Lord was commanding him to speak to the mountain.

In all his reading and studying of the Scripture, all he'd read indicated God's sovereignty over life and death. Jesus had healed all those who'd come to Him. And yet, had Ian prayed in faith? Had he truly believed in God's willingness to heal *him?* Had he seen so much sickness and death in his life, he found it hard to believe that God was the same God in his day as the one who healed all those who came to Him in Judea, Samaria and Galilee?

He focused on the words again, covering his left eye to block out the blurriness. "Whosoever shall say unto this mountain . . ." God was telling him to command the mountain.

Slowly, feeling self-conscious despite being by himself, Ian raised his hand to his head. Grasping his forehead and squeezing it as if to squelch the pain ever present inside it, he spoke in a voice still gravelly with sleep.

"I speak to this tumor inside my head and I command it to be removed and cast into the sea." With each word, his voice became stronger. "I command it to be removed and cast into utter darkness, in the name of Jesus."

He reclosed his eyes and rested his head, feeling a little foolish that he, the rational man of science, had spoken like a prophet of old. Who did he think he was? Feeling the doubts resurface, Ian read the Scriptures once again, knowing his only salvation lay in them. He remembered the imperative command of the voice that had awakened him. *Search the Scriptures.*

He reread the passages and felt more confident. Then his eyes followed the next verse: "And when ye stand praying, forgive, if ye have ought against any: that your Father also which is in heaven may forgive your trespasses."

The words were like a sledgehammer against him as he pictured Eleanor's smiling face earlier in the evening, her charm directed at d'Alvergny. Loathing swelled within him, choking him. Could he forgive her? Must he forgive her? He knew the answer even before he finished the questions.

"I forgive you, Eleanor . . . I forgive you, Eleanor," he whispered to the night. "I forgive you, Eleanor . . ." His voice broke as tears spilled over the rims of his eyes, and his heart felt rent in pieces.

When he awoke again, the room was light, and he realized it was late. Memories of the night returned and he touched his head. The pain was still there though diminished. He covered his good eye. The same fuzziness blurred his vision, perhaps even more acutely than before.

As he sat up in bed, he recalled the commanding voice once more. *Search the Scriptures.* He couldn't have imagined it. He reopened the Bible to Mark and reread the passage. Once again, he spoke into the silence of the room commanding the tumor to be gone. This time he cursed it as Jesus had done to the fig tree.

After he'd washed and dressed, he decided to go to the dispensary as he'd normally do. If he truly believed the Scriptures, he must believe God had heard and answered his prayer.

He spent the morning assisting his partner in the dispensary. Denton seemed surprised to see him at first and asked him how he felt. They discussed his condition a few minutes, but then a patient was brought in and soon they were too busy to concentrate on anything but the day's patient load.

In the afternoon, Ian went to the mission and looked in on the patients there. Afterward, he and Althea sat together over a cup of tea. Ian told her about his experience in the wee hours of the morning.

"God has given you a word," she said, her eyes alight.

"How can you be so sure it wasn't something my own thoughts conjured up?"

"Because, 'all things are possible for them that believe,' " she quoted to him. "You haven't been studying the Scriptures diligently to no avail. The Word says if you seek the Lord with all your heart, you shall find Him, and if you turn to Him and be obedient to His voice, He will not forsake you, nor forget His covenant with you."

"Do I have a covenant with Him?" he asked, feeling himself too low and unworthy to be called into that kind of relationship.

"Indeed you do, one that has been ratified by the blood of Jesus."

Ian stared at her, the words ringing in the stillness. The blood of Jesus. He'd always seen it as the means of his forgiveness from sins, but not as the sign of a special covenant with God. "I want to know more of this covenant."

Althea nodded. "I'll jot down some Scriptures for you to read."

Eleanor's life had become a living nightmare. She dared not even look at another man in a friendly manner, fearing the reprisals to come in the night when she entered her house.

D'Alvergny was two people, the suave, urbane man about town he appeared in public and the insanely jealous lover who guarded his possessions ruthlessly from any perceived encroachment.

He was careful never to leave marks on her where they would be visible, but he delighted in treating her roughly, goaded on by her stoic silence, not satisfied until he'd made her cry out. Then he'd let her go with a triumphant sneer. In public he was as gentlemanly as when he had been wooing her.

Her only thought was of escape, but it was almost impossible. He'd replaced Clara, her maid, with a towering brute of a woman who had previously been a warden at Bedlam. She cooperated with d'Alvergny in humiliating Eleanor — "priming" her as she called it.

Eleanor lived in terror of losing her job in the theater, knowing if she did she would be finished. All she could think of was Sarah and her future. So Eleanor submitted, willing to sacrifice anything for her daughter's future.

Althea came to visit Ian one day when he didn't show up at the mission on his accustomed day. She found him in bed, the pain in his head too severe to allow him to focus on anything.

After she prayed for him and read him some Scriptures, she asked him, "Whatever happened to Mrs. Neville? The last time I saw her she was recovering from the fever. I went by to visit her last week but her house has been let out."

He turned his head away from her. "Yes, she recovered."

"Praise be to God," she replied softly. "I was grateful for her help with the children. She seemed to have a real affinity for them."

"Yes," he said with a weary sigh, covering his eyes with his hand.

"I'm sorry, I shouldn't be talking to you."

"It's all right. It distracts me."

"Have you any idea where she's gone? We truly miss seeing her at the mission."

"She landed a leading role at the Drury Lane. I'm sure the mission is the furthest thing from her mind."

"I see. I suppose that's what she wanted."

"More than anything, it seems."

"I hope she is happy."

"The last time I saw her, she certainly looked so."

"Was that . . . very long ago?" she ventured.

"Quite recently."

"I'm sorry, Ian." He felt her hand cover the one lying on the counterpane. "You cared for her."

"Cared?" An anemic word to describe what he'd felt for her. "Yes, I suppose I did."

When she said nothing more, only continued to rub the back of his hand softly, he asked, "Tell me, Althea, have you ever fallen in love with the wrong sort of person?"

She was silent long enough for him to think she wasn't going to answer. When he opened his eyes, he saw her partially blurred and partially clear, but was still able to distinguish a bittersweet smile.

"Yes, I'm afraid I have."

He hadn't expected that answer. Althea was to him the epitome of the truly spiritual Christian. Carnal passions seemed so beneath her that they wouldn't offer the least temptation. "It must have been long ago," he filled in for her.

"It was actually quite lately."

He stared at her in disbelief. He had seen no signs of the lovesick maiden as she went about her duties at the mission, or during her work at the chapel or at the street meetings. How could he have been so unobservant? He tried to think back despite the throbbing in his head.

"When you went away?" he asked finally, the effort exhausting him too much to say anything more.

"Yes. I let my heart be stolen by an unbeliever, can you imagine that?" she asked with quiet irony.

"Your employer in Mayfair?" he asked sharply, remembering the man whose young daughter had died and whom he'd seen only a few times. "Aguilar — that was his name, wasn't it — the M.P.?"

She nodded, looking down at her lap.

"I'm sorry, Althea," he said finally, knowing well how inadequate the words were.

Her smile didn't quite succeed. "It's all right. The Lord sustains me. I continue to pray for his soul," she added softly. "He's quite broken up about the death of his daughter."

Ian nodded and reclosed his eyes, feeling only a deep sadness. If someone — an unbeliever — had affected Althea so deeply, what hope had he that this laceration in his heart would ever heal?

A few nights later, Ian was again awakened
from a deep sleep. He had heard a voice,
this time a distinctly audible voice in the
dark room, not a voice from inside his head.
He craned his neck, peering into the darkness, his ears attuned to the faintest noise.
But he heard nothing. It had sounded like
— but no, it couldn't have been — Eleanor's voice, calling to him.

What did it mean? Eleanor calling him?
He began to pray for her. As he asked the
Lord to guide her and lead her into the
truth, he began to feel an urgency for her.
He prayed for God's protection over her.
The sense of danger wouldn't leave him.
Was she in trouble? He pictured d'Alvergny,
and his stomach muscles clenched in futile
rage.

The sense of uneasiness persisted so much
that Ian got up and knelt by his bed, continuing to pray for Eleanor. He felt an urge
to go to her and assure himself that she was
all right. Where would he find her? Most
likely with d'Alvergny. What a fool he'd appear if he found her at the duke's residence.
Eleanor would probably dismiss him as a
scorned lover.

The next day, the pain in his head was

lessened, but his disquiet over Eleanor continued. He decided to go to the mission that night and ask Althea's advice.

They were conducting an open-air street meeting and he stayed on to help. Afterward, he felt invigorated by the service. To everyone's surprise, Althea had ended up preaching when the visiting preacher had been held up by an accident. Ian had never heard a woman preach, but he could not deny that the Spirit of God was upon her. The words held conviction, and many of the listeners came forward to repent and accept the Lord Jesus as their Savior.

When they returned to the mission, he said to her, "The Lord used you tonight."

"Yes," she answered, the awe evident in her tone. "It was all right, wasn't it?"

"Yes," he reassured her. "You truly were anointed to preach."

She turned to him. "Yes, I could never have done it on my own. Ian." She gazed earnestly into his eyes. "Simon Aguilar was there. He heard the message the Lord gave me to preach."

He stared at her. "He was there?"

"Yes! He didn't acknowledge me, but, Ian —" Althea's eyes shone with hope. "I believe God must be doing something. Will you pray with me for Si— Mr. Aguilar?"

"Of course I will," he promised.

She grabbed his arm. "We must pray for Mrs. Neville, too," she added. "No matter who she is or what she has done, we must pray for her salvation."

He felt a conviction pierce him, and he realized he had been more concerned with his hurt than about her salvation. Again he remembered the sense of danger that had assailed him in the night. By day, he had managed to convince himself it was only the effect of darkness.

"Yes," he replied slowly, "we must pray for her."

"You take me for a fool! Well, it shall be for the last time." D'Alvergny yanked her toward him, his menacing face looming over her.

"I did nothing," she protested.

"You went off with Lord Alistair while I was in the card room."

"I did nothing of the so—" Before she could complete the denial, his beefy hand shot out and backhanded her across the cheek. Her head snapped back. She nursed her cheek with her free hand, the only thought going through her mind that the bruise would show. He had promised nothing would mar her face.

Before she could wrench herself out of his grasp, he hit her again. She cried out and tried to cover her face. "Stop it. I swear I've done nothing against you —"

"Tell me what you promised Lord Alistair and Viscount Stanley and every Tom, Dick and Harry who surround you like a bevy of flies to meat!" His voice rose with each word until he was shouting and shaking her as if that would produce the truth. No entreaty would convince him. It was as if he wanted to make her admit a lie, just to give him a reason to punish her. His saturnine face was contorted with rage, and for the first time she truly feared for her life. When his hold slackened a fraction, she grabbed up her skirts and bolted for the door, but she had no hope of escape that night.

His heavy footsteps overtook her and he dragged her after him to the bedroom.

Eleanor heard the scrape of curtains against the rods. She opened her eyes to the bright morning sun. It was then it all came flooding back to her, as one eye barely cracked open and the other was caked in crusty tears. When she tried to move, pain everywhere brought an involuntary moan to her lips.

"You're awake, then?" The maid's coarse

voice jeered at her. Eleanor pulled the sheets up higher, not wanting the woman's eyes on her naked body.

It was a fruitless gesture. The large woman took an end of the sheet in one hand and flung it away from her, baring her face and half her torso.

She chuckled. "I see His Grace did a fine work on you. You look like the inmates at Bedlam, them that misbehaved." Her laughter deepened. Before Eleanor could say anything, she turned away and wrung out a facecloth in a basin.

"Here." She threw the rag onto Eleanor's exposed cheek.

"Oh!" Eleanor sucked in her breath as the frigidly cold, damp cloth hit her bruised skin.

"You'd better keep it on if you want the swelling to go down on that pretty face o' yours."

Eleanor clutched the cloth to her throbbing cheek, pulling the sheet back up to cover herself.

"Well, I'd best draw you a bath, as 'Is Grace expects me to have you ready for him tonight. I don't know as you'll be up to anything by then!" Again she laughed as she left the room.

When Eleanor was alone, she tried to

stand. Her legs threatened to buckle under her. She wondered if she had broken anything. She felt her rib cage. Although everything felt sore and swollen, it was nothing to the pain she had felt after her fall in the theater, so she was reassured. She examined her body. It seemed mostly welts and bruises from d'Alvergny's riding crop and manhandling. She shuddered, preferring to block out everything from the previous evening.

All she knew was she had to get away. She must think. Where could she go? What was she to do? What about Sarah? Feeling the threat of tears, she bit down on her lip, willing herself to be calm.

Wrapping herself in her dressing gown, she began to pace the confines of her bedroom, trying to come to a resolution. She peered at her bruised face in the mirror. She wouldn't be able to be seen in public, much less onstage, for days.

Her life was over. The stark reality stared back at her. Despite her reluctance to go back into the past, she couldn't help remembering how many times her face and body had shown similar marks from her stepfather. *Stepfather* was too good a word to describe him. Her mother's lover. She shuddered, feeling the nausea rise again.

Suddenly she covered her face with her hands and collapsed in her chair. How many times she'd sworn after she'd escaped him that she'd never let a man do that to her again, and here she had fallen for this man's promises. How could she have been so fooled? Her shoulders shook with the sobs that finally came forth.

When she could cry no more, she knew she must act. She would not stay under this roof another night. When another maid, a young girl, came up later in the morning with a breakfast tray, Eleanor turned to her. "Can you send a boy from the mews to deliver this message?" She handed the sealed note along with a guinea to the wide-eyed girl.

"Oh, mum, yes, mum, straightaway," she stammered, curtsying, her eyes fixed on the gold coin.

Eleanor waited impatiently all day for some sign that her note to Betsy had been delivered, hoping against hope the note wouldn't be intercepted, that Betsy wouldn't have a performance that night, or a rehearsal in the afternoon.

At last, in the late afternoon, Betsy arrived. By then, Eleanor had packed a small valise with some overnight things. She glanced in distaste at the many dresses that

429

hung in her dressing room. The majority had been purchased with d'Alvergny's allowance, and she wanted to take no reminder with her.

When Betsy arrived, she took one look at Eleanor's face and brought her hands to her mouth. "What happened?" she asked in a shocked whisper.

Eleanor brought her fingers up to her jaw, feeling afresh how awful her face must look if it horrified her friend so. Another wave of despair swept over her. "I . . . I . . . can't explain," she faltered. "I need your help."

Betsy came to kneel beside her. "Did the duke do this to you?"

Eleanor pressed her lips together, fearful of saying too much. She was terrified of what d'Alvergny could do in retaliation. She had made the mistake of having Sarah visit her in her new home, and she didn't know how much the duke could deduce from her friendship with the girl.

"Don't ask me that," she finally said to Betsy, taking her hand. "Just help me, please."

"Of course, Eleanor. I'll do anything for you."

"I need a place to stay . . . for a few days . . ." For how long? She had no idea where she could go. She'd have to find a place far from d'Alvergny's reach.

As they were sitting together, Eleanor heard the sound of a carriage down below. Panic gripped her. He couldn't have arrived so early. She sprang up from her seat and rushed to the window.

"What is it?" Betsy called after her.

Not bothering to answer, Eleanor stared through a crack in the lace curtain. It was d'Alvergny's coach. She felt the terror suffocate her, rendering her immobile.

Betsy came to join her at the window. "It's the duke." Glancing at Eleanor, she exclaimed, "You look terrified."

"You've got to help me get out of here before he sees me," Eleanor managed through stiff lips.

Betsy glanced back into the room. "Is there any other way downstairs?" she asked finally.

"The service stairs," she managed.

"Is your carriage in the mews?"

"Yes." She turned to leave the room and her glance fell on her valise. "I've packed a few things." She could hardly think beyond the dread of seeing d'Alvergny.

Betsy scooped it up by its handles. "Come, then," she said, taking Eleanor's hand as if she were a child.

Eleanor didn't dare wait for her carriage,

so the two exited into the alley and made their way to Piccadilly from there.

When they finally arrived at Betsy's small room, Eleanor didn't notice her mean surroundings. Her only concern was whether d'Alvergny knew of its existence. She would not rest easy, but sat in a hard-backed chair, staring out the window to the street below. No matter how much Betsy tried to coax her to lie down, she didn't move from her place of vigil.

Ian sat alone in his study, meditating on God's words of healing. "I am the Lord that healeth thee . . . He sent His word and healed them . . . bless the Lord, oh my soul, and forget not all His benefits . . . who healeth all thy diseases."

He covered each eye in turn and focused on the words in the Bible. For a few days now he'd noticed an improvement in his vision. His headaches also seemed diminished in their intensity. Was it his imagination? He had told no one, doubting his own feelings.

A soft knock on his door interrupted his examination. "Yes?" he called out.

Mrs. Duff poked her head in the doorway. "There's a young woman asking to see you."

The fact that she didn't use the term "lady" led him to believe it was a woman from the neighborhood, perhaps someone seeking medical attention, although the hour — he glanced at the clock face, which read ten — was late.

"Did she give any indication of what she wanted?"

"No, sir. She seems nervous, though."

He pushed away from his desk with a sigh, wondering what it was about. "Very well, I'll be right down."

"I've put her in the front room."

"Very good." His housekeeper knew where to put unexpected callers.

When he entered the dimly lit sitting room, he drew in his breath. Miss Simms hurried forward, her gloved hand outstretched, a look of relief on her face.

"Mr. Russell, please excuse the lateness of the hour, but I had to see you. I didn't know where else to go —"

"That's quite all right, don't trouble yourself," he replied, taking her hand in his. "What can I do for you?"

"I would have come by earlier, but I had a show tonight, and I couldn't get here any sooner. I was awfully worried, you see, and wasn't sure if I should even come, but I think she needs medical attention, and . . . oh, I don't know quite what to do!" she ended, almost in tears.

"What is it?" he asked more urgently, leading her back to a seat. "Come, sit down. Let me get you something to drink to calm your nerves."

"No, that won't be necessary. I must be getting back, and I was so hoping." She looked into his eyes earnestly. "Oh, please, can you come with me?"

"Tell me clearly who needs help."

"Eleanor. Oh, sir, it's awful . . ."

CHAPTER NINETEEN

Ian heard nothing more after the word *Eleanor.* His heart hammered in his chest and his hands unconsciously gripped Miss Simms's more tightly. "What's happened?"

"She's hurt, sir. Oh, she looks awful, like someone beat her."

He dropped her hands, stepping back, feeling as if his gut had been punched in. "Tell me everything," he whispered sharply.

"She sent for me, and when I went by this afternoon she was — oh, sir, her face was bruised, and her neck. I couldn't see any more, but she seemed terrified, and when His Grace drove up — that's the Duke d'Alvergny —"

His jaw tightened. "I know who he is."

"Well, she panicked. She said we had to leave. She asked me if she could stay at my place. I said of course. But she wants no one to know. She is terrified he will find her."

"Is she there now?"

She nodded.

"Take me to her."

"Oh, thank you, sir. That's what I was hoping you'd say."

They walked quickly through the dark streets, Ian remembering the night he'd been summoned to her rooms. When they arrived, nothing had changed. The squalor and filth were the same. When Miss Simms opened her door after a soft knock and "It's Betsy," and heard the door open from within, Ian pushed it open farther, unable to wait any longer.

He flinched when he saw Eleanor's face. Her pale skin was mottled an ugly bluish-green along one cheek and around one eye. She stepped away from the door as soon as she saw him.

"What is he doing here?" she whispered, her glance going from him to Betsy.

"I thought he could help us. I thought you might be hurt."

Eleanor didn't listen to anything more, but turned and retreated to the opposite side of the room.

"I'm sorry, Eleanor. I didn't know it would upset you." Miss Simms sounded close to tears.

"Forget it, Betsy." This time Eleanor's

voice sounded indifferent.

Ian closed the door softly behind him. "It's all right, Miss Simms. You did the right thing to summon me." With a soft squeeze to her shoulder, he left her and approached Eleanor.

She stood in a corner of the room. In the dim light, he observed her more closely, shutting out his personal reaction and dealing with her as he would with any patient.

"Who did this to you?" he asked in a neutral voice.

She shrugged. "I was beaten and robbed on my way home from the theater."

"Was it d'Alvergny?"

Her only reaction was to look farther away from him.

"Will you let me examine you? For anything broken or injured internally?" he added.

She hugged herself with her arms, shaking her head.

"Were you hit anywhere else on your body?"

She made no answer but looked down, her lips pressed together as if to prevent any words from betraying her. She began to rock slowly back and forth.

"Are you afraid whoever did this to you might find you?" he asked softly.

At that her eyes widened and she looked up at him in fear. She was terrified, he realized. In those few seconds he knew he would protect her in any way he could.

"I have nowhere safe to go," she whispered, and he could see her control was slipping.

He thought quickly. "Let me take you to the mission. Althea will know how to look after you. You'll be safe there," he promised, using the soothing tone he used with children.

She said nothing, but finally after a moment, she gave a single nod of her head, which he would have missed if he hadn't been observing her so closely.

"Miss Simms," he called out, "could you get me Mrs. Neville's belongings? I'm going to take her with me."

"All right, sir. She only brought a small valise." She hurried to bring Eleanor's cloak and bag.

"Thank you." He wrapped the warm cloak around Eleanor's shoulders, marveling at her docility. Was this the same woman he had seen scarcely a month ago? Something — someone, he amended, his jaw tightening at the thought of d'Alvergny — had frightened and abused her badly.

He put his arm around her shoulder and

led her out of Miss Simms's room. "Can you manage to walk at all?" At her nod, he added, "I think we can find a hackney a few streets down."

He rode opposite her in the dark, musty-smelling coach for hire. She volunteered no more information, and he asked for no more. He watched her, asking himself what she had gotten into. He didn't believe for a moment her explanation of being beaten and robbed. He'd seen too many women beaten by their own husbands or lovers to believe any differently in this case.

But . . . d'Alvergny? The man was an aristo. Ian's mind rebelled at the idea that the man would actually beat a woman the way Eleanor appeared. His gut twisted at the thought of the man's hands on her. The man, for all Ian's dislike of him, must behave with some gentlemanly conduct toward the fairer sex. Ian could scarcely accept the evidence before his eyes. The men who routinely hit their spouses were drunken louts, often unemployed, or unskilled laborers, brutish sailors . . .

Ian felt his thoughts going round and round in frustrated circles, wanting only to find the man who had done this to Eleanor and beat him to a bloody pulp.

When they arrived, he decided he must

know the truth. Before they exited the coach, he put his hand on her arm, and noticed her flinch at the touch. He removed his hand immediately. "Do you want me to inform d'Alvergny of your whereabouts?"

"No!" She started back in terror.

He'd had his answer. "Very well. No one shall know. Come along. You'll be safe here."

When he'd left her settled with Althea, briefly explaining the circumstances, Ian got back into the coach.

He had a purpose, which he vowed would be accomplished before dawn. After receiving directions from Betsy, he headed to the West End, to Eleanor's new town house. D'Alvergny was not there, but he got the address to d'Alvergny's residence from a footman. It was a palatial house only a few blocks away on St. James's Square.

The duke seemed to be entertaining that evening. Every window was lit, several coaches lined the street in front of the house, and music floated out the door each time it opened.

Ian approached the door and had no need to knock as a couple preceded him up the steps. After they were announced and the butler gave them admittance, the frosty man looked down his aquiline nose at Ian.

Ian handed him his card and said, "Please

inform His Grace that Mr. Russell is here to discuss Mrs. Neville's case with him."

When the butler finally returned, he said to him, "The Duke d'Alvergny wishes me to inform you he does not discuss Mrs. Neville with an obscure surgeon."

"He doesn't?" He imitated the butler's supercilious tones, feeling the temper he'd barely held in check overflow. He marched up the remaining steps and attempted to walk past the butler.

"Wha— see here! What are you about?" he sputtered, planting himself more firmly in front of Ian. Ian shoved him aside and continued on down the wide, carpeted foyer.

"I'll call a footman to throw you out!" the man threatened behind him. Ian ignored him and stepped through the first doorway he found. Several people looked at him. He spotted d'Alvergny sitting at a card table with three other men in evening dress.

D'Alvergny glanced at the butler hurrying after Ian.

"I'm sorry, Your Grace, this man burst past me."

Ian gave him no chance to explain further. "A word with you. If you prefer I not say it here in company, you'll do well to give me a moment of your time."

Two footmen came up behind Ian and

took his arms. Ian shook them off. With a flick of his fingers, d'Alvergny waved the servants away. "Leave him," he said, before turning his attention to Ian. "Very well, you may have one moment of my time." D'Alvergny unfurled his body from the chair and laid down his cards. "Excuse me, gentlemen, while I take care of a small matter having to do with an investment of mine."

He turned to Ian, looking down at him from his superior height. Without a word, he led him to another door and they entered a smaller room. At the click of the door behind him, Ian faced d'Alvergny.

"To what do I owe this intrusion?" d'Alvergny asked, taking a pinch of snuff and inhaling deeply.

"I could bring criminal charges against you."

D'Alvergny raised a dark eyebrow. "On what grounds?"

Ian wanted to hurl himself at d'Alvergny and knock the arrogance out of him. But he took a deep breath, knowing he wouldn't get very far. Instead, he made himself speak calmly. "I am here to inform you that your arrangement with Mrs. Eleanor Neville is over. She has removed herself from the premises at Jermyn Street and will send someone over to fetch her belongings on the morrow. I want your assurance that she will no longer receive any of your — attentions. Ever again."

D'Alvergny laughed, a deep baritone sound that was absorbed by the satin-clad walls. "So she has run away to the good doctor, is it?" he asked, as if not quite recalling who Ian was.

"What you have done to her is unpardonable, despicable, unworthy of a gentleman —"

D'Alvergny's eyes hardened. "Have a care. What goes on between Mrs. Neville and myself is no one's business but my own. If you need feminine companionship, there are plenty of other female patients, I'm sure, who are willing and eager for your services."

Ian lunged at the man, grabbing him by the lapels of his evening jacket. The duke flung him off as if he were a pesky gnat. Ian stumbled backward barely keeping his balance.

"I've had enough of this nonsense," d'Alvergny said, turning toward the cross-stitched bellpull hanging on the wall beside the door.

"You will not come near Mrs. Neville again," Ian continued in a low tone. "Leave her alone, or she will bring a suit against you, and I will testify in court of your brutal treatment of her."

"May I remind you there are no witnesses?"

"There are the servants."

"Who are in my employ."

"Nevertheless, I will describe her bruises on the same night you visited her."

D'Alvergny gave him the insolent smile that had never quite left his face since the first mention of Mrs. Neville. "Have a care, surgeon, I can have a word with the Royal College and have your license revoked. I have friends in high places."

"And I have a *Friend* in a higher place. Proof or not, I don't think it will take long for the sordid details of a trial to reach all the gossip columns and be the talk of the ton."

The other man laughed again. "Who will believe you, a surgeon of no repute? If you bring my name up in court, I'll sue you for libel and make sure you never practice medicine again."

The two men stared at each other in a draw. At last, d'Alvergny shrugged. "If Mrs. Neville no longer desires my attentions, it's her loss. She's a fool. No one will hire her now that she has abandoned the Drury Lane Company."

Ian straightened his jacket, having to be satisfied that d'Alvergny would leave Eleanor alone. The man deserved a hiding, but the anger had drained from Ian, leaving only an abhorrence for the self-satisfied man who stood before him.

Without another word, he turned on his heel.

Before he had reached the door, d'Alvergny's voice stopped him. "You are welcome to the little baggage. She has been well worn. Let her tell you how much she enjoyed being manhandled. She'd beg me to overcome her. She called it her 'punishment' for misbehaving."

His laughter rang in Ian's ears long after he'd quit d'Alvergny's mansion.

If Eleanor thought her despair had been severe following the fever, she had never known anything like the depths she found herself in after arriving at the mission.

Althea Breton was nothing but kindness itself, but that did nothing to assuage the utter sense of hopelessness that engulfed Eleanor. She tried to feel gratitude and knew she must, but it could barely rise above the gloom pulling her down.

Althea had put her in a room far above the mission, under the eaves of the roof, next to her own room. The first night, she'd slept with Althea, too scared to be on her own, but by the next night, she began to believe d'Alvergny wouldn't find her here. She smiled bitterly — he'd never step foot in this forsaken end of London. Even Betsy didn't know where she was, although Mr. Russell had promised to assure her that she was safe.

Mr. Russell. She'd gone back to thinking of him as Mr. Russell. The formality served as a good barrier against seeing him as anything but a surgeon — not even hers anymore. She'd allowed Althea to examine her bruises, but no one else. She felt so dirty and vowed never to let herself be touched by a man.

What a stupid dupe she'd been. How could she have let herself be so fooled by a man's gentlemanly facade? Her despair was so deep not even tears would diminish it.

Being out of the play because of the accident was one thing. And all those weeks convalescing hadn't helped. But now? After just opening at the Drury Lane, to suddenly disappear from sight? She was now a joke. No one would ever hire her.

She couldn't have returned even if she'd been brave enough to face d'Alvergny. Her face was too battered. By the time the bruises faded, her reputation would be irreparably ruined. So her career was finished. She'd be lucky if she could find a bit part in Bath or York.

She spent the days sitting at the narrow dormer window sticking out of the slanted roof, staring at the ugly building opposite. She refused to go below. Her shame was too complete. Her only action since arriving at the mission had been to ask Althea to deliver a note to Sarah's family telling them she'd gone away on holiday and would write more fully at a later time.

She couldn't bear the thought of facing anyone — not even Sarah. How could she ever look her daughter in the eye knowing how far she'd fallen? Her daughter deserved better.

"She refuses to come down or see anyone," Althea told Ian. It had been three days now, and he hadn't seen her since the night he'd brought Eleanor here.

"Are you sure she is all right?" he asked yet again.

"Physically, I believe so," Althea replied, as she sat across from him in his cramped office at the mission. "I detected only bruises and . . ." She looked down and bit her lip.

447

"And?" he insisted.

"Lacerations," she answered reluctantly.

"Lacerations! Why didn't you inform me sooner?"

"I —" She shrugged helplessly, as if having no adequate response. "I'm sorry, but she didn't want me to say anything to anyone. I cleaned and dressed her wounds. I . . . I think she'd been beaten . . . or whipped," she added softly.

Ian wanted to kill the man. He wanted to throttle the life out of him. His hands quivered to wrap themselves around the man's fleshy neck and squeeze until the veins popped on his forehead and his eyeballs bulged out. He wanted to see d'Alvergny suffer, his lips distended in helpless agony.

Ian stood from his desk, the chair scraping back harshly from the abrupt movement. He shoved a hand through his hair, turning away from Althea, who watched him in concern.

What had gotten into him? Where was the man called to love his enemies and exhibit Christ-like love to mankind? Nothing would satisfy him but that d'Alvergny pay in kind for what he'd done to Eleanor.

And she? What did she deserve? How could she have submitted to such a monster?

He'd asked himself the question so many times he didn't expect an answer anymore.

Althea had already told him Eleanor didn't want to see him — feeling too ashamed, according to Althea — but Ian was no longer sure he wanted to see Eleanor. What was there to say? She'd proved herself every bit as ambitious for worldly gain as she'd appeared when he'd first met her. She'd stopped at nothing to achieve her desire for acclaim and her West End address.

Ian felt nothing but disgust . . . and sadness.

"Are you all right?" Althea's soft voice came to him from behind.

"Yes, I'm perfectly well," he replied through stiff lips.

"How are you feeling, physically?" she asked, coming to stand near him.

He glanced sidelong at her, almost afraid to speak the words. "My headaches seem to . . . have lessened."

Her eyes widened and she brought her hands up to her mouth. "Praise God," she whispered.

He said nothing, afraid to speak his hope aloud.

"I shall continue thanking our Lord for this miracle," she said.

"Thank you," he said, truly grateful for this sister in Christ.

Eleanor turned from the window. "Come in," she said, recognizing Althea's soft knock.

"I brought you some supper," she said with a smile, entering the twilit room. "Let me light a lamp." Eleanor let her gaze follow Althea's movements, setting down the tray, lighting a lamp, smoothing down the counterpane of the bed where Eleanor had been lying down.

"There, that's better, a bit cozier, isn't it, with the light?" she asked. Eleanor knew she didn't expect a response anymore. "Come, I've brought you some slices of bread and butter, a nice hot bowl of soup, and a cup of tea." She gave her a smile of encouragement.

Eleanor sighed, unable to disappoint the expectancy in the other woman's eyes. She sat obediently like a child, but the effort of lifting knife and spoon seemed too much.

Althea bowed her head and was saying grace over the simple meal. "Come, let me cut this bread for you. Cook just baked it this morning." Althea held it out for her. Lifting her hand as if it weighed a stone, Eleanor took it from her and bit into it, the texture feeling like crumbling clods of dirt in her mouth. She chewed until she could finally swallow it, but the effort of another bite was too much.

"Sometimes it helps to talk about it," Althea said softly.

Eleanor suddenly couldn't abide the kindness and consideration a moment more. "What could you possibly know about it? You are — a — a good woman." She said the words like an insult. "You're the kind of woman Ian is waiting for — pure and gentle. You've probably never thought an unkind thought in your life."

Instead of the protest Eleanor expected, Althea's gray-blue eyes only looked more kindly at her. Eleanor turned her face away, covering it with her hands. "Oh, why don't you go?" she asked wearily. "Just leave me. I don't deserve anyone's attentions."

"Oh, my dear, there's nothing so terrible it can't be forgiven."

Eleanor felt her lips trembling, but she wouldn't give in to tears. "What did you ever do to deserve forgiveness?"

"Once I felt as vile as you do right now. I felt I'd never be clean again."

Eleanor looked at her against her will. "What did you do, tell your parents a little white fib?"

"I was used as abominably as you by a man who passed himself off as a gentleman to the world." She gave an ironic chuckle. "I don't know why it seems it would have been any more acceptable if it had been a man who didn't hide the fact that he was a scoundrel."

Eleanor swallowed, her throat suddenly too dry. "What happened? I can't imagine you sold yourself to a man in return for some material gain."

"No." She looked down at the dinner tray, her fingers folding the cotton napkin she had brought for Eleanor. "He forced himself upon me."

Eleanor stared at the other woman. "How did it happen?" she finally asked, her voice as low as Althea's.

"He pursued me and pursued me. Everywhere I went, he was there. It was my coming-out, you see. He insinuated that I was no better than my mother." She looked at Eleanor. "A chorus girl at the opera in Paris."

Eleanor looked in wonder at the woman she'd thought a paragon of virtue. Her background was not so very different from her own.

"He terrified me with threats of exposing my background to my fashionable friends if

452

I didn't return his favors. He finally cornered me one night and took from me what he had no right to take."

Eleanor brought her hand to her mouth, her eyes filling with tears.

"I wanted to die. I felt more shame than I could possibly bear. I thought I had deserved this vile abuse, because I believed this man's words that I was tainted from birth."

"No!" Eleanor cried out.

Althea gave a sad smile. "Nevertheless, for a long time I believed it so."

"Is that . . . is that why you came here?" Eleanor asked at last.

"No, that came much later."

"What . . . how . . ." Eleanor found it hard to articulate what she wanted to say, not sure she knew, herself. "How did you bear it?"

"I found that there was One who could love me. In spite of my filth, in the absence of any self-worth, He found me worthy of His love."

Eleanor looked confused. "But you're not married . . . ?"

"No, but I am loved and cherished beyond measure."

Eleanor waited, puzzled.

Althea leaned toward her, taking one of

her hands in her two. "Eleanor, Jesus loves you so very much that He gave His life for you. He wants to wash you as you've never been washed. He wants to give you a new life. He wants to show you how very lovable you are."

Althea's voice broke, and Eleanor found she couldn't restrain the tears she'd been holding back until now. The words held such promise, although Eleanor found them impossible to believe. But they sounded so lovely. *To be loved.* The little girl playing in the gutter, her face smeared with dirt; the young girl, her body beginning to display womanly curves, being groped by rough masculine hands in the dark of night; the young woman, willing to sell that body to the highest bidder in order to achieve fame and fortune. How could there be someone to love that person?

"No, it's not possible." She hung her head, the tears splashing atop their joined hands. She couldn't wipe them away, her hands held captive.

"It *is* possible. Oh, Eleanor, all you have to do is open your heart and receive His love. He's waiting for you to ask Him in."

"He can't want me. No one wants me, not now."

"He does. He was willing to be brutalized

for you. He suffered for you. He gave His very life in the cruelest death, so that you could partake of His life."

Eleanor stared at Althea. How much she wanted to believe.

"All you need to do is ask Him to come into your heart. Tell Him you want His forgiveness. He'll cleanse you of every man's touch."

Eleanor shuddered, remembering each sordid act she'd ever engaged in. "Help me, Althea. Help me! I don't think I can do it! You were an unwilling victim. I defiled myself willingly, time and again. You can't know what kind of life I've led. Oh, God, I deserve to die," she cried, her head down.

Althea pressed the napkin to Eleanor's face, and smoothed the hair away from her brow. " 'Though your sins be as scarlet, they shall be as white as snow; though they be red like crimson, they shall be as wool.' "

Eleanor stared at Althea. The words were like a balm to her battered soul. They convicted her and yet promised life. They dared her to believe.

"Oh, God, forgive me," she sobbed, feeling Althea's arms come around her and hold her. She clung to her.

"Tell Jesus you accept that He died for your sins."

Eleanor nodded acceptance.

"Tell Him you receive Him and His sacrifice."

Eleanor sobbed the words.

Althea prayed some more with her. When they had finished, Eleanor felt calmer. She wasn't sure what impact her prayer would have with God, but she felt the burden of self-hatred had lightened as she prayed.

"Oh, Eleanor, the angels are rejoicing in heaven right now." Althea laughed and gave her another hug.

Eleanor hugged her back, feeling for the first time as if Althea was a sister.

"Come, you must eat something."

Eleanor looked down at the food, realizing for the first time in days she felt hunger.

As she ate, she realized nothing had changed. She was still in hiding. Sarah had no idea where she was. She couldn't go back to the theater. D'Alvergny was a subscriber to the Drury Lane. If he was capable of orchestrating an accident at her old theater, what wouldn't he do to make sure she was dismissed from the Drury Lane Company?

Yet she no longer felt the fear and despair that had gripped her since d'Alvergny had terrorized her so ruthlessly.

She smiled tentatively at Althea. "No one knows I am here, not even my friend Betsy.

I don't know what I'm going to do. Why do I feel suddenly . . . unafraid?"

Althea smiled. "Because you have an army on your side."

CHAPTER TWENTY

Ian didn't go to the mission for a couple of days. He forced himself to stay away, knowing there was nothing he could do to help Eleanor, except pray for her. He divided those days between praying and meditating on Scripture verses in his room and visiting the dispensary for only a few hours each day. He'd never felt so useless in his life, and yet he'd never felt so close to God.

He took the Lord's words "Seek ye my face" to heart, and replied like the psalmist David, "Thy face, Lord, will I seek." One night he felt God's presence; it was like being filled to overflowing and for the first time in his life he understood the term "filled with the Holy Spirit" the apostles spoke of in the Book of Acts. At that moment all he desired was to fall to his knees in worship. He could spend the rest of his life in worship.

He stood and raised his arms heavenward

and began to thank God for His goodness and mercy. After a few moments, he felt it was not even himself praising God, but the Spirit of God within him flowing through his mouth in a paean of joy, the words no longer intelligible to him, known only to God, his entire being consumed by worship for his Creator.

It was then he really began to believe that the Lord was *Jehovah Rapha,* the Lord, his healer. *I am the Lord that healeth thee,* the same words spoken to the children of Israel in the desert, were beginning to be true for him.

The night following her praying with Althea, Eleanor accompanied her to a service in the chapel. It was the first time she'd ventured from her rooms since she'd arrived. She sat close to Althea and met no one's eyes as they squeezed into the crowded pews.

She didn't participate in the singing, unlike the times when she'd come before and had joined her voice to the ones around her, taking pride in its purity in contrast to the unschooled ones. Now she felt unworthy to sing words like "And in all our praise of Thee may our lips and lives agree."

But when the preacher began to deliver his message, she forgot those nearby. He preached Jesus Christ and the gift of salvation He came to bring the world. With every point he made, she felt the walls around her breached. When he spoke of a woman who thought her sin so black it couldn't be forgiven, Eleanor sat riveted, wondering how he knew her. But he wasn't speaking of her, he was referring to a woman in the Bible.

"She deserved to be stoned to death." The preacher's forefinger pointed to the crowd. "How many of us didn't deserve death for our sins?

"But her Savior, Jesus Christ, took that vile sin of hers on the cross with Him. He shed His blood on the cross that she might be set free from the law of sin and death. Hallelujah!" The preacher's voice rose, his forehead glistening with perspiration from his exertions.

"Jesus shed His blood on the cross to cleanse us from our sin. No one loves you with that kind of love. The Word says your father and mother may forsake you, but then the Lord will take you up . . ."

His words went on and on, but Eleanor sat stunned by that last statement. She who'd known no love from father or mother, she whose father had forsaken her before she'd ever been born, and whose mother had turned a blind eye to what her lover was doing to her daughter, felt the last wall come down.

"Come unto me, all ye that labor and are heavy laden, and I will give you rest. Come!" The preacher's voice rose. "Come to the altar. The Savior's voice is calling you."

Eleanor rose, needing no one's prompting, and followed the many who were going forward. At the altar she knelt and the tears began to flow as the preacher led them again to pray to receive Jesus as their Savior.

As she finished the prayer, someone came over and laid hands on her head and began to pray for her. Eleanor felt a warmth flow over her body, and all she could think of was the blood of Jesus washing away her sin, making her clean for the first time in her life.

The shadows and oppression, like serpents being untwined from her heart and mind, slipped off her, and she felt God's love enveloping her.

Ian observed Eleanor's kneeling figure from the rear of the crowded chapel, and he prayed that God would make Himself real to her as He had to him. He could only feel profound gratitude to God for leading her to Althea and a place where she could hear the gospel.

All those months he'd known her, he'd made no inroads. The Word said some were to plant, others to water, but that God was the one to give the increase. Ian could rejoice that God had used others to bring Eleanor into His kingdom.

The days following were a revelation for Eleanor. She spent her days reading about Jesus in the gospels. Little by little, she emerged from her shelter and came down to visit with the children. They were over-joyed to see her and soon she was helping out again.

Even though she knew the Lord would protect her from d'Alvergny, she did not go back to the house he had given her. She sent for her coach and a few of her belongings. She was not ready to return herself, how-ever. After another few days had passed, she went to the Drury Lane.

"You are resigning from the company?" Stephen Kemble asked in an incredulous tone. "What has happened? You didn't show up and d'Alvergny sent round word that you were indisposed, and now you come almost a fortnight later, saying you want to resign. The show is doing very well, I might add."

"Yes, I know," she said quietly, having read

the reviews. "Congratulations."

"You don't seem overly interested that Miss Parker has filled your role quite satisfactorily."

"I'm glad she was able to do so."

"What are you going to do? Are you getting married?" he asked, stating one of the few reasons a young actress might quit the stage. "Did you find a rich man to support you in style?"

"No, I'm not getting married."

He raised an eyebrow. "Well, then? Come into an inheritance?"

"You could say that. But I'm not sure what I'm going to do with it yet."

"Well, I congratulate you. I hope you'll become a patron to the theater, then."

She rose and bade him farewell, amazed at the indifference she felt at leaving the place she'd worked so diligently toward for more than a decade. "Goodbye, Mr. Kemble. Thank you for the opportunity you gave me here."

When she emerged into the pale February sunshine, she smiled up at the sky. She felt free — from the past, from her dreams, from every living being. The future was before her, a nebulous sea, and the present was to be lived.

■ ■ ■ ■

As the days passed at the mission, Eleanor saw Ian every few days when he came to see patients or to attend a meeting at the chapel. She observed him from afar with a deep sadness, reluctant to place herself within his notice after the way she had treated him and how he'd seen her.

Only now did she fully appreciate his selfless service to others. When they'd been in almost daily contact with each other, she had been too wrapped up in herself to truly see how dedicated a doctor he was.

She had certainly been right about one thing, she thought to herself. He could never have given his heart — not fully — to one such as she. And he was right. She would never deserve a man like that.

But he had been tempted by her, of that she was sure. She had done everything to entice him. She vowed never to behave in such a manner again. Ian Russell was a good man, and she would rather die than see him fall from his purity and faithfulness.

She didn't miss the irony that now that she could appreciate his goodness, she was determined not to throw herself in his way again.

One morning as the two were folding laundry, Althea asked Eleanor if there was anything amiss between Ian and her.

"No, of course not," she'd answered hastily.

"You seem to avoid the sickroom when he comes on his rounds. I hope you no longer feel any shame about . . . the way he found you."

"No." She spoke the word firmly, although inwardly she questioned the truthfulness of her response.

Althea held out a large sheet. Eleanor took the opposite ends of it and helped her stretch it out to fold.

"Ian has been enduring a severe trial these last couple of months," Althea said.

"What's happened?" she asked, her hands stopping in their actions.

"He was feeling terribly ill. Headaches, dizziness, his vision blurring, even losing consciousness at times."

Eleanor felt her heart encased with a sudden chill. "What does it mean?" she asked in a whisper.

Althea looked at her steadily. "Something very serious. As a surgeon, he has done enough dissections to know that a tumor must have been growing in his brain."

"Oh, no!" she breathed, collapsing in a seat.

Althea came beside her, crouching beside her. "God be praised! He has healed Ian."

Eleanor's eyes widened as she struggled to understand what Althea was telling her.

"It's true. God has delivered him from certain death. The headaches have disappeared, his eyesight is back to normal, and he has not fainted in almost a month, he told me the last time he was here."

"I had no idea . . ." Eleanor began, her feelings so mixed she didn't know what was uppermost — relief . . . shock . . . sadness that she had known nothing and could have done nothing to help a man she cared for so deeply.

"Of course not. He hadn't let any of those close to him know anything until it was unavoidable. I reproached him for that. I told him he needed his brothers and sisters in Christ to pray for him."

"Did you?"

"Of course we did. But everyone, including his uncle and other family members, I'm sure, has been terribly concerned."

"You say he is all right now? Are you sure?"

"I'm as sure as I'm sure God's Word is true."

Eleanor nodded in understanding.

She was only beginning to learn how strong that statement was. She read the Bible as her source for life each day, hungry to know her Savior and to understand God's purpose for her.

One day as she read the words of Jesus, she felt convicted by a particular passage. "Therefore if thou bring thy gift to the altar, and there rememberest that thy brother hath ought against thee; Leave there thy gift before the altar, and go thy way; first be reconciled to thy brother, and then come and offer thy gift."

She felt Ian was justified in having much against her, and that she must ask his forgiveness. The last time they had truly spoken she had said terribly cruel things to him, and she felt them as a barrier almost as great as the shameful way he had seen her.

She prayed for a few days, continuing to ponder the meaning of this Scripture, until finally she knew she would know no peace until she had asked Ian to forgive her.

She waited until he had finished his rounds and was in the small room he used to keep his supplies, before knocking on his door. Her heart was beating like a kettle-drum and her palms were moist, but she knew she had to go through with it.

Ian finished packing his instruments into his bag and closed it up. He stood for a moment by a narrow window. Once again, he felt a deep gratitude welling in his heart toward God. *You delivered me out of the pit,* he said silently, bowing his head and thanking God for His goodness and mercy. He didn't seem to want to do anything these days but thank Him. The world seemed a new place. He had new hope, invoking God's Word with each patient he came in contact with.

He was so immersed in his prayer of thanksgiving that he didn't hear the soft knock on the door, which he usually left ajar. It wasn't until he heard the diffident clearing of someone's throat that he started and looked up.

Eleanor stood in the doorway, her hands folded meekly in front of her. Her beauty never failed to take his breath away. Despite the fact that she was dressed simply, almost severely — he wondered if the dress was one of Althea's — she still had an ethereal beauty that caused him pain. No matter how much he tried to put the past behind him, her presence opened up the wound afresh.

"I'm sorry. I didn't mean to interrupt you —"

He shook away the fruitless thoughts and drew a deep breath. "No, not at all. You weren't interrupting."

When she said nothing more, he asked, "Is there something I can do for you?" He kept his tone with her as impersonal as possible, when he wasn't managing to avoid her.

She moistened her lips, and he realized she was uneasy — perhaps as much as he.

"I've —" She stopped and cleared her throat, then began again. "I've come to ask your forgiveness."

He frowned. "For what?" They'd hardly spoken to each other since the night she'd arrived, and he couldn't think what she could be referring to.

"For how I treated you . . . before." Her voice lowered on the last word and he had to lean forward to hear it. His face reddened as he realized what she was saying. He thought it had been put firmly into the past, and here she was bringing that awful day to the present.

"I know I said — did — some unpardonable things."

"You don't —" he began, unwilling to remember those times.

She stopped his interruption with her next words. "I have no excuse, except to say I was a different person then." Her lips lifted in a slight, bemused smile. "I hardly know that person anymore. I hope you can forgive me for the awful way I behaved toward you."

He said nothing, not knowing what to say. A plea for forgiveness was the last thing he'd expected. What did she mean exactly? What was she asking forgiveness for? Her cruel taunts the day he'd kissed her? Or for having made him fall in love with her? His lips twisted. Unfortunately, she couldn't be held responsible for that — only his own stupid folly.

"Well, I'll leave you. No doubt you have many patients awaiting your attentions elsewhere."

Wait, he wanted to say, unwilling to have her to leave yet. In a bid for time, he asked, "What are your plans now?"

"I'm not sure. I'd like to pay a visit to Sarah."

He nodded. "She'd like to see you, I'm sure."

She looked down at her clasped hands. "She's my daughter, you know."

He stared at her, astounded by the sudden revelation. Of course . . . he should have guessed. "I didn't know," he replied slowly.

She met his gaze. "Yes. It happened when I first ran away from home. The manager of the traveling theatrical troupe who took me in and gave me work —" She looked past him, as if unable to endure his regard. "He fathered her. He must have seen some talent in me, because when I began to increase, he didn't want to lose me. He could have abandoned me then, but instead he paid a couple from the troupe — the Thorntons — to take me in. They were tired of the life on the road and were ready to settle down so they agreed. I stayed with them just until Sarah was born, and then rejoined the troupe.

"I only got to hold Sarah a few days and give her suck —" her voice cracked, and Ian's heart wrenched with pity "— before having to say goodbye to her." She cleared her throat. "Louisa and Jacob have been good to her, and they've let me visit as often as I can. I was waiting until she was older to bring her to live with me."

"And now?"

"Now?" She spread her hands wide in a shrug. "I don't know. I don't know if I can ever be a mother to her at this late stage, but perhaps I can live close by. I had such great plans for her," she said with a sad smile. "Now," she repeated, "who knows?

God knows," she ended with a calmer smile.

"Was that why you went with d'Alvergny?" he asked, wanting to know. It was the first time he'd named the duke in her presence.

She flushed and looked down at her hands again. "That was one of the reasons. I was waiting for the day to have enough money to bring Sarah to live with me. But don't fool yourself. It wasn't the only reason. I wanted a part at the Drury Lane. He promised it to me, and he kept his word."

"Were those the only reasons?" What was he looking for? For her to admit that what d'Alvergny had said was true?

"The Lord has shown me how I also did it out of contempt for myself."

Ian didn't expect that answer, and he had to struggle to make sense of it.

"He has shown me it has been that way each time, although I never realized it until now. That is why I hated those men." She dabbed at the corner of her eye with a fingertip. "The only time I thought I was in love, with the gentleman who taught me the manners of a lady, it was a desperate kind of love. By the end, I probably hated him more than anything because I felt he'd taken everything from me and given me nothing of himself in return. I hated feeling helpless . . . and abandoned." The last word was said almost in a whisper.

Ian felt sickened by the disclosure, not thinking anything could have disgusted him more than d'Alvergny's words. Now he wiped a hand across his mouth, not sure he wanted to hear anything more. For her, this might be cathartic, but for him it was a torturous ordeal, showing him afresh how hopelessly wrong she would have been for him.

He remembered his uncle's words. *It takes a strong man to resist the role of rescuer to a damsel in distress.* Was this what his uncle had meant? To resist would have saved him countless agonies, but had coming to her rescue been inevitable, requiring a much stronger man? Was he just as big a fool as every man who'd admired her?

Her next words surprised him, pulling him out of his hopeless questioning.

"You once asked me what my real name was."

"Yes."

"It was Maisey. Rather common, don't you think?"

"No, it's a pretty name," he found himself saying almost automatically, still too stunned by everything else she'd told him to take it in.

"Maisey Moore. Not very elegant for a

stage name."

When he said nothing, she waited a bit. The silence hung between them awkwardly. She sighed. "Well, that is all I wanted to say. Goodbye, Ian."

Before he could stop her, she had turned and left the room.

He let the hand he'd lifted drop back to his side. What was the point of detaining her? He'd already settled that she could never be the one for him.

Eleanor sat with Sarah in the farmhouse parlor. After Sarah's delight in seeing her, Eleanor had taken her hand and told her she had something serious to talk about. She proceeded to tell her that she was her real mother.

Now she sat back, waiting for shock and accusation. Instead, Sarah's face looked radiant, and she threw herself into Eleanor's arms. Eleanor braced herself to keep from falling backward and returned the hug tightly.

"You mean you are my real mama? Oh, I always hoped it to be so! And now it is. I can scarcely believe it!"

"Are you sure you are not disappointed?" Eleanor asked, when they'd loosened their hold on each other. "All those years I told you such a lovely tale of your parents, and now the truth is your mother is only a simple actress on the stage — not a very good one at that —"

"Oh, no," she breathed, still looking at Eleanor in awe. "Not a simple actress. You are the most beautiful, the most wonderful person in the world."

Eleanor could feel the tears welling up in her eyes again. "Oh, dear, no . . . I'm not that." Her lips trembled so that she couldn't continue speaking.

Sarah, as if sensing her mother's uncertainty, took her two hands in hers and said, "I have always loved you above anyone else. Even more than Mama and Papa Thornton or my brothers and sisters." She hesitated a moment. "Even more than those imaginary parents you told me about all those years."

The tears were rolling down Eleanor's cheeks, but she didn't bother to wipe them. "Did you really? But you always seemed so eager to have me tell you the story about them."

"I was. I loved hearing it. It was like a fairy story. But I still loved you best of all. You were real. You were here. Those people seemed so perfect, they couldn't have been real."

Eleanor fumbled in her pocket for her

handkerchief and blew her nose and wiped her eyes. "You're right. They were too perfect. That was my mistake, wasn't it? I should have given them each a slight flaw. Perhaps a mole on your 'mother's' cheek and crooked teeth for your 'father.' " She smiled at Sarah through the tears welling up in her eyes once more.

Sarah laughed with glee. "Or a limp when he walked. He could have been wounded in battle." After they both laughed heartily, Sarah asked seriously, "Tell me — Mama." She hesitated only a moment over the name. "Why did you make them up?"

"Because I wasn't good enough for someone as perfect as you. I was only a lowborn actress. And what I told you just now is true. I wasn't married. I couldn't even give you a papa."

"So I don't have a papa? It's not Papa Thornton after all?"

"No, my dear," Eleanor said quietly. How could she explain to an innocent ten-year-old the truth? "Papa Thornton loves you as his real daughter." She looked down at their hands. "Please don't ask me about your real papa. Someday when you're older I'll tell you about him. I promise," she whispered, too ashamed to look at her daughter.

"Oh, Mama, don't be sad. You mustn't be

sad when you've just told me the most wonderful thing." She squeezed Eleanor's hand. "You are my mama. You don't know how often I wished it so. Every time you spoke about how you and my make-believe mama were the best of friends and told each other everything, I would think afterward how true that was of the two of us. How could we not be related when we thought about the same things and liked the same things and told each other all sorts of things?

"Can I come and live with you now?" she asked eagerly. "Is that why you told me now?"

"Partially. I do want us to live together. I just don't know where that will be at the moment. I was thinking perhaps of getting a little cottage out here and living near you . . ."

Sarah looked disappointed. "Oh, I was so hoping to come to London with you." She brightened. "But if we live here, I will still be next to Papa and Mama Thornton."

"We don't have to decide this minute. We'll talk with Papa and Mama Thornton and see what they think."

Eleanor embraced Sarah once more, grateful to the Lord, who had restored her daughter to her after so many years.

She didn't know what else she would do

with her life, but she trusted the Lord would make a way for her to be with her daughter soon.

CHAPTER
TWENTY-ONE

Eleanor knew it was time to get on with her life, although she didn't yet understand which direction it would take. She'd already told Althea of her departure from the mission. Although Althea had expressed regret at her leaving, she promised to do all she could to help her. In the days following, Eleanor continued to help at the mission, finding peace in the simple rhythm of everyday chores.

"Hello, Eleanor," Althea greeted her when she stopped by the small medical office to get some supplies.

"Hello."

"I need your help." Althea was standing in front of a table laden with medical bottles.

"Of course. What would you like?"

"I need to get some prescriptions from the apothecary. Ian usually brings them from his uncle's but he won't be in today, and I'm afraid we're a bit shorthanded this morning."

"Would you like me to fetch them?"

"Could you? His uncle's apothecary is at St.Thomas's."

"I know where that is. I'll go immediately."

Eleanor found the herb garret easily enough, but when she entered, there was no one there but the young apprentice.

He recognized her right away and smiled broadly. "Mrs. Neville! What are you doing here?"

"I came to collect some prescriptions for the mission."

Jem looked around. "Mr. Russell, Sr., didn't tell me of anything that needed to be collected. Maybe Ian already took them."

"That's possible."

"You could ask Mr. Russell himself. He's in the herb garden just down the road a bit."

Ian's uncle. Suddenly Eleanor felt a curiosity to meet the man. It might be her only opportunity. She smiled at Jem. "Yes, I shall go there."

"Would you like me to accompany you there?"

"No, that's kind of you, but I think I prefer to find it on my own, if you'll direct me. It's a beautiful day to visit a garden."

"That it is. Spring is finally making an appearance. Too bad I'm cooped up here."

She smiled in understanding.

Eleanor followed the street to the building he'd indicated. When she stepped under the thick stone arch, she gasped in delight. Through it lay an oasis of green. The first tender shoots of grass lined the brick walkways. Rectangular beds of dirt were set out in rows down the length of the hidden courtyard. Bright clumps of yellow edged them where the first daffodils were opening up. Birds twittered in the bare branches of the trees.

She stepped through the arch and emerged into the sunny courtyard. As she walked past the beds, she saw a man bent over one of them with a garden fork. As she neared him, he turned. Shading his face with a hand, he watched her progress, as he rested against the fork.

"You must be Mr. Russell's uncle," she said, already feeling a welcome in the older man's genial face.

"Yes, indeed. Oliver Russell, at your service. And who might you be?"

"Eleanor Neville."

He smiled. "So you are Eleanor Neville."

She blushed, thinking he was referring to the actress. She shrugged. "I don't know," she answered honestly. "I don't feel like

481

Eleanor Neville these days."

He chuckled. "Why is that?"

"She wasn't a very nice person, you know," she replied, wondering at how easily the words came out.

"Wasn't she? Beyond redemption?"

"Yes. Thankfully, a new person has been resurrected in her place. I feel brand-new." She looked down at the freshly turned earth. "But it means learning things all over again."

"That could take some time."

"Yes." She sighed, returning to the reason she was there. "I've come to fetch some prescriptions Mr. Russell left for the children at the mission."

"Ah yes. He already collected them. I'm sure he'll drop them by the mission today."

"Yes, I'm sure he will." She would probably miss his visit. It was for the best, she told herself.

"Do you have a moment?"

She turned her attention back to Ian's uncle. "Yes, why?"

"Why don't you take a few minutes and sit in my garden? It is a place of discovery."

She smiled. "Thank you. I believe I will. I shan't disturb you in your labors, shall I?"

"No. I was about to return anyway. I must see what Jem is up to," he said with a chuckle.

They bade each other goodbye and Eleanor turned back to the garden. Here and there she discovered a clump of crocus or a border of daffodils.

Ian stepped into the quiet of his uncle's garret.

"Hello, Ian, I wasn't expecting you today," his uncle greeted him from the worktable.

"No, I just left the ward. There was a surgery patient I needed to look in on."

His uncle was pressing a medicinal dough onto the pill tile with a long, grooved rolling pin to make a fresh batch of pills. Ian breathed in the scent of eucalyptus.

"Well, I'm glad you've come. No, don't sit down," he said as Ian prepared to take a seat at one of the stools. Before Ian could inquire why, he explained, "I suggest you take a walk down to the herb garden."

"Why ever for? Did you leave something behind?"

"No, but perhaps you did." Before he could figure out the meaning of his uncle's cryptic words, Uncle Oliver added, "There's someone down there I think it worth your while to see. Leave your other cares for the moment and spend some time down in the garden."

"I suppose you're not going to tell me any more than that?"

"You suppose right. Now run along before you miss this individual."

Ian retraced his steps down to the ground floor. When he emerged in the street, he hesitated. Well, there was no harm in it, and he knew his uncle wouldn't waste his time playing jokes on him. He turned in the opposite direction he'd come and walked toward the garden.

His first thoughts as he came through the arch into the sunshine was that the trip had been in vain, for there was no one there, then he squinted, seeing someone at the far end, partially obscured by a yew hedge.

Eleanor! What was she doing here?

Ian found himself walking toward her. She didn't hear him approach, and as he neared he saw that she was kneeling in front of an outcropping of colorful lavender and yellow crocus.

She looked like a girl in prayer.

He had been praying the day she'd come into his office. The significance hit him like a bolt from the sky.

Isaac beholding Rebekah. Ian's asking God for a sign. Had that been it, and he'd missed it? Was Eleanor indeed the one?

He felt a sudden jubilation, just as quickly

followed by a conviction of guilt. She leaned forward and broke off a flower stem and twirled it in her fingers.

Had he truly forgiven her?

She'd come to him in humility and what had he given her in return? In a split second he recognized his true nature, petty, unforgiving and arrogant. God had forgiven Eleanor and washed away her past as surely as He'd healed Ian. Her sins had been put away from her as far as the east is from the west.

These thoughts crystallized in the few seconds Ian stood watching Eleanor in the sunshine. He must have made a sound because she turned and saw him. Her smile of greeting faded and he read uncertainty in her eyes. Is that what he made her feel? Uncertain? Unloved? Afraid? . . . the way every other man had? The knowledge pierced him.

He stepped toward her, unsure what he was going to say.

"What a beautiful spot your uncle has here. He invited me to stay a few moments," she said, as if to excuse her presence there.

"Yes, it is a beautiful spot. Please feel free to stay as long as you'd like."

She made to rise and he immediately came forward and held out his hand. As

soon as she was standing, she let his hand
go.

"There is a bench over there. Would you
care to have a seat?" he asked diffidently.

She watched him the way a patient would
who was awaiting a diagnosis. With a quick
nod of her head, she accepted his suggestion and he led her to the bench.

"There is not too much sun for you?" he
asked when they were seated side by side.

"No. It's nice to see the sun and feel its
warmth after the long winter."

He nodded.

They sat for some minutes. Just as Ian was
ready to speak, she began, and he fell silent,
preferring to hear what she had to say.

"I shall be leaving the mission soon."

His heart sank, but then he remembered
she still lived in London. Her next words
dashed those hopes.

"I am going to live with the Thorntons for
a little while, until I can find a cottage
nearby for Sarah and myself."

"You and Sarah."

"Yes."

He watched her profile as they spoke.
"What will you do?"

"I don't know yet." She gave a slight
smile. "The Lord hasn't revealed that much
to me yet."

"Will you resume your . . . acting career?"

"I don't think so."

He was stunned. "I thought it was so important to you."

"It was." She looked down at the crocus in her hand. "I believe if I ever appear in front of an audience again it will be in the Lord's service, but that's as much as I know."

They sat a moment longer in silence, Ian wondering how he could say what was in his heart.

She turned to him slightly. "May I ask you something?"

"Of course."

"Why haven't you married Althea? Isn't she everything you are looking for in a woman?"

The question startled him, and he struggled to find the answer. Her face was so close to his as she awaited his reply. He looked into her eyes and was caught anew by their amazing color, a gray so translucent it was like glass. The dark pinpoints of her pupils contrasted sharply, adding to the effect of light.

"She is such a worthy woman," she added.

Her words gave him the opening he needed.

"She may be worthy, but I'm not in love

with her." He paused. "There is only one woman in the world for me."

She swallowed. "Oh." She sounded disappointed. "What is she like?"

"She is so beautiful it makes my heart ache."

Her lashes came over her eyes to hide them from his view. "What is the matter, then? Does she think she is too good for you?"

"No, on the contrary," he replied slowly, "she has never known her true worth. But I am certainly not good enough for her and never will be."

Her eyelids flew up and he could see the protest ready on her lips.

"I would never ask her to share the life I lead. I would never ask her to give up the recognition she's gained over the years through her talent and determination and hard work on the stage."

The look in her eyes told him she was beginning to understand that he was referring to her.

"Why haven't *you* ever married, Eleanor?" he asked her softly.

"Because I never trusted men . . . until now," she whispered.

"You had good reason not to."

"But the Lord showed me there was one

man who was trustworthy. He thinks he is a mere surgeon, but I've never met a truer man, or better friend, or . . . protector."

"Oh, Eleanor," he breathed, "I can offer you so little except my love."

The smile began in her clear gray eyes and reached her lips. "How can you say that when we've been given wealth immeasurable?"

He leaned forward until her face blurred and he inhaled the freshness of her skin and finally felt the softness of her parted lips.

Some moments later, she giggled beneath his lips.

He opened his eyes. "What do you find so amusing about my kisses this time?"

"Your kisses are perfect," she assured him with a quick peck to prove the fact. "What I find funny is the fact that you're going to make an honest woman of me."

"No," he replied seriously. "The Lord has already done that."

She sobered, bringing up a hand to stroke his cheek. "So, what is left for you, then?"

He smiled. "To enjoy it."

As her smile grew in response, he leaned toward her again. "I have, after all, a lot of time to make up for."

Her laughter was smothered by his kiss.

A little later she pushed away from him

again, a look of sadness on her face.

"What is it, my love?" he asked, his fingers framing her face.

"I'll never make a good wife. I don't know how to do anything housewifely. All those things like cooking, sewing, knitting . . ." Her voice grew mournful as the list grew longer.

He laughed. "I don't expect to marry my housekeeper. I don't need a servant, but a soul mate. I may be a poor surgeon compared to your manner of living, but I do have an adequate income, enough to pay for at least a servant or two."

"Where shall we live?" she asked, snuggling against him as he put his arm around her, amazed at how right she felt beside him.

"Here in London or near the Thorntons if you'd like. Sarah will live with us, of course." She squeezed his free hand in response.

"You remember that gentleman, Digsby, you dragged to the anatomy lecture?"

She giggled at the memory.

"He has become interested in my work after all. He's offered to line up some backers to put up the money for a children's hospital — the first of its kind here in London."

She turned glowing eyes to him. "Oh, Ian, that's wonderful."

He looked deep into her eyes, whose goodness he could now trust. "I don't expect to tell you what to do. God has given you a wonderful talent — to entertain people and make them laugh — even cry. I won't dictate to you whether you should leave the theater or not."

"Thank you, Ian. That means a great deal to me." She traced the line of his jaw. "But I think the Lord has another course for me now. I want to join you in this new endeavor to help the children of London, if you'll have me."

"Nothing would make me happier." He kissed the top of her head where her bonnet had fallen back. "May I call you Maisey?"

She smiled up at him. "You alone."

"Will you be my Maisey? Can you really want to marry me, Maisey mine?" he asked in a teasing voice, touching his nose to hers.

"I should like that above all, Ian, my love," she answered shyly.

His lips met hers once more and he hugged her close to him, rejoicing in what a blessed man he was.

His future wife had been worth the wait.

EPILOGUE

Announcement in the Morning Post

Married: Ian Russell, doctor of surgery, to Maisey Moore, spinster, April 3, 1818, at the Morningstar Chapel, Whitechapel.
Witnesses present: Jacob and Louisa Thornton and their offspring.

QUESTIONS FOR DISCUSSION

1) What is Ian Russell's first impression of Eleanor Neville? Hers of him? How can first impressions be both accurate and inaccurate?

2) Both Ian and Eleanor have preconceived notions of what the other should be in their respective professions, the doctor and the actress. How does each break the stereotype in the other's mind? What kind of parallels do they see in each other's professions?

3) What is Eleanor's real opinion of men? Why does Eleanor want to tempt Ian to fall from his pledge of purity? How is this related to her cynical view of men? In her opinion, is any man capable of the ideals Ian holds?

4) How is the Bible story of Isaac and Rebekah significant to Ian?

5) How do Ian's attentions to Eleanor differ from other men's? How does this confuse Eleanor?

6) When Ian escorts Eleanor to a show at the Drury Lane, how does this event begin to change Eleanor's ambitions from being accepted by the high society of London to being merely a respectable member of society?

7) When Eleanor attempts to do good — working with the children at the mission, attending church — how do things backfire?

8) What does Ian's "apprenticeship of faith" consist of? What kinds of things does he have to unlearn from his religious upbringing? How does the faith of his parents and elders begin to be transformed into his own faith?

9) After all her years of separating herself from her shameful past at the hands of her stepfather, Eleanor's life comes full circle when she finds herself at the mercy

of d'Alvergny. What is the ultimate result of the degradation she is made to feel at his hands?

10) How does Ian finally realize Eleanor is as pure as the woman he has held up as his ideal?

AUTHOR'S NOTE

I apologize for causing any squeamishness in my readers when describing some of the medical procedures in 1817 London. I, too, am squeamish and found them difficult to write about! But I have tried to portray an accurate picture of medicine, including its many advances, in the Regency period. I was privileged to visit an operating theater in London, as well as an herb garret, both of which were part of St. Thomas's Hospital in Ian's day.

I've also found much useful information in many books on medicine and theater at the time, which I list following. Although I have tried to respect dates, I did take a few small liberties. For example, although Rene Laennec did invent the stethoscope in 1816 in Paris, he didn't publish anything on it until 1819, so it was probably *not* in use in London at the time of my story. However, I believe it to be a reasonable scenario that someone could have heard about it from a French colleague and even received a sample one, the way Ian does.

It was true, also, that at the time there existed no hospitals to treat children. The first "dispensary" specifically for children opened in 1769, but disappeared in 1789 when its founder, Dr. George Armstrong, died. The idea of a dispensary was like our modern-day out-patient clinic. Few of these treated children. The second one for children, the Universal Dispensary for Children, opened in 1816, and grew to eventually become the Royal Hospital for Children and Women. It didn't actually admit children as inpatients until 1856.

As for the theater world, the male leads in some of the offshoot productions of *Don Giovanni* did go to women, but not until 1820. One of the most popular was Madame Vestris, whom I mention briefly in the story. But it was not unusual for a woman to land a "breeches" part prior to 1820.

For further reading on the medical and theatrical worlds of the period, I recommend the following works (this is not a complete list):

Bosworth, F.F. *Christ the Healer.* Grand Rapids: Baker Publishing Group, 2004.

Buchan, William. *Complete Domestic Medicine 1849.* Gloucestershire: Archive CD Books.

Clinton-Baddeley, V. C. *The Burlesque Tradition in the English Theatre after 1660.* London: Methuen & Co., Ltd., 1952.

Hitchcock, Tim and Heather Shore, eds. *The Streets of London from the Great Fire to the Great Stink.* London: Rivers Oram Press, 2003.

Hood, Paxton. *Portraits of the Great 18th Century Revival.* Greenville: Ambassador Books, 1997.

Houtchens, Carolyn W., contrib., Lawrence H. Houtchens, ed. *Leigh Hunt's Dramatic Criticism, 1808–1831.* New York: Columbia University Press, 1949.

Loudon, Irvine. *Medical Care and the General Practitioner 1750–1850.* Oxford: Clarendon Press, 1986.

Mandel, Oscar, ed. *The Theatre of Don Juan: A Collection of Plays & Views, 1630–1963.* Lincoln: University of Nebraska Press, 1963.

Nuland, Sherwin B. *Doctors: the Biography of Medicine.* New York: Vintage Books, 1988.

Porter, Roy. *Quacks, Fakers & Charlatans in Medicine.* Gloucestershire: Tempus Publishing, 2001.

ABOUT THE AUTHOR

Ruth Axtell Morren wrote her first story when she was twelve — a spy thriller — and knew she wanted to be a writer.

There were many detours along the way. She studied comparative literature at Smith College, met her junior year in Paris, taught English in the Canary Islands and worked in international development in Miami, Florida, where she met her future husband, who took her to the Netherlands to live for six years.

It was in Holland, in 1990, that Ruth began seriously crafting her first story, between having children: Justin, Adaja and Andre. It was there, too, that she gained her first recognition as a writer — as a finalist in the Romance Writers of America Golden Heart contest in 1994.

Ruth's first two novels, *Winter Is Past* (2003) and *Wild Rose* (2004), both won awards in contests sponsored by the Romance Writers of America. *Wild Rose* was recently selected as a *Booklist* Top 10 Christian Novel for 2005.

After living several years on the beautifully wild "down East" coast of Maine, Ruth and her family decided to move back to the Netherlands so their children could learn about the language and culture of their birth. You can get in touch with Ruth through her Web site, www.ruthaxtell morren.com.

The employees of Thorndike Press hope you have enjoyed this Large Print book. All our Thorndike and Wheeler Large Print titles are designed for easy reading, and all our books are made to last. Other Thorndike Press Large Print books are available at your library, through selected bookstores, or directly from us.

For information about titles, please call:
    (800) 223-1244

or visit our Web site at:
    www.gale.com/thorndike
    www.gale.com/wheeler

To share your comments, please write:
    Publisher
    Thorndike Press
    295 Kennedy Memorial Drive
    Waterville, ME 04901